EX L

VINTAGE CLASSICS

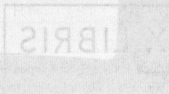

YOU CAN'T DO BOTH

Kingsley Amis was born in south London in 1922 and was educated at the City of London School and St John's College, Oxford. After the publication of *Lucky Jim* in 1954, Kingsley Amis wrote over twenty novels, including *The Alteration*, winner of the John W. Campbell Memorial Award, *The Old Devils*, winner of the Booker Prize in 1986, and *The Biographer's Moustache*, which was to be his last book. He also wrote on politics, education, language, films, television, restaurants and drink. Kingsley Amis was awarded the CBE in 1981 and received a knighthood in 1990. He died in October 1995.

FICTION BY KINGSLEY AMIS

Lucky Jim
That Uncertain Feeling
I Like It Here
Take a Girl Like You
One Fat Englishman
The Anti-Death League
I Want It Now
The Green Man
Girl, 20
The Riverside Villas Murder
Ending Up
The Crime of the Century
The Alteration
Jake's Thing
Collected Short Stories
Russian Hide-and-Seek
Stanley and the Women
The Old Devils
Difficulties with Girls
The Folks that Live on the Hill
The Russian Girl
Mr Barrett's Secret and Other Stories
The Biographer's Moustache

KINGSLEY AMIS

You Can't Do Both

VINTAGE BOOKS
London

Published by Vintage 2004

8 10 9

First published in Great Britain in 1994 by Hutchinson

Vintage
Random House, 20 Vauxhall Bridge Road,
London SW1V 2SA

www.vintage-classics.info

Addresses for companies within The Random House Group Limited
can be found at: www.randomhouse.co.uk/offices.htm

The Random House Group Limited Reg. No. 954009

A CIP catalogue record for this book
is available from the British Library

ISBN 9780099461029

The Random House Group Limited supports The Forest Stewardship
Council (FSC®), the leading international forest certification organisation.
Our books carrying the FSC label are printed on FSC® certified paper.
FSC is the only forest certification scheme endorsed by the leading
environmental organisations, including Greenpeace.
Our paper procurement policy can be found at:
www.randomhouse.co.uk/environment

Printed and bound by Clays Ltd, St Ives plc

To Virginia and Michael Rush

1

Robin Davies crossed the landing and went into the bathroom, where his father, a stocky dark man in his early fifties, stood at the washbasin shaving. It was exactly half-past seven and, under terms he had himself laid down, Mr Davies should have been just off to finish dressing. But he lingered, left hand in trouser pocket, going over tricky bits again with his razor and looking at his melancholy face in the folding mirror on the window-sill. 'Morning, old boy,' he called cheerily enough to his son's reflection there.

'Hallo Dad,' said Robin without much warmth.

'I shan't be a moment. You can start on your teeth.'

There was not much room to reach past for his brush and the tin of pink powder, but Robin managed it and was soon cleaning his teeth into the bath. Its taps were at the window end, so to do this he had to stand a little closer to his father than seemed natural. But Mr Davies was in no hurry to leave, slowly washing out his razor while still staring at himself in the glass. After a moment he broke into song in his pleasant light baritone:

> This ill-fit*ting* cuirass
> Is *but* a useless mass:
> It's made of steel
> *And* weighs a deal . . .

In time to spare himself a repeat of the first piece of information, Robin interrupted in a louder and harsher voice:

1

> I know for certain
>   The one I love;
> I'm through with flirtin',
>   It's you that I'm thinking of . . .

'Here, half a minute, old chap, I think that's very uncalled-for,' said Mr Davies reasonably.' There I was, quietly singing away to myself, almost under my breath you might say, and you come butting in half bawling your head off. Did you have to do it or what?'

'I don't know.'

'Worried about exams, are you, is that it?'

'No.' Robin had seen all along he would have to apologise, but felt no repentance, so he said neutrally, 'Sorry, Dad.'

'You don't sound very sorry to me,' said his father with more emphasis.

Robin rinsed his toothbrush under the bath-tap and said again, 'Sorry, Dad.'

'Well, all right, we'll agree to call that adequate for this time in the morning, though I must say it doesn't sound so very different to this pair of ears.'

With an air of great weariness, as though every movement went deeply against the grain, Mr Davies laid out his shaving-kit on the tiles of the window-ledge: razor, current blade, open packet of blades, soap-stick, brush, glass tumbler round the inside of which he would rub blades past their best but with some life left in them. He went on:

'It's not much fun, you know, being on the receiving end of one of your attacks of EMP. Dear oh dear, it reminds me so clearly of how your Uncle Peter used to behave when he was a boy.'

EMP, Robin knew well enough, stood for Early Morning Peevishness. He said quickly, 'I don't know what I can have meant.'

As hoped, this form of words was taken as an adequate apology, though he could have done without being heartily assured that that was more like it. Anyway, Davies senior now quitted the bathroom with no more than a routine caution against hanging about half the morning.

Having removed traces of his father's beard from the washbasin, Robin poured into it from an enamel jug the now lukewarm leftover of shaving-water and soaped his hands and face, not forgetting his neck. He was not in fact an only child, but the absence from the household of his married sister and employed, digs-inhabiting brother certainly helped him to understand what it was like to be one. At fourteen years old to sister's twenty-three and brother's twenty-one, he supposed himself the child of his parents' middle age. It was not that he felt unwanted in any way, far from it, so far from it that before now he had thought with longing of what it must be like to be unwanted at least some of the time, like six days a week. He had reckoned that offered the choice he would have agreed to be wanted on Sundays. Now he took a little of his father's brilliantine and splashed water more generally on his fair hair. Peering round the door, he saw the landing was empty and hurried across to his bedroom. A moment afterwards he heard his father, now on his way downstairs, dispensing further data about the ill-fitting cure-arse.

In the dining-room, Robin scattered sugar, then milk, over his bowl of cornflakes. These had had malt used in their preparation and on most mornings would have caused him some trouble to dispose of, but today a letter from his sister Margery dominated the breakfast-table. It seemed that Margery's husband Roger had been spoken to encouragingly by his immediate boss. This meant little more to Robin than that one bore known to him and amiable enough had had such-and-such treatment from another, one he had never met but felt fully entitled to regard as worth avoiding if matters should ever come to that pass. Not that the encouraging words that had supposedly passed between the two were the whole story. Far from it. Mrs Davies's manner, pitched somewhere between that of a messenger of God and a delighted scandal - monger's, was an unequivocal guarantee that something about That was imminent. He tackled his cornflakes with the

3

concentration of someone about to make an important discovery in that general field.

His mother said, 'Margery's been to see that chap again.'

'What chap?' asked his father, who seemed to have noticed nothing special.

'You remember, Tom, the chap she went to see last *month*.'

'What? Oh, oh, that chap, of course. How was he? I mean, what did he have to say?'

'Everything was fine and going along just as it ought to.'

'All quite normal, in fact.'

'Everything was *fine*, said Robin's mother again, making a face he had no need to see. It and her tone rebuked her husband's choice of a risky adjective like normal.

'Oh, good. Has he said anything about when?' After some seconds of blank silence, Mr Davies went on, 'That's to say when . . . when he's going on his holidays.'

'Yes, well, he thought about the middle of March.'

'I see.'

'But it's difficult to be precise in the circumstances.'

'M'm,' said Mr Davies, clearly giving that one up as a bad job.

'The circumstances being that this is going to be Margery's first baby and the boy who sits next but one to me in my maths set's sister had her first baby in the Easter break, and it was three weeks late and according to her doctor first babies are quite often late but not always, you bloody old fool,' said Robin inside his head. Having followed the conversation without difficulty, unlike his father, he could think of plenty of other things he felt like saying, and out loud too, such as that he could cease imitating a prodigy of ignorance and a monster of incuriosity if his parents would agree either to treat him like an average boy of nearly fifteen or, if that was too much to face, to operate a self-imposed ban on all references to That, however indirect and well hidden and whether deliberate or accidental. No one could have wanted more fervently than he did to bawl slowly and immediately, on the spot, right away, now, a demand to be told what the hell was being talked about. The fact that he refrained from doing so witnessed not at all to any desire on his part to refrain from embarrassing his parents. It was due entirely to his reluctance to be told, as his father would assuredly tell him, to be a good chap and not poke his nose into matters that were none of his business. Well, possibly he did feel a small desire not to embarrass his mother.

Perhaps Mr Davies guessed or deduced what turn his son's thoughts were taking, because as they were getting up from breakfast he said to him sharply, 'Have you done your bigs this morning, Robin?'

'I went last night, Dad.' This was true, but Robin tried to make it sound like a lie. He took the question as a shrewd reminder of his only-just-out-of-nappies status.

'Give your mother a hand with clearing the table.'

Half an hour later, Robin was standing on one of the Up platforms of the railway junction. His father stood at his side. That was where his father had continuously been while they walked from the house to the corner, down the hill, into the side entrance of the local station, up the slope and on to the platform there, while they waited for their connection and while they rode to the junction. And that was where he would be, or as close as he could get, all the way to the terminus and along to and down the stairs to the exit, only parting company on the pavement outside, a bare hundred yards from the school steps. Why? His father had very little to say to him at these times, almost nothing to justify lifting his eyes from the columns of the *Morning Post*. Probably some instinct had told him to go on keeping his son under surveillance as long as he could within reason, without also telling him what his son might be nefariously getting up to in the street in broad daylight, on a crowded train, etc., if left to his own devices. Once or twice Mr Davies had seemed to try to explain himself.

'Has it ever struck you as funny that I go up with you on the train in the mornings? After all, you're getting to be a big boy now.'

'M'm, not really.'

'It may sound odd to you, but I'm glad of your company. I don't see anything of you during the day, and by the time I get back from the office you're usually deep in your homework. Of course, if you'd rather go off with your pals I should quite understand and you've only to say the word.'

If the word had been shit or fuck, Robin would have found it no more impossible to say to his father, even when, as now, his schoolmates Wade and Hurrell were to be seen waiting for the very same train as themselves some yards down the platform. Wade grinned and waved to Robin and Hurrell touched his cap to Mr Davies.

'They look nice enough chaps, those chums of yours.'

'Yes, they're very decent,' said Robin at once.

'Perhaps one of these days,' said his father, managing to introduce a wistful note, 'I may be allowed to meet them.' Robin was quite glad that their approaching train was still some distance off at this point, too far for pushing the old fellow under its wheels to be a practical proposition. When it finally stopped, his father got a touch of intrepidity into the way he set about boarding it.

In the third-class compartment Robin had to sit right next to him, but as against that he had by him some genuine homework, a chapter of Robinson on the Peloponnesian War. Next year he would be doing Roman history, which was generally agreed to be far worse than Greek, all about corn laws, so he settled down to the Athenian disaster in Sicily with redoubled eagerness.

At his side, Mr Davies made an occasional sound of dissatisfaction with what he was reading, but forbore from actual conversation with his son. At the same time he made it plain enough to whom it might or might not concern that they were travelling as a party of two, if not simple lunatic-and-keeper then medium-grade mental deficient with trusty or other attendant. When they separated outside the terminus, he said good-bye with a smile radiating absolute confidence in his son's ability to complete the journey unaccompanied without serious mishap.

Robin soon caught up with Hurrell and Wade. Hurrell was in the form a year ahead of Robin, Wade in one of the same year but on the Modern side. Like Robin, both wore the navy-blue school cap and tie with a white shirt and black shoes; unlike him in his black jacket and grey trousers they were in grey flannel suits, this being the summer term. Like Wade, Robin carried his books in a leather satchel; Hurrell, in token of his superior status, affected an attaché-case. Considering how little they had to do with one another in school, the three got on very easily together.

Wade's opening remark perhaps stretched matters a bit. 'How's the pater this morning, Davies?'

'Thank you for your interest. The pater, as you choose to style him, is no worse than usual.'

'No doubt when you see a chance you'll be getting down on your knees to thank your Creator for that. Is he, that's your dad, not the Creator, is he still sticking to his non-story on why he travels with you every day?'

'As far as is known.'

'He looks a nice old boy,' said Wade. 'Do you seriously maintain he goes to all these lengths simply to humiliate his young son before the uncaring multitude?' Before the last word was fairly out of his mouth a long loud ripping noise followed it, to be described for convenience as a belch and as usual taking precedence over whatever was being talked about.

'Thank you again,' said Robin. He said no more while the three finished passing the imposing offices of a firm of industrial chemists and being overtaken by a greatly disliked prefect of the school who, with a grown-up air of having much on his mind, ran urgently up its front steps. 'As regards to my parent's behaviour, it repays study.'

'You certainly give it plenty,' said Hurrell. He was a gloomy-looking boy, an impressive fast bowler for one not yet turned sixteen.

'That's to keep it from driving me mad.'

'Don't take it too seriously,' said Wade.

'You haven't got to put up with it. Look, I don't really think he does things like sticking to me like a leech in the mornings just to embarrass me, though if you were in my shoes you'd wonder sometimes, it's just, it's more he doesn't go to enough trouble not to. Like taking five seconds off to think about it.'

Wade grinned. 'How you do go on, to be sure.'

'Hey, I like that, it was you brought the subject up.'

Hurrell said to Robin, 'Some people are supposed to go through life looking for their father. You've found yours already, haven't you?'

The three went in by the side gate of the school and were soon dispersed among the crowds of boys making for the assembly hall on the first floor. On the landing of the stone stair there was a large tablet commemorating those ex-pupils, masters and staff who had been killed in the Great War. Here wreaths were laid for Armistice Day and a bugler in OTC uniform sounded the Last Post. The tablets in the hall itself bore the names of pupils who had attained academic distinction. Idealised stained-glass depictions of Homer, Sophocles, Plato and Aristotle stood at the end behind the platform. A heavy brass lectern was situated on the platform itself and it was from here that the headmaster, with the second master next to him and the senior assistant masters ranged on either side, started reading announcements to the school. Today these concerned the dates of examinations, the weekly gramophone recital, the League of Nations Union. When they were over, the Head nodded as always to the senior Jewish boy, who led from the hall the others of his faith, the Roman Catholics and the Dissenters. Bringing up the rear and a little apart, again as usual, went a boy in Science V named Easton. Throughout the school Easton was known for an unbeliever, or perhaps more truly as the unique possessor of a father who had successfully petitioned the Board of Governors for his son to be excused attendance at school prayers on grounds of conscience.

When the swing door had closed behind the departing Easton, those still present looked at the floor while the Head recited in his fine but rather monotonous voice the General Confession from the Book of Common Prayer:

Almighty and most merciful Father; We have erred, and strayed from thy ways like lost sheep. We have followed too much the devices and desires of our own hearts. We have offended against thy holy laws. We have left undone those things which we ought to have done; And we have done those things which we ought not to have done; And there is no health in us. But thou, O Lord, have mercy upon us, miserable offenders. Spare thou them, O God, which confess their faults. Restore thou them that are penitent; According to thy promises declared unto mankind in Christ Jesu our Lord. And grant, O most merciful Father, for his sake; That we may hereafter live a godly, righteous, and sober life, To the glory of thy holy Name. Amen.

Our Father, which art in heaven . . .

Robin could not remember ever having seen any of this written down, not even the contents of the Lord's Prayer, though they were familiar enough to him from countless repetitions within his hearing. He was not sure that it was indeed health whose absence was confessed, not that the point had much interested him at any time. He had a blurred memory of a visit or visits to church in his childhood, but nothing more recent. His parents visited no place of worship and neither of them had made any sort of suggestion that he should do so himself. During the first phrases of the Confession his attention wandered from the unremarkable events of the day so far to what he expected to be the no more remarkable ones of the rest of a day in the summer term; he certainly devoted no thought to whatever might have been meant by the words the Head was saying, or been taken for granted in them. With the beginning of the Lord's Prayer, many or most of those present added their soft mumble, but not Robin. If induced to explain why not, he would most likely have talked vaguely about seeing no reason why he should do something just because it was expected of him. Nevertheless he was refusing or denying something and knew it. And then he kept his head and eyes lowered and envied Easton not at all.

'Amen,' said the Head and almost everyone else at the end of the prayer. For three seconds, five, there was virtually complete silence, not much of it, in Robin's estimation, the result of any real feeling. In the company of Embleton, his desk-mate, he joined the general steady movement out of the hall and along the corridors. He supposed that for a crowd of boys aged from eight to eighteen, for the moment not under the direct eye of authority, they looked docile enough, even perhaps verging on the well behaved. In this and in other ways they were quite unlike the boys in his favourite kind of school story. These fictional boys either behaved like men of forty or carried on like comic lunatics or were wasters, scapegraces, bounders. Such characters smoked Turkish cigarettes, drank brandy and soda, ate duck and green peas, played poker for money and betted on the horses when they were not balancing pails of water over the door of the masters' common-room or setting fire to the Head's trousers on Speech Day. Sometimes they stole. Robin enjoyed such stories as he enjoyed tales of pirates or the Wild West, and had little time for stuff about licking the House cricket XI into shape, outwitting rotters and slackers, etc. But he was very well pleased with his own real school and tended to follow its rules and customs instinctively. You knew where you were at a place like this.

Embleton had shared Robin's desk since the beginning of that school year, not from choice nor from compulsion, but because a boy with a surname beginning with E was likely to find himself sitting next to another with one beginning with D when it was taken for granted that a class sat alphabetically. Robin saw nothing unexpected in the fact that this system had presented him with the companionship of somebody he would have had some difficulty in specifying, let alone seeking out. For Embleton was not only handsome in a dark, solid, unpretty way but gave an impression of being equal to any likely challenge, well within his depth at rugger or chess or Latin but also free of any anxiety about what he wanted to do with his life, whether he had it in him to do it, and other puzzles Robin would have had to struggle to find words for. At the same time there were large parts of Embleton he obviously meant to keep to himself. These were not the things people first noticed about him and Robin sometimes wondered if they were really there at all. He was certain only of liking him and being afraid of him and finding, when unsure of what he thought himself about a Fats Waller record or a Charles Morgan novel, that finding out Embleton's opinion simplified matters greatly.

While the class waited for Mr Oakley to come and start teaching them about the fateful night battle on the plateau of Epipolae, Robin said to Embleton:

'Why do these Hollywood film stars keep getting divorced all the time?'

'Well, Americans are much more free and easy about divorce than we are.'

'But do these women keep falling in love with a new man every couple of years? Or do they all keep making the same mistake and trying to put it right? Or do they just want to get more and more money?'

'I think they just want a new man to, you know, go to bed with.'

'But why can't they just go to bed with him when they feel randy and go back to their husband when they've had enough? Why do they have to get divorced all the time?'

Embleton showed signs of impatience. 'You've got to remember they're very stuffy and puritanical over there. Everybody's got to abide by the rules.'

'But a moment ago you were saying—'

At that point Mr Oakley arrived and Robin had to concentrate on what he proceeded to tell the class about how the presence of Theban troops on both sides caused first misunderstanding and then panic among the Athenian forces, how this led to the loss of Epipolae, how the besiegers of Syracuse soon became the besieged, how defeat in Sicily helped to bring about the fall of Athens, and how the history of the world might have been changed by the events of a few seconds in a remote corner. Robin fought to get it all down in his notes. He turned to Embleton again when the departing Mr Oakley was barely through the door.

'You said Americans were a free and easy lot about divorces and a minute later you were telling me they were a puritanical lot that always played by the rules. How can the—'

'Sorry,' said Embleton. 'The rules say you can only go to bed with someone you're married to, then it's all right. They don't say anything about how many husbands or wives you may have had before.'

'What are you talking about? People like my parents would be very firm, bloody firm on people sticking to the person they were married to. And they're against, well, going the whole hog with anyone before they're married, which has always struck me as too much to live up to and jolly dreary too.'

'You're talking about a different set of rules, Davies, you owl. All that's to do with sin.'

'What is the difference, Embleton?'

'Eh? Sin's against religion, crime's against the law.'

'So what?'

'It's against the law to go to bed with anyone but your wife in California, which is where Hollywood is.'

'It can't be.'

'You'll find it is.'

That was one of old Emble's ways of declaring an argument closed. He had perhaps shifted his ground somewhere in it, but before Robin could cast his mind back, Mr Pearson had turned up for Latin unseen. Boys went up to him in turn at his desk to have their last week's efforts briefly gone over; the rest of the time they translated another of his selections from the much-hated book they used for this purpose. It was a random selection, presumably on the reasoning that predictability would constitute an invitation to look up the hard words illegally ahead of time, which might have been good enough as reasoning but underestimated schoolboy innocence and laziness.

Robin had as usual pretended to think he had done badly with last week's unseen but again as usual had done pretty well, having been marked at beta-alpha in a rather tough week. Today's piece was an almost insultingly easy couple of paragraphs of Caesar and he finished it with ten minutes in hand. He was not quite secretly glad to see that Embleton took a little longer.

When the papers were collected it was time for break. The bell rang and in no time the tall bare corridors and identical stone staircases were full of boys in movement. Robin went to the tuckshop on the ground floor and from habit got into a queue of boys of about the same size as himself. From it he had a good view of the celebrated Milnes of the Economics Sixth, a sub-prefect of small intellectual distinction but known as a fast and violent wing forward and an enviably debauched character who, it was said, had once shown one of the tuckshop girls a french letter and made her cry. It was also said or believed that his use of french letters by no means stopped short at showing them to girls, which was felt, by Robin for one, to cast an unfavourable or at least ironical light on his father's national fame as a broadcasting sage. At the moment Milnes the younger was wearing what Robin took to be a well cut grey suit, and rather flaunting an outsize ring on his middle finger while he sipped at a glass of milk. No doubt he carried a french letter at all times in case he should happen to run into one of his many girls. Robin felt not so much envy as acceptance, a resigned feeling that Milnes was following a mysterious path that he himself might never find however hard he looked. When his turn came at the counter he paid a penny for a kind of chocolate bar called a milky lunch and hurried out of the shop, along the cloisters and into the main part of the playground. Here he was about to join a scattered group who were kicking an old tennis-ball about when he was hailed by a boy in his form called MacBryde. He stopped and turned and saw it was too late to run away.

Not that Robin would ever have done so in fact, but it was undeniable that MacBryde was a goof, a chump, a stodge. At anything of a distance he looked quite normal, even rather impressive with his upright way of holding himself. It was only when he drew closer that you took in such things as the large loose knot of his school tie, always a bad sign, his juvenile waist-belt, horizontally striped, with gilded snake-buckle, and his highly polished shoes. These must have got into such a state either by his own hand, which would have been bad enough, or by his mother's or father's, which in different ways would have been worse still. Then a little later you noticed that the upright bearing went with a gruesome habit in conversation. He would turn himself bodily to face each new speaker in turn after the lapse of what seemed like three-quarters of a hour or so, but in all probability was no more than some seconds. He somehow managed to bring off this effect even when, as now, there was only one of you.

'Where are you rushing off to, Davies?' he eventually asked in his unexpectedly high voice.

'I'm not rushing off anywhere. Not at the moment.'

'Oh, I thought you were rushing off somewhere. Tell me, Davies, will you be going to the branch meeting of the League of Nations Union after school?' Others of the smallish company that might have brought the matter up at all would probably have called it the LNU meeting, but then that would have taken less time to say. 'It's being held *there*,' added MacBryde, no doubt referring to the neighbouring premises of the girls' school that shared nothing much besides its badge and part of its name with the much older boys' grammar school. Uncharacteristically, he left it at that for now.

'Will you be going anyway?' asked Robin to gain time.

MacBryde brought himself to bear on this question with the deliberation of a dreadnought's primary armament. Then a smile lit up his face and he spoke almost animatedly. 'What about you?' he said. 'I asked first.'

'I haven't made up my mind.' At that moment the tennis-ball came bounding directly towards him. His movements given precision by having no time to think, Robin kicked at it with both feet in the air, got it at just the right spot on the instep and sent it unimprovably into the top left-hand corner of the goal chalked on part of a nearby wall. Those within sight raised a caricatured roar of appreciation. On impulse Robin said to MacBryde, 'I suppose I might as well. We could stroll round there after school.'

At intervals during the rest of the morning and the earlier part of the afternoon Robin scrutinised this decision of his, from time to time assuring himself untruly that he could always change his mind up to the last minute. Fear of boredom and embarrassment finally succumbed to mingled curiosity and lust, and when lessons ended for the day he was ready to tell himself with more truth that it would at least look shitty if he let silly old MacBryde down. But just then fate intervened in the person of a boy named Chalmers of Classical IVB. Chalmers looked and sounded all right, but he was godly, something that could never have been held against MacBryde with all his faults. Like a fool, not paying due heed to the Crusader badge in Chalmers's lapel, ignoring Embleton's advice, Robin had refrained from instantly telling Chalmers to sod off at his first mention of the Deity, and the Crusader still made fitful attempts, as today, to persuade him to come along to one of the weekly after-school gatherings of his club or sect. Robin was too tickled at the idea of sheltering from a God-botherer behind a goof to take this surely golden opportunity for delivering a brief but definitive sod-off speech. Anyway, at a quarter to four he and MacBryde were making their way towards the girls' school in question.

Robin knew the address of this girls' school because he knew things like that, not because he had been there before. As they approached, he felt contentedly that it was an inferior place away from traffic and the river, more like a block of flats or offices than his notion of a school, it turned out, with a low wall and railings between it and the pavement behind which rose-bushes grew. Oh well, he thought, rose-bushes and glossy serrated leaves went with real girls, an order of being he had experienced almost nothing of except in the plural and at a distance. A member of it, a rather fat person in grey flannel that included a hat with an encircling emblematic ribbon, passed Robin and MacBryde on the steps up to the entrance. She gave them a glance of very limited curiosity and was gone.

The entrance hall switched the thoughts to hospitals as much by its inorganic smell as by anything to be seen. Here the two boys were soon accosted by a bald-headed man in a serge suit, no doubt some form of porter, though visibly of inferior standing to the liveried officials at their own school. The bald man, who must have been taken in by MacBryde's consequential manner, quite readily and politely directed them to what he called a library room just round a corner from where they stood, and they went to it.

After less than a minute inside this very citadel of girls, Robin had had sight, fleeting as it was in most cases, of several dozen of them, in fact had had time to switch his policy twice, from pretending no one was there to 'behaving naturally', with frank interest, no-bones-about-it curiosity, etc., and back again. Half a dozen further girls were already in the library room, sitting among the rows of chairs arranged for the meeting, looking at books on the shelves. Those who took any notice of the boys' entry paid about as much attention as one customer at an ironmonger's might give the arrival of a couple more. While he pretended to consider where to sit, Robin asked himself what he had expected. That all the girls in the place should rush at him, tearing off their clothes as they came? Regretfully no. Such things took place only in America.

When another boy or male person arrived, some dim, barely recognised senior from the thin wastes of Science or Mathematics Sixth, sanity and boredom were restored. There really was going to be a talk about the rise to power of the National Socialist government in Germany and he was on the spot with plenty to spare. The sudden loud braying utterance of MacBryde, whose presence he had quite forgotten, to the effect that they might as well sit down, came too late to restore any sense of higher reality. Not for the first or even the hundredth time, the thought suggested itself to Robin that very likely babies were indeed found under gooseberry bushes, or that the stork's part in their production had been gravely underestimated, or that under certain conditions it was the doctor who brought them in his little black bag. What else?

The seats mostly filled up with boys, girls, and schoolmasters, schoolmistresses, other adults whose identity was not worth the trouble or the humiliation of trying to guess. Some senior female in a chair facing the audience introduced another one as a famous writer just back from Berlin, somebody everyone was lucky to have with them that afternoon. Whether this would turn out to be strictly true or not, there was a good deal of applause. The famous writer stood up and very soon was talking of Munich and von Papen, Brownshirts and Ludendorff, Reichstag and Hindenburg. Robin, who had joined in the applause for something to do, knew almost nothing of Adolf Hitler and his Nazis except that he and they were giving the German Communists a bad time, which was obviously much to be welcomed. Hence he was mildly surprised to gather, from what the famous writer was saying, that it was more complicated than that and that the Communists had a case, to do with some election on 5th March 1933. As well as being mildly surprising, this was mildly irritating. If the famous writer had been about fifty years younger, Robin might have dismissed such obvious perversity as only to be expected from a bloody woman. As it was, he took a mental note or two to use in a grown-up style of report to Embleton, then abandoned the project as too much like hard work and not what he had come here for.

What he had come here for was spread out all round him, easier to look over now that general attention was fixed elsewhere. He had soon eliminated some candidates on grounds of taste, others as inaccessible to view in the absence of mirrors, periscopes and kindred novelties. It took him a little longer to make a final selection from his short-list of three. The winner was about his age, he decided, but with a thin face that might have made her look older. The visible portion of the rest of her was not thin, but it was not fat either. He dutifully tried to conjure up the invisible portions that he nevertheless knew on excellent authority were to be found under the grey gym-tunic and light peach-coloured blouse, but found himself unable to fuse the imagined with the real. He felt among other things like a recruit improving his knowledge of the enemy by watching a film of him performing barrack duties. Perhaps the girl sensed Robin's interest, because at no particular moment he saw her head start to turn in his direction. Instantly he faced his front, easing his neck inside his shirt-collar for no reason he could think of.

He had read somewhere that, because of relative speeds of metabolism or something, time seemed to elapse more quickly for the old than for the young. Over the passage of the next substantial fraction of eternity he wondered a few hundred times if perhaps he had stumbled across a genuine advantage of age over youth. But all things come to an end, bad as well as good, and in the result he felt little more advanced in years when the previously unbelievable happened and the famous writer asked for questions and got some and answered them and was done and finally received thanks. Robin's legs brought him to his feet when required as if nothing had happened.

The room emptied slowly. He had to wait his turn to join the stream making for the door. He found he had done so at exactly the same moment as the girl he had looked at. Then he found he was standing side by side with her at a temporary standstill. She was quite tall, nearly as tall as he. If she had had a friend with her, no such person was to be seen just then. She turned her head towards him and this time he could not have turned his away. She had nice eyes, he noticed, though he failed to take in their colour.

'I thought that was never going to end,' she said in a semi-classy voice.

'It did rather go on and on.'

'I expect it did us all a power of good.'

'I expect so.'

The girl drew a skein of straight brown hair back towards her ear and put a couple of books under her arm. In the other hand she carried a black felt hat with the ribbon of her school round it. 'I haven't seen you before, have I?' she asked. 'What's your name?'

He told her and before he could stop himself added the needless information that he attended the boys' grammar school round the corner. 'I'm in Classical IVA,' he finished helplessly, feeling his cheeks flushing and, it seemed, quite incapable of asking the return question.

'Oh yes. Tell me . . .'

After less than half a minute's deadlock, small but swift and inescapable events got going again. There was scattered movement; somebody stepped between Robin and the girl; he called over to her that he would see her again; MacBryde appeared and claimed him; they were leaving the room. In the corridor Robin looked to and fro but without much intention: it was clear to him that he could not have ridded himself of MacBryde. The girl was gone.

Turning his top half towards his companion, sometimes dangerously far, MacBryde went on about the talk and the speaker until they had reached the outdoors, and about the speaker and her talk thereafter. More than once he explained that an old friend of his father's was closely involved with the trade development in Germany as some sort of diplomat. By the time they parted outside the Underground station, it had become clear to Robin that he had been on the point of going off with one of the girls who had been at the meeting when bloody old thick MacBryde had butted in and of course mucked the whole thing up. That at least was going to be the version Embleton would hear the next day.

Hurrell and Wade would have gone back by an earlier train, so Robin cheered up his journey home by buying a copy of *The Humorist*. Its contents did not so much make him laugh as reassure him that there was a whole world beyond his experience and most of his imagining, but one he would be certain to inherit merely by waiting for time to pass, however long it took or seemed to take. What was puzzling or frightening or simply vacant now would become manageable and commonplace.

Robin walked up the hill towards home in bright early-evening sunshine and let himself into the house with the latchkey he had taken from under its stone on the narrow flower-bed below the front window. Enjoying the silence all around him, he went through to the kitchen at the back. Here on the white enamel-topped table there stood a dinner-plate with another lid inverted over it. Robin's eyes widened in theatrical surprise and wonder. Moving cautiously, one crouching stride at a time, he approached the table. When in range he halted, lunged abruptly with his arms, gripped the upper plate by its circumference, stood stock-still for a moment, then snatched off the covering plate and with extended arms raised it above his head, meanwhile doing his best to imitate the sound of a cheering multitude. Finally he put the plate aside, raised his right hand to quell the applause and proudly extended his left to indicate to his audience the now revealed six well buttered slices of brown bread and marmalade, cut in two diagonally, his mother had prepared.

There was also a note from her on the table, in pencil on the sheet of the light-azure paper she liked to write her letters on. Am at Joy Carpenter's for cards, it read; back by six – have a nice tea. As usual, two crosses followed but no signature. While he waited for the kettle to boil he took a handful of larger and smaller table-knives from the drawer, lined them up along the dresser and set each of them spinning on the raised ring between handle and blade. At one time, he remembered, he had really pretended they were the propellers of aeroplanes. Long ago. Since then he had gone through a phase of seeing how many he could keep turning at once. These days he just did it, to pass the time, small amounts of time.

The kettle boiled. He made tea in the little chocolate-brown pot and turned off the gas. Soon he had everything he needed laid out at his place at the dining-table, including a copy of the *Aeneid* opened at the passage to be construed the following day. The clock on the mantelpiece reminded him that there were still some minutes of the BBC Dance Orchestra to be caught on the National Programme, enough for him not to be deterred from turning on the wireless-set by the trouble this took. Accordingly he went and lay face down on the carpet while he fished under the sideboard for the plug at the end of its flex . . . got it, found the power-point in the wall. . . . Robin's father was not the man to go as far as forbidding the use of the wireless when he was not there, but neither was he the man to allow this to happen whenever any Tom, Dick or Harry took it into his head to try it. And it was remarkable how little difference there turned out to be in practice between something being forbidden and its being merely very difficult.

A puny electromagnetic squealing and nothing else became audible when the receiver had warmed up. This was unusual, and it made Robin feel slightly flattered to think that perhaps a detuning process had suggested itself to his father as the next step in his campaign to make unsupervised listening to the wireless too much bloody trouble. But a few seconds' twiddling of the knobs produced first some remarkably human wails, then the sound of what was called a comedy number ending. Robin did his best to settle down with bread and marmalade, a chap singing a song with violins, tea and *macte nova virtute, puer.*

By the time he had finished eating, the band had struck up its end-of-relay tune and had been faded out. Six o'clock. Robin started to rise from the table, meaning to look out of the french window, but sat back again. The most interesting thing to be seen from there would have been the man next door digging his garden. Robin sat on. By now he had decided to tell Embleton tomorrow that MacBryde had been a bit of use for once in his life by unintentionally rescuing him from the clutches of a very plain girl who had been trying to pick him up. Well, it was not so far from the truth.

With the wireless turned off, the silence of the house no longer pleased him. It seemed to him that there was nothing in the world he wanted to do that lay within his power to do. Bar the old exception. Robin had no sooner thought of it than he began to ask himself pressingly why he had not thought of it the moment he found himself alone in the house. His mother had written that she would be back by six, but she was never back from one of her whist afternoons less than a half an hour late. Plenty of time.

He went upstairs and locked the bathroom door after him. It would not have been his first choice of venue if the lock on his bedroom door had had a key to it, but somehow it never had. He

21

promised himself he would take a long time over the next bit, and then suddenly found he had taken as little time as possible. A couple of minutes later it occurred to him almost as suddenly that to say he had been rescued from a very plain girl was actually far from the truth. The truth was that his own cowardice and incompetence, fuelled by vanity, had led him to turn down the chance of a lifetime with a girl who, if not exactly beautiful, was a bloody sight closer to it than somebody like him deserved, somebody who had last kissed a girl when he was ten years old at her tenth birthday party and made her run out of the room calling for her mother. He would never be able to tell anybody any of that.

'I only saw her for a few seconds,' said Robin, 'but as far as I could make out she was pretty good. If only I'd had a bit longer to get my ideas in order I know I could have thought of something, but I had bloody MacBryde on one side waffling about his uncle at our embassy in Berlin, and somebody's aunt taking up a lot of room on the other, so I just . . .'

Embleton made whistling noises and fanned his face with spread fingers, 'What a shemozzle,' he said. 'No wonder you fluffed your lines.'

'I don't mind telling you I felt a bit of a twerp, you know, coming a complete mucker like that.'

Now Embleton shook his head in the manner of one who knew. 'Don't,' he said emphatically. 'That's how they want you to feel, you silly ass.'

'What who want?'

'Oh Lord, *they,* the powers that be, park-keepers, schoolmasters, cinema commissionaires, that sort of person, guards on the railway. People who want to stop you having a good time.' Embleton's dark eyes seemed to flash. It was hard to be sure how serious he was being. 'You must have come across plenty of people like that.'

Looking back on this conversation of the day after the LNU meeting, Robin thought to himself that he had done more than come across a couple of such, then decided he was being unfair to his mother. A moment later he conceded that, on the whole and taking a long view, he might have been being slightly unfair to his father as well. It was easier, or less difficult, to make that concession, as now, on a Saturday morning, the only one in the seven that contained no school and no father. The school, for some complicated reason to do with Jews, was shut; Mr Davies's office, like many another office, was open, and until 12.30 (in summer, 1.00 in winter) he would be in it, helping to buy or sell or originate insurance. Sometimes, his family knew, he would not be strictly in it, just close by it in a teashop getting down to a good chat with his pals about stocks and shares as well as insurance. One of Robin's definitions of being grown up was that it started when you started looking forward to chats about things of that kind.

It was a beautiful morning. In his bedroom getting ready to go out, Robin played his portable gramophone, using a loud steel needle as always when Mr Davies was out of the house and putting on the turntable a record known to be especially displeasing to him. The piece was in the style of a folk-song for violin with accompaniment, performed by a musician of international repute once described by Mr Davies as that gipsy fiddler fellow. It lasted for the time it took Robin to choose one of his non-school ties and put it on in front of his dressing-table mirror. As he pinched and pulled at the knot, he examined a question hitherto unexplored: why his father had ever bought him a gramophone for his birthday in the first place when he must surely have expected not to care for the sounds apt to emerge from it. Wrong: he could not have expected it, unless perhaps he had been looking for a new means of harassing his son. Rather an expensive means. And no normal man would think like that. But then no normal man would have expected his son's musical taste to be agreeable to him. 'I know,' said Robin aloud, 'I'll understand when I'm older.' He set the gramophone going again with an accordion band playing *The Bluebells of Scotland*.

What Robin liked about Saturday mornings was not only no school and no father, or at least no corporeal father, it was the time when for a couple of hours he was his own boss. He could call in at the shop that sold bikes and bike-lamps and stuff and where the not very friendly man nevertheless allowed him to look over the stock of model aeroplanes and gliders, call in at the gramophone shop, where the very friendly and quite pretty girl – aged at least eighteen, but still – let him play a record or two without expecting him to buy one, change his book at the 2d-a-volume-a-week library, and keep his eye open throughout for girls both possible and impossible. For that short space of time his father's policy of round-the-clock chaperonage was in abeyance. His mother abetted his evasion by letting it be thought he had spent the time with her or in her charge. Now and again she gently required him to spend an hour or so with her at the coffee shop where she met her pals. That was set to happen today.

Although he might have said to himself he would rather die than admit it, he was not sorry when one of these occasions came round. In his thoughts he might have pleaded that some of the pals must have suitable daughters to whom this was a possible route. It had signally failed to be any such thing as yet, but you never knew. It had never occurred to him that his mother might enjoy his company and the chance to show off a son of hers who was doing well at a highly esteemed school. But under duress he might have admitted he enjoyed his mother's company.

They walked together down the road at the end of which, five mornings a week, Robin turned left with his father towards the station. The thought of that imparted pleasure to turning right today with his mother. Soon they passed a sweetshop he had once longed to enter but knew now to be much too grand for the likes of him, selling as it did chocolates and chocolate and stuff like sugared almonds rather than aniseed balls or those marvellous little round yellow packets of sherbet with the liquorice tube. After waiting a moment or two they crossed the main road near the almost-new public lavatory, a facility Robin's father had forbidden him to use on the surely dubious grounds that you were liable to pick up nasty infections in such places. Three boys of about Robin's age were skylarking in and around the Men entrance, one of them being a vampire and the other two his terrified quarry. On catching sight of Robin all three of them elaborately pulled themselves up and went quiet and put on goody-goody expressions.

A little later, as they stood at the bus-stop outside the green - grocer's, Robin said to his mother, 'Mum, I've been meaning to ask you something.'

'I'm listening, dear.'

'Mum, I was thinking, I don't seem to have many friends. I've got plenty at school but I don't seem to have many round here.'

'Well, of course it isn't easy for a boy in your position, with your brother and sister so much older and your school miles away like it is. I remember your father telling you before you started going there what you'd be in for.'

'I understand that.' Robin considered saying he could not remember seeing much in the way of company outside school in the days when the school he went to was within walking distance, but decided it would do no good. Instead he went on, 'But I . . . Sometimes I think he doesn't really want me to have friends much.'

'Robin, please don't talk such tommy rot. Of course your father wants you to have friends, what nonsense.'

'But he won't leave it to me to choose them. He wants to choose them himself.'

'Oh dear. Isn't it natural and right that a father should, well, keep an eye on his son's companions?'

'Yes, but not that sort of eye. Sorry, Mum, but he sort of makes up his mind they're not suitable before he's had a chance to see if they're suitable or not. And in any case . . .'

Robin had started to get quite worked up, but his mother disarmed him with sympathy and concern. 'I know, dear, I know what you mean, he can be a bit of a one for laying down the law, it's just his way. Now listen, I've got a suggestion to make.'

'Oh, goodo.' It was hard not to sound impatient now their bus was in sight, coming up the hill towards them not more than a hundred yards off.

'It's your job to find somebody you like, but when you have

25

we'll invite him over to tea and I'll make it all right with your father.'

'Oh, Mum, that would be super.'

'Mind you, I'll expect you to pick somebody reasonable, not some awful common creature.'

So they were back where they started, thought Robin morosely as he and his mother climbed on to the bus, but he forgot his grievance in enjoying the excellent sunlit field of view from where they were soon installed, in the left-hand front seat. The bus moved on past the little old cinema and the big new cinema, the public library where he sometimes went, his first school and his second school where he was glad to think he would never have to go again. On the pavements people moved to and fro on their obscure errands. The sight of them filled him with impatience to be grown up. He savoured the thought of that distant state until, inevitably, he remembered from several occasions his father telling him to enjoy his boyhood and its freedom from care, responsibility, money worries, etc., for all too soon those happy days of youth would be no more. That memory took Robin straight back to his grievance, but again he soon forgot it, this time because his mother furtively squeezed his hand, meaning what she could not very well have put into words, that she sympathised with what he had been saying and would not go back on her promise. He was not the sort of boy to admit to loving his mother but quite often, like now, he experienced a surge of liking for her, not hard to feel for such a cheerful, nice-looking woman, nice-looking both in the sense of looking a nice old thing and quite pretty too, not so very old in fact, mid-forties perhaps, and with her mostly auburn hair and bright brown eyes declared attractive by that rigorous tribunal, an ad hoc selection of his schoolmates (who had had a look at her at speech days and other such functions). Now, the moment their stop came in sight she stood up to leave the bus. It was her disposition to leave plenty of time for everything.

That morning at the Dainty Shop revealed no relevant girls, not even a spoken reference, let alone a physical manifestation. Actually it produced something worse than just no girls in the shape of an invitation to go round to Joy Carpenter's 'for say an hour' that evening.

'Are you sure you want us, on a Saturday?' asked Robin's mother.

'Oh yes,' said Mrs Carpenter, and went on to explain, perhaps unnecessarily, that something else had fallen through at the last minute.

'Do you mind if we bring Robin with us? He'll be all alone otherwise.'

Mrs Carpenter stared at him for a few seconds. 'Oh, he doesn't want to come to us, it'll be all grown-ups. Terribly dull for him.'

'No, honestly, I'd love to come,' said Robin, reflecting that there was nothing like a stiff dose of the truth for bringing out the lies.

Mr Davies, at any rate, had no doubts about the plan when it was put to him on his return home. He was a little later than usual and already in genial mood, which suggested he had put away a couple of quick glasses of beer with his pals while discussing stocks and shares with them. The prospect of a free evening out might have cheered him up further.

'We might pop in for one at the Swan on our way there,' he said. 'Fizzy lemonade for you, youngster, if you're good. I doubt if there'll be anything more exciting than a cup of cocoa where we're going.'

He was leading the way to the dining-room for lunch when the telephone rang, not a frequent event in this household. The instrument stood on the sill of the little stained-glass window to one side of the hall. Mr Davies approached it frowning, not at all inclined to think well of the unexpected caller. He took off the receiver in gingerly fashion. The hairs on the backs of his hands were noticeable.

'Hallo, yes? I'm sorry, I wasn't able to catch your . . . Who? One moment, please.' Elaborately covering the receiver, Mr Davies fixed his gaze on Robin. 'Some . . . somebody seems to want to speak to *you*,' he hissed.

27

Robin approached the telephone with a show of nonchalance. He very soon heard a voice he recognised.

'Oh, Davies, it's Wade here. I was just finishing my homework when I wondered if you'd like to come over to tea this afternoon? Hurrell's coming and threatening to bring his sister, so I thought . . . Here's the address.' It was short and easy to remember. 'Facing the common. What shall we say, about four? Very good, if I don't hear from you I'll take it that's okay. Bye.'

Robin put the receiver back on its hook and turned away to see his parents facing him side by side. Their expressions seemed to combine curiosity and vexation. 'Who was *that*?' demanded his father, as if the caller had accused him of something serious, like stealing a stock or a share.

'Wade, that school chum of mine we see every—'

'Never heard of him.'

'We see him every morning on the train into town, the one with glasses. He asked me to—'

'Through no fault of my own I've never managed to make Master Wade's acquaintance. Anyway, what did he want?'

'He asked me over to tea this afternoon. That other chap—'

'This afternoon. What did you say?'

'I said that would be fine. You heard me, Dad.'

'Oh, so that would be fine, would it?'

'Well, I thought . . .'

Mr Davies sighed deeply. 'I can see we'll have to discuss this.'

Mrs Davies, who had been looking from one to the other as they spoke, now concentrated on her husband. 'Can we do it over lunch? I'm starving.'

'I'm sorry, my love.' Mr Davies quite tractably went along into the dining-room and took his place at the table, but flung up a detaining hand when his wife seemed about to go out, very likely in order to bring in food from the kitchen. 'What's in store for us?' he enquired.

'Oh nothing, Tom. Just a bit of ham and salad.'

'Very suitable for the time of year, my love, and it means you can afford to sit down for a moment, there being nothing to go off the boil, as it were. Now, Robin old boy, this shouldn't take us more than a few seconds to sort out, given a bit of good will. Er, you, er, as I understand, accepted an invitation from Joy, from Mrs Carpenter that is, to go round to her place this evening in the company of your parents, I believe that's correct?'

Robin, heroically as he saw it, confined himself to saying, 'Yes.'

'And now you tell me you've accepted *another* invitation to go out to tea with this friend of yours, this Cade or Spade or Shade or whatever he's called.'

'Wade. So I have.'

Mr Davies raised his head sharply at what he might have seen as a signal of defiance. Then, as if a bright light had suddenly been shone into his eyes from near at hand, he covered them with his fingers and, his face working, seemed over the next half-minute or so to stroke them back to a normal state. He said, 'You see . . . the point is . . . the sad fact is . .. you have a previous engagement. Perhaps it slipped your mind in the excitement.'

'Oh, but that's not till this evening, as you said. A quarter to eight or eight o'clock, which means leaving here about half-past seven. I'll be back from Wade's by half-past six at the latest, probably earlier.'

His son had hardly begun this speech when Mr Davies started shaking his head in wide, slow swings. When it was his turn again he said, the remnants of his Cardigan accent showing, 'I'm sorry, old boy. You can't do both. I'm sorry.'

Robin sat at the dining-table, small and square-topped without its leaf, in his usual place, back to the window, father on right, mother on left. He had foreseen the entire course of the conversation from the moment he had put the telephone down, including details like the slipped-mind suggestion. His father's invoking of a phantom law of nature, one seeming to deny the possibility of a person's presence in different places at different times, was just the sort of thing he could never quite get Wade or Hurrell to believe. Foreseeing what was to follow not much less closely than what had already passed, he nevertheless said, 'Why not? There's long enough in between for me to polish all the silver if I feel like it.'

'Don't try to be flippant with me, my lad. When you forget your duty it falls to me to remind you of it.'

'Duty? What duty?' Robin knew, but still had to ask.

'I'm referring to your homework, or had you forgotten that too?'

'I say, do you mind if we start lunch?' asked Mrs Davies. 'My tummy's rumbling.'

'This'll take two minutes, no more. Well, Robin?'

'My weekend homework will take me two hours maximum. Even if I don't do any of it today I still have all tomorrow, say ten hours allowing for mealtimes and an early night.'

'It used to be a rule you finished it by Saturday teatime, but I suppose that too has gone by the board. In addition to which, what sort of fellow is this Wade, broadcasting invitations to tea off his own bat over the telephone? Pretty casual, isn't he?'

'I don't know.'

'Oh, you don't know what sort of fellow you were proposing to spend half your Saturday afternoon with? Well, you'll have to forgive me for saying I think perhaps I may have a provisional idea. Somebody pretty casual, not concerned with the niceties of life, with the forms of common politeness in such matters as invitations to tea and so on, which in cases such as this ought surely to be delivered by one parent to another . . .'

It was obvious, it had always been obvious, that Mr Davies was not going to let his son go and have tea with a schoolmate of that son's. Why not? Perhaps he really thought that schoolmate might start swearing or smoking or gambling or grabbing at son's winkle. Swear, smoke and even gamble, yes, schoolmate might well have set about doing, but as regards the other he was significantly less unlikely to tear off Hurrell's sister's knickers. Perhaps Mr Davies really thought he had a personal obligation to try to maintain standards of behaviour. He said so often enough.

'I suppose he just rang up on the spur of the moment,' said Robin.

'Yes, that's rather what I thought. Which is this Master Wade, anyway? Of the two I see every morning. Is he the one with the sticky-out teeth?'

'He's the one with the glasses. Neither he nor Hurrell has sticky-out teeth.'

'Then he must be the one with the sticky-out ears. Anyway, to me at least, in one way and another he looks a bit of a hobbledehoy. Also, to me just now over the telephone, he sounded a good deal of a hobbledehoy. Do I make myself clear?'

You do, thought Robin. So clear you were quite right in thinking you had no need to bother to make it sound like a question. Crystal clear. Even bloody clearer than you thought. To you at least Wade is a rough, a rowdy, a hooligan, a johnny whose mother sews him up for the winter, who habitually makes rude noises in front of people and shouts at them from up or downstairs or the next room instead of going where they are and speaking politely, who picks his nose and eats it and has never learnt to talk proper. 'Yes, Dad,' said Robin. 'I just didn't think. Sorry.'

'That's better. I was pretty sure you'd see reason if I put the point to you squarely. Now if I were you, old chap, I'd go and ring up and just say you can't come to the tea-party after all.'

Robin heard his mother draw in her breath and let it out again. He said, 'You mean now?'

'What's wrong with that? Get it done. No time like the present. More considerate too, to give plenty of warning.'

'But what shall I tell him?'

'Tell him the truth, I would. Always best, you know. Tell him you had a previous engagement that slipped your mind for the moment.'

'But I . . .'

'The quicker you do it the more natural it'll seem.'

Robin saw the force of this argument immediately and went to the telephone in the hall. It was just as well that, in a fit of energy or boredom some months back, he had entered Wade's number along with the three others he knew in the handsome leatherette register, emblazoned with the words *Telephone Numbers* in gold italic script, that hung by the instrument. Otherwise there was no knowing what he might have had to do. Wade answered on his second ring and took in the message with unimprovable readiness tempered with concise regret. Perhaps he would lend a readier ear in future to Robin's accounts of paternal persecution.

When this part was over Robin felt quite flat, as if nothing would ever stir him again. His mother, standing in the kitchen doorway, went through a little mime of sympathy and helplessness that made him want to run to her and be held in her arms and also, separately as it felt, to cry. But he managed to do neither, though he did feel a momentary envy of girls, who were more or less expected to burst into tears when something turned out badly for them.

So he got his homework finished by Saturday teatime after all, with just his *Alcestis* vocabulary to swot up in the train on Monday morning. Mr Davies congratulated Robin on his conscientiousness when at twenty minutes to eight he assembled his family by the front door, a process he called getting the troops on parade. Out of either compunction at having deprived his son of his tea-party or satisfaction at duty done, he was more amiable than usual, though nothing further was heard about popping in for one at the Swan. In his brown suit, striped shirt and tie and brown shoes, an outfit not to be seen during the week, and with his still-thick dark-brown hair carefully brushed, he looked younger than his age. This was never divulged, but Robin estimated it to be about fifty, which made him as old as he himself was in the last years of Victoria's reign, which in turn might have accounted for some things.

'Well, youngster,' he said as they left the house in late sunshine, 'after poring over your books all afternoon you'll need to stretch your legs and get some air into your lungs, so I suggest we toddle round to the Carpenters' on our own two feet. Won't take us long, and it's a fine evening.'

Mr Davies's last statement, at any rate, was accurate enough. Indeed, the evening was so fine that its light made the long straight street look almost inviting, instead of just being what connected a house where nothing was ever going to happen to a wider world where nothing was ever going to happen either. Even the visible people had briefly given up their air of uselessness and seemed to be looking at something or thinking of something. Departing from a rigid tradition, they numbered among them several attractive females. In vain Robin told himself that he had been here before with never a result, that the promise of adventure would vanish in an instant at the first breath of reality. The thought offered him a glimpse of the future, one from which he shrank away.

The Carpenters' house had a kind of miniature drive in front of it, separated from the pavement by a low wall surmounted by ornamental loops of black-painted spiky chain. On the gravel of the drive there stood a dark-green car Robin had seen before and knew to be an Austin Six, a mystifying designation since it was a couple of sizes larger than another type of car he could name, the Austin Seven. Just such a conveyance regularly occupied the small garage adjoining his own house, belonging not to Mr Davies but to a jovial red-headed neighbour, said to be an Irishman, who rented the place from him. Robin had developed an imitation of his father's expressions of tolerant superiority, of fleeting puzzlement that anyone should go to the trouble and expense of owning a car, whenever Mr Higgins was detected driving into or out of the garage or was mentioned. It was a pity there was nobody to perform the imitation in front of, especially on cold wet mornings with a walk to the station in prospect.

Standing on the Carpenter doorstep with his parents, Robin consciously tried to hold on to his sense of expectation. Before it could quite pass away, the door opened abruptly and somebody he had never seen before appeared, a young man of twenty or thereabouts.

'Welcome, Davieses,' he said, smiling. 'For anybody who doesn't know, I'm Jeremy, the son of the house. Come in.'

Robin never forgot his first sight of Jeremy Carpenter. It was not so much that he was good-looking as that his face and its sur-roundings seemed made out of classier materials than most people's, what with smooth skin, eyes with very clear whites, fine hair, well-shaped ears. There was nothing delicate about the rest of him, which was tall and rather broad and clad for the most part in the kind of blue sports coat and grey flannel trousers Robin sometimes dreamed of wearing himself when he was older. He thought Jeremy noticed him too to judge by the quick straight look he got from him, polite but in some way more than just polite. Now he came to think of it, he remembered Jeremy's mother speaking of a son who was 'up' at Cambridge, and had briefly imagined a toff in a crested blazer swilling champagne and flourishing an oar.

The Carpenters' house started with a hall that amounted to a room, with an open fireplace, a chest made of some dark wood and a large china vase full of pampas grass, instead of being a mere passage where outdoor coats were hung. In the same way, the drawing-room had scores of photographs in silver frames and no fewer than two cushioned couches or sofas. A pile of illustrated magazines and a cigarette-box with mirror-glass on top and sides were arranged on a low table. The Carpenters themselves were to match, Mr Carpenter moustached and rather stout in a ginger-coloured plus-four suit, Mrs wearing an impressive green summer frock and in general more elaborately got up than Robin's mother, though in his view nowhere near as pretty. All three Carpenters had posh accents, posher than the Davieses, who again according to Robin were among the very few people with no accent at all.

Robin found himself sitting in a leather armchair while the parents talked, but quite soon Jeremy leaned over towards him and said quietly, 'Would you care to join our fathers in a discussion of Wednesday's Ratepayers meeting?'

'No, not particularly.'

'Or perhaps you'd prefer to take part in our mothers' conver-sation about the summer sales?'

'How do you know that's what they're talking about?'

'All right, do you want to take a bet on it? We'll get out of here in a minute but we can't move straight away. Where do you go to school?'

It was easier to answer that and add a bit as evidently expected. Then Jeremy said, 'No doubt my mother's told you more than once I'm at Cambridge.'

'Well yes, she didn't say you'd be here tonight.'

'I'm on vacation. No, I wasn't going to be here tonight, only a date fell through. Actually I'm quite glad it did,' said Jeremy, and hurried on, 'I think we can decently make a break for it at this stage.' He raised his voice, 'Mummy? Mummy, Robin here says he wouldn't mind a look at my books. Would it be all right if I took him up?'

Mrs Carpenter hesitated for a moment, but then said, 'All right, darling, just for half an hour.'

Rather against Robin's expectation, no roar of dissent and veto arose as he looked imprecisely towards where his parents were sitting. He tried not to hurry to the door.

'Isn't that typical?' said Jeremy as they passed through the hall.

'Isn't what typical?'

'A parent can't say yes, it's always yes but, that's if it isn't plain no. My ma likes to think she's got a say in everything I do. Pa's the same, not so obvious about it though.'

'Are you the only one?'

'How did you guess? Are you?'

'As good as. As bad as, I mean.'

Robin explained about his sister and brother. He noticed there were framed pictures even on the wall beside the staircase and more of the same along the first-floor passage. He was mildly disappointed to find Jeremy's bedroom fell short of being the Aladdin's cave he had looked forward to. But it had yet more pictures, ones with a look of dating from earlier that same year instead of being over and done with long ago, like the few at home, and a radiogram and a shelf of records, and a small desk with a portable typewriter on it, and a great many books, some of them in ragged piles on the floor. Robin caught sight of the title *Brave New World*. He took it for an omen and felt a little surge of excitement.

'Would you like one of these?' asked Jeremy.

These were the contents of a yellow packet of twenty cigarettes. 'I bloody well would,' said Robin. 'Thanks.'

Jeremy looked at him with unmistakable friendliness but said only, 'Sorry to sound like somebody's mother, but do remember to put your ash in this tin if you would.'

'Aren't you supposed to smoke?'

'In moderation. It's another form of yes, but. In theory, five a day is my limit, but it's always more than that, especially when I'm working.'

'What's your college at Cambridge?' Robin asked this not in the hope of useful information but to show he knew about colleges at Cambridge.

'King's, and a very nice spot it is. So's Cambridge as a whole, even though it's full of silly buggers who say they can't stand Cambridge. I take it you'll be going there yourself, won't you, or the other place?'

'Well, obviously I'd like to, but it would be a hell of a struggle for somebody like me to manage it. I'd have to get a scholarship and they don't grow on trees.'

'Oh yes they do.' Jeremy frowned momentarily and seemed to flash his eyes at Robin, 'I got one myself, so I ought to know. You should walk into one from the Classical A side of a school like yours. The only question is, do you want to go to a university?'

'I suppose so.'

'Never *suppose* a thing like that, Robin. If you only suppose it you don't really want whatever it is and that means you won't get it.'

'Are you saying if you do want something you will get it, Jeremy?'

'I'm much closer to saying that than you probably think. Oh, someone who's struck by lightning, they're not going to get anything regardless, I realise that, but yes, I'm certainly saying the first essential for possession or achievement of any kind is a strong will.'

'You never know what you can do till you try.'

'All right, but do try not to make it sound like a sneer, there's a good boy.'

'Sorry.'

'Oh, don't be ridiculous. Of course I should have remembered to say there are other limitations on what the will can do. If you really want to be a painter you'll probably learn to draw all right and put colour on and so forth, but it's pretty safe to say you'll never be another Matisse or Braque however hard you try. Would you like to look at my books? After all, that's what we're supposed to have come up here for.'

'I'd sooner hear a record if that's all right,' said Robin, who had had a quick glance at Jeremy's collection.

'Sure. William Walton or Louis Armstrong?'

After some hesitation, Robin plumped for Armstrong. Jeremy gave no sign of whether he approved of the choice but, first remarking that most of the best stuff was in Cambridge, put on his radiogram something quite fast and very raucous and subversive. At an early point one of the trumpet men produced a ferocious, clearly intentional discord that made Robin draw in his breath and also acted on him as a tremendous encouragement, as if thousands of good chaps were telling him they understood exactly how he felt about life and that he was right and would win. The rest of the record had obviously been designed to cause not just a very great deal of offence to Mr Davies but, in every rasp of the trombone and thud of the double-bass, the maximum possible in the time. When the bash on the cymbal announced the closure, Robin asked what was on the other side.

'A horrible bit of dance music,' said Jeremy. 'Different band.'

'Oh, well, could we have that again, then?'

'All right. You'd better give me that cigarette-end before you swallow it.'

The record seemed even better the second time round, at least in one way: it assured Robin that he had been completely justified in feeling about it as he had and had not been carried away by sheer noise. 'How marvellous to be able to play the trumpet like that,' he said at the finish.

'Armstrong or Henry Allen? They were both there.'

'Yes, I thought there must be more than one of them. Well, either. Both.'

'I'm afraid that's another case of no matter how hard you try . . . No, forget I said that. Sorry, Robin.'

'Whatever do you mean?'

'I've got a terrible urge to teach, I'm certain to end up as a schoolmaster or a don. I mean if I happen to know something I think's interesting I can't resist blurting it out. So with Henry Allen, who by the way was only – Oh God, there I go again, blast it.'

'Surely it's all right if the other person wants to learn.'

Jeremy smiled and said, 'Perhaps it is, Robin. Would you like another record now or would you sooner talk?'

'I think I'd sooner talk.'

'You don't sound very certain.'

'I was going to ask, if you really want something you, well, you stand a decent chance of getting it, is that right?'

'Near enough. Here, have another cigarette.'

'Thank you. Well, I mean there must be more to it than that.'

'Oh, there is. There's a lot to do with if you really want some - thing you should have it, you ought to have it, you must do it or take it if you can.'

Robin puffed smoke. 'I don't think I quite understand that.'

'Look, on the most elementary level, if you're thirsty you ought to drink, you'll feel better, it'll do you good. Obvious.'

'Yes, I understand that.'

'But the real point is, whatever it may be that you really want, however . . . outlandish it may seem when the idea's new to you, then get it or do it and you'll feel better, altogether different.'

'How did we get on to this?'

'It started with you wanting or not wanting to go to a university, but never mind that. It's enough that we're there.'

Robin blew out more smoke and said, 'Suppose what I really

want to do is strangle my wife, would I feel the better for having done that?'

'I don't know, do I? But I should think so, wouldn't you? For really want read deeply want, passionately, pre-eminently want.'

'Want so much it rules out everything else.'

'Such as what?'

'Well, conscience'll do for a start.'

'Oh, conscience, that trade-name. Another way of saying weakness. Weakness implanted by training.'

The cigarette was making Robin feel dizzy. He took one or two deep breaths. It was not clear to him where this conversation was leading, but he felt vaguely it might be somewhere he would rather not go. By way of diversion, he asked, 'Have you worked all this out for yourself?'

Jeremy seemed relieved. 'Yes and no is the answer to that, or rather no and yes. No, I've read some books and I've chatted to a couple of people in Cambridge and London and so forth. And yes, that sort of thing has merely pushed me a bit faster and further along the road I'd already chosen off my own bat. I don't think I'd have taken in what I read and what I heard if I hadn't been tuned in to receive it. Wouldn't have been able to take it in.'

'I see. Have you got any of those books here?'

'I haven't really thought. I expect I have. Why, would you like to borrow some?'

'If I could.' Robin moved over to the shelves beside Jeremy. 'I promise to bring them back.'

'I'll trust you. Well, there's this, of course, if you haven't read it.'

'D. H. Lawrence. I can't take that one, I'm afraid.'

'Why not, it's perfectly harmless? Oh, I suppose your parents wouldn't have it in the house.'

'That's right, they've never read a word he's written but they know it's all filth.'

'Oh dear. Well, we won't pursue the point. What about this chap, and this chap?'

'They're all right, I haven't heard of them myself. And this one's poetry, verse I mean. Guaranteed parent-proof.'

Jeremy turned to face Robin. For a moment he looked at him with his clear eyes, then dropped their gaze. When he spoke, it was to say something different from what he was going to say, something about there being no rush to return the books.

'What should I be looking for when I read them?' asked Robin.

'I'm not saying. You might anyway see different things in them from what I see. No, your immediate spontaneous reaction is what counts. But I'll be fascinated to hear. We'd better go down in a minute. God knows what your parents think we've been getting up to.'

*

Lawrence, Blake and Homer Lane, once healers in our English
    land,
These are dead as iron for ever; these can never hold our hand.
Lawrence was brought down by smut-hounds, Blake went dotty
    as he sang,
Homer Lane was killed in action by the Twickenham Baptist
    gang.

Robin paused in his reading. Perhaps these three were like Newman, Ciddy, Plato, Fronny and the others in the list on the previous page, real people mixed up with made-up ones or nicknames. So Lawrence was no doubt the famously filthy D. H. Lawrence, but who were the other two? Might Blake be the poet and artist, who could just about be said to have gone dotty as he sang? But he had been born in 17-something. But then Plato had been BC. And what about this Homer Lane? And who, if anybody, were the Twickenham Baptist gang, though they sounded promising? And . . . Well, more things to ask Jeremy.

The poems as a whole had baffled Robin but stirred him too, had here and there seemed to promise some great enlightenment and then withheld it – 'Yours you say were parents to avoid.' Like the ones he had himself? 'Learn to leave ourselves alone.' Did that mean . . . ? And, in the last poem in the book, a passing reference to the distortions of ingrown virginity. Could that refer to . . . ? And where was it, whatever it was, all supposed to be happening?

The house was quiet. Robin's mother, he knew, was in the drawing-room with her knitting and her book. His father, he also knew, was out at a Ratepayers meeting, for which as usual he had left abruptly, as if on the spur of the moment, perhaps reasoning that to have advertised his intention in advance would have left that much more time to bring about some deed of pillage or arson in his absence. Anyway, he was not about. It was a week night and Robin had finished his homework. He left the book of poems on the lowered flap of his little deal bureau and went downstairs to the drawing-room where his mother was sitting in her usual place in the bulgy brown leather armchair on the far side of the grate, where she could catch the light from the window. She looked up over the tops of her tortoiseshell spectacles and smiled at him.

'Mum, I was just wondering . . .'

'Yes, dear?' She laid her substantial knitting aside.

'I was wondering, you remember on Saturday you said I could invite somebody over to tea, as long as they were responsible, you said? Well, I just thought we could invite Jeremy Carpenter over some time, what do you think?'

Robin braced himself for a reluctant negative full of phrases, before he saw his mother was smiling again, in a rather apologetic way. 'Well . . . of course he is a very nicely spoken young man, anybody can see that, he must have a lot of calls on his time, but if you really think he'd care to . . .'

'I don't think Dad would object, do you?'

'Oh no, dear, I'm sure he'd be all for young Jeremy coming round here, in fact he said to me on Saturday night what a fine boy he was and what a wonderful thing it would be if the two of you were to see more of each other.'

'Good. Well, I could give him a ring now, unless you feel you'd like to.'

41

'If you really want me to, but perhaps you could do it.'

'No time like the present.'

Robin gave his mother a glassy smile and went out into the hall. While he looked up Carpenter in the leatherette register and waited for the number to answer, he was shouting inside his head. Yes, just because he talks posh and lives in a big house and has a father who drives people home in a luxuriously appointed *limousine,* you'd go on thinking he was a fine boy while he tore my clothes off and shoved his— 'Good evening, could I speak to Jeremy Carpenter, please?' he said aloud.

'Who's that speaking?' asked an incredibly hostile male voice that went with a moustache and a brown plus-four suit.

'It's Robin Davies here, Mr Carpenter, we met when my parents—'

'Oh, oh, oh, oh oh oh oh yes, oh yes, Robin Davies, yes. Well, young fellow, I'm afraid I'm going to have to disappoint you. He isn't here. The scurvy Jeremy isn't among us. No, he's gone off to stay with a friend of his somewhere in Shropshire, I fancy. Sorry.'

'Er, when will he be back, Mr Carpenter?'

'No idea in the world. To tell you the truth, I doubt whether he knows himself at this stage. Likes to come and go as he pleases, our Jeremy does. Hates being tied down.'

After a pause, Robin said, 'Well, thank you very much, Mr—'

'Half a minute, I was to tell you he'd drop you a line in a couple of days. I knew there was something. Mind you, if I were you I shouldn't lay any money on actually getting a letter from the fellow. Well, you never know. Well, give my regards to your parents, boy.'

Mr Carpenter rang off. After that first irritable query, he had been remarkably pleasant, with no talking-down. That was the secret of getting on with people younger than yourself. Except with babies, presumably. Robin pursued this line of thought in an attempt to block off his disappointment at Jeremy's indefinite absence. He had even found time for a surge of hope in the few seconds while a letter from him had sounded likely. Of course he had been rather counting on going through those poems with Jeremy, must have set more store by the prospect than he had realised.

'He's away,' Robin told his mother.

'Oh, what a shame. You'd been looking forward to having him over, hadn't you, I could tell.'

'I suppose I had, yes, a bit.'

'Come and sit down. Your father'll be disappointed too.'

'I should have asked Mr Carpenter to get him to ring me when he gets home.'

'Oh, Robin, sit down, do. You make me all nervy, standing there fidgeting like that.' His mother smiled to soften her words. 'There'll be plenty of time to have him over to tea or something before he goes back to Cambridge. They have a long summer holiday there.'

From where he now sat, opposite his mother in the twin bulgy brown leather armchair, Robin could see most of the room where they were, quite enough anyway for him to visualise bringing Jeremy into it. No more than anyone else, Jeremy would hardly be able to miss those chairs and the matching sofa that faced the grate, nor the mysteriously dubbed occasional table in some dark polished wood, with a sizeable glass bowl at its centre standing on a green crocheted runner, nor the shiny upright piano that at the moment had a very old-fashioned-looking piece of music on its rack, nor the uncrowded bookshelf where Mr Davies's cheap editions of detective stories leaned against his wife's sold-off library copies of love stories. Nor the awful pretend-velvet curtains and gold-bordered pelmet.

The reason why Jeremy would hardly be able to miss these articles was not that, apart from the curtains, they were really bad in themselves, but they would all be so close to him the moment he crossed the threshold. But again, Robin saw, that was not far off saying that this was a shoddy little house, and he already knew Jeremy well enough to be sure he never thought in such terms and would be contemptuous of people who considered themselves too grand for their surroundings. All the same, it could not be gainsaid that, by another mysterious locution, the glass bowl was known to Mrs Davies as a wish-bowl, that it had once held not only water but a pair of small fish that had died for lack of oxygen in it, and that its bottom was still covered with sea-shells, pebbles, pieces of artificial coral and other relics of the time of the fish.

'. . . otherwise you'll still be off on your trip to Wales.'

'What, Mum? Oh yes of course, I'd forgotten, I'm off there, aren't I?'

'You don't sound very keen. You know very well it's lovely where you're going. Get your lungs full of good healthy country air.'

And empty out all that stale cigar-smoke and the brandy fumes they get full of in the bars and night-clubs and gambling-dens I spend my time in the rest of the year, thought Robin. He recognised that he had started on a chat with his mother, one of a series of such things, all called chats. Sometimes she hesitantly boasted about this institution to her mates at the Dainty Shop: 'Oh yes, Robin and I quite often settle down and have a *chat*, you know.' He felt pretty fond of her for never adding anything along the lines of 'don't we, darling?' like somebody's mother in a play. What she got out of the chat-having was probably less the chat in itself than satisfaction at the thought that chats were quite often had. He himself had grown used to not expecting much from them in the way of content, though he had still not given up hope that, preferably before his wedding-night, she would use such an occasion to blow the gaff on the buggering birds and the bleeding bees.

'You know you always enjoy it when you get there,' his mother was saying.

'I suppose I do.'

Robin spoke with a reluctance that was largely assumed. In fact he had a special reason for rather looking forward to his stay this year. It was the kind of reason you kept strictly to yourself, in fact you tried to keep it at a distance even inside your own head or bad luck might result. So he put on a sort of gloomy frown.

'Of course in a place like that you have to make your own fun.

Gorgeous country round about there, I remember, though I haven't been for years.'

'M'm. Cousin Emrys takes us to church a good deal.'

'Oh, I thought it was all chapel in Wales.'

'Where he takes us is a church, I promise you.'

'That only happens on Sundays, though, doesn't it?'

'Twice. And he talks about it on other days.'

The man Robin had called Cousin Emrys was his cousin once removed, his father's aunt's child. Emrys Williams was Davies senior's only kinsman of his generation still living in Wales and still on speaking terms. Robin stayed with him and his family once or twice a year, in the Easter and summer holidays.

When his mother had ventured something to the effect that talking about church probably did very little harm, Robin said with the pretended grimness he knew his mother enjoyed, whatever she might have thought of his sentiment, 'It is Emrys who does the talking, Mum. I'm the poor mug who has to do the listening.'

Mrs Davies chuckled for a few moments before willing solemnity upon herself. She had more colour in her cheeks than usual and looked at her best. Soon afterwards Robin asked her, more casually than when he put the question to himself, why his father was so keen on these trips of his to Wales.

'Well, dear, I expect he likes to think you're keeping in touch with the place, which is where he comes from, after all.'

'Where he came from once upon a time. Why doesn't he keep in touch himself? He told me not so long ago he hadn't been back for over twenty years.'

'He's a very busy man, your father. There's a lot to keep him here.'

'But why does he go all serious when it comes to me going down? He goes on as if it was really important, not just quite a good idea.' From his financial point of view, he added silently and perhaps unfairly.

'Well...' Before saying any more, Mrs Davies went to the window and pulled the pretend-velvet-curtain curtains over it, though there

45

was still hours of daylight outside. It was the sort of thing she would have done as a signal to the world in general that she was declaring a chat, putting paid to any hopes Robin might have had of an early escape. Then he saw his mother was looking serious, even possibly troubled. Perhaps this was going to be birds-and-bees time at last, he thought, and tried to look innocently expectant.

'I know your father keeps on at you rather a lot,' she said when she was back in her chair. She kept her voice lowered, as if the man referred to might have been lurking somewhere near. 'But you must admit he does leave you alone about religion.'

'Religion in the sense of . . . So he does, yes.'

'Have you ever wondered why?'

At one time or another, Robin had wondered why his father did a lot of things, but never that particular one. He shook his head slightly.

'Well, I'll tell you. He made a sort of vow, oh, years ago it must have been, not long after Margery was born. He told me he said to himself, he had God and the prophets and hell and damnation shoved down his throat when he was a youngster, the least he could do was to see to it that no child of his had that to put up with. And as far as I know he's always stuck to that, with Margery and then George and now you. Another time he told me it was one of the main reasons why he left Wales, he couldn't stand the way his parents never let up about the Bible and so on. Of course, we're talking about before the war now, a long time ago, but he's never gone back on what he decided then, he's not that sort of man.'

'He's never gone back on being against all that, you're saying.'

'Yes, that's right, I am.'

'Then why, when he's really fed up with me, why does he tell me the trouble with me is I've got no religion?'

'I don't think we ought to sit here discussing your father behind his back,' said Mrs Davies, but she said it doubtfully.

Robin heard the doubt, which encouraged him to press on. 'Oh, we're not doing that exactly, are we? We're not saying anything we wouldn't say to his face.'

'No, I suppose that's right.'

'So that's cleared that up.'

'Where had we got to?'

'I was just wondering why it was Dad ticks me off for having no religion when he's against it himself.'

'Oh yes.' Having voiced her scruples, Mrs Davies looked briefly over her shoulder and leant forward. 'Oh, your father's not against religion, not at all, he wouldn't like to hear you say a thing like that. It's the Church he doesn't like. He was brought up to hate Roman Catholics because, well, he was always being told they never let people alone and tried to bring religion into everything, and then he realised his father and mother and so on were just as bad. No, it's all the mumbo-jumbo stuff he can't stand, not religion sort of in itself.'

Rather than concede that this seemed to him reasonable, Robin said, 'There's a boy at school called Chalmers, according to him you can't really have religion on its own, not without the things that go with it, and the first thing you come to is the Church.'

'Well, your father doesn't agree, and I wouldn't mind betting he knows more about it than your friend Chalmers, who I'm sure is a very clever young man.'

'Actually he's not as clever as all that. But I still, I'm trying my best, Mum, but I still don't see quite why Dad's so keen on my keeping on going to a place where all they seem to have done for him was fill him with religious mumbo-jumbo he left there to get away from.'

'That's easy, he and I were discussing it only the other night. Your father wants you to get that solid early grounding in the facts of religion that he can't give you himself. He's a very fair-minded man and he thinks it's only right you should have the chance of accepting something he found he couldn't accept. Of course you'll say no to the whole thing the way he did, but that's up to you, Robin. Your father thinks that everybody has a right to go into the question for himself and work out what he believes in a personal way. That's what he did and I know that's what he wants you to do.'

47

Robin nodded his head. He said nothing for the moment because he was afraid of disturbing the equilibrium he and his mother seemed to have arrived at. But his mind was busy with a preliminary survey of what the last few minutes had brought him: entry into a major new area in which he would be able to harry and tease his father with relative impunity, and there were none too many of those. At this point he heard the paternal key grate into the front-door lock and left the room with his mother's silent approval. As always, neither of them had any wish to be caught in mid-chat.

Robin and his mates revised, sat exams and were duly marked on their performance in them. These exams were of local importance only; School Certificate would not come until next year; even so, Robin performed well as usual, even at Scripture. He had hardly had time to be told so and to enjoy the sensation of not working when he found it was teatime on the day before he was due to be trundled off to Wales.

After some thought he approached his mother in the kitchen. 'I'm away in the morning then, Mum.'

'I'll be up to do your case in good time, dear.'

'I know, I was just thinking . . .'

'Yes, dear?' she said, turning from the gas-stove where a large metal pot audibly bubbled.

'Well, before I go, I still haven't heard from Jeremy, but I wasn't sure how it would look if I rang up again.'

'To see if there's any news of him, you mean?'

'Well yes, sort of.'

'Leave it to me. I was going to ring up Joy Carpenter anyway about a recipe. I can ask after Jeremy at the same time.'

'You are super, Mum.'

'You'd better go up and decide what books you want to take and put them out.'

Super again of her, to give him somewhere to be while she telephoned, but he left that unsaid and went to his bedroom. The sun shone brightly in at the window. On the plain blue bedspread he laid out one by one *Just William, The Island of Dr Moreau,* Durell on algebra, *British Battleships,* a bound volume of *Chums* and, with a low growl of resignation, Bury's *History of Rome,* in a second-hand copy bought off a fifth-former who was going into the Maths Sixth and had taken his last look at Bury with ominous relief. On consideration Robin added an almost-empty exercise-book. If he had got to read about corn laws at all he would do his damnedest to make sure it was only the once. When he heard the telephone-bell clink he went slowly downstairs again.

Without preliminary his mother said, 'He's still in Shropshire and they still haven't heard from him and they still don't know when he'll be back.'

'Oh well, there we are.'

'Don't worry about it. There's no point in worrying.'

'I know.'

In the gloomy hall, partly lit by the non-ecclesiastical stained-glass window that Robin considered on the whole should be done away with, she gave him an odd look, not just of a passing sympathy but, he fancied, of some deeper regret or concern. Then it was gone and they went up to his room together and started packing his suitcase for the morning.

When the time came, which was a good deal earlier than some might have judged necessary, father and son left the house together. Robin thought himself quite capable of finding the way to his train for Wales without guide or escort, but evidently Mr Davies disagreed. Or perhaps he felt that while he could not justly be expected to make the entire trip himself, there and back, he might be found guilty of something or other if he failed to stay around as long as he plausibly could. On that view of things he did his best to cordon off his son by finding him a compartment with a parson and two old ladies in it, and by staying on the platform keeping guard until the train was on the move. He would have been trusting in God, assuming there was such a figure in what he personally believed, to ward off all card-sharpers, scoutmasters and other malefactors while the journey lasted.

Altogether, including the branch-line stretch at the end, the journey took six hours. Unmolested, unswindled, but feeling he had done enough travelling for one day, Robin was reminded that there was more of it to come when he left the little country station to find Cousin Emrys waiting outside it with his pony and trap.

Cousin Emrys, with his round red face surmounted by a grey tweed hat and barrel chest muffled up in a thick bottle-green jersey against the August afternoon sun, looked like an unimaginative caricature of a farmer. He seemed pleased to see Robin, hugging him, bidding him welcome in strangely accented English and stowing his heavy suitcase deep in the trap's interior. He resumed his seat behind the pony and with his muscular arm hauled him up beside him.

So, according to his young cousin once removed, he bloody well should have done and to spare. In the minute and a bit between getting down off the train and being carried away in the trap, Robin had felt his spirits sinking low enough for him to remember what it was generally like here. Boring was what it was like, boring in a way that had a strong tendency to destroy the will to resist it. Every time he came to Wales he promised himself he would congratulate his father on having had the foresight and courage to run away from the whole shooting-match, a promise he always seemed to forget on returning within range of the old fellow.

The trap drew out of the station yard. Shaking the reins, Cousin Emrys clicked his tongue and called to the pony in an annoyingly put-on way it was not even worth trying to do an imitation of. With its drooping head and scanty mane, the pony had a look of being the confederate of bores, or perhaps their butt. Other such creatures, under the name of sheep, infested the bright green hillsides. Seen close to, they looked to Robin incredibly run-down, a very long way from the bonny white beasts to be found in illustrations. Some seemed bloated as well as undernourished, perhaps a token of pregnancy, a state normally of some intrinsic import to him but in this case not worth a second thought. One of them, identifiable as a ram, was sort of hanging about near another, doubtless a ewe, and Robin remained stonily indifferent.

Having extracted and supplied some family news and such stuff, Cousin Emrys started glancing at him and away in increasing tempo. The first time this happened, Robin had taken it as prelude to some fearsome question, as it might have been about self-abuse, and even now it was not easy to convince yourself otherwise. But all Emrys said was, 'Dad all right then, is he?'

'Dad? Oh of course. Yes, thanks, he seems fine. As I said.'

Here the pony offered a comment, and a very trenchant one it was, Robin considered, in the form of releasing from its backside a succession of roughly spherical turds. While this was taking place Emrys remained silent, possibly in deference to some local superstition, and held it until all was probably over for the time being. Then he said,

'What I meant, is he *all right*, see?'

'I'm awfully sorry, Cousin Emrys, I'm afraid I don't quite see. My father seems perfectly fit and reasonably contented as far as I can tell. There's nothing much more I—'

'Ah, now that's what I was trying to get at, Cousin Robin, no more and no less. You say your father seems *reasonably contented*, right? Well, what I'd like to know is, how contented is reasonably contented? That's what I'd like to know.'

This must be the sort of thing people meant when they said the Welsh still practised the art of conversation, before it was destroyed elsewhere by the wireless, the gramophone and quite likely the talkies. Robin went pluckily on, 'I suppose I mean *averagely*. My father is about as contented as any other man of however old he is, you'd have a better idea than I would about that, in a safe office job in London that he seems not to mind too much and the sort of home life that evidently suits him, anyway he doesn't seem to want to change it, and he has friends. So yes, he seems, what was it, reasonably contented if you ask me.'

The next section of road, though not wide, contained no traffic or other hazard visible to the unpractised eye, but all the same Cousin Emrys steered them carefully along it before saying, 'Does he speak of Wales at all?'

Robin was tempted to reply that his father spoke of Wales as seldom as a man could who was constantly bundling his son off there, but decided to change the tone in a different direction, so he merely said, 'Very little,' trying to make it sound as though Mr Davies was afraid he might burst into tears if he ever let himself go on the subject.

'Will he ever come this way again, do you think, pay us a visit. It's years and years since he was down.'

'I don't say he'll never come, but . . .' Gravely, Robin shook his head a couple of times.

'I wish I knew what it was that prevents him so totally. But there, no doubt he wouldn't be letting on to you about a thing like that.'

This assumption nettled Robin slightly. 'Maybe not, but even so I think I've a fair idea. It's, how shall I put it, it's a question of religion.'

'Religion. Oh. What's the difficulty there?'

'He, my father, seems to think he had it stuffed down his throat when he was a youngster.'

Cousin Emrys laughed, showing what Robin felt were unusually good teeth for a rustic. 'Come on, boy, don't pull my leg now. Stuffed down his throat, what a pack of nonsense. Your da and I, you've heard me say, we practically grew up together, and nobody tried to stuff anything down my throat. Of course we went to church, we went to Sunday school, we talked to the rector, everybody did, oh, you were left to make of it what you could and would. Naturally there was guidance if you needed it, we'd have been a poor old lot without it, I can tell you, but there was no what, no how shall I put it, no *compulsion*. That's never been our way round here.'

Apart from a touch of indignation at the close, and an occasional glance to make sure Robin had not silently cast himself into the road, Cousin Emrys had spoken in a quiet, reasonable tone and kept his eyes on the insanely repetitive movements of the pony. An acute bend with a derelict wooden hut in the angle, a smooth grassy bank with a line of bushes along the top, a clump of trees isolated in a small hollow stirred memories in Robin, but they were indistinct and fleeting. He tried with little success to imagine what it would be like to be given a solid grounding in the facts of religion by the green-pullovered peasant next to him. Rather than go on trying he said placatingly, 'I shouldn't be surprised if the main reason my father hasn't been down for so long is the thought of all the explaining he'd have to do. There's no doubt he's a bit of a—'

'Aw, he needn't worry about explaining himself to us, his own people. In my father's house are many mansions. One of the things I've always presumed that means is that there are many ways to God and a man must find his own.'

'Dad would agree with you there.'

'Provided of course he believes in God and in the divinity of Jesus Christ, which I take it applies to your father?'

'What? Oh yes.'

'Again, please.'

'Well . . . yes, of course.'

'You don't sound very certain, Cousin Robin. Now. I want to hear you say that you have no doubt that first of all your father believes in God.'

'Well, to be completely honest I—'

'No excuse for being anything else when it comes to a matter of this importance. Well?'

Robin thought it to be at any rate a matter of sufficient importance to make the case for telling the truth a strong one. 'I'm sorry, to be completely honest, I don't know.'

All too predictably, Cousin Emrys pulled the pony up at that, with such a shock that Robin was quite lucky to escape being pitched out of his seat. 'You don't know! *Duw, Duw,* a son honestly doesn't know whether or not his father believes in God.' After nearly half a minute wondering aloud what the world was coming to and kindred expressions, during which the pony shook its head to and fro a certain amount and made blowing noises, Emrys suddenly demanded, 'Have you asked him? I mean you have asked him?'

'No, I never have.'

'I should have thought the point was at least an interesting one.'

'My father doesn't encourage questions of that sort.'

'There is only one question of that sort. However.'

A single-decker bus painted pale blue, that had been approaching from ahead, now made to pass them, no exacting task in that not very narrow stretch of road, but it seemed the driver thought different. He slowed right down and crawled forward studying the yard-wide gap, his large pale face rigid with conscientiousness. The passengers crowded the right-hand windows and stared with concern and wonder at the remarkable sight of a couple of people halted on a country road. Robin longed for London, where vehicles flashed by with just enough room to spare and probably a honk and a snarl and forgot all about it at once.

But Cousin Emrys had used the interval to cool off. He got the pony going again and said in a considered tone, 'I want you to answer a question with a straight yes or no.' After leaving ample time for Robin to have passed his peak of curiosity, he went on, 'Will you promise me that at an early opportunity you'll ask your father if he believes in God, will you do that for me?'

'Yes,' said Robin loudly and without hesitation.

'And drop me a line to tell me what he says. Believe me, cousin, I'd never have mentioned it if it wasn't such a serious matter.'

'I understand.'

Robin chiefly understood that he had effortlessly secured official backing for the project he had conceived at the end of his last chat with his mother, that of disconcerting his father with theological probings. He might have expected something of the sort from Cousin Emrys, though admittedly not quite so soon after his own arrival. Well, most likely the bloke's mind was never off it, as if it had been sex. At the same time it was far from impossible to doubt whether he cared as much as he said he did about the state of Mr Davies's beliefs.

At last they came to the smallish village just before the Williams's farm. It, the village, still contained the stationer's where they would only speak Welsh though they sold English newspapers, the cinema where the sound was either deafening or inaudible, and the music shop where none of the three not-all-that-old people admitted to having heard of Louis Armstrong. On the other hand, there was now a garage where the shooting/fishing place had been and the teashop had had a lick of paint without looking much less desolate. Not much of an other hand. But in a day or two Robin guessed he would be wandering unproductively up and down here as he always did.

The pony stopped at the side of the road by a five-barred gate between bramble hedges. Robin jumped down to open this gate before being asked to, but was not quite quick enough to shut it after them without a reminder. One all. Then he thought it was silly and peevish to think along such lines, and returned Cousin Emrys's smile when they were moving up the drive or cart-track that led to the house.

Having explained that the gate needed shutting to prevent animals from getting out into the road, he said, 'I'm afraid we got down to weighty matters rather soon after your arrival. Let's proceed on the assumption, shall we, that we've got them out of the way for this time. I only hope you'll enjoy your visit as much as we all enjoy having you.'

'It's very nice of you to say so, Cousin Emrys. I'm sure I shall.'

'And that's very nice of you, boyo. We'll all have a good time together.'

Boyo! That word, which he had encountered no more than half a dozen times, had by some mysterious process come to seem to Robin not only absurd and offensive in itself but also to sum up so much that was not there in the Welsh people he had met. No doubt they had a lot to be said for them, but what they were not was chummy or chatty, nor free and easy. More like cautious, inquisitive, even, if Cousin Emrys was any guide, stingy. And what about the way he went on about being called what he insisted on being called? The Emrys part was comparatively harmless, being nothing worse than the Welsh form of Ambrose, as he had several

55

times explained. But Cousin, Cousin anything, was different. Cousin and boyo somehow did not mix. It occurred to Robin that his father might have agreed with him there, but that mattered less than it might have done with the old shag a couple of hundred miles away.

The trap pulled up on the oblong of thin gravel in front of the house. As Cousin Emrys had explained at some length, the main part of the building was no more than a hundred years old, but there were traces in it of a much more ancient habitation, one that went back to Tudor times. Robin had asked what sort of traces they were. Well, for instance the south-west corner of the ground floor and the window just next to it, in the underlying structure rather than what was actually to be seen. The same lack of immediate visibility was a feature of the probably medieval eastern wall and door-frame of an outbuilding now used for storage, and the possibly even earlier underpinning of a vestigial manger in what had perhaps been a cowshed. Really? Robin had been and was fully prepared to believe that the dark interior with its medium-strength niff of damp and its low ceilings dated from some bygone age. The low general temperature, however, such that the chief living-room and kitchen was only really comfortable in summer, might have been upgraded by putting down something on the bare stone flags and replacing the authentically ill-fitting doors and windows, if not one or two log fires or even a bit of central heating. No wonder a man who lived there wore a thick jersey as a matter of course.

But at the moment arrival was everything. Cousin Emrys sprang down from his seat, strode to the unlit, low-level entrance to the house and called through it something unintelligible, something doubtless in the Welsh language, one he rarely used in conversation. By the time Robin had taken his case out of the trap, two kinsfolk of his had arrived at the front door, offspring of Cousin Emrys. Dillwyn was about thirty, wore metal-framed glasses, was going bald and had on a cream-coloured shirt with its open collar turned down flat all the way round his jacket collar in a style Robin's mother said was common; nevertheless he shook hands warmly and took

Robin's case. Dilys was probably into her twenties, unencumbered by glasses and quite pretty enough in a freckle-faced way to have constituted Robin's special reason for looking forward to that summer visit. It would not have been quite true to say that he had forgotten about her since arriving in Wales or thereabouts, more that the boring qualities of the place had blotted her out for the moment. Now, on the doorstep, she kissed him humorously, jauntily and gave him a sort of wink. He would give her something to wink at him about pretty soon.

At that moment she staggered, not overcome with passion but because something had barged her behind the knees. The something was the shoulder and lowered head of the dog Fido, a bulldog cross, in this case meaning half bulldog, half an unknown assortment. If he had had a more genteel heredity he might not have acted as he now did, pushing his way between brother and sister and sticking his blunt muzzle into Robin's crotch. Either this in itself or his embarrassed writhings and shovings caused Dilys to burst out laughing. Dillwyn gave a sympathetic grin. Cousin Emrys clicked his tongue impatiently and, in another rapid movement, seized Fido's collar and dragged him off into the house. Rather late perhaps, Robin managed a laugh of his own, but made it a reasonably dirty one and also Dilys-aimed. The dog's initial absence from the scene had misled him into thinking the brute must have been dead. He was certainly quite old, though it seemed not old enough.

In the kitchen it was pleasantly cool after the outdoors, and might have been more generally pleasant but for the circling presence of a lot of flies, many of them with shiny blue or green bodies, and in aggregate sounding like a not so distant mob. Bunches of foliage, strings of vegetables and several immaculate flypapers hung from the ceiling, low enough in some cases to brush the faces of the unwary. But what held Robin's attention most firmly was the considerable tea now being laid on the large scrubbed table. The layer was a small grey-haired woman apparently dressing the part of some Oriental person of political or religious consequence. This was Menna Williams, Cousin Emrys's wife and the mother of Dillwyn and Dilys. As soon as Robin appeared she stopped what she was doing as if its essential pettiness had suddenly been revealed to her, and hurried to embrace him with resolute urgency. While she did this she cried out in nonsense syllables or Welsh or a mixture of the two. Others might have underrated the importance of Robin's arrival but nobody was going to be able to say that she had.

In the course of time six persons assembled at or near the tea-table. The sixth, who sat on an unusual chair of therapeutic tendency, was a very old lady known as Gran. Robin remembered her and was nearly sure she was Menna's long-widowed mother, but had let the question slide for too long to make certain. She was toothless and the lobes of her shrivelled ears had holes pierced in them that seemed to him a size or so larger than normal earrings would have required. In the course of trying not to look at them he managed to sit down next to Dilys.

The tea was as serious as he had expected, what with ham, boiled eggs, slab cake and Welsh-cakes, tinned fruit salad and tea poured from a large yellow pot. They had all started to eat when a small middle-aged man came into the room through the yard door. On his upper half he was wearing a frayed white shirt with thin dark stripes on it and no collar, its neck secured by a brass stud. Visible parts of him, especially his long prominent nose, were deeply tanned. After shaking hands with Robin, who remembered in good time to stand up, he took a seventh laid place at the table. This was Dai Stephens, said by Cousin Emrys to be indispensable in the running of the farm. The two now began to discuss some agricultural point.

After a minute or two of this, Cousin Emrys extended his forefinger, leaned across the table towards Robin, who was eating a boiled egg just then, and said, 'In the bird not twelve hours ago.'

Robin, having heard him use such phrases before, knew that the bird alluded to was a hen, if not the self-same one that had laid this very egg then another member of the same group. He nodded his head enthusiastically and said, 'You can taste the difference.'

'Well, I can't, can I, 'cause I'm eating the identical article every day of the week, see.' Cousin Emrys laughed. Dai Stephens joined in.

'No, of course I mean me,' said Robin.

'Oh, now, that's a different matter altogether. I'd expect *you* to notice the difference, coming from London.'

'That was what I . . .'

'The eggs you get in London, they may call 'em new-laid but they're not. They can be days or even weeks old. And I was reading where they're keeping hens in boxes now to cope with the demand from the big towns.' There was accusation in Cousin Emrys's look at Robin. 'Factory farming they call it. Well, that's honest anyway.'

Dillwyn had been listening to this. Now, in a voice that seemed to bear no trace of a Welsh accent, he said, 'No use complaining, that's how things always go whether we like it or not. Under our system, whenever there's enough of anything to go round it's nowhere near what it used to be. But never mind that – at least for the moment people in this part of the world have enough to eat, we should think ourselves lucky. It won't always be so tolerable, I promise you.'

'Don't let's get ourselves into an argument now, Dillwyn boy,' said his father. 'In particular, you'd be wise to avoid sounding positively pleased at the prospect of some sort of political trouble. And anyway I'm sure you're wrong. This spot of bother in eastern Europe, for example, I can't see that coming to anything. If after all there is a bit of a dust-up, well, that's their look-out, isn't it, nothing to do with us, and I thank God for it.' He spoke devoutly but without slowing his delivery, as if he really did thank God for it and would return to the point as soon as he had time. 'We're all right here, and we'll go on being all right as long as we keep ourselves to ourselves. What does history show? History shows that we in this island should steer clear of all foreign entanglements.'

'But that's just an excuse,' Dillwyn managed to interject. 'We in this island, or rather not we, not we but our lords and masters are terrified of ideas from outside. The French Revolution . . .'

During this exchange between father and son, Robin had been surreptitiously moving his right leg outwards in search of Dilys's left leg. A vertical member in the infrastructure of the table had forced on him a cautious detour. Inch-by-inch progress after that had brought nothing for so long that he stopped to reconsider. Had he somehow given something away? A casual glance to his flank showed Dilys apparently listening to what her mother was telling her about a funeral service perhaps in the next county. She turned her head for a moment and gave him a bright friendly smile, then turned it back for more listening. Well, what now?

Always a fast lateral mover in his own way, Cousin Emrys had got on to the village war memorial. Addressing himself now chiefly to Robin, he said, 'One name carved there is that of Evan Williams, my brother, uncle to these two children here. And he died for what? He died for many things, including the love of God and man, but one of those things, alas, was and is a foreign entanglement. For God's sake, let us have no more of them and no more senseless squander of lives in the name of empty slogans.'

'I entirely agree.' Dillwyn seemed to Robin to be using an altogether different set of speech-organs from his father. 'In the pursuance of which let's see to it that we prevent any such necessity from arising. And how do we do that? First, by identifying the chief enemy, which is not difficult and can be summed up in two words: Adolf Hitler. And second, by devising counter-measures, as follows. Collective security. If you want a slogan – united we stand.'

'Surely you couldn't be alluding to the League of Nations?'

'Of course not – I mean a defensive alliance of the British government, the French, Czechoslovakia, Poland, Russia for a start. In the face of such a—'

'I'm sorry, Dillwyn boy, but, er, I was almost beginning to come round to your way of thinking, and then you have to go and rope in Russia among your knights in shining armour, a Communist country. That won't do for me, I'm afraid. As you may know, I'm no great *fan*, is it, of Adolf Hitler, Esquire, but, as everybody knows, he saved Germany from Communism and that rather puts him in my camp, I'm afraid. Need I say why?' Cousin Emrys glanced at Robin and presumably decided he had better say why after all, just to be on the safe side. 'Well, Hitler is against Communism and Communism is against God. QED. Simple. Straightforward. Plain as the nose on your face.'

Dillwyn swallowed Welsh-cake and said, 'I think you have to take a closer look at the position of the Church in Russia before the Revolution.'

He went on about that. After no more than a couple of seconds Robin felt something press with some force against his right knee, but he forbore to rejoice. For one thing, what was doing the pressing failed to suggest another human leg at all unmistakably. Could it have been part, a major part it would luckily have to be, of the dog Fido, who was nowhere to be seen? It could. Robin was still considering what, if anything, to do next when whatever it might have been was totally removed from its lodgement against his knee. In any event nothing had been lost, and yet he felt he had suffered a reverse, though not one to interfere with his enjoyment of the slice of Dundee cake he was munching. He wished even so that he had not been forcibly reminded of the magic-lantern episode that had taken place the previous summer.

The magic lantern itself, which also went by some grander name, was owned and operated by an old school chum of Dillwyn's. Its advent had been welcomed by Robin as at any rate a probable diversification of boredom. The curtains of a seldom-used parlour were drawn across and the lights put out. After a short delay, slides of foreign places and people began to be shown on the screen at the end of the room. Robin paid them little attention, having secured a seat next to Dilys with no idea at all of how to turn this to account. He was still wondering when he felt Dilys's hand shyly insinuate itself into his. He looked up at the screen and saw a tribesman in a burnous and holding a long rifle, a fine figure of a man with luxuriant whiskers, sitting on a reliable-looking camel. Looking down instead, he saw in the gloom that Fido, having approached unobserved, was licking an exposed portion of Dilys's thigh. So matters continued for perhaps half a minute, while he asked himself what was happening, what she thought he was doing and much else besides. He had reached no conclusion when there came from behind him a sharp fizzing sound, the screen became blank and the lights went up. The performance in all senses was over, nor had he ever devised an explanation or found a way of mentioning the episode to Dilys, and he had been left feeling dissatisfied in some way. As he did now.

Now Dillwyn soon made his escape. Tea had not long been over when he said he had promised to look in on old somebody-or-other and disappeared, at first pounding upstairs, soon afterwards apparently taking off on a motor-bike. He taught something non-literary, like maths or physics, at the polytechnic. Why had he still not got married? Perhaps he was having too good a time with the girls to want to, though it seemed unlikely. It seemed unlikely too that Dillwyn could not face the prospect of leaving home, thought Robin; he himself could hardly wait for that day. But perhaps father and son really got on quite well, despite . . . Robin quietly said a rude word. Had he come all the way to Wales to think about fathers and sons?

Nevertheless they would not go away yet. More than once at the tea-table he had been reminded of his own father and his way of seeming to put on a sort of performance at times when there was no audience at all, no third party. But his father was Welsh too. But one who had renounced his Welshness and would admit only to having been born in Wales. Perhaps then it was temperament, something inherited from their grandfather, old Morgan Davies, who according to Robin's father had been born in the year the Duke of Wellington first became prime minister and had never spoken a word of English in all his life.

Cousin and father were alike too in being near over money. This was brought home to Robin that evening in the course of sitting unable to read in the steadily darkening kitchen. Surprisingly to anyone who knew its owner, some parts of the house were fitted with perfectly good electric light, had been so fitted for well over a year if he remembered correctly, but Cousin Emrys hated having it on. If challenged, something not likely to happen, he would obviously have started muttering about newfangled gadgets not being really suited to country ways, or vice versa. Robin's father tended to react unfavourably when any light was turned on in a room he was not himself occupying at the time, plunging hall or landing into darkness while he in the drawing-room basked in the radiance of a standard lamp. Both men, too, were permanently on the alert for taps left running, bread being sliced in advance of immediate need, etc. It might all be due to their being Cardies, natives of Cardiganshire, famous throughout Wales, so tradition said, for being tight buggers.

Later, unpacking and undressing by candlelight in his quite nice little bedroom with the doll's-house curtains and the funny step in the floor, he found his thoughts returning to Dilys. Whatever exactly the magic-lantern episode had consisted of or betokened, whatever had happened or not happened under the table that afternoon, her room was next but one to his. Imagining her going to bed in it, as she was presumably now doing, set the rest of his thoughts oscillating at such a rate that any rational content in them was starting to boil off.

He put his pyjamas on and listened, though he could hardly have said what he expected to hear. Anyway, he heard nothing distin - guishable. He opened his door with great care and listened again. Still nothing. It was pretty dark. Treading close to the wall, where somebody had said or written that creaking floorboards were least to be expected, he moved quietly along to Dilys's door and quietly knocked on it. After a moment her voice spoke in not much more than an undertone from close to her side of the door asking who it was and at a similar pitch he told her.

Another pause followed. Robin knew he could never have got even this far if he had stopped to consider. Whatever was to follow, if anything, he could only leave to Dilys and her supposed experience of these matters. Instinct said that, perhaps after some tidying up, it would do all right as a tale to tell the boys.

The door in front of him opened at a normal speed. Dilys was to be seen largely in silhouette against the light of a candle. When at her invitation he stepped into the room, he saw that she was wearing a very clean white nightdress that was rather small for her.

She shut the door carefully and said in a neutral tone, 'Well, what can I do for you then, Robin?'

He found himself saying, 'I think my watch must be wrong. I know it wouldn't be the end of the world if I came down to breakfast too early or a bit late, but I still . . . Could you help me, I mean could you give me the right . . .'

The last couple of phrases were haltingly delivered and his voice soon petered out altogether. The tight fit of Dilys's nightdress had caused quite extensive parts of her breasts to be clearly visible. Never before had he seen anything like as much of a female bosom in the flesh, so to speak. It was not merely that he looked, he seemed unable to prevent himself from fairly goggling, or so he was to suppose afterwards.

Dilys evidently thought something like that at the time. Saying something recriminatory but otherwise unintelligible, probably in Welsh, she pulled the top parts of her nightdress together. This move duly hid her breasts from view but at the same time had the effect of raising the garment (why was it so short?) and revealing below it a substantial part of what he only theoretically knew to be there. If he had fallen short of goggling before he certainly made up for it now.

After seeming to have halted indefinitely, time, or events in it, now speeded up. It must have taken several seconds in fact for Dilys to say something furious, pull down the front of her nightdress, open the door again, seize him by the shoulder, half manhandle him out into the passage and shut the door firmly behind him, but it felt like less than one. Aware of a nearby light, he looked round and saw but could not identify someone standing there with a candle raised.

'What are you doing, Robin?' asked Menna Williams's voice.

'Oh yes,' he said comfortably, as if in satisfaction at having guessed right. 'Just checking the time with old Dilys.' And without more ado he plunged into his bedroom.

Dismissing from his mind as many considerations as possible, he got into his bed and blew out the candle. In the dark, then, he stretched out and started thinking about Dilys in a purposeful sort of way, a way that somehow improved the complexion he had just seen, put more colour and lustre into the hair, enlarged the tits, and so on. A little more time and effort finally got that nightdress (if indeed it could properly be so described) altogether off, and what happened after that was jolly good fun, so much so that he rather forgot about Dilys.

Three days went by which not only contained nothing but offered a guarantee that nothing would ever happen again. At the end of mornings at market, at sheepdog trials, going round the farm, afternoons walking to the second-highest point in the county, scouring the woods for wild flowers, evenings playing Happy Families or rummy with strangers Robin was expected to say of course he remembered from last year – all these conspired to make him uncertain even of death. Resisting any sentimental appreciation of the trouble taken on his behalf, let alone being touched by it, he thought more and more seriously of running away to join the Foreign Legion or a circus. Almost the only course he never contemplated was return home. Then, on the fourth morning, something did happen.

The fourth day started much as its predecessors had, with breakfast in the kitchen: bacon, sausage, fried eggs, fried bread, all plentiful. Cousin Emrys liked his food and had evidently failed to devise any way of systematically indulging himself while stinting everyone else, though he did what he could to discourage seconds. Taken completely by surprise as always by the coming of the postman, Fido went from contrabass growl to falsetto squeal and back in the intervals of casting himself unflinchingly against the outer door, but he left intact a letter addressed to Robin.

At this house you were not supposed to open any item of mail before naming its probable sender and a considered guess at its contents or message. Under Cousin Emrys's eye at the table, Robin was gearing himself up to performing along these lines when he saw there were two handwritings on the envelope before him. One was his mother's, forwarding the letter here, the other unknown but, with its straight uprights and flattened loops, instantly recognisable. Pausing minimally to note that it styled him Robin Davies, Esqre, with the last two letters above the line, he tore it open.

Inside there was a single sheet with writing only on the front. In unexciting mode it praised the weather, the surrounding country-side and the general conditions of life where the writer was staying. He expected to be home 'in a few days' and 'hoped to be in touch' not long after that. Robin had the disagreeable feeling that this was just one copy of a standard bulletin Jeremy had sent to a couple of dozen people he felt he ought to drop a line to, a pest to have to write out over and over again but less of one than having to start from scratch every time. Then he saw that under the almost-illegible signature something had been written and lightly crossed out, lightly enough to be still legible as the letter's PS. So Jeremy had con-templated a personal message, thought better of it and not even bothered to hide the traces. Then at once Robin told himself that it was a bit spoilt-childish of him to take that sort of line. There were any number of reasons why . . .

At this point he remembered the presence of Cousin Emrys taking his time over a final cup of tea, so he gave a satisfied nod and stuffed letter and envelope into a pocket,

'Everything in order then, boy?'

'M'm? Oh yes. Just a pal of mine letting me know where he is.' Robin tried to make it sound as if one unit in his intercontinental intelligence network had routinely checked in.

'Good, good. Now this morning I'm afraid I shall have to leave you to your own devices. I'm going to have to go into town to see a solicitor fellow. You know, legal matters and so on. I'll be taking the trap so I can drop you anywhere that's on my way.'

'What about that village down the road from here? Is that on your way?'

'It could be,' conceded Emrys. 'It could be.'

That was how Robin came to be pottering about that unrewarding centre of population, between the cinema with its eye-catching stills of *Queen Christina* (featuring Greta Garbo) and the Welsh-speaking stationer's shop, when a car pulled up and a well remembered voice said, 'Robin? Surely it can't be you?'

'Oh, Jeremy. What on earth are you doing here, Jeremy?'

'It is you. I've driven over from where I'm staying. Not all that far, just the other side of the border. Where's the place where you're staying?'

'A couple of minutes' drive,' said Robin, pointing. 'How did you know where to come?'

'My ma got it off your ma and so on. Well, after that I hope you're pleased to see me.'

'I don't think I've ever been so pleased to see anyone in my life.'

Robin had barely had time to recover his composure after his first sight of Jeremy, who had just joined him on the pavement. Those clear eyes widened for a second. Then Jeremy smiled and said,

'My goodness, I had no idea it was as bad as that.'

'I'm sorry, I didn't—'

'Those relations of yours, you make them sound pretty dire.'

'Oh. Well yes, their favourite topic of conversation seems to be God.'

'Christ,' said Jeremy, laughing, and Robin joined in. 'Look, is there anywhere round here where one can get a cup of coffee or something? Or do Welshmen just stand in the street when they want to have a nice quiet chat?'

'There is a sort of teashop round the corner where they certainly serve tea and you can sit down to drink it if you feel like it.'

'Why shouldn't I feel like it?'

'Well, there's just a couple of tables sort of *in* the shop, if you see what I mean.'

'Clearly enough, thanks. Isn't there anywhere else? What am I talking about, with a bloody great pub sitting where I can almost reach out and touch it. Can I leave the car where it is?'

'I should think so, but will it be open, the pub?'

'Only one way to find out for sure.'

'But they won't let me in, will they?'

'Why not, you're over fourteen, aren't you? Perfectly legal as long as you stick to soft drinks. If you start knocking back double brandies they might get a bit restive. Come on, let's have a look.'

To Robin's eye, the front parlour of the Hafod Arms looked like the unreconstructed but clean and tidy waiting-room of a small country railway station. There were even elderly travel posters fastened with adhesive tape to the buff-coloured walls. At first sight nothing suggested that alcoholic or any other kind of liquor was sold and consumed here. Then you noticed that the three middle-aged men sitting vigorously smoking over by the window had half-full pint glasses in their hands. At the same time, no bottles or beer-pump handles or barrels were to be seen, just a serving table spread with a not quite spotless white cloth and attended by an oldish woman in a sort of dressing-gown clasping her elbows. She looked at the two newcomers in silence and without either welcome or hostility.

Having wished her good morning, Jeremy asked for a pint of bitter and 'a glass of lemonade for my brother', upon which she turned and left the room by a door that had been behind her, without any sign that she had understood or even heard. Then he looked over at the three by the window, smiled and inclined his head, something that until that moment Robin had only read of. Their drinks arrived on a circular metal tray, quite soon and as ordered. Jeremy paid with a half-crown and the old woman gave him change out of her dressing-gown pocket. He and Robin went and sat on a wooden wall-seat within reach of a wobbly table to stand their glasses on.

'Jolly nice place here, what?' said Jeremy loudly.

'Oh, terrific'

'I call this really living it up, don't you?'

The three by the window began talking among themselves in a language that, not being English, was presumably Welsh.

'Can you follow what they're saying?' asked Jeremy more quietly.

'Good Lord no. I doubt if they can either. They're doing it on purpose. They were talking English when we came in.'

'Wonderful ears you've got. But surely you must have picked up a bit of Welsh. This isn't your first trip to these parts, is it?'

'No, but for God's sake Welsh is like Chinese, not French or German. All I've got to know is just good morning and good night and a couple of rude expressions.'

'Tell me later.'

'Jeremy, what's turned me into your brother?'

'Oh, that. Quite clever in a way, I thought. It saves a lot of explanation in places like pubs. And things like "my young friend" don't sound quite right, somehow.'

'No.'

'Don't your relations speak Welsh?'

'Not so's you'd notice. I suppose they might among themselves, when I'm not there, but I doubt it. Too near the English border or something.'

'Anyway, tell me about them.' As he spoke, Jeremy took out a yellow packet of cigarettes and helped himself to one, which he lit.

'Aren't you going to offer me one?'

'Not at the moment. Regulars at this sort of place don't like to see boys under the age of consent smoking cigarettes.'

'You've been to Wales before too, then.'

'Oh, a couple of times, but country people are the same everywhere. I'll consider giving you a fag when you've told me those unclean Welsh phrases. Now, you were going to tell me about the people you're staying with.'

'Oh, was I really? All right, here goes. A few random remarks.'

When Robin had made them, Jeremy said, 'Very interesting. To be told about, that is. You certainly seem to have found yourself a home from home, or somebody's found one for you.'

'Somebody has: my dad.'

'I thought he didn't much care for your going away.'

'Did I tell you that?'

'You may have done, or perhaps it was your ma gassing to my ma.'

Robin would have liked to hear more of what they gassed about, but said only, 'I expect he thinks I'll be safe with relations.'

'Safe from what? Or who?'

'I don't know. He never discusses things like that.'

'I see.' Now it was Jeremy who seemed to change his mind about what to say next. What he did say was, 'Excellent beer, this. Anyway, I seem to be ready for some more of it. What about you? It's a pity you can't have a proper drink.'

Robin reached for his pocket. 'Thanks, but let me—'

'No, you need to hang on to every farthing you've got. Right. Back in a moment.'

The three men across the room stopped talking among themselves and stared with some concentration at Jeremy on his way to be served, as if they half expected him to blow up between one stride and the next. Then one of the three got up and came over to Robin, who for a moment took him for Dai Stephens, but no, he was just generically similar with a more closely similar brass stud at the base of the neck.

'Excuse me,' this man said diffidently and in a heavy local accent, 'Excuse me, but are you English, are you an English boy?'

'Yes,' said Robin, getting ready to lie about his surname.

'Oh yes, you are, yes, I see. Thank you very much.'

'Not at all.'

'I hope you don't mind my asking.'

'No, not in the least.'

'Now good morning to you, thank you.'

When Jeremy came back with the drinks he put them down on

the table and, still on his feet, asked, 'What did that fellow want?' He was frowning.

'He asked me if I was English and I said I was and that was that.'

'Really. How very odd.'

'I thought it was rather, myself. He'd probably got a bet on with his mates. He was perfectly polite.'

'So he bloody well should have been,' said Jeremy, but he sat down and seemed to relax. After a pull at his beer, he said, 'We were talking about poor you in your home from home. Oh. Terrible expression, that. Two very terrible words in it.'

'Which are they?'

'Well, I was thinking of "home" and "home". All right, I agree, I suppose they are the same word when you come down to it. But, well, take your home from home first, Cousin Taffy's place, pretty dire, you agree.'

'They're quite nice people really, or that's what I'd think they were, that's what they'd be, if only I . . .'

'If only you weren't related to them and weren't living with them – sure, just for the moment but that's what you're doing. It's the home business that's wrong. I like my parents, I get on well with them, I think they're both very decent, the trouble is they're my parents and when I'm not at Cambridge I have to live with them, wherever I go I have to go back home. It's not the way to get the best out of people, is it?' Jeremy put down his glass of beer and looked into Robin's eyes. 'You feel the same, don't you?'

After some hesitation, Robin said, 'I probably will, I might when I'm your age. At the moment I quite like home, I like being there. Oh, my father and I rub each other up the wrong way some of the time, but that's only to be expected, isn't it, anyway from what I hear it happens in a lot of families with sons growing up. And what's the alternative? If living at home's wrong what would be right? Where else am I to live?'

'I do believe you're sticking up for your old pa. Sorry. In answer to your question, life's full of bad things without a good alternative or any alternative at all. Take war, for instance, or rather on second thoughts don't let's take war, for the time being at least. However. In your case there may not be a good alternative but there is a worse one.'

'Like my father giving me a bloody good hiding every day and twice on Sundays. He's always telling me I've a lot to be thankful for.'

'Well, he's certainly right there. Anyway, the worse alternative I was thinking of would be if you took a different view of your experience of home, a more lenient one. If you had the same father and mother and the same circumstances, everything, and when you thought about your life at home, if you ever did in a sort of detached way, you thought it was very agreeable, not perfect perhaps but the best you were ever likely to have, well, *then*, it would be worse if you felt like that, wouldn't it?'

'I see what you mean. Yes, I suppose it would.'

'The worst thing that can happen to a prisoner is for him to fall in love with his prison.'

'I'm in no danger of doing that.'

'Don't you be too sure, my dear Robin. Home is very powerful. Think of yourself as a spy in enemy territory, pretending to be one of them but secretly plotting their overthrow. Bear it in mind all the time. Otherwise you're liable to turn out like your father.'

'Do you mind if we talk about something else?'

'All right. Your turn for a bit. Tell me how you get through the day at kind Cousin Taffy's.'

'The first excitement is what there'll be for breakfast. The second is breakfast.' Robin mentioned some later excitements. 'Of course if I get a moment to myself ever, I might play a bit of book cricket. Well, you take a book, any book, and go through it letter by letter noting what happens at each one as if they were balls bowled in a cricket match. You've decided what happens at each letter beforehand.'

'I think you'd better start again.'

'So do I. Each letter of the alphabet stands for something that can happen when a ball is bowled, like no run, one run, two, three, four, six, and wicket down. The twelve commonest letters give no run, the next six commonest one run and so on.'

'Which are they?'

'The twelve commonest are the five vowels plus D, H, L, N, R, S and T. The next six commonest—'

'I'll take your word for it.'

'When you've settled all the letters in the alphabet you go through a book, as I said. "The cat sat on the mat" would give you three overs less one ball with no score except on M, which would give you a single. For instance.'

'Go on, Robin.'

Robin went on to explain about teams and bowlers and how you shifted the wicket-down letter from uncommon to less uncommon as the innings went on, but he was pretty sure Jeremy was not taking it in. And yet he went on not interrupting now, his eyes seemingly not so much on Robin's as on his mouth, almost as if he had been getting some lip-reading practice. Eventually he said, rather dreamily Robin thought, 'I get the general idea. No wonder you were glad to see me if book cricket's the sort of thing you're driven to.'

'You must know it was more than that.'

In another moment or two Jeremy pulled himself upright. 'Don't you do any reading? Or haven't you brought any books?'

'Certainly I have. Simultaneous equations are now my strong point and I'm just coming to agrarian policy in the 130s BC'

'Good for you, young 'un, said Harry Wharton gruffly. What about those books I lent you, did you bring any of those?'

'No, I was afraid they might get lost, but I had a good look at them before I came away and I've got some things I want to ask you about them.'

'Such as what?'

'Well, such as what the chap was getting at with that stuff about Lawrence, Blake and Homer Lane, or were they not real people?'

'Oh yes, they were real people. We'll come to them later. We ought to be off in a few minutes.'

'Off? Where to?'

'First of all to chez Cousin Taffy so I can introduce myself and ask him about hotels in the vicinity, being very agreeable all the time. And before you ask, the point about hotels is so that I can take you out to lunch.'

'No need for that. There'll be lunch at chez Cousin Taffy.'

'You deserve a treat. You need cheering up.'

'I feel cheered up already.'

'Ah, but you can't have too much of a good thing.'

'Is that your motto, Jeremy?'

'Call it a working assumption.'

Jeremy was as good as his word about being agreeable. In fact he was so agreeable that it took him only a minute or so to win over Cousin Emrys, who had had to be summoned from the cowshed, or so he volunteered more than once. At first he had been very suspicious of Jeremy, of his looks, his accent and most of all his irregular manner of encountering Robin. 'Just happened to catch sight of him walking along the street,' he echoed, also more than once. Not for nothing was he cousin to Davies senior, as Davies junior thought to himself.

'I would of course have telephoned,' said Jeremy in extenuation, 'but I couldn't find your number.'

'Oh, you couldn't find it, Mr Carpenter. Well, that doesn't surprise me. It doesn't surprise me in the least, I tell you.'

'No, really?'

'Yes; really. Because, do you see, we're not *on* the telephone in this house. So naturally we haven't got a telephone *number*, Mr Carpenter.'

This led by degrees to talk of the present difficulties of farming and farmers. In its course Dai Stephens turned up with some item of harness in his hand. Jeremy was particularly agreeable to him, asking him questions about his work and at one stage taking him a little aside. At the mention of hotels Cousin Emrys turned suspicious again, but was finally led to disclose a couple of possible names and locations.

'Do you know much about farming?' Jeremy asked Robin as they drove away.

'Not a blessed thing. Sheep give wool and in due course turn into mutton and here endeth the lesson as far as I'm concerned.'

'That makes two of you.'

'How do you mean?'

'I spent a couple of summers on a farm rather like that one when I was about your age. Cousin Taffy would be with you on the wool but he might not be absolutely sure that sheep didn't eventually turn into pork. Well, almost as bad as that. That nice little fellow, Stephens is it, he runs the place. I'm strongly tempted to say Cousin Taffy doesn't want to farm, he just wants to be a farmer. Like poets who just want to be poets. You may remember, he went on about sitting up all night with a cow that was having trouble calving. That must have been about the pinnacle of his stock-breeding experience.'

Robin groaned. 'I've heard about that cow enough to last me.'

'It's no great surprise. Tyrants are always frauds.'

'Oh come on, draw it mild, you can't call him a tyrant.'

'I was exaggerating there, I agree, but the principle's the same. You'll see.'

The Prince of Wales Hotel looked quite grand for the main square of a pretty little border town. Or rather, thought Robin, it must have looked so when its last customer entered it in about the year 1912. Since then it had perhaps declined, though a relatively undilapidated board by the entrance told not only of morning coffee and afternoon tea but of luncheons and dinners. It was very dark inside and smelt of generations of haddock and parsley sauce, but in a few minutes Jeremy had found their way to the dining-room and to one of the kind of motherly middle-aged Welshwomen who made it worthwhile to be Cousin Emrys's cousin. He and Robin sat alone in a dining-room full of worn crimson plush and greying but spotless table-linen while she brought them successively oversalted meat broth, dried-up white fish and, presumably by some oversight, a perfectly eatable casserole of beef, root vegetable and potatoes. With the casserole came a dark bottle and two glasses.

'My God,' Jeremy had said on looking through what he called the wine-list, 'a Château-Latour 1924. I'd never have thought I'd come across it anywhere, let alone in Wales. And at eight-and-six if you please. My God, we must have a bottle of that.'

Robin kept quiet while some of the wine had been poured into the glass nearest him and the waitress had gone away. Then he said, 'Why is it all right for me to drink this?'

'Ah yes. One sort of answer is that it tastes delicious. Then, it'll do you good. It's not very strong, so you can drink a glass or two of it without falling down. It's all right in another way because the lady who brought it doesn't realise it's a proper drink, and fourthly or wherever we've got to she wouldn't dare intervene anyway or wouldn't even think of doing so because of my classy English accent. If called to account she'd say she trusted me to see you came to no harm, which is a long way from my intention but comes in handy at times. Go on, dear boy, have a sip.'

Robin had a succession of sips. The taste of wine, of any wine, was unfamiliar to him, but he very soon got used to it, though he could have wished there had been less of it per sip. His mother had once got him to try something called Emu Burgundy, which she said would be good for his blood, but that had been wine of a completely different sort from this and rather nasty. Jeremy vetoed the offered suet pudding and treacle and called for cheese, observing that it would go well with the last of the wine. Robin tried it and agreed.

Through the meal, Jeremy had kept him entertained with tales of his activities at Cambridge and of the people he had come across there. He turned out to be a wonderful mimic, at least the voices and faces he did were hilarious in themselves, whether or not they were close to the originals. He gave some of the dons a specially hard time, making them out to be senile idiots to a man, stooping, peering, frowning, deaf, perpetually puzzled, still living in a Victorian dreamworld: 'I want you all to wemembah . . . you owe a duty not only to your college . . . not only to ush, your pahshtorsh and mahshtersh . . . not only to thish great university . . . not only to king and country . . . but alsho to shome uvver fing altogevvah which I sheem to have completely forgotten her her her blesh my shoul absholutely, shlipped my mind what.' The best thing of all really was something with no words to it, a killing upper-class-moron face with a lot of blinking and as many as possible of the lower teeth showing. Jeremy put it on when he looked into a cigar-box the waitress was holding in front of him, and Robin thought he would burst or at least have to go out. He was in no doubt that Jeremy was just the most marvellous and amusing companion anybody could ever have wished for.

As they were leaving, Robin said, 'Oh, Jeremy, I did enjoy that. All I can say is thank you.'

'There's no need to say anything. It was lovely to see you enjoying yourself.'

'Was it very expensive?'

'No, actually it was incredibly cheap. Now I thought we might go for a little drive before we wend our ways back to Cousin Taffy's.'

Outside the hotel yard it was immediately very hot and sunny. Robin got into the passenger seat of the car as if he had never sat anywhere else in his life. The town square must have been near the edge of town, because it seemed only a couple of minutes before Jeremy was driving the car into a shady spot that had some low fencing on the side away from the road.

'I thought we might go for a little stroll before we get on the move again.'

They came out from under the trees on to the top of a slope above a gentle valley and walked slowly along it. The air seemed full of birdsong and somehow thick. Neither of the two showed sign of wanting to go very far. Quite soon Jeremy stopped and said, 'Well, I don't know about you, Robin, but I feel as though I've done enough walking for now.'

'Oh, me too.'

'Okay, then, let's sit down for a bit.'

'What, you mean here?'

'Certainly I mean here. What's wrong with it, as good as anywhere, isn't it?'

'It might be—' Robin abruptly stopped speaking and in no more than a second was sitting on the warm grass of the low bank where they had halted.

Jeremy sat too, more deliberately. 'Were you demonstrating something by precipitating yourself to the ground like that?' he asked with a grin.

'Got it in one. I suddenly realised I was on the point of refusing to sit on the grass because it might be damp and cause me to catch a nasty chill on my kidneys, or some small venomous creature might give a painful bite in the buttock, et cetera. So down I went pronto. My dad would cut his throat sooner than sit anywhere not specifically designed for the purpose. It's a twenty-mile walk to the next oasis, Mr Davies, so I suggest you take the weight off your feet for a few minutes. Thank you no, I do not wish to get sand on my trousers. My mother would let me sit on the grass but ask me nervously every fifteen seconds if I was quite sure I was comfortable. Thank heaven they're neither of them here now. Oh, what a lovely day it's being.' Robin found a good place for his head and lay back.

Jeremy looked down at him. 'No reservations? Nothing missing?'

'Only the obvious thing.'

'Which is what?'

'Well, what do you think? A girl. No sign of one so far.'

'What? I mean, you have got a girl, surely?'

'Alas, no.' Robin closed his eyes. 'I suppose you couldn't conjure one up for me, could you? You seem to be able to do practically anything you want.'

Jeremy's voice said, 'No, Robin, I'm afraid even I couldn't manage that. Sorry.'

Robin gave a long sigh. His shoulders relaxed.

'Ever tried the other?' Jeremy sounded as if his face was turned away.

'I'm sorry, you'll have to speak up.'

'I just wondered if you'd ever tried, you know, the other.'

'What other?' Silence. Then Robin opened his eyes and hastily sat up. 'You mean *blokes*, do you? No bloody fear, mate! Good God! Why, do you think I look like one of that lot, or talk like one, or what? Honestly!'

'Calm down, Robin, come on. Nobody's accusing you of anything. Just a thought that happened to occur to me. I'm sorry, I didn't mean anything.'

'I don't know. Why, have you tried it?'

'As it happens, no I haven't, just to put your mind at rest. But I'm not as upset by the very idea of such a thing as you seem to be. Look, it's no longer the abominable, vile suggestion you evidently think it is, not today. Perhaps you don't realise, Robin, it's getting on for fifty years now since they clapped Oscar Wilde in jug for you-know-what. Now, will you answer me quite truthfully about something?'

'I'll have a shot, yes.'

'Now don't be cross, but are you absolutely certain that you weren't, how shall I put it, showing yourself to be your father's son in your first instinctive reaction to my original question?'

'No,' said Robin almost at once. 'No, I'm not certain. In fact I'm a damn sight more certain of the opposite. I think I was indeed saying the sort of thing my father would have said. Though I hope I put it in my own sort of way.'

'The general response may quite well have owed something to Davies senior, but rest assured that its expression bore the unmistakable stamp of his son.'

'Well, that's some consolation, I suppose. Oh dear. Sorry, Jeremy.'

'Don't be ridiculous. A harmless misunderstanding between friends, over in a moment. Now you see it, now you don't. Right, you have forty winks while I take a look at the ignition of that motor. I fancy it needs retarding.'

When Robin woke up on his grassy couch, he felt some shame at having answered Jeremy's question in such a blustering way. But that feeling lasted only a moment. He found he no longer thought he had said or done the wrong thing when Jeremy made his suggestion about 'the other'. It was hard to believe that somebody as grown up, as much at ease, as experienced in the ways of the world had – how could he put it to himself? – tried it on with him – in his mind he shied away from ruder expressions – thrown a pass, had a go. But that somebody had. Somebody as amusing and as nice as that. But he had. And had been building up to it half the morning and all the afternoon till some minutes ago. It was quite as hard to believe as it had always been to believe that his own father had done what he must have done with his mother in order to produce Margery, George, Robin. But he had.

It was not very easy to believe either that such a short time away from the problem should have produced such a turn-around in attitude. Nevertheless such was the case, and with an immediate consequence, namely that he was going to have to go on as if he still stuck to the unfortunate-misunderstanding account of recent events. But that was what he was going to have to do, and do it as resolutely as he could. Well, no time like the present.

Robin quailed a little when he got back to the car to find Jeremy in the driving-seat, not only reading a book but apparently set on continuing to read it for an hour or two. He quailed rather more when Jeremy raised his head with an abrupt movement and stared at him impassively. Then with equal abruptness he performed a tremendous wink that seemed to involve every muscle on that side of his face and dissolved into silent laughter. So that was all right, for the moment anyway.

On the way back, Jeremy said, 'You were asking about those fellows, you know, Lawrence and the other two. By the way, what did you think of the poem they turned up in?'

'I enjoyed it. I thought he must have enjoyed writing it, too.'

'Which is more than can be said for some of the others.'

'But number whatever-it-was, does he really mean there ought to be a revolution?'

'Sort of, yes, but not necessarily political. More a big change in the way people think and feel about things.'

'What things?'

'Sex chiefly,' said Jeremy crisply. That's where our three pals come in. Take old Lawrence. He's the only writer I know who writes about it in a completely honest and straightforward way and keeps just the right balance between, well, what you think and what you feel. I'll lend you some of his books when we get back home, that's if we can find a way of smuggling them past your parents.'

'Is he very, er, what can I say, I suppose he—'

'Very dirty, you mean. Your father would certainly think so if he were ever to read him. With all due respect, dirt is in the eye of the beholder. Reading Lawrence certainly isn't going to corrupt anyone. Not even you, Robin.'

'It says he was brought down by smut-hounds. He wasn't hunted down or put in prison or anything, was he?'

'I think that would be taking it too literally, you know. It was written in the heat of the moment, the year Lawrence died, not so long ago. He certainly had a lot of trouble with the law and the police and so-called guardians of morality who tried to shut him up.'

'Oh I see.' Robin felt a sense of anti-climax. He had pictured something more concrete and dramatic than that, not actual dogs of course but more dangerous foes than fat-bellied chairmen of committees in morning coats and top hats.

'But Blake did go well and truly mad,' said Jeremy, as if aware of Robin's disappointment. 'They thought he was enough of a threat to be had up for high treason, serious stuff.'

'Oh really. How was he a healer?'

'He would have been if he'd been listened to. He said or wrote some amazing things. Such as, "Sooner murder an infant in its cradle than nurse unacted desires." What about that?'

'I can see why they thought he was a threat.'

'He was deliberately using shocking language. Would it have been as effective if he'd said something like, "It's like a monstrous crime to cherish, to hug to yourself the thought of what you want to do sooner than simply go and do it"?'

'No, obviously not, I see that all right,' said Robin. He also saw, or thought he saw, that if Blake had wanted people to listen to him rather than be shocked by him, he might have considered something nearer the despised second version, but he shut up about that.

'In some ways,' Jeremy was going on, 'Homer Lane is the most interesting of the three. No, not quite that: he has the most to say for us, that's better.' He looked at Robin with a smaller version of his grin. 'Shall I have a stab at telling you what he said?'

'Yes, please.'

'Sure you want it, are you? All right, here goes. Well, sorry, Lane was an American psychologist who spent some time over here. Not long ago I tried to boil down what he taught for my own benefit, which'll come in devilishly handy, what? Now. Stop hating and fearing your desires. If you feel bad, depressed and bored and so on, all that means is that your desires are putting pressure on you to go and do what you really want to do, instead of what you think you *ought* to do. If you follow that principle, even if it seems bizarre or shocking of you to, then it'll be like recovering from an illness, you'll feel well and start to be happy.'

The car ran on through the afternoon. Presently Robin said, 'Have you tried putting that into practice?'

'A bit. A certain amount.'

'And has it had the promised effect?'

'Oh yes. In a limited sort of way.'

Robin left it there because he thought Jeremy might go on to tell him in what sense the man Lane had been killed in action by the Twickenham Baptist gang. But this never transpired. On consideration, he would have been lucky if what had really happened had been as much as Lane's discomfiture when, giving a lecture at Twickenham, he had narrowly missed being thumped on the shoulder by a fierce umbrella-wielding Nonconformist lady. He tried to elaborate this image. Doing so helped him to swallow his immediate sense of let-down. Once again a piece of poetry that had looked and sounded marvellous on first reading would have turned out to mean something quite commonplace. He was not far off the thought of his father's voice telling him he would forget all about that sort of thing among others when he was grown up.

They were now approaching Cousin Emrys's farm. Robin said to Jeremy, 'If you want to ring your friends you can do it from the village. There's a public telephone in the post office.'

Jeremy looked at his wrist-watch before answering. 'I don't think I need bother, thanks,' he said in a preoccupied way. 'I'll be back in not much over an hour.'

This threw Robin into some confusion. 'Oh, Jeremy, I thought you were going to come back for tea at least. Nothing at all grand, just—'

'I'd love to but I'm afraid I simply can't. There was an arrangement that some people are going to come in early this evening and I promised I'd be there for them.' Then Jeremy's voice softened. 'I would like to stay, but I honestly can't.'

'Yes of course, I understand.'

'In fact' – Jeremy looked at his watch again – 'I think if you don't mind I'll drop you just along here and you could walk up to the house, if that's all right.'

'Fine, easiest thing out.'

'Say good-bye to Cousin Taffy and the others for me.'

'I will. Thank you for a super day.'

'I certainly enjoyed it. I'll give you a tinkle at home.'

'Have a good journey.'

Robin had shut the five-barred gate carefully behind him and taken a few steps up the track before he started to cry. At first he thought he would not have needed to at all if it had been understood from the outset that he and Jeremy were going to part when they did. Then he asked himself what he was crying for. Out of a sense of relief, he told himself, relief that any further embarrassment between the two of them had been avoided. But after that, turning round and looking back the way he had come from the gate, it dawned on him that his tears were about something more selfish and almost more important. Too late, he saw that Jeremy Carpenter had been going to be the best friend he had ever had in his life, with a lot to teach him about more important things than the Twickenham Baptist gang, as well as being entertaining and inspiring and just a marvellous chap. He had thought that his own store of such qualities might well have been small or non-existent, but anyway that what had attracted Jeremy, even to the extent of driving miles and miles in the hope of seeing him, had been no more than what any ordinary youngster might feel for another. He had been wrong, but would never know to what degree, except that it must have been more than a little, quite enough to make impossible any ordinary friendship, however intense. Now all he could do was be sorry.

Thinking that there was nothing more than that to be done brought some consolation. His tears had stopped. He blew his nose and told himself it was a good job there had been nobody there to see him crying. He silently vowed that he would try to grow up and not start piping his eye as soon as things seemed to be going wrong. A change of heart. One of those poems had ended like that.

After that it was no trouble at all to be rather grand and tolerant to Cousin Emrys while telling him just a little less about the day's excursion than he saw as his due, to be effortlessly charming to Dilys instead of avoiding her eye and to simulate some respect for Dai Stephens. Only eleven more days to go.

Twelve days later, Robin got off the afternoon train from Wales and not unexpectedly found his father waiting for him at the barrier. As always on the rare occasions when they had been parted for some time, Robin was impressed by the extravagant normality of his appearance: appropriate office get-up, folded newspaper under arm, bowler hat on head, no Red Indian's eagle feathers or pirate's cutlass and eyepatch. Even his expression on catching sight of his son told only of simple pleasure, without a hint of sadistic relish. The two shook hands, on Mr Davies's side with a parade of man-to-man seriousness and absence of fuss.

'Had a good time, old boy?' he asked, and added, 'You're looking jolly well,' after assuring himself that Robin had no limbs missing and bore no obvious marks of dissipation.

'Good, I got out into the fresh air a lot.' Robin kept it simple too, not letting his candid smile degenerate into an anticipatory grin.

'Finest thing in the world.'

'Worked wonders in my case.'

They continued in this vein, eked out with abundant pauses, while they crossed from one terminus to another. In the full compartment of the suburban train, his father and himself sitting on opposite sides and at a slight diagonal, Robin waited for his father to ask after Cousin Emrys, which he did almost at once.

'Oh, he was fine, they all were. He wanted to know if they could expect to see you down there one of these days.'

'And what did you tell him?'

Robin took his time about answering that one, peering round the other passengers, who all looked as though they worked in offices, and hoping some of them had started to listen. 'Oh,' he said weightily, 'I told him I couldn't be sure, but I thought it was pretty unlikely. I hope you think it was the right thing to say.'

'Oh, rather, quite right.'

'Good. But then he asked me something else, which I, er, I didn't find so easy to answer.'

'Oh? What was that?'

After waiting for as long as he dared, Robin said, 'I don't know whether this is quite the sort of time and place to bring it up.'

Also prepared in advance, that was a devilishly shrewd move, given father Davies's reiterated theme that, far from anything being said between him and his son that would not stand public scrutiny, whatever passed was so entirely normal that it could be shouted from the housetops and welcome. He in his turn hesitated no more than an instant before declaring robustly, 'Oh nonsense, lad, let's hear it.'

Into a carriage suddenly voiceless, Robin said, 'All right, well, he made me promise I'd ask you as soon as I could' – short interval for gulp and batting of eyelids – 'whether you believed in God.'

'Oh. I see. And what did you say to that?'

'What could I say? I said I would.'

'Quite right,' said Robin's father in a reassuring voice. 'You did absolutely right. I can put your mind at rest straight away.'

'Oh thanks, Dad. What about his mind, Cousin Emrys's mind?'

'What?'

'What do you want me to tell Cousin Emrys?' said Robin more loudly.

'Oh, that. Don't worry about that. Don't worry about *that*. I'll, er, I'll take care of it myself. As good as done.'

The girl opposite was making no bones about listening to this conversation. Robin had decided she must have been a typist and stared at her with theoretical salacity, but only for a moment, because rather to his relief she soon looked away. 'There is just one thing, Dad,' he said.

'What is it?'

'Sorry to keep on about it, Dad, but he made me promise, Cousin Emrys made me promise I'd drop a line myself, telling him what you said.'

Mr Davies hesitated a little longer this time. 'I don't think we can make a start on that till I've made up my mind what I'm going to say. Now, unless—'

'But, Dad . . .'

'Yes, Robin.'

'Dad, another thing Cousin Emrys said, he said it was a very important question, and I agree with that, so much so I wish you'd tell me now which way you'll be answering it.'

'Which way? I'm afraid I don't quite—'

'Yes or no.'

'That's all very well, old boy, but I can't help thinking that what

86

we're talking about is one of those ticklish questions that's easy to ask but darned hard to answer this way or that in a few words or a hundred or even a thousand. In fact—'

'Yes is only one word and it's a complete answer to the question and you're saying it won't do for you, aren't you, Dad? I think that's marvellously honest of you, it can't have been easy for you to admit that.'

'I think if you don't mind we'll defer this discussion to a more suitable time.'

After some pretended consideration, designed to prolong his father's suspense for a few more seconds, Robin heaved a sigh and said, 'Right-oh, Dad.'

Victory! He knew he would suffer a reprisal or so before long, like being sent to bed early on some technicality or other, but it was worth it. He stood up and took Bury's *History of Rome* out of his suitcase.

2

It must always be remembered that, whereas the desire of the male is soon aroused and soon reaches its peak, that of the female is normally slower in both respects. To put the matter in different words, the male reaches the state of full preparedness for sexual intercourse an appreciable time before the female is so prepared. In the case of an informed and considerate male this interval will be occupied by FOREPLAY (see also ch. VII, sections 1–3.).

As its name implies, FOREPLAY is preludial to the act of sexual intercourse and is to be considered and employed only in its light. Should foreplay come to be enjoyed and practised for its own sake, without direct reference to the act of sexual intercourse which is to follow, then to this degree the participants have become engaged in an act of PERVERSION (see also ch. IX and ch. XII, sections 3-8.).

Robin Davies, second-year undergraduate at Oxford University, laid aside his copy of Vanderdecken's *Happier Love* (1937, printed in Holland). It was strange to be reading it in search of serious information instead of the vague but sometimes effective sexual lift he was used to getting from it or its likes. In fact, as he felt at the moment, he could hardly believe that he had ever found such material anything but mildly sedative.

The room Robin was sitting in was the sitting-room of his set, the other component of which was a bedroom. The rooms together would not quite have fitted into a full-sized Rugby fives court. Not counting the pot kept under the bed, the nearest lavatory or lavatories could be reached down four flights of stairs and across most of a quadrangle. When it came to shaving you had the choice of the bath-house at a slightly greater distance and the bedroom washstand, for which hot water was meagrely and briefly supplied by your scout in the early morning. The only heating device in the set was the coal fire in the sitting-room, which you were not supposed to light before 6.00 pm. The time at the moment was not quite four o'clock and the fire, now venting grey smoke but with a small glint of red at its heart, had been lit since three, but this was a minor illegality in the present circumstances.

All too soon, Robin heard the sound he had been hoping for and dreading, an unusual one in these parts, that of not obviously masculine footfalls climbing the uncarpeted stair towards his room. For a moment, having no other sign to make, he crossed his fingers. When the knock sounded at his door he went to open it at what he hoped was a normal pace.

Barbara Bates stood there. She was a rather tall girl with glossy black hair cut so that it curved forward in points just below her ears. She and Robin had first got into conversation at a meeting of the Classical Society earlier that term. At the same time he had also got into conversation willy-nilly with Barbara's chum Patsy Cartland. Of the two, Barbara was the more attractive without coming much higher than half-way up Robin's Category 2, that comprising girls it would be jolly nice/perfectly all right to find yourself in bed with but not worth serious trouble to get them there. Then, at an apparently fortuitous encounter with Patsy minus Barbara, Patsy had confided to him that any advances he might make to Barbara would be well received. What, *any* advances? Patsy's saying yes to what he meant had sent Barbara's stock zooming up into Category 1. At her next visit for tea in his room he had made successful but limited advances to her. This afternoon it was understood that he would be giving her more than tea.

Trying to tell himself that it was the most natural thing in the world and that anyway he was not really noticing what he was

89

doing, Robin put his arms round Barbara and gave her a medium-intensity medium-duration kiss. He tried to get into it something he really felt, that he liked her as well as being committed to what now seemed a mysterious ritual with her, but he probably failed. At any rate she was kissing him back. Until a couple of hours ago he had half believed, had thought it more than barely possible, that at about the present stage something would snap in his brain and he would find himself if not actually carrying Barbara into his bedroom then lugging her there by some method that would suggest itself when the time came. The other half of what he believed was that he would never in his life feel less than anything of the kind, and unfortunately that was the half that had got it right.

'Shall we go and sit down?' he asked, and added, 'for a minute' just to show there was no ill-feeling.

'Okay.'

He knew that any interference at all with the fire was likely to make it lose any hold it might have gained, but none the less he poked at it cautiously from a crouching position. A small piece of coal, smoking slightly, clattered into the hearth. With his back turned to Barbara, he said, 'I've never done this before, you know.'

Barbara had a hearty but quite agreeable laugh. It was to be heard briefly just before she said, 'If I hadn't known it already, I did the moment I clapped eyes on you just now. Anyway, ten out of ten for owning up like that. Now you can take your own advice and sit down.'

Robin would have liked to laugh back, or at least grin, but all he could manage was a rueful grimace. 'What about you?' he asked. 'You must have had plenty of—'

'Don't worry about me, darling. Or about yourself either. I see you've been doing your homework.' She indicated the copy of *Happier Love* she had lent Robin, prominent on the desk in its purple binding. 'What did you make of it?'

'It is rather like homework.'

'It can't have been an easy job writing it. I hope he got well paid for his trouble. It's not very warm in here, is it, darling?'

'I'm sorry, no, it isn't. But I've put a hot-water bottle in the bed.'

'Oh, you have, have you? Tell me, did you fill it in your communal wash-house place? I'd love to see round it some time.'

'Actually no, I did consider it but I decided I'd get a hotter bottle by boiling up my tea-kettle on that gas-ring on the landing. And I think I was right.'

'Very likely. Now you stay where you are while I go and get into bed. I won't shout out to you that I'm ready in case the Dean or the Senior Tutor is listening. So just you count a hundred slowly and then come sauntering in.'

'Right.'

'Better make it a hundred and fifty in case something gets stuck.'

She was gone, carrying the little tartan-covered handcase she had brought with her. He counted the prescribed hundred and fifty at top speed and then hung about. During part of this time he quietly closed the outer door of his rooms and no less quietly prepared a contraceptive device. These employments helped to alleviate his sudden feeling of having woken in the middle of the night with nothing to fix his attention on. Nothing: he could not have thought for two seconds together about what was to come. Never mind, old chap, said Robin D. silently, it'll all be over in half an hour. It won't be that long, mate, answered R. Davies, but just make sure we don't get into this again.

He heard a bed-spring twang, got up and started to march for the door before he remembered being told to saunter. Even so he was nearly there when it occurred to him that he was still fully clothed. Having rectified this with amazing speed and efficiency he sauntered into his bedroom.

As expected, Barbara was in bed, but so thoroughly, with her face turned to the wall and mostly covered with bedclothes, that she might have been asleep. That remained a theoretical possibility for the first half-minute after he joined her. Then she rotated quickly and put her arms round his neck and took his outer leg between both of hers. It was the first time in his life that he had embraced a naked person. He was struck by the extreme smoothness and delicacy of her skin, several times greater than he had expected, and wondered if it was a special beauty of hers or characteristic of women in general. At one moment her body seemed to him large and heavy, filling the bed, at the next so slender he could have enfolded it in one arm, but it was steadily warm. By now he was kissing her without any thought at all, certainly not of intensity or duration, and he was ready for her and very willing.

At this point a thought entered his head. He had undoubtedly reached the state of preparedness for sexual intercourse, but what about old Barbara? Probably she was still working up to being so prepared, and would let him know when she was. As an informed and considerate male, at any rate he hoped a considerate one, he should now be paying more attention to what Vanderdecken had called the female erogenous zones.

After some interval, Barbara changed her position and whispered to him to come on. He responded at once, but almost as soon it became clear that his state of preparedness for sexual intercourse was not what it had been. He did his best regardless.

'Sorry,' he said after a moment.

'Wait a minute. . . . Now try.'

'Sorry,' he said again after another moment.

'It's all right.'

In the end, after an appreciable time in fact, an act of sexual intercourse did definitely take place, though not one satisfactory to either Vanderdecken or Robin Davies. The latter at least felt absolutely terrible, conscious the moment it was over of a sense of humiliation greater than even he, an authority as he had supposed on that state of feeling, had supposed attainable. Nor had he any clue to what Barbara might be feeling, since she had gone back to seeming asleep. He had no inclination to blame her for anything, but recognised this only later as a small sign of righteousness. For the moment, blame or no blame, he wanted to be on the move, but a few yards had better do.

'Would you like a cup of tea?' he asked.

'M'm.'

He went out on to the landing in dressing-gown and slippers, thinking it was one of the comparatively few good things about Oxford that at any time of day or night you would attract no particular notice by appearing in dressing-gown and slippers. There were warmer outfits, though. He moved closer to the lighted gas-ring, whose slight roar and sizzle covered any sounds likely to be coming from the bedroom. He had no desire to blot Barbara out of his mind, but was afraid that any reminder of her existence now would make it harder to forget the dejected look he had seen on her face some minutes earlier. He had not considered carefully enough what might be involved in going to bed with a girl. Unless he had considered it too carefully.

The kettle boiled and he made the tea. Barbara was not in the bedroom, so unless she had gone climbing down the face of the building to get away from him she would have had to be in the sitting-room. There indeed she was, reading a copy of *Poems from Spain* she had presumably found on the shelves of his job-lot bookcase. When he appeared in the doorway with the teapot she looked up and smiled at him.

'If you give me that I'll pour it,' she said. 'I can find a cup.'

'I'll put some trousers on.'

'That's the idea.'

There was a little warmish water left for him in the thermos. Having been exposed only to women's public behaviour he was astonished by the speed and thoroughness with which she had resumed her out-of-bed self. By the time he had donned a shirt and the promised trousers among other items and returned to the sitting-room, Barbara had the tea-things set out on his shoddy little round table, together with biscuits exhibited on the only possible plate in his cupboard.

'I'd have made toast,' she said, 'only I didn't think the fire was quite up to it. I can see it's an excellent fire in other ways.'

Robin laughed. Just then he really liked her quite a lot and found it easy to say, not too heavily, 'I am truly sorry for not doing better. But the important point is you're not to think it was in any way—'

'It was any reflection on me because it was all your fault. I know.'

'So you have done this before.'

'Let's just say I keep my ears open. But what have you got to go by?'

'Nothing but intelligence, perspicacity and imagination.'

'Drink your tea.'

When they had finished the biscuits Robin offered cigarettes. They were small and made with inferior tobacco interspersed with bits of straw or hay, but in those days of shortage you took what you could get. The fire had burnt up a little by now and it was quite pleasant to sit there and chat, although conversation could not have been said to flow freely. After a short silence Barbara leant across and put her hand on his, their first physical contact since getting out of bed. Robin had wondered whether he was supposed to keep the ball rolling, so to speak, by somehow bringing about a cuddle on the couch, but had decided that would be rather a non-adult idea, and at the moment not an eminently appealing one either.

Perhaps Barbara had guessed some of that. She said now, withdrawing her hand, 'I've got to go soon. If you find yourself still feeling dissatisfied with how you performed, rest assured it isn't at all a bad sign. It shows you're imaginative, and imaginative men make the best lovers in the end.'

'In the end?'

'Well, just not necessarily straight away.'

'Does Vanderdecken say that?'

'I think so. Something to that effect.'

'Who does that book actually belong to? You only told me it wasn't yours.'

'Oh, just one of the girls in college. It was lying about in her room.'

'When was this?'

'I don't know, beginning of this term I should think. Why?'

'Nothing, just curiosity. Anyway, you obviously think it's good and agree with it and everything or you wouldn't have passed it on to me with instructions to read, mark and inwardly digest.'

'When did you decide to drop classics and read for the Bar instead?'

'Sorry, I suppose I was working up to saying I think, I was wondering if the Vanderdecken approach was necessarily the right one or the only one, scientific or trying to be when the whole thing is supposed to be to do with instinct and the unconscious mind and feeling rather than thinking and . . . all that.'

'And D. H. Lawrence. I know. The trouble with that is that no amount of instinct and feeling and the rest of it will make a man understand that for instance a woman has a different sexual and psychological make-up from a man. That's a fact that has to be learnt like the exports of Finland have to be learnt.'

'In the same way? But that's—'

'Of course I didn't mean it was the same sort of fact with the same sort of importance, I meant it was just as much a fact as that the Finns export timber and stuff.'

'All right, Barbara. Point taken, old girl.'

'Vanderdecken isn't giving you your stage directions and lines like a playscript. Just guidance, that's all. Like a tennis manual, say. You wouldn't expect one of those to lay down exactly how a game should go. I mean every game's different, but they all have some things in common.'

'For example, the overall purpose of each party is to defeat the other.'

'Of course it wasn't meant to be an exact analogy.'

'I think that last difference is essential, fundamental, don't you?'

'You can always find things like that if you look for them.'

Over her last couple of remarks Barbara's tone had sharpened. What little Robin knew of her included a tendency on her part towards getting fed up when disagreed with, really fed up. She had come within sight of walking out of their last tea-party when the two of them had differed over the structure and meaning of one of the Euripides plays, he could not for the moment remember which one. Since presumably sex mattered to her more than Euripides, she might quite walk out now instead of just nearly, and he guessed that no small effort would be needed to induce her to walk in again. And even after the recent part-fiasco he was still better placed to get into bed with her than with anyone else he knew. So, perhaps in the nick of time, he let a tentative smile appear on his face.

'I owe you an apology,' he said. 'Another one.' He would have given something, not too large or valuable, even so something, to have been able to touch hands as she had some minutes before, but he could not.

'Let's have it,' she said, her manner lightening at once.

'I was getting at you because I was still feeling rotten myself because of, you know.'

'It's nice of you to say that. It may not be quite true but it's nice of you all the same. More so, in fact. Now I really must be away. If you find you still want me to, I'll come round one afternoon next week. Afternoon. What makes them think people wouldn't ever think of fornicating in the afternoon?'

'I suppose they think they've got to do something. Of course I'll still want you to.'

'Drop me a note on Monday. Don't one or two of the posh colleges let women in in the evening as well? I'd ask you round to my place, but you probably know if we have a man to tea we have to push the bed out into the corridor, which I suppose is more of them thinking they've done something or something. Anyway I don't think you and I are quite up to doing it on the floor yet awhile, do you? See you at Pissy Percy's get-together at Univ at ten tomorrow.'

She was gone, leaving behind a faint fragrance of herself. At once the belated consciousness of a thousand ineptitudes rushed in upon him. He piled up the tea-things on the top of his cupboard, trying to make them seem even more than they really were. While he was doing that he remembered that the Euripides play he had argued about with Barbara was the *Alcestis*. Robin had more or less passed over what he saw as the psychological absurdity of the main story, which has Alcestis unhesitatingly agreeing to die in place of her husband, the king Admetus, and taking most of the play to do it.

He had concentrated instead on the kind of coda in which Hercules, an old mate of Admetus's who happens to be in town, unhesitatingly goes down to the underworld, challenges death to a wrestling-bout and beats him, claims Alcestis as his prize and delivers her back to Admetus, all but the last part taking place off-stage. When he described the Hercules part as absurd in a different way, Barbara had retorted that any absurdity in it was purposeful, designed to emphasise the absurdity of the main story; there, the intention was to attack the subjection of women by portraying an absurdly extreme instance of it. A funny way to set about entertaining a theatre audience, he had said, adding for good measure that he wondered where she had picked up such an unlikely idea. The good measure had torn it, or very nearly. Jumping to her feet, she had accused him of supposing her incapable of thinking for herself. Voluble and persuasive protestations of the contrary had been required to get her to sit down again.

Had he meant them? What, in any case, did he think Euripides had been getting at in the play? Seven years' study of Greek literature had furnished the insight that with a few exceptions, of which the *Alcestis* was not one, those fellows had either been getting at something beyond a modern understanding or, just as likely, had not been getting at anything in particular. No doubt, but could she think for herself? Did it matter? What about her views on sex? She had made them sound like the fruit of experience, but were they? Did that matter? Yes. He had assumed she was not a virgin, but he thought he remembered that she had never in so many words said she was not. And if she was not a non-virgin then her feelings and instincts on the matter were as likely, or unlikely, to be well founded and interesting as his. More than that, she had pretended to the authority of experience when in fact the two of them had been equally ignorant and innocent. She had – what was it? – kept her ears open, she had probably read Vanderdecken through when he had certainly not. That was the extent of the difference between them.

By now, Robin was convinced that his theory was right,

convinced enough anyway to want to hurl Vanderdecken out of the window. That he resisted this temptation was due to his respect for books, any books, plus the fact that, once opened, the window was the very devil of a job to get shut again. To reinforce his new feeling he turned to a random page near the end and read:

serious as to be insuperable. This is a clear warning that the contemplated sexual union has not proceeded from a marriage of loyal minds, in the words of Shakespeare. It cannot be stressed too much that where there is incompatibility of feeling there can be no compatibility of sexual performance. It would not be going too far to say that a lovemaking is unlikely to be successful or even pleasurable unless each party is able to contemplate with serenity the state of marriage with the other. Indeed, experience suggests . . .

'Pah!' screeched Robin, and made to hurl Vanderdecken to the floor at least, but again checked himself. 'I've had enough of you, you pietistic Netherlander. I won't make the same mistake again, never fear.'

And he did not. The next morning he wrote and sent off a note asking Barbara round for tea on the following Monday. After some thought he added a PS promising to give her some of the strong tea she had said she liked, a message he thought nicely poised between incomprehensibility to Barbara herself and notional impenetrability to her Dean or Senior Tutor or whatever official might set eyes upon it.

Either he had put something more than that into the text of his note, or Barbara had grown to suspect something on just thinking things over, or someone else had got to her. Whichever it had been, mistrust radiated from her when she turned up not long after four o'clock on the Monday. Having stolen some coal out of the communal bunker on the landing, he had built up a better fire than formerly; he had also, by dint of plundering the jam reserves of Cornish, the snivelling Christian biologist who inhabited the set of rooms under his, laid the foundations of a tea with elements of lavishness. She wore a dark garment that resembled, and perhaps in former days had actually been, a page's tabard in some historical pageant. He ignored her diffidence as far as possible, kissed her with some fervour, gave her no chance to sit down and half hauled her into his bedroom, where he set about undressing her as far as he conveniently could.

'We are in a hurry today, aren't we?' she said a little shakily, nevertheless going on with what he had started.

He sat down on the edge of the bed to take off his shoes. 'Correct, but not so much of one that I've forgotten about the hot-water bottle.'

'The Lord bless you, kind sir.'

Vanderdecken's first objection to what followed might well have been that it followed rather soon, though he would have found it hard to fault Robin's performance in point of enthusiasm and evident enjoyment. To judge by externals, Barbara scored slightly less in these departments.

'Was it all right for you?' asked Robin.

'All right, yes.'

'Good.' He kissed her. Then he said, 'I meant, was it, you know, *all right*?'

'If you're asking me did I, the answer's no, I didn't.'

'Sorry, darling.'

'You don't sound very sorry to me. You sound as if you've trodden on my foot.'

'I'm sorrier than that. What can I say?'

'You were much more considerate last time.' Barbara wriggled herself round a bit so that she was looking more directly into his face. 'What's happened?'

'I didn't have nearly such a good time myself last time, in fact if I'd gone on being considerate much longer probably neither of us would have had any sort of time at all. And what's happened is just that I've decided Vanderdecken has got it all wrong from the start.'

'From your long and wide experience.'

'Not much shorter and narrower than yours, is it?'

'I don't know what you mean,' she said, turning half-way back to where she had been before.

'Why didn't you just say you had had a – you know. Lots of women do when they haven't, I'm told.'

'I think people should always be honest about things to do with sex.'

'Should they? Anyway, I thought you'd say that. Let me remind you that people can be honest and dishonest in what they do as well as what they say. And what they don't do and don't say.'

'Go on, let's hear what's on your mind. And don't tell me there's no more to come, and if you think that's me showing off my woman's intuition you're wrong. A child could see it.'

'All right. Why didn't you admit you hadn't done it before either, when I said I hadn't? Then we could have started off level.'

'I see, you're accusing me of pretending not to be a virgin.'

'Not accusing. Just saying it's what I think.'

Barbara looked at him sorrowfully. 'Darling, could you possibly go and make the tea?'

In dressing-gown and slippers he did as he was asked and in due course carried the loaded teapot into the sitting-room. Barbara would have had to be in the bedroom, but she stayed there only for the length of time it took him to put the teapot down on the table and to scratch his backside, for at that moment he heard her come trotting out on to the landing and make for the stairs. Without thinking he started in pursuit and just caught a glimpse of her before she had turned the corner and vanished. Then he did think, especially about what it would be like, dressed as he was, to chase a sufficiently nimble girl down four flights of very steep stairs and across the front quad, not to speak of out into the street. Halted on the stairhead, he tried to frame some appropriately contrite and abusive message to bawl after her, but found none for the moment. Misery fell upon him when he looked into the bedroom and found no visible trace of her but the cooling water in the hand-basin, and a second descent followed at about the time he glanced over at his

desk and saw that the copy of *Happier Love* was gone. His only con -
solation was that he had not thought to signal a belated deduction
of his by thundering after Barbara something like, 'Be sure to give
your conniving chum Patsy Cartland a ram up the duff from me!'

That was surely not much to feel better about. He went back to
his bedroom and got dressed most of the way; he could not summon
the heart to put on a tie. Nor could he face sitting down to tea on
his own, so he merely poured himself a cup and took it to the chair
at his desk where he wrote his essays for his tutor and his letters
home. Darkness was starting to fall, but before he put the light on
he would arrange the black-out over his windows, so he sat on and
looked out into the street, where there stood an ancient memorial
and a cabman's shelter and a clock-tower of honey-coloured stone.
Dozens of strangers walked the pavements in ones and twos.

Robin's elation at rejecting and bypassing Vanderdecken had not
lasted long. However conscientiously he might try to, he could not
stop himself from putting himself in Barbara's place. After a near-
rape which she tried to make the best of but refused to lie about,
she had been ticked off, first for telling the truth and then, almost
in the same breath, for not telling the truth about her sexual
experience. It mattered hardly at all that he was more than ever
convinced she had indeed concealed her virginity and used Patsy in
a little stratagem (not a very brilliant one but good enough to fool
him). What mattered was that she had been at least as nervous as he
the first time and treated in a way that must have seemed to her
callous the second. Only *must have seemed to her*? Very well: *had been*
callous, and it would not help her that he was sorry now.

Although he fought hard to keep it off, he could not avoid the
thought that sexual inexperience must include contraceptive
inexperience, and it would be just his luck to turn out to be
approaching parenthood so early in the game. Time for a change,
Davies.

Until the end of that week, Robin sent Barbara carefully written
but unavailing notes of apology and pleading by post as well as by

the college messenger service and twice tried without success to get her on the telephone. On the Friday he attended a talk to the Classical Society on the non-Latin languages of ancient Italy, but even this desperate recourse brought no sign. Every hour or so of the day he crept into the porter's lodge to assure himself that there was indeed no word. An observer of his behaviour, had any such person been conceivable, might have thought he had been disappointed in love, and now and then he caught himself on the point of believing this was so. Well, the phrase had a more genteel ring to it than disappointment in lust.

When not being lectured to or tutored he stayed in his room as far as possible. No one came to see him or got into conversation with him. From time to time he saw one or other undergraduate of his college, dressed in rowing or football gear, hurrying across the quad and heard him calling brutishly to his mates, or just heard a group of such persons yelling and thumping at some party on his staircase, perhaps in mockery of his isolation. Alternatively, Robin would pass a stooped figure shuffling along in carpet slippers and corduroys and conversing in quavering, goatlike tones with a similar type, both apparently far gone in senility but proving on investigation to be no older than himself. Some young men might have found in those sequestered days a good chance to get on with some heavy work, but not Robin. Straightforward brooding took up some of his spare time, the rest he filled in with reading a long book on the Hellenistic age from the college library. This was admittedly work of a kind, but of a very lowly kind, not truly justifiable unless he expected to be sitting his final exams some time in the 1950s.

By the Sunday afternoon he was no less downcast but fed up to the teeth with solitude and self-pity. The day had turned out fine and he decided to drop in on his old schoolmate Embleton, now his best friend in Oxford. If he found him busy or absent he would walk the half-mile or so back again. Do him good.

The porter at Embleton's college was either not in his lodge or, if present, had fallen down insensible somewhere out of sight. In pale sunshine Robin walked through and across the front quad, where in a central circular bed evergreen shrubs made a brighter show than anything he could remember at his own college. At one end of a cloister on the far side and beyond a low arch lay Embleton's rooms, grander in themselves and their surroundings than Robin's, as befitted the pricier classical scholarship their occupant had won. The very door he knocked at and went in by was statelier than his.

Perhaps it was the brass knick-knacks and coloured china figures as much as anything, or the journals and magazines on the obviously imported revolving bookcase, that made it look like somebody's room rather than a camping-out sight. You could put it another way by muttering, as Robin had done once or twice in the past, that a bit of parental cash always came in handy, though in general he resisted any tendency to be classed as a bright lad with a humble background, because all the people he had met who could have been called that were either thick with it or soft as lights.

'Robin! You're just in time for a cup of tea.' Embleton had grown in height since leaving school and dark hair showed under the skin of his jaws and upper lip. He had the air of being somebody with very little left to do by way of growing up and wore a heavy maroon sweater in possible acknowledgement that it was indeed Sunday afternoon. There was a girl with him, rather a pretty one, whom he efficiently introduced as Jean Bell.

'I don't want to be in the way,' said Robin. 'I only dropped in on the off-chance.'

'Nonsense, how could you be in the way? Come and sit down.'

'I've heard a lot about you from Mark,' said Jean Bell, referring to Embleton. She was fair-haired and had large breasts which she seemed not to know about.

'Jean's reading English,' said Embleton, and named the women's college she attended.

'Is it fun, reading English?' asked Robin, 'I hear conflicting reports.'

After some more of this, he thought to himself that the trouble

103

with having manners like Embleton's was that you behaved exactly the same whether you were just about to go to bed with your girl, had just done so or were simply starting to have tea with her, providing no clues in the shape of consternation, fury, relief or real though perhaps mild pleasure. All the same, it was clear enough that Jean was in some sense Embleton's girl and not, say, the literature secretary of the Labour Club or some family connection being kindly entertained. Robin's friendship with Embleton was limited by his continued ignorance on that sort of point and his virtual inability to ask about it. Not everything became simpler as you grew up.

Anyway, very soon the tea-party was going like a house on fire and almost as soon Robin upset his teacup. This he did at the extreme limit of his reach but thoroughly. Embleton and Jean began mopping up, leaving him to reiterate apologies and stand ineffectually by. He was thus well placed to go and open the door when somebody outside knocked on it and, though at once urged to come in, stayed there.

A girl his own age or a little younger stood smiling half-heartedly at him. 'Excuse me, are you Mr Embleton?' she asked him in a rather thin voice with, he fancied, something of a Welsh accent.

'I'm Embleton,' said Embleton, moving forward. 'Do come in.'

'Hallo, Nancy,' said Jean Bell.

'Sorry I'm late, I got held up.'

'You're not late.'

In the next few minutes Robin established that Nancy was called Nancy Bennett, that she was not quite eighteen, that she had become friendly with Jean through the riding-school (called a pony club) they both went to and that she lived in North Oxford with her parents and belonged to no part of the university. If anything the last bit was a faint surprise to Robin, who had vaguely supposed that the only girls to be seen in Oxford without also being at Oxford were either whores or dons' daughters. Nancy Bennett was clearly enough not in the first category and, far from being a don of any sort, her father had an office job in the large vehicle factory on the edge of town. She released these pieces of information in low tones and a throwaway, almost listless manner, as if she could not be bothered to make them sound interesting.

Robin was mildly disconcerted by this approach, or lack of one. In the circumstances he had been half expecting something more alert or at least fully awake. Perhaps he was boring to meet, if not later on as well. His attempts to get a proper look at her were frustrated at first by the way she kept her head down and only momentarily flicked her eyes up at him. They were blue eyes, he noticed, and her hair was very dark brown, almost black, and rather good. The rest of her seemed strongly made, with broad shoulders for a girl and capable-looking hands ending in squarish fingertips. What he saw was enough, other things being equal, to get her into his Category 2.

When she paused, something she had not done much of for all her uninterested air, he said, 'Tell me, are you Welsh?'

That got her attention all right. The quick glance she sent her friend had alarm and appeal in it, as though he had asked her if she was a Hottentot. 'Yes,' she said quickly, 'both my parents are Welsh and I was born there, didn't I say? – sorry, I meant to. How can you tell?'

'I just thought I could hear a faint Welsh accent. I'm Welsh myself, I suppose, at least my father is. So I can—'

She turned briskly in her chair. 'Jean. Excuse me, Jean, this, er . . .

'Robin Davies,' said Embleton.

'Thank you, Mr Davies's father is Welsh, what do you say to that?' Without waiting for a possible reply, she turned back to Robin and looked straight at him. 'Of course, a name like Bennett, it doesn't give you much of a clue,' she said, her accent intensified, especially in the last word. 'There are lots of English names in our part of Wales. I thought I'd quite lost the accent after more than four years. You weren't born in Wales yourself, were you, Mr Davies?'

'Robin. No. London.'

'Oh, I thought it might be London, yes.'

By this time (never mind what she had been saying) Nancy Bennett had effortlessly ascended into Robin's Category 1, Division B. The B indicated not so much relative inferiority as just not-A, A being reserved for females whose good looks had an intimidating quality, enough of it to keep the Robin Davieses of this world at arm's length and preferably further, like film stars and the estate-agent's daughter who lived at the far end of the road at home. This 1-B specimen had a wide mouth, hundreds of little square white teeth, a beautiful complexion and a perfectly adequate though not quite distinguished bosom. She wore no make-up. Robin hoped very much to get into a position soon where a decent chap would have to keep reminding himself that, hang it all, the girl was still not yet eighteen years old. But for the moment all he reckoned he could do was be wonderfully funny and mature, but at the same time basically respectful, about Cousin Emrys and his family. He was unprepared when, after not much more than half an hour, the two women exchanged looks and announced that they must be going. 'We promised we'd drop in on some friends near Folly Bridge,' they said firmly.

Left to himself, Robin would have made sure he had a way of reaching Nancy Bennett somewhere, but Embleton's presence seemed to have inhibited him. 'Nice girl, that Jean Bell,' he said idly to him when they were alone.

Embleton grinned. 'Indeed she is, but the one you thought was a *really* nice girl is called Nancy Bennett, you remember. Sorry, by the way – I'd forgotten she was coming.'

'That's all right. Could you get her telephone number for me off Jean?'

'Oh, no doubt I could,' said Embleton, still smiling, 'the question is whether I should.'

'Should? I don't understand.'

At this point the scout came in to clear away the tea-things. Robin felt tense. He had always been slightly afraid of Embleton when they were at school, but this was the first time since then.

Without much success he tried to work up some anticipatory resentment as an anticipatory counter-measure.

The door closed. Embleton said, 'Where were we?'

'Just where you were about to give me a ticking-off for having nefarious designs on the person of little Miss Bennett.'

'That's right, Robin, that's exactly where we were, I remember. I'm glad you didn't say I'm objecting to your feeling what you presumably do feel about her, she's a very attractive girl, I can see. She's also very young.'

'She told me she was seventeen. Anything I might get up to within reason would be perfectly legal.'

'Of course I didn't only mean young in years.'

'Are you telling me you're not going to get that number for me? Because if—'

'What I'm telling you now is to calm down and have a glass of sherry.'

'All right. I mean thanks.'

'Good. Now I'll get you Nancy's number, for one thing because it would be ridiculous of me not to. But please think about what you're doing.'

'Christ, Mark, if you mean take it easy, go slow et cetera, I'm not a fool, you know.'

'No, that's not what I mean. I was leading up to advising you to hang on till somebody more suitable comes along, somebody older, not only in years. Cheerio.'

'Oh, cheerio. Surely you don't imagine you can talk me out of, well, what, following my own free choice in a thing like this?'

'No, I didn't, that's to say I wouldn't bother to say anything at all if I thought I was the only one on my side. But I'm not. There's you as well.'

'Me?' said Robin.

'Part of you. A piece of you agrees with me that Nancy isn't the right sort of girl for you to persuade to follow your confounded intentions or whatever they are. What I've been saying is designed to strengthen that piece and do some damage to the other piece, the one that says it's all right to go after something you want if you really want it. It doesn't sound too imposing put like that, does it? But that's—'

'A different type of fellow would have told you to mind your own business an hour ago.'

'A different type of fellow wouldn't have blabbed so freely about his general outlook on this kind of thing. It's a great mistake to talk about yourself like that, you know. A bad habit to get into. And it is my business a bit, after all. If you lead Nancy astray, Jean will hold me responsible.'

'In that case you'd better keep out of it altogether and I'll find out that bloody telephone number some other way and you can truthfully say you had nothing to do with it.'

'You don't know much about women if you can see that cutting any ice. I seem to remember one of your buddies writing that a truth that's told with bad intent beats all the lies you can invent, or words to that effect.'

'Oh come, Mark! Bad intent?'

'With intent to get me out of something I shouldn't be allowed to get out of. Now that's enough arguing. Have a drop more sherry.'

The following Tuesday morning there was a note for Robin in the porter's lodge of his college. It comprised a telephone number, the words 'Mens tibi conscia recti sit' and Embleton's initials. Two minutes later, an unknown female voice was saying that Miss Bennett was out but would be back by six. At several minutes past six Nancy came on the line, distant at first, then friendly. After apologising to Robin for having been out at work when he first rang, she said she had promised to have lunch with a girl pal the next day but would love to go out with him on Thursday, but she hoped he did realise she only got an hour for lunch. Robin said he did and arranged to pick her up at twelve-fifteen that day at her place of work.

This, Nancy's place of work, had turned out to be Nicholson's, known as Nick's in the university, a gramophone shop on the south side of the High Street. The ground-floor part sold musical instruments as well as gramophones, and an undergraduate in a college scarf was making wounded-bull noises by way of a bright brass trumpet when Robin passed through on his way to the stairs at exactly twelve-fifteen on the Thursday.

Up on its first floor Nick's sold gramophone records, of several styles to judge by the jarring mixture of sounds issuing from the half-dozen little glassed-in cubicles, known to some as audition booths, where you tried stuff out. They were also the places from which, with the aid of somebody's special tweed jacket and its unusually capacious inner pocket, you could in certain circumstances steal records. By its agency, Robin himself had walked off with a couple of rare Fats Waller discs, but he looked as if butter would not have melted in his mouth when he walked in to collect Nancy. In a natural-coloured pullover and sky-blue apron dress, she was ready for him. So were two colleagues of comparable age and appearance. Only somebody who had never seen a girl before could have failed to guess that they had been told all about him, or at least as much as Nancy knew. He hung about while she failed to sell a Bach partita to a middle-aged foreign-looking swine, then drifted towards the counter.

'Here I am,' he said.

There was another brief interval during which Nancy introduced her mates. Robin made himself be very marvellous during it, things like half shutting his eyes as he smiled, partly to try to look good for Nancy's sake, partly in case one or both of the mates should turn out to look good on a closer look, which neither did. Just as well, really. As soon as he started to move, Nancy snatched a raincoat with a quilted inside from a peg behind her and trooped out after him. It was raining in the street and cold too. He took her coat from her and held it up and she punched her way into it as if he was everywhere famous for his short temper. He wished he knew how to tell her she could afford to slow down.

'I thought we'd go to Joe's,' he said, observing truthfully that it was just round the corner. He meant the local one of a national chain of lowbrow eateries and explained as much, but not that calling it Joe's was deemed to rescue you from the odium of choosing to lunch (cheaply) among the proletariat. Too finespun, for one thing.

It was not until they were sitting down to their plates of ham and baked beans and salad that Robin became aware of the immense tract of time and conversational distance to be traversed before he could hope to arrive at Stage 0 of any imaginable scenario for seduction. He remembered from his far-distant schooldays a story about a man and a woman in a trans-Siberian train who by the third day had got as far as his third question. 'Ever been to Nijny Novgorod?' and her reply, 'No.' He had followed up with, 'Enough of this flirting – strip.' As often in life, what had seemed nothing but a jest became a glimpse of a large and painful truth the second time round. He himself had yet to ask Nancy if she had ever been to (1) Omsk, (2) Tomsk.

'Where do you live exactly?' he asked her, if anything more apropos than any chatter about Omsk could be. She answered his question and then shut up, which was commendable and a bit boring of her. What would the world be like if everybody stuck to the point all the time? This sort of unspoken question suggested itself more than once while he struggled to keep up some sort of conversation, or rather set one going. 'What exactly does your father do?' He forbore to start even roughly on what his own father did. An aphorism from his schooldays, probably culled from the tuck-shop talk of the french-letter-exhibiting Milnes, came approximately to mind. It advised him that, for every second not spent in somehow driving or dragging a given female towards bed, you were going to have to put in an extra minute later on. On that reckoning he could quite soon have been able to look forward to several unbroken hours of seductional inducement at some indefinite time in the future. 'What's it like, working at Nick's?' If only she would ask him something that gave him a chance to be wonderful or marvellous! 'Did you go to school in Oxford?'

By the time Robin had run up a couple of days on the Milnes

scale, he had accumulated more than a few valueless and yet indispensable facts. Nancy seemed quite satisfied with the way things had turned out; though silent for several stretches she had merely been quiet, not gone quiet. At the door of Nick's she stopped and turned towards him. The rain dwindled almost to nothing.

'Don't bother to come up,' she said. 'Thank you for a lovely lunch, Robin.'

He drew in his breath, wishing he could call her by some word of endearment. 'Oh, Nancy, please, it was nothing, I'd have liked to take you to a nice place but I couldn't afford it, absolutely nothing to thank me for.'

'Usually I just have a sandwich. You didn't half let me talk, though, I didn't give you a chance to tell me anything about yourself.'

'We'll put that right next time.'

'Oh. All right. You've got my telephone number.' She had taken her purse out and now opened it. 'I'd like to pay my share.'

'What? I wouldn't hear of it, a snack like that.'

'Please.' She looked at him in appeal, part of it an appeal not to be asked to explain.

'If you insist. It came to . . . You owe me one and five.' He never thought of understating the figure. 'But there's really no—'

'Here we are: one. And two, three, four . . . and a half, five. There. Now I must fly or I'll be back late. Good-bye, Robin, and thanks again.'

She gave a deafening kiss too close to the ear and hurried into the shop. By way of its window he saw her running up the stairs. Another Milnesian apophthegm drifted along, this one to the effect that liking them got in the way.

Over the next few days, Robin fought down an inclination to report to Embleton and tell him what a good boy he was being. Instead, he took Nancy out for a cup of tea after work, and acquired some rock-solid information about how she spent her holidays. But when it was nearly complete she asked him if he would like to meet her parents. Bravely and in defiance of Milnes's teaching he said he would.

The Bennetts lived across the river in a part of town rarely visited by members of the university, apart from those visiting the Communist bookshop there, whether to buy or to confer. Arriving after darkness had fallen, Robin made little of the house except that it was part of a probably Victorian terrace and was a size or two larger than his parents' place. A large dark-coloured car stood at the kerb outside it. He went up several stairs to the front door, above which a great light blazed.

Nancy answered his ring with a promptitude that suggested she had been awaiting it in the hall. She made a move to kiss him, then drew back. As he followed her he passed a kind of public telephone fixed to the wall, complete with black metal box to receive coins and directories on an enclosed shelf. The two halted by a tall cupboard in polished wood where she found room for his coat among a lot of others. He fancied the hangers in it were fastened on to the horizontal rod to guard against their removal. A considerable roaring cough came from an inner room into which Nancy now led him.

It was less easy to see what was what in here, largely because there was no central illumination; instead, a number of lamps at different heights lit up their more immediate surroundings. Such a lamp shone on what Robin recognised without serious difficulty as a comparatively small but businesslike bar, with variegated bottles and glasses and a very small refrigerator behind it, an absorbent runner along its top and a couple of actual stools with round red-leather seats on its outer side. Also behind this bar was a big man in his late forties smoking a cigarette, his shoulders continuing to shake as his fit of coughing died away but with no sound to be heard beyond a faint rhythmical wheezing. He looked up and gave a sudden smile of welcome.

'Good evening, sir,' he called in an unexpectedly high voice with a Welsh accent, 'and what is your pleasure? If you do not see what you fancy kindly ask for it nevertheless, because we unfortunately lack the space to display our stock in its entirety, you see.'

'Oh, Dad,' said Nancy. 'Dad, this is Robin Davies who I was telling you about.'

'Oh, how do you do, my dear fellow.' A large hand came over the bar and gripped Robin's for an agonising half-second. 'I'll have you know that was a serious offer of mine just now. What can I get you? What would you say to a Gene Tunney cocktail, now?'

'I think it might pack more of a punch than I could cope with.'

'Oh, very good. I mean that. Actually at the moment we seem to have no source of either fresh orange-juice or fresh lemon-juice, and I wouldn't dream of fobbing you off with the artificial article, so perhaps you could suggest something a little simpler.'

'Would a gin and tonic be possible?' Robin thought this sounded less of a soak's drink than whisky, say.

'Yes indeed, well within our humble capacity.'

'Oh, Dad.'

'Easy now girl – Mr Davies is quite capable of taking care of himself.' Nancy's father grew a shade less affable for a moment, but he went on readily enough to Robin, 'In America, you know, they wouldn't dream of serving you a drink of that general status or description without ice in the glass. Just wouldn't occur to them. I was over there for six weeks last year. Place called Detroit, in the state of Michigan. I can tell you that if my experience of that city is any guide, we must face the conclusion that in Great Britain the art of alcohol-consumption is in its infancy. At the college, are you, Mr Davies?'

'Yes.' Robin sipped his drink, which had been mixed out of his view, and found it remarkably bland. It must have been all that ice that did it.

'Or do you call it the university? Yes, girl, I know you told me, but clearly Mr Davies is more than capable of answering for himself. And while I think of it, go and find your mother and tell her Mr Davies is here. Go on, now.'

After a moment, Nancy went on her way, showing the kind of reluctance of someone leaving a friend (like Robin) in charge of a large domestic animal of not absolutely certain temper (like her father). The latter had moved further into the light shed from above him, so that his round pale face and almost hairless skull were to be seen more clearly. 'Make yourself comfortable on that stool, Mr Davies,' he said, and went on within a couple of seconds after Nancy had definitively left the room. 'Well now, I expect you're wondering a bit what I've got in store for you, aren't you?'

Only violent or anyway total disagreement with that seemed worth putting on record, so Robin nodded his head and made affirmative noises.

'There wouldn't be any point in my asking you about your intentions towards my daughter, for one thing because I doubt whether you have any settled view at the moment of what they are, and for another you'd be bound to confine yourself in your reply to what you thought I'd like to hear, of course you would, it's only human nature, I understand that. So . . . *so*, I think probably the best thing I can do, is tell you a few things, just make you a present of some information, right?'

Robin, who had only just succeeded in clambering on to the offered stool, freely gave his assent.

'Yes, well, er, as Nancy may have said to you she has two sisters, neither of whom seems to have turned out in *quite* the way their mother and I might have thought suitable for them, considering the matter in the broadest, most general sense. The eldest ran off with an artist. Now it might surprise you to learn, Mr Davies, that I've nothing against artists as such. After all, it takes all sorts to make a world. But this particular artist, well, I think even a member of the modern generation would have grave doubts there. And the less said about the middle girl the better, I suppose.' There was reluctance in the way this was said. 'So we come to the youngest. I don't think I'd be giving anything away if I told you she occupies a special place in my heart. That being so, I'll also tell you that if I find you've trifled with her affections, to use a pompous but

114

expressive phrase, I shall be greatly upset and also very cross with you indeed.'

In the pause that followed this pronouncement, Robin reflected that its content was less easy to set aside than that of some earlier ones. 'I understand,' he said.

'I hope you do, not for your own sake especially but for my daughter's and my own sake and my wife's. But good boy for not trying to tell me I've nothing to worry about.' Mr Bennett glanced at his watch. 'You've been very patient. Now I will ask you a question.' At this point there was another pause, no more comfortable than its predecessor. 'Can you . . . identify for me the state of the American union . . . the name of which could be applied to a miscellaneous heap of dentures, that's to say false teeth.'

Robin tried his best to think, but in vain. 'Texas,' he said at random.

For once his host showed a touch of irritation. 'No no man, you're not trying. Have another go. Take your time about it.'

'North Dakota. No, it's no use. I haven't the slightest idea.'

'Do you give up?'

'Yes, I give up.'

'Well and good, well and good. The answer is . . . Massachusetts.'

'I'm sorry, I don't quite . . .'

While laying out his riddle Mr Bennett had been bringing out a fresh cigarette and a large square lighter. Now he said loudly, 'Mass . . . o'. . . chew . . . sets,' put the cigarette in his mouth and lit it.

The series of hallooing coughs immediately following bothered Robin not at all when it began and for some time afterwards, but when it showed no signs of abating in its second minute he felt some discomfort. But what was he to do? He supposed he could descend from his stool and run round behind the bar, but that in itself would achieve little. 'Can I get you something, Mr Bennett?' he asked unavailingly, and was relieved when Nancy and another female who would have had to be her mother entered the room. They cheered him up further by doing so at an ordinary walking pace rather than in any desperate hurry-scurry. Very soon they had found Mr Bennett a glass of water and set him down on a relatively straight-backed chair in one of the lesser pools of light issuing from overhead. Robin had no better success than before in finding a way to be helpful. He noticed that Mrs Bennett had shiny black hair arranged in a number of overlapping layers or ridges, as in photographs he had seen of Assyrian or ancient Persian statuary. Otherwise she quite strongly resembled her youngest daughter but, he judged, without ever having been her equal in looks.

'I'm sorry about my dad,' said Nancy to Robin a little later when they found themselves alone for a moment.

'I hope he's all right?'

'Oh yes, he's had these turns before. He smokes too much, you know.'

'Yes, I think perhaps he does.'

'He told me that as a youngster he got through eighty a day. They were only Woodbines, of course, but still. He started earning good money as soon as they put him on the tracking.'

'The tracking?'

'It's to do with the distance between the wheels. He used to say every car that left the works had been through his hands, but I reckon he was boasting. I hope he didn't do his Welsh act too much for you.'

'No, we had a very nice chat in those few minutes. He told me he was very attached to you.'

'Did he say anything about, about my sisters?'

'A bit. Not much.'

'M'm. Did he say anything about my brother?'

'No he didn't. I'd forgotten you had a brother, is it Ivor?'

'Dad probably didn't mention him because there's not much to say about him. He's not a worry to anybody, Ivor's not. He's so much not a worry he's boring.'

'But I gathered your sisters are a worry.'

'Winnie, she's the eldest, she's more or less all right. Married to an artist, I must have told you. I mean he does paintings and sculptures but she is married to him. It's Megan that's the worry. What did Dad say about her?'

'Nothing at all. He just said he wasn't going to say anything about her.'

'M'm,' said Nancy again. This time it sounded a little sceptical. 'She was my dad's favourite in the days when we were all still at school, but there's a lot's happened since then. You know Robin, my dad, actually he's not such a . . .' Nancy stopped speaking.

'Not such a bad chap, were you going to say?'

'More or less. But he would be so much better without the Welsh. I'm afraid we won't be able to go, you and I, until you and my mum have had a word.'

That word came not long afterwards. With a smoothness that told perhaps of prearrangement, Mrs Bennett segregated Robin in the very place where he had enjoyed his chat with her husband, at the bar. Behind it, she now speedily mixed him a second gin and tonic and gave herself one too. This supplementary drink tasted distinctly stronger than the one before. He thought she saw him notice this, and also wondered if her brisk way at the bar came from former professional experience, but mentioned neither point, not that much small-talk proved to be required of him.

'I think I've got a pretty good idea of what my husband would have said to you.' The remains of her Welsh accent were socially elevated by comparison. 'He's always been one for speaking his mind, that's to say some of his mind. There are things he won't talk about, doesn't like talking about even to me. For instance I don't suppose he said anything about our other children, did he?'

It was hardly a question, but Robin said, 'No he didn't,' and added encouragingly, 'Nancy told me something but not much.'

'There's not much she could have told you. Our eldest now, Ivor, he'll be twenty-five next birthday and he's got quite a good job in a biscuit firm in London and he's steady. He's never been a worry, young Ivor, bless him.' Mrs Bennett efficiently lit a cigarette, her comfortable, confidential demeanour behind the counter again suggesting the ex-barmaid. 'Have you read about these experiments they've been doing?' she went on, 'trying to control the sex of unborn rats and so on? In one of these laboratories, you know.'

'I think I did see something about it.'

'Yes, well when they get there as eventually they will, you know, Robin, it won't just be rats, oh dear me no, give it five minutes and it'll be people as well, and couples'll be able to choose whether they want their children to be boy or girl, you mark my words. It won't come in my time, and it may not in yours, but when it does, what's the betting it'll be ten boys or more for every girl? That's if people have got any sense. Because let's face it, girls are so much more trouble than boys, so much more worry. Take our Megan now, one of the prettiest little things you ever saw in your life, prettier than Nancy and me, sweet-natured too and not a care in the world. And her father and I, we worshipped her, we gave her everything two parents could have given. And what does she do?'

Robin shook his head wordlessly.

'What does she do, in her first job, she hadn't been in it more than a couple of months, she goes and starts carrying on with her boss, who I needn't tell you's a married man, and before her father and I know anything about it they're, well, I don't know what you're supposed to call it nowadays, but it used to be called living in sin. Frank, that's Mr Bennett, he did what he could about it, her being under twenty-one still then, but it just went on like before. Do you want to hear the rest of the story?'

'If you want to tell me.'

Mrs Bennett had perhaps rather lost touch once or twice with who Robin was while she talked, but she was fully aware now. Some anger showed in her glance; he hoped as much as possible of it was directed at Megan's boss or even Megan herself and a minimum at him, Robin Davies, and that minimum solely because he was a man. Surely Mrs B could not have guessed the extent of his interest in this Megan, who sounded more and more like the very thing he was looking for. Should he volunteer now to go and see her and try to straighten matters out? No, that was not what he should do. Just as well, perhaps.

Mrs Bennett had been leaning against the shelves behind the counter, but she was standing upright when she went on, 'Yes, Robin, I'd like to tell you, but you may not want to hear after all. Even somebody your age must know it by heart already. The girl got pregnant, of course she did, and the fellow tells her not to worry, they'll start a new life together before the baby comes, but when the baby does come he's not there any more, is he, because he's gone back to his wife. Oh, it's a very boring story except when it happens to happen to one of your own.' Mrs Bennett poured tonic water into the dregs of her drink. 'Actually that's not a good part but it's not the worst part of it. We asked her to come home and bring the baby with her, and we said to each other, Frank and I, we said we could do what they do in Wales and give out the baby was mine, born late in the day. Nobody believes it, of course, not at first anyway, but nobody says anything in public, and after a bit it starts getting taken for granted.

'But it didn't work this time, because Megan wouldn't come, not on any terms or conditions. We went down on our knees to her but it didn't cut any ice, nothing did. She wouldn't even come and stay or let us go and see her and the baby or as much as talk on the telephone. She's in Bristol now with our little grandson who we've never seen except the once just after he was born. Or that's where they were when we last heard, five weeks ago. I hope for your sake, Robin, you never have to go through it, any of it.

'Well, so, we worked it out, Frank and I, we worked it out we'd got it wrong somewhere, not just so she went off the rails in the first place but so she wanted nothing more to do with us afterwards. We'd tried to bring her up with a sense of right and wrong the same as we had ourselves, but obviously we'd made a mess of it. We'd forgotten we weren't still living in 1910. What had been all right for me and Frank wasn't a bit all right for somebody of Megan's generation. She'd rebelled against her upbringing, that's what she'd done. In no uncertain fashion.

'Well, we'd lost her, we'd lost Megan but we still had Nancy and we weren't going to make the same mistake twice over, catch

119

us. No, we're not going to be at her all the time asking her where she's been and what she's up to, telling her what she should and shouldn't do. If she doesn't know what's right and wrong by now no words of ours will tell her. She's a free agent and that means she's got her own life to lead and Frank and I won't be fools enough to interfere. Not after Megan.'

Mrs Bennett's tone had bitterness and disappointment in it rather than the liberalising beneficence her words might have seemed to promise. But Robin was busy weighing up how and how far the free-agent programme for Nancy would affect him, too busy to pay attention to such stuff.

When he looked back, Robin was grateful to Mr Bennett for not pressing him to declare his intentions towards Nancy. But the fellow had been uncomfortably close to the mark with his guess that those intentions were not in a settled state. They had been strictly dishonourable at all times between his first sight of Nancy and some time in their small trip to Joe's. Since then he had not ceased to follow his own unhindered choice, as he had perhaps rather grandly put it to Embleton, but that unhindered choice itself had changed. It had moved very close to being an unhindered choice in favour of keeping his hands off Nancy.

What had not changed was something Robin could never quite admit even to himself, the fact that he was shy of women, of literally getting to grips with them. Indeed, the first time he so much as kissed Barbara had been after she had agreed to go to bed with him. If she had not taken the initiative at a distance, so to speak, he would quite possibly never have tried his luck with her at all. Even this he would have more readily conceded than that he was beginning to see and feel the weight of Embleton's stated view that Nancy was not suitable as somebody to have a sexual fling with, this while he still knew almost nothing about her. It could not be, he was sure, that he regarded her physically with less than irreproachable carnality, most of the time, at least. But at certain other times . . .

A couple of days after being brought into contact with her

mother and father, he had taken Nancy to a dance in the town, in other words in a non-collegiate milieu. Considering how much he detested dances and going to them, the bare fact of his voluntary attendance at such a thing surely witnessed to the strength of his attachment or of his hankering after one. He had got ready to go and pick up Nancy in a condition of measurable sexual excitement, and had had to think about Gilbert Murray's translation of the *Medea* for several minutes before deciding he was in a fit state to be seen in public. He was even afraid of a renewed onset when he took Nancy in his arms at the edge of the floor. Nothing of the sort had happened. He had never felt so far away from her as when he was actually closer to her than ever before. He had tried to tell himself that the close proximity of a hundred or more other people could not but have a sedative effect, that in any case what he had hoped to feel like doing was unlawful in present circumstances, but these considerations had done little for his morale. Only when he was back in his college had he been capable of any kind of return to form.

Far from weakening his resolve to have his way with Nancy, such experiences only strengthened it. But what had raised his determination to fresh heights had been his sessions with the Bennett parents. It seemed to him a simple point of what had been implicitly recommended by Mr, whom he now saw as an old-fashioned heavy father imperfectly disguised as an old-fashioned comedian. Mrs was a tougher nut to crack, so much so that, although certain of eventual victory, he might have had a hard time overriding her cautionary tale of Megan and appeal for tender treatment of Nancy if she had not brought her case into disrepute by giving it the boo-hoo treatment, topped up when he left with a mute look of piteous entreaty. It might have been fair to add, however, that he found he had to think fairly hard about Nancy's charms before reassuring himself that her parents' wishes for her fully deserved the drubbing he was going to give them.

Robin tried to go over some of this in his mind while he waited at the barrier for her arrival by train from Oxford as preliminary to a long-weekend stay with his parents and himself. The day was sunny, mild for December, everything was in place, his mother seemed to be looking forward to the visit, his father at least reconciled to it, and yet he could not get away from how wrong he felt. On waking up he had felt so tense that he had had to avoid breakfast and felt he would never be able to eat again, weighed down as if by having already committed some resounding atrocity instead of once upon a time contemplating holding a girl's hand. All right, since it seemed to be an occasion for unpalatable truths, what would he really most like to happen next? The arrival of a message saying that, for some painless reason, Nancy could not come. He began to hope the train would arrive before he turned and ran away altogether.

The train arrived and almost the first to get off it was Nancy. Instantly it seemed to him that he had felt nothing of any consequence but eager expectancy at the prospect of seeing her. She had had her dark hair cut in a fringe with what in effect were little curving sideburns and looked healthier than ever, also pleased to see him. They kissed in a familial sort of way that would have drawn at least a wince of disapproval from Milnes. His teaching on the point was that every display of affection made real progress more difficult, and Robin had never before seen so clearly what he meant, though he did have time to wonder how Milnes would have handled greeting a well-wrapped-up girl of seventeen in a crowded station with her hand-luggage to be taken care of. No doubt he, Milnes, would have known how to turn to amorous account subjects like a train arriving on time and parents being well and sending their best wishes.

'Hey, it was a good job you thought of writing to my father as well as me,' said Nancy.

'My own father's training.'

'He might not have let me come otherwise.'

'On what grounds?'

'He might have said he thought it was just your idea, having me over. He's very free and easy about most things but not things like that. You writing to him made it sort of official, I suppose. Aren't parents funny?'

'Well, my pop's a scream,' said Robin. 'Not a patch on what he used to be, but still pretty deranged. Sorry, all I mean is there are still times when I can't make him out or start thinking he's off his head, but mostly he's just boring and set in his ways like all that generation. Or most of them,' he added, hoping that would be enough to make him seem to be excepting the senior Bennetts.

'Shall I be able to get on with him all right, do you think?'

'Oh, he'll be as nice as pie to you, or he'll do his best to be, especially if you keep saying what a badly behaved crowd the youth of today is and calling him Mr Davies.'

'He doesn't sound very deranged so far.'

'I shouldn't really have said that, I suppose. It's just his attitude to me as it used to be and as I'm quite sure it still bloody well is only he doesn't feel he can let it show now I'm meant to be grown up. That makes me think he's a bit barmy, I was going to go on to say. What you might call over-protective if you wanted to let him down lightly.'

'What would you call it? I mean you haven't ever said anything like this about him before.'

'You haven't been going to meet him very soon before. I don't think I'd better tell you what I'd call it. Well, here's something that ought to give you some idea, he was very keen on me going to Oxford, always on about having promised himself I'd get the chance he never got and if he had one wish, et cetera, but when the time came for me to actually go there he turned out not to be so keen after all. He said he wasn't as sure as he'd have liked to be, what, of the wisdom of such a grave step. You'd have thought I was going into one of those monastery places where they don't let you speak for the rest of your life.'

'Trappists,' said Nancy. 'I was reading about them somewhere.'

'Sorry to go on about this but we might as well get it out of the way now. Now. If I'd pressed my father harder than I've ever known how to press him, then he'd probably have talked about the dangers of falling into bad company up there at the jolly old varsity. Dangers like smoking, drinking, spitting, gambling and telling dirty jokes, with some stuff about a father's duty being more than ever something-or-other in a godless age thrown in. Nothing much wrong with that as it stands, anyway nothing to make a song and dance about, he was just trying to see I turned out all right, in other words like him. I suppose all fathers of sons have that a bit. But there was something else as well. He was trying to cover up a straight-forward piece of what-you-may-call-it. Snobbery won't quite do. In fact I can't see any way of not bringing politics into it. He, my old dad, he's always been afraid of sinking into the working class, he's set on me being the kind of middle-class gent he'd have liked to be, so it wasn't so much he was afraid I'd waste all his money backing the gee-gees and sink into debt, it was more I might pick up a cockney accent off the bookie's runner. The objection to which accent isn't of course that it's common but that it's lazy and also ugly, and that'll do for now. I hope it wasn't too boring for you.'

'No, it was fascinating, and a bit extraordinary too. Wouldn't it have been an Oxford accent you might pick up rather than a cockney one, and wouldn't your father have thought that was quite a good—'

'That's exactly the sort of thing I mean when I call him deranged. Of course most people who know as little about it as he does would think something like that, but not my dad, who prides himself on being realistic. *He* knows you don't acquire an Oxford accent at Oxford but from your nurse and governess and Eton. By the time you actually get to Oxford it's too late. Just as well according to him, because all it does is mark you as a TNT, and, before you ask, that's a Toffee-Nosed Twit, a bloody fool of a would-be aristocrat. My father's always been a great one for assuming that what he hasn't got and can't have isn't worth having. Sorry, I'll shut up about him now.'

'Not on my account. It's a relief to think I've heard the worst. I mean I suppose if there was anything more objectionable about your father than him worrying about your accent you'd have told me first. I mean for instance he doesn't drink, does he?'

'No, not in that sense. In a way I wish he did.'

'You wouldn't wish he did if he did,' said Nancy. 'I mean you'd wish he didn't. My dad drinks a bit, not much compared with some, just now and then, but the rest of us all wish he didn't. Nobody minds him enjoying himself but sometimes he gets a bit nasty with it. Well, sort of sullen.'

'That doesn't sound like any father of yours.'

'It's true what I'm telling you. But I wouldn't want you to think it's a big thing with him. Just sometimes he gets home late and he's been with his mates and sits behind that bar of his, you saw it. Doesn't drink any more as a rule, just sits and broods.'

'What about?'

'I don't really know. Megan perhaps. He hasn't said anything to me about it and neither has my mother. I suppose he might have a whole lot of reasons or none at all. That must happen now and then. Maybe I'll understand when I'm older, but if I don't it won't matter much.'

'Better not mention your dad's drinking spells in front of my dad.'

'Don't worry, I wasn't going to mention anything. Teetotaller, is he, your dad?'

'No, that would make him too much like a lay preacher from Ystradgynlais. No, he openly has a drink in the pub, and he gets home late like your dad on Christmas Eve and sometimes on a Saturday afternoon, but no one's ever seen him the worse for drink, or so he says. You only get like that when you're a Welsh oick from Ystradgynlais.'

'So he doesn't really have spells.'

'No. I don't think he's a proper drinker, his heart's not in it. I'd say he only has a drink to be sociable if I thought he had any interest in being sociable.'

Robin was aware that his last remark was a little hard on his father. Now and then he found it not altogether easy to concentrate on what he was saying to Nancy, let alone on what she was saying to him. At their first meeting he had thought her voice thin, now he would have called it quiet, even gentle if nobody like Milnes was about. Anyway it, her voice itself, distracted him slightly from her actual words. Then there was her Welsh accent, which unusually for him he found positively pleasant. Her looks, though, made a more powerful impression on him than anything in what she sounded like.

By a familiar process, Robin had gained his ideas of female attractiveness at least as much from still photographs of strangers as from seeing live people he might or might not be acquainted with. This arrangement gave film stars an unfair advantage over girls seen serving in model-aeroplane shops or in motion on street corners. An impression that womanly appeal was an entirely pictorial, static thing was beyond doubt to be derived from literature, as when Shakespeare had written that a frantic lover could see Helen's beauty in a brow of Egypt, which was to say in an Egyptian cliff or hilltop. That imaginative leap was bolder than any Robin could or would have taken, but he thought he caught the general drift. At the moment, sitting next to Nancy on the Underground, he had an unusually good chance of properly taking in and estimating her looks, but found it a difficult task. The trouble was that, whether talking or listening, she refused to keep still. He was forced on to particulars such as the very small mole low down on her left cheek, the clear outline of her lips, the straightness of her nose and as before her fine complexion, together with impermanent stuff like the way her fringe was cut slightly askew. By the time the two were settled on the suburban train, he had decided that either she was too lively and amiable-looking to count as beautiful or, perhaps alternatively, that if she was to be squeezed into that category after all it would have to be conceded in a way nobody else was.

Now and then Robin remembered he would have to make clear his dishonourable intentions over the weekend or probably never, and it was like being reminded of an old disgrace.

*

On his entrance, Mr Davies put on what was for him a tremendous show of cordiality and welcome, which meant he was reasonably civil, as his son might have put it. It led without interval into one of the sustained bouts of clowning he went in for a couple of times a year and would describe afterwards without detectable penitence as a case of letting his sense of humour get the better of him. On this occasion he performed a not very well observed take-off of a gallant Continental gentleman, bowing low, making as if to kiss Nancy's hand, loudly delivering a flowery speech of welcome in a generic foreign accent at a speed that precluded interruption. Every few seconds he pretended to trip over his own feet. For what in theory was a comic turn it was a remarkably effective means of disconcerting someone meeting him for the first time, like Nancy. As any sane adult might have done, she evidently ruled out in the first seconds all possibility that such a performance might hold anything in any way funny and so had only to wait until it was over. This duly happened after the longest half-minute Robin could remember spending even in his father's company. After doing a certain amount of laughing about something or other, the latter said in an unapologetic tone,

'I'm sorry, Nancy, I'm afraid my so-called sense of humour ran away with me rather. You must have thought I was off my rocker.'

'Well, no, not really.'

'Either that or young Robin here hadn't let on about me having been brought up abroad somewhere. That would have been typical too, in a way.'

'What on earth is the old fool talking about?' said Robin to himself.

'I just never know when my husband's going to start playing the fool in his own inimitable fashion,' said Mrs Davies. 'What a way to greet a poor girl in a strange house.'

'I told Nancy I was sorry, but she didn't really need it, did you, Nancy? She didn't turn a blessed hair, just played up like a good little trouper. Good sport, Nancy dear girl, jolly good show all round.'

127

Mrs Davies smiled briefly in agreement. 'I expect Nancy'd like to pop up for a moment before we sit down to eat.'

Robin followed her. On the landing he said, 'I'm sure you remember you sleep in there and I sleep in there and that's the bathroom in there. Sorry about . . . let's hold it just a moment.' They went into his bedroom, for the moment her bedroom, where her stuff was on the bed. 'Sorry about my bloody old fool of a father. I should have warned you but I didn't reckon on him putting on one of those fearful acts of his. Next time it'll probably be the BND.'

'What's the—'

'The BND's the bugger next door. Used to be the blighter next door until I was deemed to have come to man's estate. Not a bad imitation actually, especially if you've had the luck never to set eyes on the bugger in question. Anyway, are you all right?'

'I'm fine. I just sort of wanted to rest for a moment before the next lot.'

'Oh, there won't be a next lot for quite a time. My mother'll be giving him what-for for that lot this very minute. Anyway, you did jolly well.'

Robin had his arms round Nancy and her mouth was no great distance from his. He kissed her, tentatively at first, then with enthusiasm. She responded along similar lines. Her face felt unbelievably smooth and soft against his and was warm too. So things stood for some seconds, until she moved her mouth off his and at once he took his arms from round her. With what seemed to him clear evidence of maturity he had reasoned that he could not in the circumstances expect to go on and conclude matters there and then; more practically, he was strongly against having to put in time thinking really hard about Gilbert Murray's translation of the *Medea*.

'We'd better go down,' said Nancy.

'You mean I'd better go down. Give my dad a chance to tell me what a splendid girl you are. He doesn't get things wrong all the time, you know. See you in about ten minutes.'

In the drawing-room downstairs, his glasses on his nose to read the *Evening News* through, Mr Davies said to his son, 'Nice girl, that Nancy, no doubt about it.'

'She's all right, isn't she?'

'And a very good girl. I mean there's a lot in her, I could tell straight away.'

'I'm glad you like her.'

'Good material is what I'm saying. Tell me – we've always been pretty close, so I know you won't mind my asking: are you, how shall I put it?' Mr Davies carefully adjusted his glasses while he pondered how. He had the advantage over his son of presumably being in no doubt about what he wanted to put. 'Well, put it this way: is it your intention to marry little Miss Nancy – is it Bennett?'

'Yes, meaning yes it is Bennett. As regards the rest of it, isn't it a bit early in the game to start talking about my intentions?'

'Robin, please, it is no game.'

'I only mean . . .'

'If you treat it as a game it's my duty to inform you that you're in for a rude awakening, my lad.'

'Sorry, Dad, I expressed myself badly. I assure you I regard it as a very serious matter indeed.'

'That's more like it now. Are you sleeping with her? Come on, Robin, don't look so shocked, you're a man now, a man of the world. You're also healthy, and normal I take it, and I'm not so old that I can't see young, er, young Nancy's a very attractive girl. Surely it's no more than a natural question to ask? In private?'

'Oh yes. And the answer's no, I'm not, sleeping with Nancy.' Robin felt like adding something on the lines of, 'and I don't half bloody well wish I was,' which might carry conviction but had its own drawbacks. So he contented himself with glaring steadily at his father and hoping he looked different this time from how he had looked on the not very numerous occasions when he had managed to get him to believe a lie.

'Don't be offended, but I've known you to turn a bit Jesuitical when it suited you and answer what people actually say rather than what they obviously mean, so if you wouldn't mind rephrasing—'

'Very well, Nancy and I have never performed the sexual act together.'

'All right, all right, no need to shout, you don't want her to hear you, surely to God. And would you swear to that on your mother's head?'

'Yes!'

Rage and frustration successfully added themselves to the power of truth and it seemed that Mr Davies was convinced. When, shortly afterwards, Nancy joined them, it struck Robin that a man of his father's supposed powers of intuition and insight might have been expected to see one thing without much difficulty: here was somebody who, whatever her potential, was for the moment not a sexually functioning person. He himself had very little idea of what to look for, if indeed there was anything constant, but he felt he knew that nothing of the sort had ever happened to somebody who looked like that, dressed like that, did her hair like that, looked at you like that. But he soon forgot about such matters.

It had naturally not occurred to Mr Davies that the younger two might have liked to spend some of the evening by themselves, and the hours went by in glassy four-cornered chatter, listening inattentively to a variety programme on the wireless, playing a very straightforward card-game called hearts, drinking cups of tea, drinking a small glass each of tonic water. Apart from some welcome interludes of boredom, Robin used up the time in impromptu diplomacy. Protecting Nancy against what his father might do or say, the quite different and comparatively minor task of protecting her against his mother, the different-again but familiar need to head off remarks from his mother that might have had an adverse effect on his father – so it went. During the game of hearts it did seem rather as if some sort of caricature of a Post Office clerk might have been on the way, but the occasion passed off without incident. Eventually Mr Davies observed that Nancy must be tired after her journey and it would do none of them any harm to get a spot of sleep. Robin had been looking forward to kissing Nancy good night, but before he could move into position his father called him back into the drawing-room.

'Just before you disappear, old boy.'

'Yes, Dad?'

'Sit down a moment. I just wanted to say . . .'

'Yes?'

'I wanted to say I've had a good chance this evening to take a really careful look at your young lady and I haven't wasted my time. I don't miss much, as perhaps you've noticed. Now, in my considered opinion, that girl is a very good girl indeed.'

One thing Robin had noticed in full was that his father took no more kindly than the next man to being told he had said something before, so he just muttered some words of agreement. He left unmentioned altogether his uneasy feeling that the old fellow was building up moral capital for the delivery of a well considered, regretful but necessary verdict of disappointment with the said young lady.

There was no sign of that for the moment. Mr Davies said, 'I said, I said that Nancy is a *good . . . girl*, and I suggest to you it's in your own interest that you pay due heed to that *fact*, which in my view it is.'

Again, Robin thought himself equal to paying heed to things unaided, but this time he said as if he meant it, 'I promise you that's something I'll never be fool enough to let myself forget.'

The next day, Saturday, saw Mr Davies disappearing to his office at the usual time. Robin came down to breakfast to find his mother and his young lady in the kitchen, already deep in culinary intimacy he could not fathom, to do with the eventual making of pickles or jam. Seething saucepans shook and rattled on the gas-stove while polyhedral glass jars underwent a severe scalding-out process in open vessels. Nevertheless it was clear that some more personal event was in prospect. Robin felt satisfactorily mannish as he put together a sort of meal of toast and marmalade and tea. There was no possibility of eating it where he was so he took it into the dining-room and sat at the table. He switched the wireless on and music from a brass band was to be heard. It was not a very agreeable noise, but he let it go on as a small celebration of being free of his father on this one morning of the week.

When after some minutes Robin turned the brass noise off there was silence from the kitchen. On taking his breakfast things out there, he found Nancy sitting on a chair close up to the sink with a towel and his mother bent over her doing something energetic to her head, which seemed covered in soapsuds.

'I thought I'd give Nancy a proper scalp massage,' Mrs Davies explained. 'It's no good if you try and give it to yourself.'

'It's marvellous,' said Nancy indistinctly. 'It's easier to do it down here.'

'And we thought we'd be out of your way.'

'I can feel it really toning up the roots of my hair.'

'Another minute or two should be about right.'

'It would cost the earth to have it done in a shop.'

'And they'd probably skimp it too.'

'Oh, again, that's wonderful.'

'Do you mind if I stay for a bit?' asked Robin. 'It's fascinating. Really being taken behind the scenes.'

'Nearly there now. . . . Right. Rinse coming.'

Mrs Davies picked up an enamel jug from the draining-board and started to pour a thickish stream of smoking water over the sudsy part of Nancy's head. As soon as the water touched her Nancy gave a sharp cry and jerked aside, and Mrs Davies stopped pouring as soon as she could, but in the nature of things some part of Nancy's scalp had apparently been scalded.

'Oh, I'm terribly sorry, dear.'

'It's all right, I'm all right, it's just it was so hot.'

'How awful of me, I could have sworn I put enough cold in, I can't think what happened, I'm so sorry. You poor little thing. How bad is it?'

'Don't worry, you didn't mean it, you couldn't help it. It's not so bad.'

'Do you want me to put something on it? What would you like me to put on it?'

'It's all right,' said Nancy again, but this time she could not go on and by rapid degrees broke into tears, holding the towel over her face and muffling her sobs in it. Robin thought he had never seen a person crying who was trying so hard not to, anything like so hard. He saw his mother think of saying something to Nancy about pulling herself together and then violently reject the thought and put her arms round her. He himself said in his mind that for this not to have happened he would have agreed to things being changed so that he and Nancy had never met, but quickly withdrew the offer as false, insincere, before it could somehow be taken up and acted upon. With that safely disposed of, he was left wishing he could think of something that would make either or both of them feel better. Well, he would say whatever came into his head. He moved closer and rested his hands on the women's shoulders.

Within ten minutes, rather to his own surprise, Robin had things back in order. He examined Nancy's scalp, found a small, not very much inflamed patch, pronounced it best left alone, sent her up to the bathroom with instructions not to come down till she was ready, soothed his mother, made fresh tea and served it to them at the dining-room table. The fine weather had held, the three had an enjoyable outing to the Dainty Shop and to all appearance, at any rate, the scalding incident was forgotten by the time they got back to the house.

Robin at least had forgotten it. He had decided that asking Nancy how she felt would be a good lead-in to grabbing her and exacting another proper kiss. A chance soon came up when she went to tidy herself before lunch. He followed her fairly slowly up the stairs and was still outside grabbing distance when she entered the room that was temporarily hers and shut its door almost in his face. He was weighing the pros and cons of following her in when he heard his father's key in the front-door lock and, almost before he was aware of it, found himself in the bathroom preparing to pee, a terrifying witness to the old man's anaphrodisiac power at a distance. Robin whispered a string of obscenities by way of exorcism, but was very soon tamely going downstairs again.

Mr Davies was still in the hall, still in his overcoat, being talked to by his wife in subdued tones. He glanced up at Robin with an expression of profound gravity, as at the death of a close relative. 'Oh dear,' he was saying, 'how very unfortunate. Oh dear.'

'I tried it twice to be on the safe side. I know I did.'

'Don't you worry, my love, we're all human, we all make mistakes.'

'I feel so bad about it.'

'Try not to,' advised Mr Davies, and added helpfully to Robin, 'Your mother's been telling me about the unfortunate accident this morning.'

Without thinking Robin said, 'Well, we needn't put on sack - cloth and ashes about it exactly, need we? Poor little Nancy got a spot of water on her head that was a bit hotter than she'd bargained for and that was it. Too bad. Actually she's made an excellent recovery.'

'Really!' said Mr Davies loudly, and Robin saw his mother turn away in something like hopeless exasperation. 'Really! Forgive me while I take my coat off, if you don't mind. Now, this matter deserves to be treated rather more seriously than you show signs of doing, young fellow-my-lad. As regards your mother's error in judgement, it may surprise you to learn that you and I are pretty much in agreement. The significant part of the story comes in what happens next, when the young lady behaves not like a young lady at all but like a child, bursting into tears on what seems generally agreed to have been not enough provocation, not enough for a grown-up person, that's to say, not even a woman. I'm afraid I was misled by—'

'What do you mean, Dad, not *even* a woman? Are they less grown-up than grown-up men according to you, or what's the matter with them?'

'Oh, Robin,' said his mother, 'please don't start—'

'Of course not,' said his father. 'It's just an observed fact of life, that women cry more easily than men, in societies like our own, at least. Perhaps when you've had a bit of experience you'll come to see the—'

'Oh, Dad, for heaven's sake, why have you got to make mountains out of molehills all the time? Everything's an observed fact of life or an error in judgement or an unfortunate accident. Nothing can be just what it is, it's got to be an example of something else. We'd all forgotten about that bit of nonsense about a drop of hot water when you came along and turned it into a court case.'

'Peggy,' said his father gently, 'it might be as well if you went up and made sure Nancy's got everything she wants, eh?'

'Oh, Tom, I don't want you to—'

'Don't worry, love, it'll be all right. Off you go now.'

In the drawing-room with his father once more, Robin braced himself for some sort of going-over, but soon found it was not one of those he was to get.

'I hope nothing's happened to upset you, old boy.'

'Nothing I'm aware of.'

'I thought you seemed a bit, you know, edgy. Anyway, we've only got a minute. Now, of *course* I realise that a splash of hot water constitutes a molehill, but your mother doesn't, or didn't. You see, Robin, I dare say you had just about forgotten all about it, and maybe Nancy had too, but your mother hadn't, oh no. I could tell straight away she was very upset as soon as I came in. She thought she'd been negligent, which is why I turned it into a court case as you accurately put it, just to assure her that she was not, after all, seriously at fault in any way. I reckon I'd just about achieved that when you went and put your oar in.'

'Sorry, Dad.'

'Oh, forget it. When you're my age and have been married as long as I have, you'll come to realise there are some times when you can just pass something off in one second flat, and other times when it's up to you to make a big song and dance about it.' Mr

Davies sighed deeply. 'I suppose in a successful marriage the bloke somehow manages to get it right nine times out of ten. Ah, they're coming down now.'

When reciting his grievances to himself, something he did quite often, Robin would complain that he had too little money to get the best out of what was still to be got out of Oxford. He certainly had less money than most of his contemporaries. He lived on the scholarship he had won at his college, the consequential bursary from his school and a grant from his local education authority. His father gave him bed and board in the vacations and nothing more, because, he said, he could afford nothing. Robin reluctantly believed this, which did some damage to his attempted self-portrait as a victim of malevolence. On the other hand, he had allowed his father to become his paymaster, receiving funds, paying college bills, physically doling out cash or rather allowing it to trickle towards its rightful owner. This arrangement, which certainly saved Robin trouble, he had in his ignorance assumed to be normal, discovering too late that his mates ran their own finances just like grown-up men. Anyway, there he was with an undignified secret to guard and ten bob a week at a time when a packet of twenty decent fags cost a shilling.

Life was a little easier at home, where Robin picked up a small supplementary income from his mother, sometimes in kind in the form of the odd drink and cigarette. Nevertheless he had had no trouble deciding against a couple of nights' stay at the Ritz for self and young lady and in favour of booking in at the parental home for that period. He had a few bob put by which he hoped to hang on to unless and until the close proximity or actual presence of the senior Davieses should become intolerable. Then the second morning turned out so sunny and mild that taking Nancy for a walk seemed plausible as well as desirable and free of charge. Robin introduced the project when his father was settling down after breakfast with the *Sunday Express*.

First consulting his wrist-watch, Mr Davies asked, 'Where were you thinking of taking her?' – prior to the citing of facts rendering the chosen objective out of the question.

'Along Willow Road to the bottom and then across the common and down past that botanical research place was where I was thinking.'

'M'm. You'll have to step it out a bit if you're going to be sure of getting back here in good time.' Mr Davies looked up and addressed himself to Nancy, standing quiescent at Robin's side. 'I dare say my son won't have thought to explain to you, but in this house the midday meal on Sunday, which I was brought up to call Sunday dinner, that was the most important time of the whole week, when we all got together as a family. Like – how shall I put it – like Christmas dinner on a smaller scale. The same spirit, the same family spirit, only on a smaller scale, naturally.'

He closed this exposition staring up at Nancy, who waited for a moment before nodding her head vigorously and saying, 'Oh yes, I see.'

'We'd better be off then, Dad,' said Robin, 'if we're to be sure of getting back on the dot.'

'Wait a minute – wait a minute, of course I could come with you,' said Mr Davies, then without any interval broke into a bout of coughing, no effect of a mere tickle in the throat but a hollow booming affair from deep within, comparable with Mr Bennett's recent efforts but sounding somehow more evolved than they. He held up his hand, made noises of apology, shook his head impatiently at offers of help, inhaled with every sign of recovery before plunging off again. Robin waited with great interest to hear the remainder of what his father had to say. It came finally in an attenuated senile quaver: 'I'd love to, but it would leave your mother alone in the house,' and everybody was well aware of the threat posed by Chinese pirates to unguarded women in the outer London suburbs on Sunday mornings. If Mr Davies felt like telling his son he could go out for a walk at 10.10 am or take his place at the family dining-table at 1.15 pm, but could not do both, he kept it to himself.

137

Robin got Nancy away as soon as he could after that. They turned left outside the front gate, bringing to his mind all the term-time mornings when he had turned right in his father's company on the first leg of their journey to the City. Long ago, why yes, but when remembered all of a sudden, as now, it had a nasty habit of seeming like last week with a revival next month under discussion. With little effort he recalled somebody in that insufficiently far-off era saying in effect that if people could really spend half their lives looking for their father then he, Robin, was lucky to have come across his so early. For a moment he wished he had thought of retorting that he knew of a case in which a man had after no great delay found his son, an easier task from the start given the quarry's limited freedom of manoeuvre, and had been able to hang on to him ever since.

Robin thought himself lucky to have Nancy there that day to come between him and such imaginings. She wore a dark belted overcoat undistinguished enough in appearance to have come straight from her schooldays, a green and white scarf crossed at the throat in a sort of military style and natural-coloured woollen gloves. On her head was a thick woolly hat of some neutral shade pulled down rather low on the forehead. Altogether it was a far cry from the sort of hat that Milnes had had in mind in the long-ago when he delivered a never-to-be-forgotten paragraph of his tuck-shop talk. The gist had been that for a woman (as a suitable female was technically known) to put on a hat in your honour was as clear a sign as any that she had decided to take you seriously. Being taken seriously by a woman meant a sporting chance she had decided to let you do as you wanted, though again in an unknown percentage of cases she meant you to marry her first.

Robin acknowledged to himself that, even as it stood, Milnes's hat para, like the rest of his talk, was fogged with ifs and buts and inapplicabilities, but at least it had been pitched at the right level. Other guides to misconduct, like Vanderdecken's, raised new difficulties while leaving old ones untouched or, like Homer Lane's, went no further than telling you it was all right to do what you wanted to do, as distinct from authorities like Davies senior who maintained it was *not* all right to, etc., whatever it might have been.

This had not taken long to turn over in his head, but he realised it was up to him to change his luck as far as he could in the time available. He wasted a good half-minute hating Nancy for not simply offering herself to him while his mind clanked and shuddered like an old donkey-engine with the effort of producing any utterance at all. Then, ignoring a strong suspicion that the words testified to irreversible derangement on his part, he said ingenuously, 'What made you choose to sell gramophone records for a living?'

'Well, I thought it sounded more fun than working in the habby at the big shop, sorry, that's the haberdashery department it's called, handkerchiefs and ties and gloves and things, and I thought you'd asked me that already.'

No doubt he had. With a lopsided smile to indicate sophistication, he said weightily, 'Perhaps I did, and perhaps I didn't. And has it turned out to be more fun?'

'Oh, yes, but that's really only because of the other girls, I said, they're very nice and helpful, at least Shirley is, that's one of them, you saw her, she's the one with the short hair, she knows an awful lot.'

'About music?'

'No, not specially about music, I was going to say, what Shirley knows is about the catalogue and what's been deleted and what's going to be deleted, and what's out of stock at the factory and what's only out of stock in the shop, and she knows all the prices just by the number, that's the number on the record, and if something's out of stock she'll suggest another record by the same artist which is in stock.'

'If you don't mind me saying so, it doesn't sound much more fun than the habby so far.'

'Or one of the same song by a different artist. No, it's not. There it was lace and collars and cuffs and with the records it's Charlie Kunz and Bing Crosby. Not all that much in it.'

'Anyway, with the records to sort out you must have plenty to do.'

'Shirley's the only really helpful one. You know, when she has to disappoint a customer she's really sorry, or she goes on as if she is, which is just as nice really. But Norma now, that's the other girl, it isn't just she doesn't know as much as Shirley, she doesn't want to learn, I think she actually likes disappointing people. Well, if you want to know what I think, I think she's thinking about boys all the time. You should see the way she makes up to some of the men who come in. I suppose you'd call her attractive with that figure.'

'I didn't notice her particularly,' said Robin, trying to turf chagrin out of his voice, aware at the same time that the you just mentioned was not intended for him personally. Even the suggestion that Norma thought nonstop about boys had been made only as one learned observer to another. Nancy had not deviated from her good-interviewee mode, conscientiously supplying clear and full information on the point specified. Against his will, and not for the first time, he found himself hankering after less pure discourse, something less literal-minded and pissier, automatic responses to questions not asked, a touch of what's that supposed to mean, who do you think you are (I'd like to know), I don't see it's any business of yours (a) quite frankly or (b) you cheeky thing. Then, merely to stop himself from enquiring if they got much call at the shop for Fats Waller or Louis Armstrong, he said, 'I don't suppose you want to go on selling records all your life, do you?'

Still keeping up her functional stride and demeanour, those of somebody out for a brisk walk on a fine winter's morning and that was that, she blushed quickly and deeply in a way that filled him with transient compunction and also made him slightly uneasy. 'I'm really only doing it because I ought to be doing something, not just living at home. My dad wanted me to train as a teacher, but that was before everybody could see how absolutely hopeless I was at school except for nature study.'

'When somebody says they were hopeless at school it usually turns out to mean they were very badly and boringly taught,' said

140

Robin, although on the whole that was not his true opinion.

'Oh, not me, I was bored all right, but that was because I couldn't follow what they were saying after about the first sentence. I just wasn't up to it, you see. The word must have got round eventually among the teachers, because after a bit they all stopped including me in the lesson and just let me sit at the back and keep quiet and read and draw. My mother taught me to read when I was quite little, but I've never learnt how to count properly. If you asked me to write down, well, er, ten thousand in figures I'd be stuck. I know it's a one with noughts after it, but I'm not sure how many noughts. And as for adding anything up . . . In the shop I have to get Shirley to give me a hand if I find I've got to cope with more than about two records at one go.'

'Which did you grow up speaking, English or was it Welsh?'

'Oh no, it was all English in our part. No way out there, though it's nice of you to try and help.' She grinned, showing some of her hundreds of little square white teeth, then turned serious again. 'I sucked my thumb till I was twelve. Very secretly towards the end, mind you.'

'That's not the sort of thing you want to go round blurting out.' Robin tried to make it clear, but not too clear, that he spoke largely in jest.

'Oh, I don't. In fact you're the first . . .'

He hurried on. 'I see what you mean about not being really cut out to sell records. Do you get on well with animals?'

'Yes. At least I think I do. I like them all right.'

'Well then, wouldn't it make more sense to get a job looking after some? In a kennels or a racing stables or somewhere?'

'I've done bits of that and loved it. The only trouble is, to do it properly you more or less have to live in, and that's pretty well ruled out in my case because my parents seem to expect me to live at home until I'm married.'

Before the last phrase was fairly out of her mouth she had started to blush even more quickly and deeply than a couple of minutes earlier. He felt rather more compunction now than then, but as against that he could readily identify the source of his uneasiness. Milnes on hats had been right after all; here was a woman who had decided to take him, Robin, seriously, whatever she might have had to say on the matter. He read fear and apology in her glance now; he could not even try to hurry on after this one. He put his arms round her and started kissing her. She responded.

So things stood for some time. Although he failed to notice it for the first second, there was no one near them to see, indeed anybody further off would have found it hard to spot them through one or other of the strips of woodland, much of it evergreen, that now partly enclosed their route. Shielded from the sun where they were, they could feel the winter cold in the air. When Robin remembered that this was supposed to be an erotic embrace, or if not then it was up to him to turn it into one, he put his hand on the part of Nancy's overcoat that must lie over her left breast, only to find he could get no satisfactory purchase on it through various layers of clothing. An important such layer consisted of the leather glove he wore, and the prospect of taking it off or equally of leaving it on to explore under the overcoat seemed somehow unattractive. He had the feeling that in either case she would ask him in a puzzled way what he was doing. Admittedly she was responding with enthu - siasm, with little moans, but they seemed to him to be moans of contentment rather than desire. He was spared the task of thinking of a next step when she disengaged herself.

'Isn't there some place we can go?' she asked.

He had no means to tell himself she meant not a place with a bed in it, not by any means, but one where she could get a cup of tea if not of cocoa, and shook his head. 'Everywhere'll be shut,' he said.

'What about the pubs?'

Where they sold lemonade. 'Only after twelve.'

'Let's walk, then.'

They walked across the common and down past the botanical research place, with more to say to each other now. At one point Nancy said, 'I'm afraid I do rather tend to go on about Mum and

Dad and my brother and sisters. I hope you don't mind hearing about them.'

It was true in a way that Robin would sooner have heard about Nancy's detailed plans for a career in indecent films, but only in a way. More realistically he felt he could have expected worse than these family chronicles, even though every sentence of them seemed to lead further away from the life of inventive fornication his fantasies designed for her in her absence. 'No, I love to hear,' he said, doing his best to jostle tepidity out of his looks and behaviour.

As they approached the Davies home, less was said about the other Bennetts, in fact on any subject at all. Nothing on the outside gave any sign of what life was like inside, except possibly for the small white-on-green tin sign fixed on the gate, which demanded or pleaded for no hawkers or circulars. The days were past when Robin wondered what a hawker would be up to in a suburb or what a circular was and did, but he still occasionally reflected how typical it was of his father to have gone to such trouble, not that the notice had any perceptible effect but at least it advertised his hostility to people who did things he or another had not explicitly empowered them to do.

When Robin opened the front door there was silence. When he advanced and called there was more silence. On the unlaid dining-table he found a note for himself in a sealed envelope. This and the folded sheet inside were of his mother's favoured duck-egg blue, but the writing on both was in his father's misleading upright and spaced-out hand. The salutation read, 'My Dear Son,' as if Davies senior had been writing from his death-bed in Wagga Wagga or somewhere. The message told Robin that his sister Margery had telephoned 'in obvious distress' with the news that little Reggie (aged five) had had a mishap with some heating device that had laid him at death's door. 'Accordingly,' Mr and Mrs Davies had arranged to be driven over by the Irish neighbour, Mr Higgins, in his Austin Seven and were not to be expected back before evening. There was soup ready to be warmed up on the stove and cheese in the larder.

At the bottom of the sheet Mr Davies had written, 'I trust I can rely on you to look after everything decently,' which for him was coming quite a long way out into the open, his son thought. He had read to Nancy most of what the note had said as he came to it, but the last bit he kept to himself.

Robin's bedroom, even when not given over to Nancy, boasted a gas-fire of curious three-dimensional design, with gnarled black burners instead of the more familiar straight white ones, a legacy of some previous owner of the house. It probably threw out no more heat at no greater cost than more conventional appliances, but its unusual horizontalised appearance made it not a thing to be trifled with, in other words not a thing to be used except at times of imminent glaciation. In a small way Robin regretted that he would never be able to explain to Nancy what a thrill it gave him to flout parental protocol by lighting this fire; its soft bang at ignition sounded in his ears like the first distant gun of a relieving army. He had other matters to think about, true. For the moment these did not include poor little Reggie's reported accident. He liked Margery and wished her no real cause of distress, but he had found her inclined to exaggerate adversity and could contemplate with fortitude most disasters likely to beset her small son.

Within seconds of lighting the singular gas-fire Robin had got hold of Nancy again and went on kissing her. This time he did far less thinking and also seemed to need less of it. When he tried to look back afterwards, he found he could not recall the stages in their move on to the bed. But there was no mistaking her pleasure and growing desire at his touch on her bare breast, nor the abrupt change in her response to his next move.

'Please don't do that,' she said in an undertone.

He muttered something meant to be inarticulate and forced his mouth back on to hers.

When she turned her head aside she could only speak half into the pillow, but if her words were indistinct her meaning was clear enough.

'Do you want me to stop?' he asked.

'Of course not, how could I, that's the trouble, but please do stop.'

If calculated, to utter that piece of truth would perhaps have been a mistake. A firm false declaration that she did indeed want him to stop might well have got him to. But it was only a matter of might well and perhaps because so much of what happened next had already been settled outside that room and long before.

At a late stage Nancy said, 'Don't let me have a baby, will you?'

'I'll make sure you don't,' said Robin, and that was true too.

Later still she said, 'That was lovely, but I feel as though I'll never want to do it again, isn't that funny?'

'Quite normal.'

'Of course you've done it with other people.'

'Not really. Not properly.'

'Good. I'm sorry, I shouldn't say that.'

'Why not? Are you hungry?'

'Starving. What about that soup?'

Robin and Nancy were in the dining-room just finishing the last of the soup when his parents arrived back from their errand of mercy, some hours before they had been expected. Mr Davies, who was wearing the lighter-coloured of his City suits, explained that little Reggie had actually overturned an electric fire and sustained a couple of nasty burns, but was quite a distance from death's door. Then, while he was lamenting his own foolishness in letting any course of action be decided by women, his would-be jocose manner fell from him. He had seen something or, being no better at seeing small things than very large ones, thought of something.

'Just a minute,' he said, still quite lightly but raising an index finger, 'just one moment if I may. Might one inquire at what time you two returned after your walk? Robin?'

'I don't really know. About a half an hour ago, I imagine. Why?'

'*Why?* Well, in the first place because about no more than half an hour ago seems to indicate that you and, er, you and Nancy took an unexpectedly long time over your walk along to the bottom and across the common and down eventually back here, do you agree?'

'If anybody'd care for a bit of bread and cheese and some pickle I could rustle it up in no time,' said Mrs Davies.

'No thank you, love, thank you very much indeed, that sandwich I had over there was quite sufficient.' Mr Davies advanced into the room at a measured pace, looking about him attentively as if he had never penetrated it before, and with a hint of asking permission took a seat at the table. 'So,' he went cheerfully on, 'the two of you returned here after a rather *extended* walk and, well, and well, what happened then? I'm only asking,' he went on with a half-laugh. He seemed uneasy.

His wife had followed him into the room but not as far as the table. Now she said, still trying to sound bright and untroubled, 'Oh, come on, Tom, it's obvious what happened, Nancy and Robin came back from quite a long walk and probably just freshened up, and, I don't know, sat about and took their time getting the lunch. Nothing *happened,* dear. You go on as though somebody's plotting to blow up Buckingham Palace.'

Mr Davies's manner had settled down. 'I only wish I could joke about it,' he said. He spoke in a heavy, mournful tone, without the touch or more of the consciously dramatic often to be detected in daddy's paddies, as his son silently called them. 'Well, there's no point in prolonging the agony. Now, Robin, while your mother and I were away from this house, did anything improper happen?'

'Improper?'

'Or whatever you prefer to call it yourself. You know what I mean.'

Mrs Davies started to say something, then changed her mind and left the room. Robin hesitated. He knew his father was watching Nancy, but dared not look at her himself.

'I wrote a few words to the effect that I was putting you on your honour in a postscript to that note I left you.' Mr Davies said this in the same way as before, avoiding any sarcastic parade of helpfulness.

'Oh,' said Robin quickly, 'no, there was nothing of that sort.'

'Nothing at all. Very well. Before I ask you again, I suggest you turn your head and see what Nancy is saying without recourse to words.'

Of course Nancy was blushing deeply and radiating guilt.

'Do you still answer no to my question?'

'Most certainly I do. She's confused and embarrassed, as anybody might be.'

'Just so. Well, as I said, there's no need to prolong the agony. All that need be done is I ask your mother to come in from the kitchen or wherever she's taken herself and you just tell us that you swear on her head you've been telling the truth and we say no more about it, or rather I have a great deal of apologising to do. I don't know how far back it goes, the idea of swearing an oath on one's mother's head as a token of solemnity, certainly to old Grandfather Morgan, probably a good deal earlier. I've often meant to ask Cousin Emrys about it.'

Robin missed the second half of that. He was discovering as once or twice before in his life, and as then with some bitterness, that while it gave him no trouble at all to tell a quick lie in passing he had acquired from somewhere a rooted objection to making a full, formal statement or declaration that he knew to be untrue, whether or not his mother or any other person or entity had been brought into it. So, not hesitating now, he said, 'No I can't say that, I'm sorry, I couldn't say that. Something, what we've been talking about, something of that sort did happen. Please don't ask me for details.'

'Don't worry, I won't,' said his father without rancour. 'For the first time in your life, old boy, I wish you'd told me a lie. I wish some other things too, but there'd be no point in bringing them up now, them or anything else. I suppose some people would say I should never have asked you, especially since I knew the answer already. But it wasn't that kind of knowing, not like knowing something for certain. And there's all the difference in the world between being as sure as you can be in your own mind and really knowing.'

Mr Davies got up from his chair and stood with his hands on its back and his gaze lowered. Anybody, even someone who was used to him, would have said he was deeply troubled. For a moment none of them spoke.

'Sorry, Dad,' said Robin eventually.

'Yes, well, I think I'll just go and find your mother and have a quick word with her.' Before going he stood where he was a little longer.

The moment they were alone, Nancy said, 'Don't start being nice to me or I'll have to cry.'

'I had to tell the truth when he put it to me like that. I honestly don't see how I could have done anything else in the . . . given the . . .'

'Of course you had to,' Nancy's hand came feeling for his in a furtive, burrowing sort of way. 'I'd have had to tell him myself if he'd known what to say to me. I managed to give it away by how I looked. I'm sorry I was such a fool.'

'You couldn't help it.' He stroked the back of her neck. 'You don't feel different about it, what we did, I hope.'

'No, it was lovely. I mean it still is. Be careful or I'll start crying.'

'A few tears from you might make him go easier on us.'

'What's he doing?' asked Nancy after a pause.

'Among other things he's trying to work out what to do next.'

'Will he tell my mum and dad? That's what I'm really afraid of.'

'Not without telling you he was going to first, and I reckon he could be talked out of the idea anyway.'

'Hope so. It was all my fault for giving it away. I should have been able to brazen it out and then he wouldn't have had to ask you.'

'He never had to *ask,* and you couldn't have brazened it out, not without being someone else, and I wouldn't want you to be someone else, not in anything.'

She squeezed his hand. 'It came a bit soon, that was the real trouble. I knew I'd have to face that side of it sooner or later, but not that soon.' She stopped and listened, but there was no sound to be heard. 'Is your dad really, what you said, trying to think what to do next?'

'That and my mother's moral support for whatever he comes up with.'

'Do you think he will tell my mum and dad?'

'I doubt if he'd get my mum's support for making that sort of trouble. And anyway, I'd stop him.'

'I know you'd do your best,' said Nancy with another squeeze. 'It makes all the difference, knowing I've got you on my side.'

'What? But how could I not be on your side? What would I do?'

'Well, for instance you could have said something like, "It wasn't my fault, Dad. She led me astray with her wicked wiles. A decent, respectable lad like me, you know I'd never do a nasty common thing like that left to myself. It was all her. She's nothing but a," I don't feel like saying the word myself but I don't suppose you'd mind if it came to it. You know, things like that.'

Oddly enough, a thing like that was very much the plea father offered son in due course. Before that stage was reached, son offered assurances that he would never take so base an option, while hoping he had never sounded even remotely like the creature of Nancy's imagination. Then there came a sharp knock on the door of the room. Immediately, Robin said in a furious undertone,

'A thoughtful warning to me to pull my trousers up and you to put your knickers back on before large packs of savage smut-hounds are released to restore the premises to a semblance of order and decency. Hallo, kindly enter,' he called in a much louder voice, 'come on in, Dad, you're not interrupting anything, I'm sorry to say,' though he quietened down as soon as he saw from his father's expression that whatever was to follow had not received his mother's moral support.

'I think the best thing we can do in this unfortunate situation,' Mr Davies told the two of them as he sat down again, 'is keep our heads and our tempers and not raise our voices. And if I say anything wrong or unnecessarily hurtful or anything, I want to apologise for it in advance. I've had a nasty shock, in fact I can't remember when

I had a nastier, and I'm not firing properly on all cylinders yet. I'd have waited until I was feeling more myself if I hadn't thought it was so important to straighten out this sorry business as quickly as possible, in so far as it can be straightened out.'

All at once, Robin saw his father half-consciously enjoying his sense of being chairman of a small committee, and felt his hatred, which had subsided a good deal in the last minute, flare up again satisfactorily. To advertise his status as a free spirit he took out a packet of cigarettes and lit one.

'Do smoke if you want to, Nancy,' said Mr Davies in a kind voice.

'I don't smoke, thank you.'

'Now I suggest there's no point in arguing the ins and outs and rights and wrongs of the way I found out, well, what I found out. The fact remains I know. As I said just now, the knowledge came as a severe shock.'

'But surely not as any great surprise,' said Robin.

'Actually, Robin, yes, it came as a considerable surprise, which information may come as a surprise to *you*. But it's necessary to distinguish between two kinds of surprise or shock. It came as not much of either to learn that you had lost your innocence – all right, substitute your own words if you like. But what did surprise and shock me both was to have it thrust upon me that you had indulged in this kind of behaviour *in my house,* that is to say in your parents' home, behind their backs, if not actually under their noses. *That* is the vital distinction. The one is, how shall we put it, no more than a common fact of experience. But the *other* . . . involves deceit, deception, dishonesty, not perhaps in the intention but in the result. A different matter altogether, as both of you are quite intelligent enough to see.

'That puts at least two of us in an impossible position, myself and Nancy. If things are left as they are, I've no option but to connive at the dishonesty and she gets away with it, doesn't she, to put it crudely. Now,' and some forcefulness entered Mr Davies's manner, 'I'll neither tolerate such a thing nor set about taking steps to prevent it from happening again. Just try to imagine what that would mean! And so, Nancy, with great reluctance, believe me, I say to you that I see no alternative to your leaving this house, no more, no less. I've tried, but I can envisage no other way of putting the matter to rights. I'm sorry, I'm deeply sorry, I can say no more.'

Nancy's head was lowered and she neither said nor did anything. It took a moment before Robin was quite certain of what his father had said. Then he asked,

'That is right, is it, you're ordering Nancy out of the house?'

'I realise it must sound like that to you, but if you'll just think about it for a moment you'll see it's not that at all. Of course I'm not ordering her to leave this house, merely—'

'She is here, you know, and she's not deaf.'

'Now, don't you start taking me to task, young fellow, I won't have it. As yet we haven't even approached the question of your responsibility in this mess.'

'You're the one with the responsibility. It's your mess, all of it. No, you've had your turn for a bit. You hadn't been back here more than a couple of minutes just now before you started poking your nose in. All right, I don't know what gave us away, but whatever it was it should have given you the tip to keep out and mind your own business. And don't feed me any of that pap about its being your business to see to it that nothing improper went on under your bloody roof. Improper, my God. How long is it since Queen Victoria went into mourning? Not a hundred years yet.'

'I thought I made it clear to the meanest intelligence that it wasn't the act, the thing itself, but the deceitful way the pair of you calmly went and—'

Nancy, whom both men had gone on mostly treating as if she had not been there, now suddenly got up from the table, on which lay two almost-empty bowls of chilly soup and some fragments of bread. She was trembling a little, but not crying. She said in a strained voice, 'Just one request I should like to make of you, Mr Davies. Would you please not tell my parents why you've asked me to leave your house?'

'They'll never know of it through me, Nancy, I promise. You have my word of honour on that.' Mr Davies indicated by a subtle arrangement of stresses that his belonged to a better class of words of honour than some people's he might have been able to mention if probed.

'Thank you, Mr Davies. I'd like to go upstairs now for a short time if that's all right. And please, I don't want anyone else to come with me.'

She looked at Robin in a way that showed she meant that but was not at all cross with Robin, or with his father for that matter. The door closed quietly behind her. Robin's shoulders slumped.

'Oh, what a sad business,' he said, not far from tears himself.

'For each one of us,' said his father.

'Go on – and it's all my fault.'

'I wasn't going to say that, Robin. I'm not thinking it either.'

'Sorry. What are your plans for Nancy?'

'My plans? I'm afraid I don't . . .'

'What do you think she'd be best advised to do?'

'Oh. Well, to telephone her parents and tell them there's been a change of plan and she'll be returning home some time this afternoon or early evening.'

'You mean on her own?' asked Robin.

'What? Well yes, on her own, presumably. But if you mean you feel like going back some of the way with her, then that's obviously up to you.'

'Oh, I see.'

'I hope you do, old boy. I don't know exactly what went on between the two of you or when or where or anything else and as I said I don't want to know, but it strikes me as distinctly probable that a decent level-headed chap like you just wouldn't have, what shall I say, lost your judgement, erm, thrown discretion to the winds, forgive the cliché, taken a leap in the dark, made a . . .' Mr Davies's voice tailed off and he looked at his son in brief puzzlement. 'Erm . . .'

'I wouldn't have blotted my nose in a china-shop et cetera

without something or if something or unless something or whatever
the hell it was.'

'Thanks for the help, in recognition of which I'll put it bluntly
and suggest you wouldn't have been or might not have been in so
much of a hurry to indulge yourself if you hadn't received something pretty substantial in the way of encouragement. You know
what I mean. I didn't want to have to say this but I'm constrained
to wonder whether that girl is as much the little innocent as we've
been tacitly agreeing to regard her as. I say you know what I mean,
and I know you do, of course you do, so please don't sigh in that
silly put-on way and click your tongue and raise your eyes to heaven
like a cheeky shopgirl. I must say I never thought I'd have to remind
you that this is a serious matter.'

Robin's chronic desire to swear at his father had risen to a height
seldom equalled before declining to its normal level. He wanted not
so much to tell him off, though he definitely wanted to do that too,
as to direct foul language at him, unclean expressions fully decorated
with blasphemies, that kind of thing. He considered he had ample
and frequent occasion for so doing and was not prudish in any
ordinary sense of the word, and yet in practice he was hardly ever
able to get beyond the occasional bloody and good God. Anything
in the nature of an ordinary fuck or Christ or shit, no more than
routine in his daily conversation and solitary mumblings, seemed
quite beyond him in the company of Mr Davies. Part of the reason
for this shortcoming was easy enough to identify, though not so
easy to explain, deriving somehow from the thoroughness with
which the old boy would neutralise any recognisable obscenity,
pooh-pooh it, effortlessly dismiss it with the wave of a hand as
childish, dated, banal, forced, abhorrent not to decorum so much
as to some higher value like sense of the fitness of things. But also
at work was Robin's feeling that to discuss anything serious,
anything of importance to himself, with his father and in his father's
repertory of words and phrases, would be next to impossible. That
repertory had grown up to meet the needs of people who had
known what they thought and meant and had been in no doubt

about what was what. It was not necessary to feel superior to such people, nor think oneself better informed than they, as a part of finding them impossible to talk to. But it helped.

For the moment, Robin did not of course push his reflections so far. Nor did he have to cope with his father much longer unaided. When his mother came back into the room, Robin's first glance removed from him any hope that she had turned up with the purpose of intervening on his side, but his second made it clear that she was not going to come out in support of the other side either. She had tidied her hair and put colour on her lips and looked quite formidable. And also solemn, subdued, as if there had been a death in the house. Mr Davies lifted a hand, reminding his son of the similar gesture he had made at the outset of his inquiries.

'Before you say anything,' he told her in a gentler voice than before, 'please understand that the matter is settled. Nancy is to leave as soon as she's ready.'

'That won't be very long,' said Mrs Davies, 'the way she's getting on with her packing.'

'She must be very upset, I suppose?'

'She certainly seems to be. As you might expect from a girl in her position.'

'If only there was some alternative, but I can't see one, can you, Peggy?'

'Not now, anyway. She can't wait to be out of here and I can't say I blame her.'

Mr Davies frowned in a despondent way. 'Why has there got to be this terrible conflict between the generations? My old father and I used to go on at each other hammer and tongs, though that was about religion. Well, I dare say when this young man starts . . .'

Here Mr Davies stopped speaking for a moment, no doubt aware all at once that in the circumstances it might be painful for himself or accounted tactless by others if he openly referred to his son's ability to sire children, just as if nothing had happened. When that son said, 'I suppose if it's not one thing it's another,' it was only in

154

the vague hope of somehow extending his father's embarrassment.

'You know, I'm still sure that girl has got some excellent qualities in her after all – I'm not usually far wrong about things like that. But then I don't want to run the risk of hurting your feelings, old boy.'

What Mr Davies was certainly running the risk of was being sworn at by his son at last, if not of being thumped in the mouth by him. Perhaps Mrs Davies sensed something of the kind. She said to Robin,

'Go up and talk to Nancy and quick about it.'

'She said she didn't want anybody else up there with her.'

'Never mind that, you go up now.'

When he got to Nancy he found her in front of the dressing-table mirror brushing her hair with a small but fierce-looking brush that had stiff black wires instead of bristles. She saw him in the glass but went on brushing. He noticed that when she lifted the brush at the end of a stroke the hair tended to curve out to follow it.

'Why are you brushing your hair now?'

'No reason really. Just filling in time. Something to do.'

Robin went over and stood behind her. She put the brush down and turned towards him.

'It's all right,' she said, looking his face over, 'you can put your arms round me if you want.'

'Do you want me to?'

'Well, of course I do.'

He still hesitated. 'Won't it make you cry?'

'No, not now.' They hugged each other and both sighed deeply. Nancy went on with her cheek against his neck, 'I only cry when I'm upset and someone's nice to me. I know I cried with the hot water on my head but that was because it hurt so much.'

'You mean at the moment you're not upset any more?'

'Nobody can be really upset for long without stopping, can they? They have to sort of fall back on being very fed up. That's what I am now.'

'So am I. But come on, love, it isn't the end of the world.'

'Isn't it?'

'I mean I'll give you a ring in Oxford as soon as I can and we'll meet.'

She stood back and looked down at her belongings, 'I'm all ready to go.'

'There's no rush, surely.'

'Sooner the better.'

He asked her how she was for money and it seemed she was all right. She added that she had brought a railway timetable and was perfectly capable of making her way to Oxford and home. He said he would see her to the local station. When he went to pick up her suitcase he saw there was after all a tear in her eye.

'You look very sad.' He could think of nothing else to say and nothing he might have done.

'I am very sad. Because it's absolutely certain to be silly or showy-offy or embarrassing or something to say it, but what happened in here not so long ago was the most important thing that's ever happened to me. It was like being given something marvellous and already I've got to give it back. That's why.' She turned aside. 'Take my stuff downstairs, will you, Robin, and tell them not to come out, and I'll be down in a minute and we'll go.'

They duly went, turning right outside the garden gate. They had not gone far when Robin heard his mother's voice calling behind them. He put the suitcase down and ran back.

'These are for you if you find you want to stay with Nancy a little longer than you said.' Not looking squarely at her son, Mrs Davies handed him two pound notes, two ten-shilling notes, a half-crown and a thin open packet containing five Woodbine cigarettes. 'And give me a ring in the morning. Not first thing.' In other words not until after anybody with an office job would have left for his place of work.

'Oh, that's super of you, Mum. What does Dad think you've come out here for?'

'I don't know what he thinks. About that. Off you go now.'

Robin kissed his mother's soft cheek and left her. After he had gone a few paces in his original direction he turned to wave to her, but she was gone.

'What did she give you?' asked Nancy.

He showed her. 'This makes all the difference. Well, quite a lot of difference. Sit down on here while I explain. You can't weigh all that much.'

She perched on the upended suitcase as ordered. 'Won't anyone mind?'

'There's not much they can do about it if they do mind. Now. You don't seriously imagine I'm going to take you down to the station and walk away from you, do you?'

'Why not? Why, aren't you?'

'Until five minutes ago I was. I didn't want to, but I was. Then when you said what you said in the bedroom at the end, I decided I couldn't, but I didn't get a chance to tell you properly, and in any case I thought I'd better hold it until I'd got some idea of what we were going to do, but I'd only got eight and twopence ha'penny on me and I felt I couldn't very well ask my father for a sub.'

At this point the three persons who had been passing more and more slowly on the other side of the road, an elderly couple and a woman of about forty, finally halted so as better to take in the spectacle of a young man talking to a girl sitting on a suitcase. Robin had just regretfully decided he was too much of a coward to shout across at them the malediction they had earned, when Nancy sprang up from her suitcase and put her arms round his neck at top speed. His response so ordered matters that he was able to extend and wag two fingers at the nearby trio behind Nancy's back while heartily kissing her. It was a very good moment, hardly at all impaired by the fact that Mr Davies was not available to make up the four.

Finally Robin said to Nancy, 'But I still haven't thought what we're going to do.'

'Never mind, we've got three pounds ten and eightpence-ha'penny plus there's a bit of change in my bag and I've got my return fare. Now can we please get along because I was about freezing to death sat there.'

They got going. Having recklessly laid out several pence on a bus journey down to the station they found themselves with twenty minutes to spare before the next relevant train. There followed a consultation in the vast gloomy hall, smelling of firelighters and decorated with posters that showed strange people in bathing costumes, where a hundred passengers might have forgathered had they thought to do so.

'Well, we could try to book in at a hotel,' said Robin, 'but I'm not sure I fancy that. In fact I am sure I don't fancy it, pretending we're married. I don't think anybody would think we were married, do you? Do you fancy pretending to be my wife, even with a curtain-ring on your finger?'

'No, I don't,' said Nancy.

She said it so emphatically that he looked at her for a moment. 'What makes you say it in such a definite way?'

'What? Well, I'd fall down.'

'How do you mean?'

'I'd fall *down,* probably on the stairs. It would be too much for me, pretending to be your wife in a hotel. I can tell it would.'

'I don't know what you're talking about, but anyway we're not going to a hotel. We'll make some phone-calls, that's it. We could start with my brother.'

'What's he like?'

'He's called George. He's twenty-six. Schoolteacher. Rather like a young version of my father to look at.'

'Is he like your father to be in the same house as?'

'Good God, no, he's much more like me. Of course he may not be in. And I hope he's in the book, I haven't got his number by me.'

But George Davies was doubly in, and in a third time when Robin and Nancy arrived at the door of the run-down house in Notting Hill Gate he occupied the ground floor of. He greeted them warmly and asked what he could get them.

'Could I have something to eat?' asked Nancy, dandling the plump tabby cat of George's she had already scooped up. 'There wasn't, we had rather a light lunch and it seems hours ago. Bread and something would do, or just bread.'

'Sardines on toast be all right?'

'Lovely, can I do them? Unless there's a lady somewhere.'

'There often is, but not just at the moment, I'm sorry to say.'

'I can find things, I saw where the kitchen is. How many for? And a pot of tea ? Right, I'll call you when it's ready. Give you the chance to get the embarrassing bits out of the way.'

'Let's have the embarrassing bits in full,' George told his brother a moment later, and when he had briefly done so said in tones of admiration, 'The bloody old self-justifying God-bothering Welsh bugger and he's not even trying.'

'You don't know how much good it does me to hear you say that.'

'I was going to call him hypocritical but held it back at the last moment. And rightly too, as unjust to *Parchedig* Thomas Davies. Nobody ever hated sex with more sincerity than that old bastard. I take it your romp with Nancy was a success?'

'No complaints.'

'I knew it. If it had been a dud he'd probably have let you off with a caution.'

'If we're going to go on being fair to him, it's not only that,' said Robin, lighting cigarettes for George and himself. 'There's snobbery too.'

'You mean if Nancy were the Honourable Nancy she could have fucked a donkey in the drawing-room and he wouldn't have turned a hair?'

'Not quite that perhaps, but he'd have asked her to make other arrangements ever so respectfully.'

'My God, I do believe you're right.'

'You remember how he used to try and prevent you from having anything to do with anybody under the age of about sixty-five unless he was there too and preferably at all ever?'

'I'd forgotten all about that,' said George, staring at his brother from the depths of an armchair that looked as if it had recently been carried indoors after several months in the open. 'I remember it well enough now, though.'

'Yeah. You see, he couldn't prevent you from going to school and so on but he could try and stop you really getting to know boys you met there so that you saw them outside school as well. On top of having bad accents . . .'

'. . . they showed you how to smoke and how to toss off because they were lower-class and . . .'

'And they gave away how lower-class they were by smoking and tossing off.'

'Well not quite, isn't it more they get lower-class through smoking and tossing off?'

'Yes, that's it,' said Robin with an air of revelation, 'smoking and tossing off make you lower-class, and being lower-class makes you smoke and toss off. Got it.'

'Well, there's probably something in it,' said George after a pause. 'You don't get away from being lower-class by living in Stepney and smoking and tossing off. You must see that.'

'It's all very well for you to laugh, you're out of it.'

'Why aren't you out of it? I mean really out of it, not this gone-one-minute, back-the-next mode of existence. You're too comfortable there, that's your trouble, boy.'

'It was easy for you.'

'You're also too lazy. It was easi*er* for me, especially as regards timing, I see all that, some of it anyway. But in one way it's easier for you, because you've got what I hadn't, a bloody good issue to walk out on.'

'And I've walked out,' said Robin, trying not to sound too pleased with himself.

'But without enough prejudice to walking in again, correct? Yeah. When the term ends, stay up and get a job in the vacation. It's not as hard as all that, and you could probably get somebody to put you up, for a bit anyway. Think of calmly announcing you won't be coming home in the vac. That would put the fear of God into Thomas Davies, Esq., BF, and I mean God. I'm not advising you to fight the good fight, just to inconvenience yourself a trifle. And before you ask, the answer's no, I haven't got any money to lend you, I'm thirty quid in the red as it is, thanks.'

'I wasn't going to ask you for any.'

'Liar. Alternatively, shame on you. You ought to be ready to do a bloody sight more than that for that Nancy. From what I've seen of her she's a splendid girl.'

'Dad said the very same thing.'

'If you think that'll make my flesh creep you're wrong. Even the Devil himself agrees that two and two are four. Right,' added George, heaving himself up from his armchair, for Nancy had been heard yelling from the kitchen. 'Do you want to ring up home to tell Mum where you are?'

Robin too stood up. 'In the morning when he's gone to his office. We don't want him getting her to talk and then stalking in here to confront the guilty couple.'

'Christ,' agreed George. Then he said, 'Putting up with him for the next few hours won't be much fun for her.'

'If I know her she'll have got some of her mates coming in later to play cards.'

Nancy had laid places for three at the kitchen table and as soon as the brothers had sat down put in front of them warmed plates bearing grilled sardines on toast, toast that had been deprived of its crusts. The tea was made, with hot water standing by but no fanciful extras like slices of lemon. Robin managed not to grin at the very unwatchful way Nancy watched for consumer reaction to what she had prepared. To be on the safe side he limited his show of approval to minor noises and faces.

George was not so inhibited, 'It's a risk, letting a strange female cook anything for one,' he told Nancy. 'Rather a pig in a poke, if you'll pardon the expression, but there's no stopping a girl once she's taken it into her head to make for the stove. Anyway, this time I needn't have worried, you're clearly the domestic sort. Which reminds me to say that another girl, the one that's often round the place but isn't at the moment, she's turning up in about an hour to

161

be taken to the pictures down the road. Some gangster thing. You two are welcome to come along if you don't mind paying for yourselves.'

Robin felt he could hardly say that he and Nancy had other plans for that evening. When he looked at her he saw she was not being in the least circumspect about being for the pictures. So he announced he would treat them all, which went down fine with George as well as with her.

George went on to say that he was sure Nancy would get on like a house on fire with his girl Elizabeth – they were the same sort of type, he thought. A little later, he said Elizabeth had domestic instincts. A few minutes after that, he said he had better tell them that he and Elizabeth intended to get married at Easter, and on hearing this Nancy blushed as deeply as Robin had ever seen her, and he felt an internal sense of alarm.

When he and George were washing up and Nancy had been sent off to get herself ready, Robin said, 'I'm afraid that girl wants to marry me.'

'Surely not.' George shook soap-flakes into the bowl before him. 'What on earth gives you that idea?'

'It's not funny, you know.'

'Isn't it? You flatter yourself.'

'I'm serious, George. I know her better than you do, after all.'

'By a small margin, perhaps. Anyway, very well, let's suppose you're right, which I have to admit you might well be if you are her first man, which again seems quite likely. What's so terrible about the idea of her wanting to marry you?'

'You're being like Dad again. Of course it's not such a *terrible* idea, it's just an idea that I regard it as undesirable she should have, because I've no intention of marrying her, not her in particular, anyone at all at this stage of my life.'

'Whereas your intention at this stage of your life is to engage in an indefinite series of fornications and you'll think about the next stage in your life when you come to it.'

'George, please, you're not that much older than me, you're

surely not going to tell me you have to try to remember having a stand up to your neck day in and day out? All right, never mind why, perhaps I was slow off the mark, but as long as I can remember I've thought about almost nothing but getting my end away and now I've managed it I intend to keep at it as hard as I can go until further notice.'

'And without let or hindrance. No need to dry that, it can go on the rack here. Of course I know what you're talking about, and what can I say, your scheme sounds a splendid one as long as you know what you're doing.'

'There's one part of me that knows exactly what I'm doing and what I'm going to be doing and it isn't my head.'

'Nor other parts of you besides apparently. Well, Robin, if you ever do find yourself contemplating matrimony I hope you'll consider Nancy if she hasn't been snapped up by that time, which I warn you is highly probable.'

'Give it a rest, George.'

'Sorry, I should have remembered when people decide to get married they start boringly trying to persuade everybody else to get married too.'

'How can you afford to get married if you're thirty quid in the red? Or is Elizabeth rich?'

'She's got a job in a bookshop, so certainly not. But where there's a will there's a way as the bishop said to the actress. Not that you need telling about that. Right, lad, thanks for your help. I'll finish these few, now you can bugger off and have a word with Nancy.'

'You do mean a word, do you?'

'Believe it or not, I do. It's your duty to convince her you like her at least.'

'You're right, and I haven't conveyed that information to her for nearly half an hour.'

'So you do know something about women.'

Robin found Nancy in the spare room, which was even more like a boxroom than the boxroom at his parents' house. She was brushing her hair with the fierce-looking brush but stopped when he appeared.

'Filling in time again?' he asked her.

'In a way, I suppose, but it's much more enjoyable than the last lot.'

He noticed that she had put out her sponge-bag, which had a sort of Red Indian or Pacific feel to it, with some of its contents, and her not nearly so enlivening handbag likewise. 'Let's have a kiss,' he suggested.

'Oh, lovely,' she accepted readily, as if he had offered her a plate of jam tarts.

A moment later he said, 'I hope you're feeling better now than when you told me you felt as though you'd been given a wonderful present and then found you had to give it back again straight away. Do you remember saying that?'

'Oh yes, of course I do, but I'm surprised you do. Anyway, yes, I remember, why? Was it awful of me?'

'Absolutely not, just that was when I made up my mind I couldn't just let you go off on your own.'

'Yes, you said. What a relief that was, I mean for me, but what about it?'

'Well, I was just hoping you weren't feeling like that any more.'

'Oh, it's sweet of you to bother, Robin, but no I'm not at all, quite the opposite. Now, you mustn't go on or I'll start to feel silly and about one.'

'How do mean, about one?'

'About one year old. A baby.'

'Sorry.'

'What's this Elizabeth girl of George's like, have you any idea?'

'No, but she must have something to her or George wouldn't, wouldn't think so highly of her.'

'I hope whatever it is she's all right.'

Robin said confidently he was sure of it. All right in this context, for Nancy, must mean something in the general area of amiable, unassuming. He too hoped Elizabeth would be all right, but in the sense of attractive, sexy, brother's property or not. In the interval between now and her arrival, he found himself devoting some time to this hope. It was not that he saw any shortcoming in Nancy in herself, and he deeply wanted not to be the sort of man who, when just getting into his stride with a satisfactory love-affair, nevertheless seriously contemplates getting started on another. Unfortunately, at other times or even at the same time, that was just the sort of man he at least as deeply wanted to be. It had even occurred to him that sticking firmly to one girl could be unethically used to obtain exemption from the sometimes gruelling task of promiscuity.

When Elizabeth finally turned up, Robin felt a surge of mingled disappointment and relief. If there was indeed something to her, it would have to have been in the social or moral sphere, not the physical. All the same, she and George seemed very much taken up with each other. Robin wished them well rather tepidly as well as silently. He could not help feeling that he remembered his brother's previous attachments, of whom there had been several over the years, as distinctly better-looking than Elizabeth, and he thought he had noticed other cases where an apparent lowering of physical requirement had seemed to go with the choice of a wife, even or especially when the bloke had been a bit of a hammer of the ladies. The discovery, if it was a genuine one, nettled him a little by suggesting there might be things about sex or women or life he had yet to understand in full.

He took special care not to let any of this leak through to Nancy and did his best to show he understood that this was her first night with a man. He knew that the way to show this was through gentleness rather than anything that could be called passion. Just before he fell asleep he thought he saw he must learn to be somebody his fully alert, daytime self would despise and shrink from.

3

'I quite thought you'd lost touch with him,' said Mrs Davies.

'That's what I quite thought too,' said Robin.

'It might be just as well if you had, what with him going to prison like that. It can't do any good for people to think of you associating with him.'

'It can't do me much harm either. Anyway, who are they, all these people? Only you and Dad know I knew Jeremy. And I rather admire him for standing up for what he believed in.'

'Oh, Robin, you can't seriously say you admire somebody for going to prison, especially for refusing to help in the war.'

'For being prepared to go there, to not just back down at the threat. It doesn't mean to I say I agree with him.'

Robin had spoken mildly. He and his mother sat in the drawing-room of the old family residence. Like the rest of the house, it seemed to him smaller but less horrible than it had when it was part of his home. After a pause, Mrs Davies, who had on a new pair of glasses that made her eyes look interestingly detailed, edged a couple of inches closer and sent him an uncharacteristic stealthy glance.

'Did you know he'd nearly gone to prison some time before that for something, you know, something else?'

'Oh yes, I did hear something like that,' said Robin cautiously. 'What actually happened, do you know?'

'It was all rather hushed up. Jeremy went in front of the magistrates for fighting an Australian in the street. They let him off with a caution.'

'Yes, I heard that. You mean there was more to it?'

'Well, Joy Carpenter didn't exactly go into detail, but I did gather . . .' Now Robin's mother sent him another unfamiliar look, one that assumed without much confidence that his recently acquired status as an adult had brought him understanding and tact. 'I rather gathered,' she went on in a lowered voice, 'that Jeremy and the soldier weren't exactly fighting, or if they were it was because, because of something else. And, well, it wasn't exactly in the street this happened. His father managed to get all that part hushed up.'

'Ah,' said Robin in a way that evinced not only full understanding and shatter-proof tact but considerable surprise. 'How extraordinary,' he said.

'You mean it hadn't occurred to you he might be, you know, peculiar?'

'Well . . . I suppose it might have crossed my mind at some stage, but I never seriously . . .'

'I just thought you might like to know about that before you went out to lunch with him.'

'Oh yes, Mum, you did quite right to tell me,' said Robin, hanging out situation-well-in-hand signals as he spoke. 'It'll be fun, seeing old Jeremy again today.'

Robin had been convinced that it would be something like that ever since being telephoned about it earlier that morning. His mother had been less whole-hearted, asking for details of when and where the suggested lunch should take place as if she meant to forestall a kidnapping or hold-up attempt. Until a few moments ago, he had thought that her uneasiness sprang from nothing more than reluctance to approve any lunch-sized project that her husband had not ratified. Now all, or enough, had been made clear, and he left on foot for his date with a comfortable sense of having chatted to his mother just long enough.

The war nobody had consulted him about had at least got him quickly and irrecoverably away from home, in return for which a few years' inconvenience seemed to him, especially when he was on leave, a reasonable price to pay. However much he might have longed to, his father could not have clapped a padlock on his flies, stopped him swearing and smoking, etc., from a couple of thousand miles away, nor arranged with the forces paymaster to have all relevant monies directed to himself for possible onward transmission piecemeal. Beyond mere quirks like reminding his son now and then that the serviceman was confined to one theatre of operations at a time, and therefore denied the comprehensive view afforded those in, for example, London, the old man (sixtieth birthday next March, ho ho ho) was apparently resigned to the change. Once or twice he had touchingly gone as far as using bad language in his son's hearing.

Having quitted the house Robin turned to his right outside the gate. He thought he remembered doing just that in his father's company every schoolday morning for years, before he reasoned that of course it could not really have been every morning, merely too many mornings. To have meekly done the whole journey under constant paternal surveillance made him out to be too much of a ninny. But he had forgotten all about it by the time he turned right into the main road. On the far side of the pedestrian lights stood the now seasoned public lavatory, the very spot, possibly, where Jeremy had run into the Australian soldier. Perhaps the truth about that would emerge at the forthcoming lunch.

For the next couple of minutes, Robin's attention was not on the shops and such about him as he walked, which surely must have changed since he last saw them but in no way that interested him or caught his eye. Instead, his mind went back nearly ten years, to an afternoon in September in the first week of school term just after he had been staying with Cousin Emrys. Robin had been on his own, walking along the Embankment towards his train home, when a rather stout middle-aged man in a smart tweed suit approached him.

'Excuse me, but isn't it Robin Davies?'

'That's right, and you're Mr Carpenter, Jeremy's father.'

'Please understand immediately, Robin, that nothing is wrong,' said Mr Carpenter, though Robin thought his voice was unsteady. 'All is well with all your family and friends. But I do want to speak to you rather urgently. My car is round the corner. May I drive you home?'

'Well, I suppose so, sir. I mean yes, thank you very much.'

It was a warm, overcast, humid afternoon, and in his suit Mr Carpenter looked as if he was feeling the heat. They had walked some yards in silence when he said,

'I apologise for intruding on you like this, but I could think of no other way of having a private talk with you that could be kept private, without your parents' knowledge of it and so on. I hope you'll understand why I regard that as important when I've told you more. I'm afraid you must find all this rather strange. If it's any consolation to you, so do I, in the extreme.'

Mr Carpenter had stopped by the dark-green Austin Six that Robin remembered and waved him into its passenger seat. Again nothing was said at first as they drove. Robin's uneasiness, quelled by Mr Carpenter's earlier reassurance, began to mount again. Experience had shown that private talks, serious talks, meant trouble for somebody, usually their recipient.

'It's about my son,' said Mr Carpenter when they were clear of dense traffic.

'Jeremy.'

'Yes, Jeremy. I believe he visited you in Wales not so long ago.'

'Oh yes, we had a very nice day, or middle of a day. I enjoyed myself no end.'

'Yes. I gather via your mother that he gave you lunch in an hotel.'

'That was really the best part, sir. He had me in fits of laughter from start to finish. I only hope he wasn't spending too much money.'

'I doubt it very much. Let's be grateful for small mercies, this is not a money matter. As far as I know. Just tell me, if you would, what happened after that lunch. My son ran you back to where you were staying. Anything else? Truthfully, please, boy.'

By that stage, Robin had understood a good deal of the reason why Mr Carpenter was again showing some agitation, but not why he had begun to sound accusing as well. 'Nothing of any importance happened, sir.' That was not altogether true, but it answered truthfully enough what the question had implied.

'What did you talk about, the pair of you?'

'I'm afraid I can't remember. As I said, it was nothing important. What are you getting at, sir?'

Mr Carpenter uttered a kind of snort and at some risk moved the car out to overtake a tram. 'So you deny . . .' he said, but failed to go on.

'Mr Carpenter, you seem ill or upset or something.' Robin tried to keep his own voice from trembling, 'I suggest you pull in to the kerb and stop until you feel better able to continue driving. I'm in no hurry.'

The other gave no immediate sign of having heard, but soon turned the Austin into a side-street by a church and stopped. After another moment he switched off the ignition.

'I'm sorry,' said Mr Carpenter, and he certainly looked and sounded it. 'I convinced myself I'd be able to carry this off, ask you and tell you what I meant to, do so without . . . and yet I haven't been able to. But I must say it and I will say it in a minute. In just a minute. I must. . .'

'It's all right, sir, take your time. Isn't there a drink you can have or something?'

For a moment then Robin had seen somebody else altogether, a different man entirely from the poor driven creature who had tried to summon the calm to talk reasonably about what was not reasonable, somebody longing to return to the world he under-stood. 'I don't know where you got that from, youngster, but you're absolutely right. I've never wanted a drink as I want one at this moment, but it's no good, it wouldn't do any good. It would still be there, worse than ever.' Mr Carpenter drew a long deep breath. Then with some return to his earlier manner, he went on, 'I had an excellent reason for getting hold of you like this. When a father finds out something deplorable about his son, or something that would be deplorable if true, he's at fault with himself if he doesn't do his best to find out more. But it's hard to know what's best to do. All I could think of was to blame someone else. You, for instance. I wanted to hear you admit that you had led Jeremy astray in the first place and so he was less at fault, less to be blamed, perhaps to be pitied. How foolish of me, of course you'd deny it, true or not. Nevertheless, now we're here I'll ask you anyhow. So, first of all, have you and Jeremy done things together, you know what I mean, be good enough not to ask me to explain what I mean. But please answer.'

'The answer's no, Mr Carpenter, nothing of what you mean has ever taken place, and I want to say I resent being suspected of it, because that's what you've been doing.' Robin had had time to prepare some of that. He kept his hands tightly clenched in his lap while he was speaking. 'And that's flat, what I've said, you can take it or leave it. And if you ask me any more questions I won't answer them, I warn you.'

'I do believe you're telling the truth.'

'I don't care whether you believe me or not, sir.' If Robin had not just realised that he was only yards from a bus-route that passed within five minutes' walk of his front door, he would probably not have had the cheek to blurt out the last bit, which by the way was not even true.

Mr Carpenter sighed deeply again before seeming to revive suddenly and restarting the car. He drove them in silence through side-streets until they were back in the road they had left some minutes before. He still said nothing when Robin asked to be set down at the next bus-stop, but pulled up at the kerb a few paces beyond it.

'I'm sorry, Robin.' Mr Carpenter seemed less apologetic but more helpless than before, 'I feel I should thank you, though I don't quite know for what. I can at least make sure you don't finish up out of pocket. This will cover your bus-fare.' A shilling was offered and accepted. 'And this is some compensation for your trouble.' He held out a much-folded piece of white paper with very black lettering on one side.

This Robin recognised as a five-pound note. 'No thank you, sir,' he said, holding up a hand, 'that's not necessary,' and prepared to get out of the car.

'Now I know you're straight,' said Mr Carpenter as he put the note away.

And he had immediately driven off. He had hardly begun to do so before Robin began to chide himself for having turned down five perfectly legitimate and as always unequivocally acceptable quid. He had behaved like a boy in a story or film, the sort of story or film that his own father would have singled out for praise as uncommonly true to life. On the rare occasions when that bizarre encounter came to mind, as now on the way to lunch with Jeremy, it was the forfeited fiver that Robin most remembered, though without keen regret. He certainly never thought of his reflection at the time, that Mr Carpenter had been silly to think that turning down a sweetener proved anything, just as silly as he had been to make his approach in the first place. Anyway, the old fellow was dead now, fallen down stone dead the previous summer.

The meeting-place was the lounge of the local hotel, which had opened just in time for the war and had had to struggle ever since to pay its way. Robin was on time but Jeremy had been early, waving as he enthusiastically was from a kind of skeletal armchair by the windows. The two had not met for over a year and their first meeting went back nine or ten years further, but to Robin's view Jeremy had scarcely changed since that first occasion, his skin still smooth and his eyes clear. He did look shabbier, though, with his unpressed jacket and a cheap tie with rucked-up lining. He stood up with a show of vigour to shake hands.

'I haven't ordered a drink,' he said, 'I thought somehow it would look better not to.'

'Have one now. I'm going to.'

'Oh good. I'll have a gin and French.'

'That sounds wicked.'

'Now you come to mention it I suppose it does rather. I like it better than gin and It, which I always feel a tiny bit awkward about ordering anyway, being such an old tart's tipple.' When the waiter had gone to fetch two gin and French, Jeremy glanced at Robin and said, 'I must say you look terrifically gallant.'

'Thanks. I'm sorry about the uniform. My mother makes me wear it on leave.'

'Does that thing above your pocket mean you were very brave about something?'

'No, just that I was somewhere in particular at a particular time.'

'I'm sure hardly anybody knows the difference. It adds an unmistakable touch of glamour.' After a quicker glance at Robin he went on, 'Why does your mother make you wear your uniform on leave?'

'She says to show I'm not a, that I'm in the services, but I know very well it's to advertise the fact that her son's an officer. She didn't make me wear my plebeian uniform when I was home.'

'How frightfully middle-class of her. I'm sorry, Robin, you know I worship your mother. She was an absolute saint to my mother when my pa died. You knew him a bit, didn't you?'

'I just met him once or twice.'

'He wasn't a bad sort of chap. We didn't get on very well for obvious reasons, but I think we liked each other.'

At this point the waiter brought their drinks. When he had gone again, Robin said, 'Well, since we're old friends, Jeremy . . .'

Jeremy nodded brightly. 'Of course. Continue. Here's how.'

'Cheerio. I was going to ask you, I can think of two entirely different sets of obvious reasons why you didn't get on very well with your father.' He paused a second time and once more Jeremy motioned for him to go on. 'One of them to do with what you went to jug for some time ago, and the other to do with what you nearly went to jug for rather more recently. Which was worse?'

'To start with, they're not as separate as you say, but any fool could start off like that. Yes, well, the second one was the worse by

far, the harder for Pa to take. There'd been troubles before, but –
me and the Australian, do you know what I mean?'

'Yes, I did hear something about that.'

'I was so pissed at the time I've only the vaguest idea what
happened. I wouldn't mind betting the chap felt like punching
somebody and led me on, but I didn't say anything about that to
the beaks, no point in it. Pa had a quiet word here and there so that
nothing rude came up at the hearing, but it was a bloody near thing
and the suspense practically killed him. When it was over he went
on about, you know, it had been worth it if I'd learnt my lesson,
let's hope there'll be no more childish behaviour in the future, what?
Would you believe it, he wanted me to promise to reform. I
promised to try and I did, too – I spent the whole of the next
afternoon trying to reform, and there was no change by teatime so
I gave up. It's like trying to have red hair. I told the old man when
he asked me, I said I'd always been like it as long as I could
remember, and do you know that quite cheered him up. He
thought he'd made me like it by being around too much when I
was a nipper, or not being around enough or something. I say, all
this talking's made me thirsty. Are we going to have another drink
before we go and eat?'

'As long as you don't start mistaking me for an Australian,' said
Robin, signalling to the waiter.

'Hark at him! You're safe from me, old bean.'

'I'm relieved to hear it. I suppose I've gone off quite a bit since
that afternoon in Wales.'

'What afternoon in Wales was that?'

'You remember, you drove over to where I was staying and after
a bloody good lunch we went for a stroll and I didn't know it at
the time but you were just about to throw a teeny pass when I said
something off-putting and you didn't. I only realised it afterwards.
Tranquillity recollected in emotion as you might say. It must have
been getting on for ten years ago.'

'I certainly came to see you in Wales but I honestly don't
remember any stroll, let alone anything as interesting as what you

describe. I thought we had lunch with your very charming but rather dull relatives.'

Until quite recently such a response might have disconcerted Robin, but not now. 'Oh well,' he said, 'there goes my chance of showing you how tolerant and broadminded I am.'

'Believe me, Robin,' said Jeremy, 'you've shown that by meeting me in public knowing what you know about me.'

'What the hell has happened to that waiter?'

At the lunch-table Jeremy said, 'Yes, well, actually going to jug wasn't nice at all, in no way whatsoever. Which is meant to include what chaps like you may have heard about the sort of life chaps like me lead in HM prisons. I'm not asking for sympathy, just stating a fact. You get more of what you want than you want, which I know sounds rather deep. It wasn't very long before I started wishing I hadn't said I wouldn't help with the war, but it was too late for that by then,'

'Why had you said? That you wouldn't help with the war. No, you go on, don't mind me.'

'I suppose to start with I fell for the stuff about its being an imperialist war and all nearly everybody was going to get out of it was being killed, also its being a great waste of energy, but by the time my case came up I'd more or less forgotten that side of it, but I didn't give in because they were so bloody rude to me, and stupid as well. What's the matter, you seem disappointed.'

'Sorry,' said Robin, 'but I quite thought you were going to say you didn't join up because you didn't want to.'

'What are you talking about, of course I didn't want to.'

'Sorry, no, I meant that business to do with the autonomy of the will. Homer Lane and all that.'

'Oh, Christ, that was in the days when I wanted moral support for wandering off the straight and narrow. Which merged with the days when I found it came in handy for persuading other chaps to wander off the straight and narrow.'

'It didn't work with me, did it?'

'No, it didn't, did it? Not in that way, at least, though it might have encouraged you to do what you felt like doing and to hell with other people, that's if you needed encouragement. But really, you know, all that sacredness-of-desire stuff was just queer propaganda.'

'Even old David Herbert? Even Blake?'

'They were straight cards in the hand, there to lend respectability and sort of universality to the enterprise.' Jeremy poured himself more wine. 'Lawrence had a great appeal for the sick and infirm. It's a funny thing, I've never come across any kind of Lawrence-disciple, queer or not, who wasn't in a proper pickle about sex. Odd, isn't it?'

'Another thing I was going to ask you,' said Robin after some pondering, 'why aren't you in clink still, or again? I thought they went on bunging you back in as long as you went on objecting.'

'They found I had asthma. That gets you off everything.'

'You don't strike me as asthmatic'

'I might quite forcibly if you saw me having an attack.'

'Why didn't you tell them about it before?'

'They didn't ask me before. Now that's enough questions.'

Before they parted, Robin asked after Jeremy's mother.

'Pretty fair,' was the reply. 'Misses my father a good deal.'

Robin could think of nothing to say to that.

'I miss him too. Not as much as she does, of course, but I never thought I'd miss him at all. I do, though. Freud says the most serious loss a man suffers is the death of his father. I could supply him with a footnote, adding that it doesn't seem to matter or make much difference when the man in question is a pretty funny sort of man.'

'Don't ever call yourself that Jeremy, even in fun.'

'I'll try and remember. What about getting together again before you go back and teach the Hun who's master?'

'Can't manage it this time around, I'm afraid. I'm off in the morning, taking a girl to Wales. Same bit of Wales as before.'

'Pity. That means we shan't see each other for quite a while. Ma's selling up here and we're off to Carshalton at the end of next month.'

'Drop me a line and we'll meet in London.'

'Sure. At the risk of mildly embarrassing you I want to tell you that as far as I'm concerned you haven't gone off at all. Quite the contrary. Sometimes I find myself thinking my sort only really likes your sort of man.'

'What does Freud say about that?'

'He says bugger off.'

The girl Robin took to Wales the next morning was none other than Nancy Bennett. He undoubtedly wanted to do that, he knew no other girl he would have considered taking, and he was totally content that these things should be so. At the same time it was clear to him that part of his reason for taking her was that he thought he should do something of the sort, and a related part was his desire to deal his father one in the eye, and he was far from content that these things too should be so. With the deliberation of some shitty Dickens mercer turning through swatches of cloth at a rotten old textile fair, he set about examining his motives on his way to the main-line station for Wales, but kept being disturbed by the memory of a voice that told him, If you take one of them away on any sort of holiday, as distinct from a dirty weekend, etc., get ready to kiss your bachelorhood good-bye.

That voice was silenced, at any rate for the time being, when the train for Wales drew in at a station near Oxford and he caught sight of Nancy, as arranged, standing on the platform. As unmeta - phorically as possible, her face lit up when she saw him. He had not thought beforehand of doing so but jumped down from his carriage and hurried to meet her. She ran into his arms still holding her suitcase.

'You're looking terrifically well,' he said.

'So are you, tremendously well.'

'Everything all right?'

'Absolutely all right.'

Still talking, they got into the train. Their compartment was not full but it had two other people in it. This rather suited Robin, because without their presence he might have yielded to the temptation to give Nancy at least a thorough kissing, and to get that far, as he could see without any trouble while he was still only tempted, would almost certainly have brought its own problems. He thought as well as hoped she was feeling the same kind of temptation as he was. She had taken the seat opposite his and kept looking at him, chiefly at his face, until perhaps she got the idea that it might be more seemly if she looked out of the window instead.

Nancy might have felt she had some catching-up to do on Robin's physical appearance after not setting eyes on him since his last leave the previous year, She had not gone to meet him off the boat-train this time because his parents had proposed to do that, and neither of the two reunions of the four parties in question had been much of a success. Mr Davies had gone on rather about bygones being bygones, as if he had invented the bloody expression, according to Robin after the first attempt. But, as he had gone on to admit to Nancy, father would have had his work cut out to manage to say anything acceptable to son in the circumstances.

Such considerations distracted Robin briefly from more immediate causes for concern. For at a time hard to fix precisely in retrospect, he and Nancy had decided they were engaged, presumably to be married, if ever, at some future date also left blank. He assured himself, with some truth, that in wartime such arrangements, or non-arrangements, were common, or not uncommon. When it came to Nancy's feelings in and around the matter, it was obvious that she was all in favour of the part of it that concerned their going off together. It was more difficult to say what she believed or thought she understood about his recent personal life. Of course he had had to leave Oxford in some hurry and be called up, spent months being trained in a remote spot, been sent hither and thither, done what had been required of him in some famous and some utterly obscure places. He considered himself amazingly lucky not to have been prevented from seeking and usually finding female consolation, up to and including a dose of clap (soon cured) in Alexandria. But it was not his internal warning voice alone that told him such freedom could not go on indefinitely.

They crossed into Wales. To Robin, Wales meant first of all his father and his father's youth, and now Nancy and her childhood, but more immediately it meant Cousin Emrys and his world, if world it could be called. The last few times Robin had entered it he had come away vowing never to go there again, and the moment when he became aware he never need go there again had marked an important step in his progress to maturity. Things had changed slightly since then. His erstwhile state of chronic penury had been alleviated by service pay and allowances, but not out of recognition. Smoking constantly and getting drunk regularly, together with other necessary expenses, had shrivelled any amount he might have put by. On leave now, he was strongly inclined to keep what he had left for anything possible in the way of riotous living. This consideration made Cousin Emrys's world quite attractive, at least as a dormitory. On the other hand he, Robin, had not set foot inside it for a year or two, and it might easily have got worse. Indeed, it might even have been worse in a way he had forgotten, and stayed unchanged. Best to play it safe and stay away. But then again curiosity worked in favour of a visit. A splendid compromise became possible when Nancy mentioned hospitable relatives living somewhere in Wales at just the right distance from Emrysworld for a day-trip to it to become possible. A couple of telephone calls had settled the matter.

It had occurred to Robin as possible that after some exposure to Nancy's hospitable relatives he might well find intrinsic merit in time spent away from them, and so it proved. The old girl, Mr Bennett's younger sister, was all right, middle forties but all right, so much so that if things had been different, Robin mused, things might have been different. The old boy was some years older and not all right, dropping to not at all all right when he declared his inability to provide any help whatever over the matter of hiring a car and in the act reminding Robin of his own father. A day away from him, if not more, was just what the doctor ordered, and Robin felt full of fun when he drove Nancy and himself off on a sunless but also rainless and pleasantly warm morning.

The day had brightened by the time they were passing the former cinema, now an office of the Ministry of Food, and the stationer's where Welsh had been the only language publicly spoken. Robin remembered how Jeremy had once come across him dawdling along that very stretch of pavement. There seemed to be no change in the five-barred gate at the entrance to the track that led up to Cousin Emrys's farmhouse, nor in the sheep that hung about the place, except that they seemed rather less numerous and a good deal dirtier even than memory suggested.

With his expected air of never having personally sanctioned the development of the motor-car, Cousin Emrys emerged as they arrived. A little thicker round the waist, a little less upright in his carriage, a little more of an obvious fucking old fool, he soon took in the situation. This achieved, he conducted the hazardous operation of moving two able-bodied adults and their luggage from outside his house to within it. He even found the detachment to inquire after the health of individual members of Robin's family and his temporary hosts, in case somebody had taken an unforeseen turn for the worse during the couple of dozen hours since the same ground had been covered over the telephone. Perhaps some such thought had come to Cousin Emrys, for just then he told Robin a second time how lucky it was in the circumstances that the farmhouse had recently had this device installed after so many years without it. In fairness, however, if you happened to like fairness, it had to be conceded that old Cousin E. was putting himself out to be friendly and welcoming to Nancy. She at least seemed happy to be where she was and, Christ, they only had to last out until teatime.

From the first moment of arrival, the barking of two dogs, yap and boom in counterpoint, had been audible at some distance. The fact that it went on being at some distance was a good indication that the dogs in question were not free to move, were tied up, and they and any other dogs that might have been around put in no appearance at any stage, much to Robin's relief. He remembered from years back the dog Fido, that snuffler into your crotch and silent but deadly farter, remembered him not well but well enough to be thankful for his absence. Also absent were Dillwyn and Dilys, Cousin Emrys's son and daughter, long married now, Robin assumed, and far away. Married Dilys certainly was, it transpired, and her husband, a merchant seaman, at the moment satisfactorily far away on convoy in the North Atlantic, but she herself was in fact close at hand, emerging now from round the corner to show herself between Menna Williams, who seemed half a size smaller than memory showed, and Gran, now so old it was getting beyond a joke. Mugs of tea and a kind of coffee were produced and handed round.

Sitting at or near the kitchen table with the others, Robin was aware that Dilys had dressed herself up and come over specially from her habitation on the far side of the village, and also that she was looking to and fro between Nancy and himself with a knowing, friendly-jeering smile. 'So you've finally persuaded a poor defence-less creature to let you have your way with her, have you, you young rip, you,' it said loud and clear to anyone else capable of picking up such signals. The only other qualified person present was obviously Nancy, who seemed to be listening to Cousin Emrys's account of farm animals and farming on his farm, a state of affairs that could not continue for ever, at least on her side. Luckily Dilys got fed up with making faces after a bit, and at about the same time Nancy told Cousin Emrys that yes, she would very much like to be shown something of the farm and its animals, and in due course a small party went out of the back door and into the yard. Dilys made one of this party, which Robin considered was sort of mildly surprising without himself finding it so.

They visited chickens and ducks, then cows, including a calf, and even a horse or two, and of course as many sheep of various sizes and shapes as anybody could possibly have wanted to know of. Naturally Robin was at all points indifferent to anything as country - fied and antiquated as livestock, but he knew from experience that a rich spectrum of unacceptable treatment of animals was available to girls. So he watched with close interest when Nancy made a medium-sized fuss of a sturdy-looking lamb or juvenile sheep. Either she was doing a marvellous imitation of a girl quite uninterested in the impression she was making, or she really was such a girl. The latter, he thought, and good for her. He saw it was bad luck on her to have got tied up with a chap who hardly knew what it was not to care how he seemed to other people.

Nancy finished with the lamb and was being led away by Cousin Emrys. Robin was about to follow when Dilys moved round to the front of him. Her way of doing this emphasised the presence of her breasts under a thin snuff-coloured jumper. He noticed too that the freckles on her face seemed less noticeable than before.

'Would you like to see something?' she asked him.

'Yes,' he said, and there was a good case for saying it, only perhaps not quite good enough.

'Round here.'

She took him off in the opposite direction to the others but not very far, just to where a smallish dark-brown horse with a black mane and tail was savagely tearing at the grass with its teeth. The creature looked to Robin distinctly puny compared with a couple of no doubt lower-class horses seen earlier. Aware that it was no longer alone, the present horse raised its head and turned its shifty gaze on the two of them.

'This is Midge,' said Dilys. 'He's my pony.'

'Is he? When will he be full-grown?'

'He is already, dull. Isn't that just like a townie, thinking a pony's a young horse. It just means he's small. He's six actually, going on seven.'

'I see.'

Robin had taken his eye off Midge for a second or two and now, with many a slobber and snort, it reached forward and seemed to be trying to push its muzzle into his jacket pocket. 'Get out of it, you bugger!' he shouted, jumping aside.

'He's only wondering if you've brought a goodie for him.'

'A *goodie*?'

'Like an apple or a carrot.'

'Well I haven't. Why should I have done?'

'Yeah? I'd say you were afraid of him.'

'That's what I'd say too.' It was one of those rare times when he forgot to care how he seemed to other people. 'Bloody brute,' he finished strongly.

'Ha!' Dilys gave a yelp of scornful laughter. 'That's honest anyway. You weren't such a funk when you came down here one time before, I remember.'

'When was that?' asked Robin guardedly.

'Oh, years ago. I dare say you'll have forgotten or you'll say you have. I remember all right, though, because of the pathetic way you went on. "Oh, Dilys, be a sport now and let me see your tits." Bloody scream you were. Couldn't have been more than fourteen either that year. Bloody cheek of you.'

'I remember something too, and according to me you did all the talking.'

'Stop that, Midge, that's enough!' Dilys suddenly bawled at the horse, which had diffidently moved its rear pair of legs a little way apart. 'Forget it, will you.'

The pony drew its back legs together again and blew down its nostrils in a refined way.

'What was it going to do, crap?' asked Robin after an interval.

'Something in that department, yes. That Nancy of yours,' Dilys went on with no interval, 'she seems a very nice straight sort of girl.'

'Oh yes, she is.'

'Perhaps we'd better be getting back to her.' Dilys gave the horse some hearty smacks on the neck. 'Quite, well, attached, are you, you and her?'

'Yes, we are, thanks.'

'How long are you going to be on leave this time?'

'Just another four days. Why?'

'You won't be coming down again, then, like on your own?'

'No,' said Robin, then rather belatedly took in the whole of Dilys's remark and added, 'What?'

'Nothing, I just wondered. Only Mervyn's away a lot now, see, and I get more free time than I know what to do with. So if you ever feel like a little excursion, you know where to come.'

Strolling along at his side, she gave him the kind of provisionally amorous glance that it was easy to visualise melting into voluptuous surrender, and at least as easy to imagine followed up by indignant and unshakeable protest that nothing of even approximately that nature had come anywhere near as much as crossing her mind, and what about Nancy? Still, what he always said to himself without fear of contradiction was you never knew.

'Have you got a telephone number?' As Robin spoke he saw a car of some sort driving cautiously up the track towards the house.

'Write to me would be better. Care of here will find me. And in case you've forgotten, I'm called Walters now. Well, it would be nice to see you some day.'

They caught up with the other two in time for a short refresher course at the hen-run. Nancy sent Robin a look void of suspicion, let alone reproach, that made him feel a shit for almost as long as it took them to get back inside the house and again penetrate as far as the kitchen. Here he found himself confronted by a pair of strangers, a man in his fifties with a mass of grey hair that he had recently washed and not done anything about since, and a small, also grey wife-like figure who watched the bloke in a beaten, devoted way. Cousin Emrys performed introductions. Although in the ordinary run very ready to dispense information several times over, he had got it wrong about the new arrivals, whom he seemed to think mistakenly he had mentioned to Robin at least twice before. Anyway, whatever their names, at once forgotten, they were soon revealed as the recently installed rector of the Anglican parish and his wife. Now that he had been alerted, Robin could make out an attenuated dog-collar at the base of the shag's neck. He seemed wary but prepared to be friendly.

Whatever the shortcomings of Cousin Emrys's household in the past, nobody could fairly have said that he stinted you when it came to food. Drink in the alcoholic sense, on the other hand, had been small and thin, though that had hardly bothered Robin in earlier years. This time, he had told himself rather grimly beforehand not to expect anything beyond a glass of sweet stout or brown ale with the meal, except perhaps for a few ccs of British sherry by way of aperitif. In the event there was enough booze to satisfy the thirstiest or most exacting of guests; gin, whisky, brandy, even rum, even real champagne, a rarity except at weddings but available here in apparently unlimited quantities from the inside of a large refrigerator of recent date. Also to hand were soda-syphons, small bottles of tonic and dry ginger, saucers of stuffed olives and cheese straws. Menna poured the drinks, inexpertly no doubt but with an endearing proneness to overdo the shots of spirits. Food was visible, but dishing-up time went on being not yet.

What had turned Emrys into such a liberal host? The answer that soon started forming in Robin's mind was given shape by something Dilys said to her mother. It became clear that, in these wartime days, the price of a carton of booze was reckoned not so much in pounds and shillings as in prime cuts of mutton and lamb and vice versa and so on. And just as when you got hold of a best end of the neck (via a generous neighbour) you cooked and ate it, so when you got hold of a bottle of gin (via a grateful neighbour) you opened it and drank it. Well, what was a lucky guest to do but go along?

Some time later the party sat down to lunch or midday dinner or whatever they called it out there. At first there was relative silence as all at their different speeds came to terms with the fact that eating was what they had to get on with now. During this phase vessels of mint sauce and redcurrant jelly and bottles of tomato ketchup and Nuits-St-Georges were passed to and fro. Before long, Cousin Emrys set himself to clarify what the office of rector was understood to mean in general and what it involved in this parish in particular. By this stage Robin was thoroughly enjoying himself, savouring his awareness that he was eating and drinking much better than at home and better even than on service, complacent about his sexual situation, telling himself that the whole occasion justified his inquisitiveness about how life was going on in this remote corner. That agreeable state of mind began to alter when the rector showed himself a true son of Wales by exercising his right to reply to Cousin Emrys's address.

All might have been well if the clergyman had had a different manner of speech, a different hair-style or a different wife, but he would have needed a different audience, one without Robin, to be sure of a generally respectful hearing. In an accent perhaps deriving from northern England, certainly not from any Welsh place, he spoke of the responsibilities of his position. Actually a different accent might well have done his cause some good or at any rate less harm.

'At a time like this,' he was heard to say, 'one obviously isn't going to stress the difficulties of religion and the demands it makes of one, which are considerable. It's no use pretending the Christian way is an easy one, because it's nothing of the kind. To read the sayings of Jesus in the New Testament is not a comfortable experience.'

Robin drained his tumbler of Romanée-Conti 1936 and refilled it from the bottle that had come to rest in front of him. 'For instance,' he said encouragingly.

'There are as many instances as there are pages in the Gospels, but I was thinking of one very famous one in particular, a quotation from the Psalms, to be sure, but so much more than that. My God, my God . . .'

The rector had once more shown himself a true son of Wales, not only by uttering these words in apparent consternation, as at some horrific sight or disclosure, but also by gazing slowly round the company afterwards, defying any bold spirit to rebuke him for blasphemy. When there were no takers he started again, 'My *God*, my God,' he said, this time making the first my-God seem like an exclamation of remonstrance, the second a rather chummy vocative. When all present still remained silent he finished in a businesslike tone, 'Why hast thou forsaken me?'

At that time a great many, perhaps most, people in the United Kingdom would have recognised these as Christ's last words on the Cross (according to St Matthew). After some initial bafflement, Robin certainly did. He scrubbed out one of the black marks he had earlier awarded the rector, now revealed as a distinguished dryballocked bugger, as some men he knew might have described it. He recognised too that, for whatever historical or other reason, Wales was what England was not, a place where matters of the deepest importance could be discussed, or at least approached, at least mentioned, without elaborate prelude, without apology. In not much more than a desire to keep the ball rolling, he said, 'Thereby blowing the gaff on the whole pretence that he was God himself in human shape.'

Someone, probably Cousin Emrys, gave a loud gasp, but the rector had had such a dart thrown at him more than once, and survived. He continued to nod his head, which he had begun doing about a quarter of the way through Robin's remark, and smiled faintly before speaking. 'Yes, as I put it a moment ago, it's not a saying one feels comfortable with, precisely because it's open to the interpretation you suggest so succinctly, sir,' he said, having a fine time with all those sibilants at the end.

'What interpretation do you suggest?' asked Robin with no overt disrespect.

At this the rector rounded his lips, but instead of starting to whistle he drew in air through them. 'Well, if, I repeat *if*, one is to take those words as an exact version of what Jesus said on that occasion, one still has a wide choice of interpretations. I for one am inclined to favour that which takes account of the fact that Jesus was man as well as God, and as a man was suffering at that moment the most extreme pain of his mortal existence. It sure is no wonder, no *miracle* as one might say, that just then he spoke as a man. Oh, there are numerous interpretations open to one as a Christian without knowing or needing to know which one, if any, is the right one. And, after all, I ask you, what does it matter?'

The rector made to go on without staying for an answer, but Robin had decided that to let him go on along his present track was most undesirable. When he broke in, however, it was not to say, 'If you must say *one* all the time, *for Christ's sake* say it properly: the word is *one*, not wan,' which he thought might have been seen as bad form, but instead, still pacifically, 'I'm afraid I sidetracked you,

Rector. Weren't you going to tell us what, er, what one should be talking about these days in preference to dwelling on, what did you call them, the difficulties of religion?'

'Now you mention it, sir, I was indeed about to embark on some sort of attempt to outline a pattern of some of the more helpful features of systematised belief,' and this, many would have agreed, he proceeded to do.

Perfectly reconciled, sipping at a sweet wine called Château Climens which Cousin Emrys rightly insisted was just the thing with bread-and-butter pudding, Robin let the rector talk on uninterrupted. He had given up any pretence of following the fellow's drift, was beginning to consider how he might reasonably hope to pass the afternoon, when some reference to mercy set him reluctantly listening again.

'No matter how painful or terrible things may turn out for one, God is always ready to help one, if asked seriously and in good faith. And in his mercy he's arranged matters in such a way that anyone, anyone at all, Christian or Buddhist or non-believer, can reach him in the twinkling of an eye. No need to ask by what means, because everyone knows the name of this method of immediate communication with God. It's called prayer.'

What Robin rather felt like saying now was, 'Everyone knows the conversational tactic of taking a long time to unveil a platitude, but not everyone agrees on the name it may go by. According to me, this one's called bullshit,' or words to that effect. But he knew without looking at her that Dilys wanted him to get cross or fussed or something, anything that would give her the chance of a superior grin or outright snigger at his unworldliness. To forestall this bad result he shut up altogether this time.

But the rector did not, anyway not at once. 'And prayer,' he was going on, 'is always answered. It may not be answered in the way one might expect, it may not be answered in the way one, er, one's wisdom may have decided one deems suitable or even satisfactory. But God always answers and always helps. That's the first thing to get straight in these troubled times. Now—'

Having first glanced at Robin as if for permission to break in, Nancy said, 'May I ask you something, please, Rector?'

The man addressed turned towards her with some emphasis. 'I have got a name, young lady. I'm not just Rector X or the Reverend Mr Blank, you know.'

Nancy started blushing. 'I'm terribly sorry, but I'm afraid I just can't . . .'

'And it's exactly the same, is my name, as it was an hour or so back when we were introduced. So if it isn't too much trouble . . .'

Robin did not stop to consider what part of this display, if any, might have been excusable as a reaction to being interrupted. He felt his own cheeks turning hot and a part of his chest seemed to have gone hollow. He said, managing to keep his voice down for the most part, 'You tell us, *Rector,* that God always answers our prayers. I've also read or been told often enough that God is love, meaning presumably that God, that same God, loves his whole creation, including human beings, loves them all like a father. Well, my own father, the man who fathered me, has certainly got a lot wrong with him from my point of view. Of course he has, he's only human if you see what I mean, and he wouldn't claim to be without fault. But in one respect his love for me is of a morally superior kind. Again, there are plenty of things I want and would say I need and think I ought to have that he doesn't give me. But he does give plenty of things I've never had to ask him for, obvious boring stuff like food and clothes and a roof over my head, which I may say in passing is a sight more than God's ever given me. What kind of love is it that has to be asked before it'll give, asked nicely too, so you're supposed to go down on your bended knees to plead for whatever it is? Art thou troubled? Yes. And what's God's answer to that? Not, In which case I've clearly fallen down on the job, but, Right, you just follow the laid-down procedure and I might consider doing something or other about it one day. And secondly, Rector, there are some situations where mere help isn't much of a help. What about ugly girls or blind people or deformed people or people with the wrong taste in sex that no amount of trying will ever take away?

When that kind of thing comes along God's answer is not, Whoops, here I go slipping up again, but, Get into the grovelling position and thank me for giving you such a spiffing chance to be brave, and if I feel like it I might give you a hand. By helping you to be brave, nothing more constructive or troublesome or serious than that. So please don't tell me how nice God is, what with him always answering our prayers and all. He can't exist without being a shit, and I wouldn't dream of saying flatly he doesn't exist, just that the world and everything in it are indistinguishable from a world et cetera in which he doesn't exist.'

Then Robin bowed his head, thinking not much more than that he was lucky to have been given the chance of having his say out. He was conscious that Cousin Emrys had very nearly interrupted several times but the rector had restrained him. A faint quavering snore could be heard now from Gran.

'Very good, young sir,' said the man of the cloth after a pause, 'very forcefully argued. And it's not often one comes across that these days, 'I'm sorry to say. Yes, I think Emrys here may have something he wants to contribute, am I right, Emrys?'

'In all my born days I'm quite sure I've never heard anything that for sheer arrogance could begin to—'

'Yes, well I think we can all take that as read, can't we? And let me make no bones about warning you quite seriously, Emrys, against arrogance on your own side. I know this is a Christian household, but that ought to mean tolerance, a spirit of give and take, respect for the other fellow's point of view. Our Church was born in conflict and if its teachings ever fail to arouse conflict it will die. It's our duty, our sacred duty, to allow a hearing to opinions we disagree with. Truth is only strengthened when it collides with error.' He turned to Nancy. 'I'm sorry if I was sharp with you a bit ago, my dear. I sometimes get flustered for a second or so if someone interposes a remark just as I'm getting into my stride. Nothing to be proud of. There was something you wanted to ask me, wasn't there? Well, ask me now.'

'It's all right, it doesn't matter, thank you,' said Nancy.

'Are you quite certain? Oh, by the way, for future reference, if any, the name's Hopkins, Arthur Hopkins, Welsh by descent only, but on both sides. And now, Emrys my lad, you'll oblige me by giving a fair wind to that excellent Armagnac.'

A moment later, Emrys had passed to Revd Arthur Hopkins the brandy-bottle and, making many an apologetic face, was vigorously shaking hands with Robin from a seated position. A moment later still, he had risen from his seat and left the room, deviating from a straight path by a couple of paces as he approached the door. Later again, he was said by Menna to have gone upstairs to rest his back. By then, rector and wife had left and Robin and Nancy were going off in the car to blow the cobwebs away before tea, or so he said.

'I didn't much care for that vicar,' said Nancy as they went jolting down the track.

'Oh, he wasn't too bad as they go, except when he was being bloody offensive to you. But I thought he wished he hadn't.'

'That was just eyewash, he wasn't taking any of it back. I thought myself he was a blasted hypocrite.'

'Any parson's bound to be that, it goes with the job. Oh yes, what were you going to ask him?'

'Quite silly really, about surely you'd feel better, or you might just sort of psychologically if you said a prayer. But I really just wanted to interrupt him.'

'Between us we managed that all right.'

Nancy looked at Robin's profile for a moment. Then she said, 'What made you go for him like you did? You were quite angry.'

'Well, I was pretty cross at what he said to you.'

'I expect that got you started, but you went on after that. You were more than just pretty cross. I meant secondly. What you went on to say. I thought you were thinking of somebody in particular, like a friend or a relative.'

'No. Not really.'

'Oh. Were you a bit, you mustn't mind me asking—'

'Yes, I was. Perceptibly pissed. Drunk to you. Must still be though I don't feel it. Anyway, drink doesn't put things in people's heads that weren't there to start with, it just makes them feel it's all right to say them. For good or ill.'

'I see. Now it is all right if I look out of the window for a bit? I don't know this part of Wales at all and I'd like to see what it looks like. Do you mind?'

'Not in the least,' said Robin, and it was true that he only minded in so far as he staunchly believed almost any human being to be worthier of an adult's attention than almost any chunk of scenery. Or nearly any. It was true that he had never seen the Alps or Arizona.

Actually Robin was looking out of his own window now and then, because he was growing increasingly certain that he had managed, partly by luck, to find the road Jeremy had taken coming back from lunch that summer's afternoon nearly ten years before. He had been slightly drunk then too, he remembered. Another mile and he was quite certain. This, seen from the opposite direction, was the patch of shade and the low fence where the two of them had got out of the car and walked a couple of hundred yards and had a conversation that had embarrassed him for years to recall, but now no longer. If the scene had changed in more detail he noticed nothing, and on that day and on this there was nobody else to be seen. At the moment even the nearest sheep were a couple of hundred yards away.

Robin pulled in by the stretch of fence and stopped. 'It's a lovely day and it probably hasn't rained for a couple of weeks.'

Nancy laughed. 'So I needn't worry about getting my shoes all muddy. Very thoughtful.'

'You're so sharp you'll cut yourself one of these fine days.'

A few minutes later she said, 'People can't see us from the road, can they?'

'Not unless we stand up.'

'In that case we'd better not stand up.'

'Not standing up won't hide us from the little grey men with field-glasses behind every hedge.'

'There aren't any there really, are there?'

'And bush. Of course. Deacons they are. This is Wales.'

Afterwards he heard birdsong from quite close at hand and was elated by it without being able to identify the birds. He was aware of the sun and its brightness where before he had been conscious only of its heat. For the first time, he wondered quite seriously and almost academically if he was in love. He knew of only one test worthy of the name, all others he had heard or read about striking him as showing off or bullshit or mumbo-jumbo or all three at once. A grandfather or at least uncle figure in his junior mess, a man in his thirties who was understood to have a Spanish wife, had once said in Robin's hearing that the physical sensation of making love when in love was different, not just superior, to that experienced when not in love. Surely, somebody had put it, he must mean different in some bullshitty or mumbo-jumboish way. No, the man had insisted, physical, as physical as any other physical thing. Robin believed that what he himself had felt just now had differed physically from all previous occasions. If you really believed you loved a girl it was surely all right to tell her so. Nobody said that if you believed that, you *had* to tell the girl you loved her, or if anyone did, there were others to deliver the warning that if you told her so you were apt to find yourself married to her willy-nilly.

At this stage, Robin forgot such speculations when Nancy leaned over and not only kissed him, but kissed him in a way that he thought told him unmistakably that she loved him. He was about to speak when she spoke first. 'I wish there was some special name or something I could call you by that nobody else has or ever will, but I don't suppose there are any left that wouldn't sound silly, or even be silly.' There was no suggestion that Robin could have made or anyway expressed at all for a time, but eventually he said, 'What exactly do you think your mum and dad think we get up to, you and me?'

'You mean sort of how well are we supposed to know each other?'

'That kind of thing, yes. Do they think for instance that we're spending the afternoon picking primroses?'

'Primroses are all over by about the end of April.'

'Oh, to fuck – sorry, but you know what I mean.'

'Sorry, of course I do. Well, I should think they both have a pretty fair idea, but I don't suppose they discuss it much between the two of them, and having a pretty fair idea of something is completely different from being told about it as a fact, isn't it? And the other thing is, you'll think it's awful but it means a terrific lot to both of them, you being an officer. They think, I know them, they think you can't be all that irresponsible or anything because . . .'

'On account of me being an officer of the King with a commission of authority and all. Sancta simplicitas, or blessed simplicity, or Christ almighty, just look at a few of the frightful shites who actually are officers, not unincluding me. Anyway, I don't particularly want to talk about this, and I assure you there's no particular reason why I should be talking about it, but don't your mum and dad ever ask you what's going on?'

'They do sometimes ask me things, but not that. My dad's said a couple of times, out of the blue really, that of course he knows people in wartime come under a lot of stresses and strains they don't get in peacetime, and they sometimes behave in ways they very likely wouldn't in peacetime, but I can't tell whether he means he'd understand if he found out that we, you know, or just I'd better take special care till it's peacetime again. He gives me a big mark-my-words look while he says it but that might go with either.'

'So it might. What's your mother said?'

'Well, she's asked me once or twice, I suppose in a way it isn't really asking, did I think you'd let me down. Ever let me down I think she said.'

'Oh.' Robin shifted his gaze to a tree in the middle distance, to give Nancy a chance to blush free of scrutiny if required. 'What did you say?'

'I said no, I didn't think you would. That was the truth, that I didn't think you would.'

'Of course it was.'

'But I don't think it's necessarily a good idea for us to go into things like that now, or at times like now, not really, do you?'

'Perhaps not,' said Robin, to say something.

'I'm very happy with things being as they are, considering. I never thought I'd be, but I am. And you've probably worked it out, but I'll be twenty-one at the beginning of next year, and then I'll be able to decide what it's best for me to do and do it.'

'Now that sounds like a good idea.'

'There's plenty of time to think about it, but it would be good if you could manage to call in on my parents. With me there too, I mean.'

'We'll have to see, but you're perfectly right.'

'I'm a bit worried about my dad. He's coughing something terrible.'

'I wish you'd tell me about it one of these days, Robin.'

'Mum, I keep telling you there's really nothing to tell you, nothing more anyway. If you think I haven't told you much it's because nothing much happens in a prison camp. No thrilling escape attempts or even boring ones. One day's pretty much like another, at the time you say sod it but afterwards you say more thank God. From what I hear we were luckier than some, and sure the Italians were the nicest hosts, but quite a few of the Germans had nothing to reproach themselves with, like our lot. Which mostly means as I said, nothing goes on worth remembering. You don't really want to hear that the camp commandant was called Colonel Weber and carried a leather-covered stick, stuff like that, and honestly if you don't mind, Mum, I'd as soon not be reminded of what it was like.'

'Oh, I'm sorry, my love, I didn't mean you to go into all the—'

'Don't worry about that, Mum, of course you didn't.' Robin hesitated. 'I've been meaning to ask you about Dad. How has he been? I thought he seemed all right in that minute this morning.'

'Yes, he says he feels all right, most of the time anyway. But he does get this feeling of fullness after he's eaten. Indigestion too, what he calls hot risings.'

'Well, he's always been a bit that way inclined, hasn't he?'

'I suppose he has, but it won't seem to go away this time. He says he thinks he's got a touch of chronic acidity. Gastric acidity.'

'Whatever that may be. I'd say he was a bit on the highly-strung side. What would you say about that, Mum? After all, you've seen much more of him than I have.'

'Isn't it funny, we've never talked about him in this strain before, as if he was just another person like everyone else. Yes, I suppose he is what you might call highly strung, I've never really thought about it. You mean he fusses over his health too much?'

'I was thinking more that if you worry a lot, live on your nerves and so on, you can manufacture more than your fair share of stomach acid, with exactly the—'

'Oh Robin, do you think it's that?'

'Well . . . it does sound rather like it to me.' He tried to get reliability and unplumbed experience into the way he tilted his head forward and over to one side. 'After all, he's never been what I'd call a real boozer. How old is he? He's never told me.'

'That's another funny thing, he's never told me either, always managed to prevent me even seeing his birth certificate. I stopped trying to find out from him years ago. But he must be sixty-three.'

'No great age really, is it? And of course medical science is making tremendous strides these days.'

'I suppose they must have found out a lot in the war, about how to patch people up and everything, I was reading about that somewhere.'

'That kind of thing.'

Robin had put on his demob suit, which had very narrow lapels on the jacket, and demob shirt, whose bright blue stripes had been printed on one side of the material only. His demob tie he had rejected, without having tried it, as having already started to come apart, or perhaps having never fully cohered, but demob socks and shoes were on his feet. So garbed, for the first and very likely last time, he was sitting opposite his mother in the drawing-room at home. The place was marvellously unchanged, with its upright piano, perhaps less shiny than it had once been, pelmet and sort of velvet curtains and occasional table, at the centre of which there stood a glass bowl subtly different from the one that had stood there in his boyhood, too subtly for him to have defined the difference even if he had wanted to. Now he was free of it he felt affectionate towards it, and half believed he had had some good times within its buff-papered walls. He thought that, whatever might have been the fact of his father's condition, he had done the proper thing by trying to persuade his mother that whatever was wrong with the old boy was containable and temporary. Both her character and her position made her fear the worst, and Robin would have gone over to where she sat and bent down and taken her in his arms if he had not felt that doing so would have heightened her fear.

Eventually his father's key was to be heard at the front door as he had heard it so many hundreds of times in the past. But was it just as before? Yes yes; it was only because he had paid full attention to the sound for once that he had fancied there was hesitation in it, and what if there had been? Exactly the same reasoning applied to what seemed the over-long time his father was taking over his arrival, before showing himself in front of his wife and son. Here he was at last.

'Hallo, Dad.'

'Hallo, old boy, hardly got a glimpse of you this morning. Well, I must say you look pretty fit after your ordeal.'

But now that Mr Davies had the chance of a prolonged inspection of Robin's appearance he passed it over. There had been the kind of brief, stylised embrace between the two that might have recalled a French general half-way down a long line of winners of minor decorations, then a hardly less brief marital one.

'What sort of a day have you had, Tom?'

'Pretty fair, dear, thank you, much as usual. Phew, it was pretty hot and sticky in the train, I don't mind telling you, so I think I'll just go and have a quick sluice and brush-up and then we might all have a small drink. I want to hear all about it,' he said to Robin, 'the whole story,' and was gone.

'How do you think he seemed?' asked Mrs Davies after some seconds.

'I didn't get much of a chance this time either, but from what I saw of him I thought he seemed all right. A bit tired, but that's natural at his age and in this weather.'

Mrs Davies looked closely at her son. 'You do mean that, don't you?'

'Absolutely, of course I do, Mum, surely you know I wouldn't pull your leg about a thing like that.'

'Oh, what a relief. Sorry, dear. So your first impressions of him are more or less all right. It's hard to tell if somebody's changed when you see them every day. Now I'll go and put the potatoes on and you can have a proper look at him.'

Before she moved, however, she frowned suddenly and compressed her lips and pressed a hand against her side. Robin stepped across and put his arms round her. 'What's the matter, Mum?'

'Just one of my twinges. Yes, I know a bit about stomach acid from my own side of the fence.'

'Have you seen the doctor?'

'I got some pills from the chemist. They're only twinges. This one's gone now.'

'I can't have you and Dad going sick at the same time.'

'I haven't told your father, it would only worry him.'

'Well, it is worrying, you know, Mum.'

'Don't talk nonsense, dear, it's only just a little twinge every so often when I forget to take the pills.'

Left alone for a moment, Robin was mildly struck by the thought that it had taken a considerable twinge of pain (not a little one, to go by his mother's reaction) to get him to embrace her. He had not always been so disinclined for physical contact with somebody as close to him as that. Or had he? If he had, perhaps that made him undemonstrative, restrained, tough. Alternatively it went to show he was a cold bloody fish, everything Blake and Lawrence would have hated.

These speculations vanished when Mr Davies came back into the drawing-room. Robin got his proper look at him then, but it was hardly needed. There was something in his father's face, no specific physical detail, just something hard to find words for that led straight to words like discomfort, distress, disquiet and further. He gave Robin a quick, humourless, almost furtive glance, as if he had in his possession a valuable secret he was nervous of giving away. But quite soon he was asking questions about Robin's repatriation in the first weeks of peace in Europe, what had followed it, what would or might follow that. After a few minutes Mrs Davies reappeared and Robin made drinks for the three of them from the bottle of gin he had brought with him. Then as prearranged, he took his parents out to dinner at the hotel down the road. There was not much to eat and Mr Davies ate little of what there was, but when he complained of indigestion it was in his traditional style, complete with insinuations that his stomach and other organs were cast in a finer mould than the average person's and hence more likely to become upset. By the time they were back in the house, Robin was beginning to believe that his mother's fears were excessive and that he himself had let his imagination fall under their influence.

She took herself off to bed before very long, leaving the two men downstairs.

'Would you like a drink, Dad? I brought a bottle of Scotch too, you remember.'

'I don't think I'd better with my wretched tummy, old boy, thanks all the same. Don't let that stop you having one, though.'

'No fear.'

When Robin came back to the drawing-room with his weak Scotch-and-water, his father put down the evening paper. 'You'll be off to Oxford soon, I suppose?'

'I thought the day after tomorrow. I don't want to leave it too long.'

'No, I suppose not.'

Robin guessed from his tone that they were about to start on what with luck would be a short exchange about Nancy without mentioning her, a convention that over the years had become rigidly observed. 'I've got to see about next term, talk to my tutor and so on.'

'Oh yes. You are set on going up again, are you? I remember you telling me you'd already done enough exams for a degree.'

'Only for a pass degree. Not good enough for what I have in mind for myself.'

'I see,' said Mr Davies, with a slight smile and lift of the hand that meant he might have expected his son to invoke some clever fornication-furthering technicality.

'I've got an advantage over the chaps who are still in uniform and serving their country in the Far East or . . .' Robin stopped speaking because in that short time he had seen his father's expression revert all the way and unmistakably to the despondency of a couple of hours before. He had only a few seconds to wait.

His father said, 'Of course it's marvellous that you're free and home after all this time and that's the important thing. But it's come at a specially, a specially opportune time for me. Now, you've gathered I've been having some trouble with my digestion, the hot risings I've been used to and losing my appetite after the first few mouthfuls of a meal. Yes, well, this afternoon at the office just as I was getting ready to come home . . .' In a gesture not at all uncharacteristic of him he went to the door and quietly opened it, listened, shut it and went back to his chair. 'Promise me you won't breathe a word of this to your mother.'

'I wouldn't dream of it.'

'Well, suddenly I had to throw up. I only just got to the lavatory in time. And when I . . . vomited, it was mostly blood. Blood with froth in it. Never happened before. I mean I have thrown up a couple of times recently, but I've had stomach upsets in the past. But not this. There must be something seriously wrong. What do you think?'

Robin had been trying to summon his resources. He spoke consideringly. 'Well, as you know I'm no sort of doctor, but what this sounds like to me is a burst or ruptured gastric ulcer. You're lucky to be still up and about with that. You'd better see the doc right away. There's probably more of the same sort of thing to come.'

'I don't like that fellow Musgrave.'

'He's supposed to be very good. If you really can't stand him, go to his partner or, I don't know who, but some doctor or other, tomorrow if possible.'

'Who told you Musgrave was good?'

'Mum, of course. Yes, naturally we discussed you, you and your acid stomach, what would you expect?'

'It'll worry her.'

'She's worried already, Dad. Again, what on earth do you expect?'

'She'll be even more worried if I go dashing off to the quack first thing in the morning.'

'Not as worried as she'd be if you have to be rushed to hospital in an ambulance for an emergency blood-transfusion. I think you should tell her everything you've told me. It'd be worse for her to realise she's not being told the whole story.'

'M'm. I'll think about it. How do I look to you?'

'You look troubled, which isn't surprising. Apart from that you look just like your old self.'

Mr Davies gazed at his son, who was grateful for having been able to tell a version of the truth. 'What do you think is wrong with me?'

'I don't know, Dad. Not being a doctor.'

This time Robin was grateful to his father for not insisting on an answer to the question he had asked, saying only, 'I'm sorry to have inflicted all this on you.'

'Don't be ridiculous. I wish I could have done more than just listen.'

'You have done more. For one thing you've helped me to make up my mind to go to the doctor as soon as possible.'

As it turned out, the unpopular Dr Musgrave was away and it was his partner, Dr Wells, who arranged to see Mr Davies the very next morning at ten-thirty, when he had an opportune cancellation. Robin sat with his mother, whom his father had evidently confided in at some stage, and read the current issue of the *Daily Telegraph* with an intensity he had never before shown that journal. He could think of no other way of passing the next hour or so, and concluded that this was one of those times when you had little choice in what you were to do. His choice of seat was similarly dictated as one facing away from the front of the house and so not advertising excessive concern. But his mother was on her feet before key had finished entering lock. Robin followed her out into the hall. As soon as he saw his father he was sure his news was fifty-fifty or better.

'He was very serious and asked a lot of questions and made a lot of notes and I could tell he was *thinking*. And I suppose he examined me, though I hadn't any idea what he was after from about half-way through. He made a telephone call, but I couldn't even make out who he was talking to. At the end he said, "Well, Mr Davies, I can't tell you for certain what's wrong with you without some proper tests, but this much I can say. Everything so far is consistent with your suffering from the results of excessive gastric acidity, what we call a primal ulcerous condition not uncommon in elderly people of your disposition. If that's the case, you have a difficult and painful ordeal ahead of you, but nothing worse." And he smiled, which he hadn't done till then. I must say I rather took to the fellow. Of course there'll be tests and X-rays and a strict diet and what not . . .'

Between then and the time fixed for Robin's departure for Oxford the next morning nothing of great significance happened, unless the delivery by post of a cyclostyled diet-sheet counted as that, so he left as arranged. For a time he had found it hard to think of anything much except his father's illness, but that now receded behind other preoccupations. The chief of these was Nancy, whom he proceeded to live with (in effect) at a lodging-house run by a rather disreputable landlady from Cardiff who also dyed her hair and painted her fingernails. He went at different times to visit the

Dean and the Senior Tutor of his college where they lived with their families in North Oxford, and his own tutor, who seemed genuinely puzzled to hear that he had not used the months of his captivity to extend his knowledge of the classical authors. In a gingerly fashion he put his nose into the works of Thucydides, Tacitus and others he had thought he had some knowledge of already, and was remarkably complacent on finding how much he had remembered.

One morning of the week following his return to Oxford he went into the porter's lodge to pick up any mail and found a note addressed to him in the porter's hand. It said that George Davies would be in Oxford that morning about 11.00 am and would Mr Robin Davies please leave a message here saying where he could be found. Robin complied and after a few minutes' walk entered by its open front door the lodging-house where he (in effect) lived with Nancy. A woman's voice, not Nancy's, called an enquiry from the basement.

'It's me, Robin, Mrs Pendry. My brother's coming to see me in about half an hour.'

'I'll send him up, love. No trouble, is there?'

'Thanks. Not that I know of.'

None that he could readily imagine, either. Trouble these days meant Davies senior, but, as established by telephone the previous evening, pills, diet and X-rays comprised the only sort of news there. If there had been something even more recent, it would hardly have reached George first. But what did he want? Robin tried to dismiss the matter for the time being and to read a none too lively work on Attic stage conventions.

After little more than half an hour, George arrived. The two brothers greeted each other affectionately. George glanced round the smallish bed-sitter.

'I'm looking at Nancy's joint, I presume,' he said. 'I don't see much of your stuff lying about the place.'

'Correct. These are unlicensed digs and mustn't be let to members of this university, sir.'

'Nevertheless you manage to put in quite a lot of your time in this one.'

'My room in college is even tinier than this. Depressing, too.'

'Not to mention being unlicensed for what you get up to in here. By the way where is Nancy at the moment?'

'Off being a kennel–maid in Botley. It's marvellous to see you, George, but are you passing through, dropping in for a chat or what?'

In an instant George's expression became as grim as Robin or anyone else could have wanted. He reached into his pocket and drew out a letter in an opened envelope. 'I suppose I might have read you this over the telephone, but I thought it might be more suitable if you had the chance of reading it for yourself.'

Dear Mr Davies (Robin read),

I am the general practitioner of medicine whom your father, Thomas Owen Davies, recently consulted with reference to digestive distress he has been experiencing. At my advice he underwent various tests the results of which have just now come to hand.

I am sorry to have to tell you that in my opinion he is suffering from an inoperable carcinoma of the stomach which may already have begun to found secondary growths in adjacent organs such as the liver. Although some alleviation of the grosser symptoms is certainly practicable, his active life is by my calculation to be measured in weeks rather than months, but I have to add that as always the most confident prognosis can be refuted by events.

In my estimation, based on several meetings with your father, it would not be advisable to tell him what I have told you. If he believes me he thinks he has some sort of ulcerous condition which can be relieved by medication. It also seems to me to be unnecessary for the moment to let your mother know the truth.

Perhaps you would get in touch with me soon to decide what is best to be done.

Yours very truly,
G.H. Wells

'Have you been on to this chap?' Robin asked his brother.

'That came this morning. I thought I'd have a word with you first. It's a shock, isn't it, even if you've seen it coming.'

'How did you manage to see it coming?'

'I rang, I often ring on a Sunday evening these days to keep in touch. Mum told me Dad had been poorly, and I thought, well, it doesn't matter what I thought.'

'Would you like a cup of Mrs Pendry's coffee, or shall we go to the pub?'

'I'd say the pub, but will it be open?'

'They open at ten here. Market town, see.'

In the pub, which was small but otherwise almost empty, Robin fetched pints of bitter. What with his gratuity and the money his college had advanced him against his government grant, he was at any rate less badly off than he had been before the war. But he would have come here for a glass of water to get out somewhere that had people in it, even people like the parsonical landlord or the diminutive fellow from the nearby cabmen's shelter who was slowly shifting a half of Burton at the other end of the bar. The brothers silently toasted each other.

'Does this make you wish you hadn't said all those nasty things about him over the years?' asked Robin. 'I know I've said them too.'

'I've thought about that,' said George, accepting a cigarette. 'Not really, no. I can't remember them all, of course, but I doubt if I'd feel I ought to withdraw more than a couple of them. Especially not the ones about him being a bloody old Welsh preacher at heart. But none of it seems to matter now. And, well, if it hadn't been that it'd most likely have been something else.'

'Yeah. Do we bring Margery into this?'

'I've had time to think about that too, and the answer's no, or I suppose I mean not yet. I see more of her than you do, and whenever it came to her turn to do anything she'd be too busy with those bloody kids of hers. And I can't stand that miserable bearded bugger of a husband who always looks as if he's going to touch you for a fiver even when he conceivably isn't. We'll tell them later.'

'All right. What about Mum?'

'Well, what about Mum?'

'This thing the quack said in his letter about it not being a good time to let her know that it's what it is. I mean, she'll have to be told sooner or later. I said to Dad last week, it'd be a bloody sight worse for her, suspecting things are being kept from her and wondering what they are. She's no fool. People in her position aren't likely to be.'

'No they're not. I agree with that.' Frowning, George looked into space and Robin wondered why on earth he had ever thought his brother looked like his father. 'Now I imagine we're in for more of phase one, during which he goes on being fed medication for what he's supposed to think is an ulcer, and then an unknown amount of phase two, which consists of him being in a hospital or nursing-home being looked after until he dies.'

'Yeah.'

There was silence while each of them tried to consider this prospect.

'How easy is it for you to get away for a morning or a whole day?' asked George.

'Easy as winking with a bit of notice.'

'Good. I'll arrange to see this doctor fellow and let you know and we'll go down there together, agreed? Good. Let's have another.'

'M'm. You don't suppose this cove has got it wrong, do you, and it is just a stomach upset?'

'That too . . . No. Other people will have looked at those X-rays. Of course they could still have all got it wrong and let's pray they have, but no. Eh?'

'That stuff in his letter about it being just his opinion and the rest of it, it must be second nature to a doctor to go on like that. Do you think he knows, I mean Dad?'

George shook his head a great deal before replying. 'He won't know what he thinks. It won't be one thing, anyway. Some of the time he'll think he's got it, and some of the time he'll think he hasn't got it. Especially the first. I'll get through this one now and then I really have to be off.'

'Can't you stay for lunch? It's Nancy's half-day at the kennels.'

'I can't, it was hard enough getting the morning off. I'm sorry to miss Nancy, though. Tell her I was asking after her. How is she?'

'Very fit. Looking after those bloody dogs seems to agree with her. I have to let her tell me about them in return for being told about the pair of lesbians who run the place. Funny sort of pair they are, I've been up there a couple of times. They're quite young but I can't see what either of them sees in the other. But I suppose that's different.'

'Oh, we all know what a cracking hetero you are, Master Robin. And seeing as how that's what you are, why don't you marry young Nancy? Why haven't you already? Why hasn't someone else by this time? You'd look a bloody fool if someone did.'

'I know. I don't want to be tied down. The thought scares me.'

'Oh, for Christ's sake, what have you been reading? What does she think of the set-up? She's not the sort of girl to put up with it indefinitely.'

'No.'

'And what about her parents, if they're at all like your description of them, what do they think they're—'

'Just shut up a minute, George, will you? Oddly enough there are seven reasons why they let this go on as it is, I was counting them up the other day.' Robin ticked them off on his fingers. 'They like me, especially the old girl. Gallant war record, which you know and I know consisted of just not quite being reduced to the ranks and never actually deserting, but the Bennetts don't. For all they know I couldn't support a wife. Their attention's pretty well occupied with Nancy's sister Megan, who's drunk all the time and has a seven-year-old boy and no husband. Nancy would never go near them again, or they're afraid she wouldn't, if they tried to break up her and me. That's five. What the bugger is six, I could have sworn, oh yes, the old boy's poorly and mustn't get excited. Not as good as seven, which is they know what's going on according to Nancy but they don't want to be told. Which now I come to think of it . . .'

'Has a bearing on other matters too. Oh dear. I think I could just about squeeze in another half if I get a move on.'

Soon afterwards Robin walked his brother down to the station. As soon as George had left him, all thought of Nancy vanished and what was going to happen to his father completely occupied Robin's attention. He found himself unable even to bear in mind that so far the outcome was still not quite certain, let alone to try to consider the odds. Nor could he think about what difference, if any, the prospect might make or had already made to the whole of his feelings about his father. He kept visualising, as clearly as if it had been a good photograph, something that to his knowledge he had never yet seen, the old man's face caught in an expression of extreme fear. The rest was all shocked emotion, expressible only in what were not so much words as cries – no, please, help him, save him, make it easy, make it not happen, but most of all how terrible, how impossible to endure. It seemed to Robin no more possible that he himself would ever be able to think of anything else.

But on his again approaching Mrs Pendry's front door other concerns, other importances came rushing back. Without much in the way of volition on the way here, he now thought he would go in and find his book and do his best to read it, perhaps until it was time to go and meet Nancy for lunch. But when he got to the room she rented he found her already in it, evidently engaged in brushing her hair.

'You're back early,' he said.

'They sent me off early. I thought we could . . . What's the matter?'

'My dad's very ill.'

She put her hairbrush down and moved over to the bed, which was made and covered. 'Come and tell me about it.'

'There's not much to tell.'

'Tell me what there is.'

He had not reached the end of what there was to tell when he tried to say that Davies senior might or might not know how ill he was, and found he could not say the words. After a moment's thought he laid his head against the upper part of her chest and she held him tight. Neither spoke for a minute or two. Then he started kissing her on the mouth, at first with no more than affection, then passionately. Nancy seemed to hold back to begin with, but before long responded. Without undressing, without even taking the cover off the bed, with the minimum of delay they made love. That too took only a short time.

'I wasn't expecting that to happen,' said Nancy.

'Neither was I.'

And he had not, at least up to about the moment when he had stopped telling her how his father saw his illness. Robin's desire had been complete and genuine and his enjoyment total. Nevertheless the suspicion occurred to him that he had had some extraneous motive too, apart from that of blotting out his preoccupation with his father. Now that his mind was no longer distracted, that feeling returned for a while.

When it was agreed by all concerned that Thomas Davies's condition had reached a point where it could no longer be treated at home, a bed was found for him in a small nursing-home a few miles more distant from the centre of London than where he had lived. Since his wife had no money of her own, the cost of the bed for the first days was borne chiefly by his employers, with supplementary contributions from his children, with an option to extend the arrangement should this be required. Soon after his admission to the nursing-home, Mrs Davies and Robin went down there to visit him.

They found him in the end bed of a rather low-ceilinged but airy ward into which the afternoon sunlight penetrated. At the time of their visit the bed next to his was unoccupied, so that when the smiling young pink-uniformed nurse had left them, Robin and his mother were left virtually alone with the sick man. When he saw them approaching, he took off and hung up on a convenient hook a pair of earphones and greeted them almost with vivacity, making a large deprecating gesture when his wife laid on the bedside table a brown-paper bag of soft fruit and a drum of crystallised ginger. Robin put there a couple of paperbacked crime novels of the slightly superior English sort that his father was known to prefer.

'I'm rather in favour of this place,' said Mr Davies. He was closely shaved, wore smart new pyjamas with green and black stripes, and looked appreciably better than when Robin had seen him last, a couple of days before his arrival here. 'I don't know what they put in the dope they've been feeding me and pumping into me but it sure smartens me up,' he went on, dropping for the moment into his harrowing version of an American accent. 'I'm beginning to take an interest in life again.'

'How are you feeling, Tom?' asked Mrs Davies. 'How's the . . .?'

'The old tum? Put it this way, it isn't well yet by a long chalk, but it's streets ahead of what it was. I haven't got to force myself to eat any more.'

'Have they said anything about letting you out?'

'Nothing in the least definite, no. The nurse prattles gaily on about "when you're home again", but I reckon that's standard stuff to keep the troops' spirits up. Of course, at places like this they can make sure you take your pills. I reckon that's part of the reason why they got me in. But that's enough about me to be going on with. What's the news of Margery and that devil brood of hers?'

On their way out of the ward, Robin's mother said to him, 'Wasn't it sweet, the way he thanked us so, so warmly for taking the trouble to pop in? As if we'd had to come all the way from Australia or somewhere. He certainly seemed better, didn't you think, better than he was, I mean.'

'No question about it,' said Robin firmly. There was no question in his mind but that his father had seemed better. Whether he had really taken a turn for the better was another matter. All the same, the slender hope that Dr Wells might have been mistaken in his diagnosis, if only in part, had expanded a little.

When the two reached the entrance hall, the young woman at the Enquiries counter looked up and said, 'Excuse me – Mr Robin Davies? Mr Davies, one of our staff would like a brief word with you in the office, if you would. Go to the back here, turn left and it's the third door on the left. Thank you.'

But having gone in at the designated door, he found himself not in any expected kind of office, but in what looked more like a small consulting-room with files, a glass cupboard and a desk. Sitting behind the desk, rising now to his feet, was the tall saturnine figure of Dr Wells, recognisable to Robin from his and his brother George's visit to his surgery two or three weeks earlier.

'Thank you for coming in, Mr Davies,' said Wells in his incongruously genial tones. 'Please sit down. Forgive the air of conspiracy, I just happened to be about when you happened to be visiting your father. This will only take a moment. How did you think he looked?'

'Much better, I thought.'

'Yes, he does look better in certain respects. His illness is in remission, but I'm afraid I must tell you that any improvement is purely temporary. As expected the – forgive me if I use plain language – the tumour in his stomach has put out secondary tumours in his liver and probably other organs. Naturally, we're all doing everything we can, but there's going to be a limit to that, as I'm sure you appreciate.'

'Yes, doctor, I do, at least I'm trying to. Can you give me an idea of when you expect that limit to be reached? How long has he got?'

'Weeks, Mr Davies. I can't tell you how many, but not very many. I repeat I wish very much I could give you more hopeful news, but I see it as my duty to tell you the truth in these circumstances. You have my number, please don't hesitate to telephone if you need information or anything else I can provide.'

'Thank you, doctor. What about my mother, what's she going to be told? Surely she oughtn't to be left in suspense?'

'The most painful suspense is less painful than knowing the worst. Let her be kept in suspense as long as possible.'

'Maybe,' said Robin. 'Does my father know the worst?'

'He can't know it, but he may have guessed it. He hasn't asked me and I haven't told him.' The doctor's voice softened. 'He strikes me as one of those people who, for more than one reason, prefer not to discuss the matter. And now I mustn't keep you, Mr Davies. Most fortunate, our running into each other like this. My regards to your brother.'

As soon as Robin's mother caught sight of him he smiled and shook his head several times. He walked up the hall to her and said, 'Nothing, just a couple of forms they wanted me to sign. To do with their accounts.'

'Oh. Was that all it was.'

'Yes, honestly.'

She did not press the point.

The next morning she sent him back to Oxford, saying he must not miss the beginning of term, and they would talk on the telephone every evening, and her woman friends would take care of her, and Margery was coming over soon, and she would be all right. Robin was unwilling to leave but thought his mother would find female company of more actual help, and also rather wanted to stay but not as much as he wanted to be off— all that without bringing Nancy into it. So he went and got in the train to Oxford.

Some days later Dr Wells telephoned, starting off by saying he had tried to make contact with Robin's brother George but had been unable to.

'Will I do instead, Dr Wells?'

'Thank you, Mr Davies, you'll do very well instead. I regret having to say that your father's condition is reaching a point at which he'll have to be put on to rather stronger drugs than we've been giving him so far. The new ones will probably have the effect of making him less lucid in what he says, less able to make sense and to follow what others say to him. That being so, or likely, would you, and or your brother, want a, what shall I say, a reasonably coherent talk with him, I expect you're busy but it boils down to the sooner the better.'

'What have you told my mother?'

'If you agree, I propose to tell her what I've just told you, no more, no less, when she comes to see me at my surgery this afternoon. But it's my belief that she now knows how matters stand and . . . has accepted the situation. If that conflicts with your own view, remember that people often behave differently in front of doctors from how they behave to members of their family, however close to them they may be.'

'I see,' said Robin. 'By all means tell my mother about the new drugs. Dr Wells, if it doesn't sound disloyal or anything, I'd like to see my father when she's not there, if possible.'

'I understand. If you can arrange to go in to see him at say four-thirty, I'm expecting your mother in my surgery at that time.'

'Thank you, I'll see him then. Well, doctor, I don't suppose I'm as busy as you are, so I'll take on the job of letting my brother know what you've told me.'

'Most kind. Good luck, Mr Davies.'

Robin tried George's number several times before he left for London, but got no reply. He wrote Nancy a note telling her where he would be. Sitting in the train he caught himself wishing he had been less informative in that note of his, because in that case he would have been able to turn tail and avoid visiting his father, which he felt very much like doing, without having to try to justify himself to Nancy. But he stopped wishing along those lines when he saw that there was no getting out of that visit whatever he might have felt about it. Besides, he could not have faced explaining to Dr Wells and hearing him say he understood.

He arrived at the nursing-home at four-twenty, checked that there was nobody with his father and was shown into a room with a single bed in it, in or on which Mr Davies lay. Robin noticed at once that the whites of his father's eyes were discoloured in a faintly yellowish direction and that the skin on his forehead and cheeks were similarly affected. Besides this he looked rather more worn since Robin had seen him two days previously.

'How are you, Dad?' he said because he could think of nothing else to say.

'All the better for seeing you, old chap. Very nice of you to come along. I expect you've heard I haven't been too well and don't look like making a dramatic recovery yet awhile kind of thing. I think if you don't mind I'll stay as I am, because do you know I find it very tiring these days, sitting up in bed the way you're supposed to. There's a stool somewhere under the foot of the bed for you to park your arse if you feel inclined.'

Robin found the stool and sat on it. From his father's weakened voice and in a different way from its tone, it was obvious that he would never be all right again, but not how long he might continue as he was.

'Your mother was here earlier on. She's tough, you know, that woman, as I've found over the years. Oh, I don't mean hard, of course I don't, you only have to look at her, but she's got a lot of backbone. I wish I had half as much. I realise I've led her a dance now and again, getting all wrought up when there was no need to, but she's never once complained. There has been one thing, though, I've never given her cause to worry about, well, she knows I've never had eyes for any other woman but her. When I was young that'd have been nothing out of the way I suppose.

'One thing we have been lucky about, your mother and I, and that's our offspring. Just between ourselves I've never seen a great deal to Margery. A bit too self-centred to suit me. I know it's a thing with women, but Margery, she goes rather far in my opinion. Still, fair play, she's a good enough mother and housewife and she puts up with that husband of hers, which must take some doing now and then. Could that be a talent that runs in the family, do you think?'

His father smiled slightly, closed his eyes and lay so still that Robin thought he might have fallen asleep, but then he opened his eyes again and said in a stronger voice than before, 'Do you see much of George these days?'

'I see him occasionally.'

'A good lad that. You know, solid. I'm delighted he's settled down at last with that nice Elizabeth. I hope he drops in here for a moment before too long.'

Robin said, 'He told me over the phone he'll be coming along if not tomorrow then the next day. I'm sure he'll come.'

'Yes, so am I sure. You're a good lad too. You and I, we've had our troubles and misunderstandings but it hasn't been too bad, has it?'

'I should say not. We've both of us respected the other chap's point of view, that's the important thing, and where would I be without what you've taught me?'

'I'm glad to hear you say that, Robin. You've been a good son to me, better than I've deserved, but I can't help feeling I haven't been much of a father to you. I feel I've let you down in all sorts of ways.'

'What nonsense, you mustn't even think that.'

'I'm very afraid it's true. Oh, I'm all too well aware I've talked a lot of perfect piffle, subjected you to all manner of out-of-date guff, and not only that, I realise there were times when I've been too hard on you, though it was all done for the best . . .' Mr Davies shut his eyes tight for a moment and gasped a couple of times, but the spasm of pain, if such it was, soon ended. When he went on, his distress seemed to come from his thoughts rather than anything physical. 'I don't seem to have ever been able to make any money for much more than necessities, none to spare for you, and I know how that puts restraints on a youngster's freedom.'

'Look here, Dad, you're not to start apologising. I've no complaints, I've done all right for myself.'

'It's a bit late in the day now, isn't it? I'm afraid I've let you down over more important things than money. I'm not blaming anybody, you understand, but when I got away from my upbringing I went too far in the other direction. I reckoned I'd had more than my fair share of training and doctrine and guidance, and so, well, I decided you shouldn't have any, I wasn't going to give you any. I didn't even send you to Sunday school, which would have been better than nothing. There are other things I wish I'd done different, but you'll have to fill in what they are for yourself, because what with all this nattering on and talking tripe, I seem to have got awfully tired all of a sudden, so . . .'

'Of course.' Robin got up from his stool and pushed it back under the foot of the bed. 'I'll pop in to see you again tomorrow.'

'If you're sure you can fit it in. But just for now – do you forgive me? For not sending you to Sunday school?'

'Dad, there's nothing to forgive.'

His father's face and voice took on some of their old faintly theatrical sternness when he said, 'Oh yes there is, Robin, as you well know.'

'In that case I do forgive you. For not sending me to Sunday school and for everything else.'

'Thank you for saying that, old chap.' Mr Davies looked as if he had something to add, but instead he smiled and looked away for a moment and shut his eyes.

After waiting a short time, Robin went out. In the hall he walked up to the Enquiries girl to ask if he could use a telephone, but burst into tears without uttering a word. She or another led him a short distance to a small empty room with several hard chairs in it and left him. It seemed to him that what made him cry was regret, or regrets, ranging from twenty years before to two minutes. When he had finished crying he found a telephone and finally got through to George.

Robin saw his father twice more. The first time, the sick man recognised him and beamed at him, gripping him by the upper arms. Somebody had taken out his father's false teeth. The second time, Mr Davies failed to give any sign of recognition and seemed mildly disconcerted or troubled, though he made no attempt to say anything.

Apart from an estranged and partly crazed elder sister, Mrs Davies had no kin of her own generation. Robin stayed with her for a couple of days after his father's death, moving rather uncomfortably about a house never empty of one or another or more than one woman friend from near and not so near. He never saw his mother alone in that time, nor did she evidently try to shed her companions for such a purpose. He came to think that, instead of his becoming closer to her as he grew up, the two of them had in fact less to say to each other than in his boyhood. Perhaps George, on the spot when needed, but now firmly back north of the river, had found the same thing. In the end Robin yielded to his mother's earnest assurances that she was all right, could manage, and moved back to Oxford.

'Do you want to talk about your father?' asked Nancy the next day.

'Not really,' said Robin. 'I haven't got used to the idea of him being dead yet.'

'That's going to take some time, I expect.'

'I've never been able to make up my mind what I think of him.'

'Perhaps now you will.'

'Of course, eventually he might simply fade into the background as far as I'm concerned.'

'Anyway, you must still be feeling very upset and suffering from shock.'

'I was when I'd just had my last talk with him but I'm over that stage by this time. There's only the funeral now and that's not till Thursday.'

Nancy swallowed noisily. 'I've got something to tell you. It's not very nice but the sooner you know about it the better.'

'You're pregnant,' he said at once.

'Yes. I'm sorry, I didn't mean to be and I'm not absolutely sure, but I am really, otherwise I wouldn't have dreamed of saying anything to you even now. I've always been pretty irregular, have been ever since I started. I really am sorry, Robin.'

They were in bed at Mrs Pendry's. It was the early evening of a windy, rather chilly day and, whereas they had gone where they were for amorous reasons in the first place, they had stayed there for the sake of going on being snug as well as out of affection and laziness. As soon as he guessed Nancy's news, there had sprung up in Robin's mind a tiny simulacrum of his father shaking its head and wagging its index finger and telling him that that just showed how no one could go on flouting decent standards of behaviour with impunity and that sooner or later, etc, and he had even had time to begin drafting a stroppy retort when he remembered that his father, being dead, was no longer in a position to formulate even the mildest dissatisfaction with his son's conduct. After fully understanding that, he waited another moment or two before trying a smile.

'Don't apologise, my love,' he said, 'if it's anybody's fault it's as much mine as yours. Let's get that quite clear at the start.'

She found his hand and squeezed it. 'Well, that time it might have been.'

'What time?'

'The time I, you know, got pregnant. You remember you'd just seen your brother and heard the news that your dad was very ill, and I'd come back earlier than usual, and one thing led to another and, well, it happened very quickly and we didn't take precautions.'

'You mean I didn't take precautions.'

'I suppose I do. I remember thinking it was like something out of a book, one life ending and another one perhaps starting. I remember thinking it'd probably be all right, we'd been careless before and nothing had happened.'

Robin's body-temperature apparently went up several degrees in a few seconds. His conduct on the occasion referred to had indeed been like something out of a book, a deeply, irremediably pissy book by D. H. Lawrence out of Bernard Shaw and celebrating the dark gods of the abdomen and the bleeding Life Force. He too remembered something from those few minutes, how at the end of them it had crossed his mind that he had acted as he had partly for some less obvious motive than desire to escape or simple amorousness. Well, he knew now what it had been and much comfort might it bring him.

'I'm sorry, Robin, really I am,' said Nancy.

He managed to reply more or less calmly, 'Don't be, it was my doing. No, I was trying to think what's best to do next. I suggest the first thing is to get it confirmed that you're pregnant. After all, you still might not be.'

'I have been sick a couple of mornings, but of course you're right.' She withdrew her hand from his. 'I can go to the outpatients at the hospital. Easy.'

Looking at her propped on one elbow a little apart from him, Robin needed no book or other aid to notice Nancy's expression or guess her feelings: serious, even stern, intent on responsible behaviour, also upset, still ashamed, frightened of more than one thing. He said, 'I want to tell you this – whatever happens I won't go away, I won't leave you, I won't let you down, ever. I know I haven't promised you anything before, well, I promise you that now.'

She came back at him with a rush, hugging him tightly even for the customarily tight hugger she had shown herself to be, kissing him with great zeal and earnestness, though not with any great passion. 'That's all right, then,' she said. 'Now you've promised that much I don't mind what happens or might happen, that is except me dying having the baby, and I don't think there's much danger of that these days. It only really happens in films, anyway.'

Robin had meant everything he had said in his promise to Nancy. He was greatly encouraged by the readiness with which she had believed him, thinking it went to show that when he was being honest his honesty shone through. It was only later that he saw the force of the rider to that proposition, namely that when he was being dishonest his dishonesty must shine through as pellucidly. Not that he could at the moment foresee any need for successful dishonesty, he just knew enough about life or about himself by this time to be reasonably sure one would be along soon.

On general grounds, his father's funeral might have been tipped as a likely occasion. The evening before, Nancy turned up to announce that, whether or not they decided it would be a good idea for her to accompany him to it, she could not in any case do so because one of the Botley old girls was laid up. In addition, she, Nancy, was indisputably pregnant.

With plenty to occupy his thoughts on the way, Robin went off to his college, where he meant to return to its library an excessively learned work on tragedy that someone else had said he wanted. On putting his nose routinely into the porter's lodge beforehand, he was approached by the porter, a well-built man said to have reached the rank of major in the Royal Marines before returning to Oxford with the rank of porter. This man told Robin civilly enough that he had just shown a gentleman across to his room.

'Oh Christ,' said Robin, remembering. 'How long ago?'

'Ten minutes, sir. Fifteen at the outside.'

'Oh Christ. Thanks, Dick.'

The visitor was Embleton. Robin had read in some university news-sheet that his old friend had been let out of uniform just in time for the start of the autumn term, and had sent a note asking him round for sherry on this once-distant evening. Seen for the first time after half a dozen years, he still gave an impression of tallness and dark good looks, though his hair had shrivelled away at the temples and he seemed in general quite a bit older than Robin, his exact contemporary. His manner now, newly snatched back from the brink of being stood up, showed that his famous tact was in good repair. No, he had had to wait no time at all; what a sensible idea to walk over to the common-room and sample the sherry there.

As they crossed the quad, two passing freshmen gawped and whispered. 'Very healthy, that,' said Robin. 'The Lower Third in awe of a couple of bloods with school colours for cricket and rugger. Gives them some kind of standard to aim at, if you see what I mean.'

'You mustn't make fun of them,' said Embleton. 'For all they know we've been out there getting shot at while they've been safe at home eating cream buns round the study fire.'

'A real gulf between the generations. I'll have you know that nobody got a fair chance of a shot at me at any stage.'

'They never even saw me. I had a Grade 4 chest apparently, no trouble breathing but it kept me in the Education Corps. At least you were a POW.'

'Dead cushy, mate, I swear. Ate like a king. Didn't drink much admittedly, but I reckon that was all for the best, don't you?'

When they both had glasses of sherry in their hands and were sitting at the quiet end of the common-room, Embleton said, 'Somebody told me you'd had some bad news.'

'Yeah, my dad went off just the other day, cancer of the stomach and elsewhere. Lucky to be over and out so soon, according to the rather decent doctor. But not much fun any way you look at it.'

'Have you done the funeral yet?'

'It's tomorrow.'

Robin did not in the least mind being questioned on this point. In fact, the more of it the better, in that it took up time that might otherwise have been spent in questioning him on the subject of Nancy. He had entirely forgotten until he reappeared in the flesh fifteen minutes before, and only hazily remembered now, that Embleton had had some hand in introducing him to Nancy and had emphatically cautioned him against even trying to enter into the very sort of relationship with her that he had enjoyed on and off almost ever since. But then probably the entire issue had passed from old Emble's mind.

No sooner had Robin reached this heartening conclusion than Embleton asked him, 'What happened to that nice girl Nancy something you met in my room that time?'

'Oh, we're still together, or together again.'

Embleton grinned. 'Together?'

'Yes. You know.'

'Yes, Robin, I know. It's no business of mine, but you're telling me you and Nancy are still together after all these years and obviously you haven't married her and presumably she hasn't married anybody else, is that right?'

'Yes. I know it sounds unlikely.'

'It does sound almost inconceivable, given an attractive and also straightforward girl such as she obviously is, except on one assumption, which before you ask is that, whether you like it or not, she's in love with you, which by—'

'I say, do you really think she is?' Robin was naively pleased for a moment before thoughts of marriage and then of pregnancy and then of marriage again came crowding in.

'To quote you just now, I know it sounds unlikely, but I really do. I was going to say a girl like that takes love very seriously, not just as a bit of fun. But still, I don't suppose you want to go into the whole thing now, or possibly ever. I'm sorry I poked my nose in. All I was really after was to make sure you'd got somebody to go to your funeral with.'

'For one reason or another Nancy won't be coming along. But my brother George whom you've met, he's going to be there. I don't need anyone else.'

'Where's it happening? South London somewhere, that, isn't it? Who's going down there with you? You'll need somebody, believe me, there and back, especially back.'

'I'll make it all right on my own.'

'Oh, you'll make it in one piece, no doubt, but why let it be worse than it need be? I'll come with you. I could do with a day away from Oxford. I promise not to mention or refer to Nancy at any time. What train are we catching?'

At first Robin thought that his acquiescence merely went to show that he had a weaker will than Embleton, and was therefore the less egotistical and so perhaps in general the nicer of the two. Then he saw that in fact he would be glad of Embleton's company, not only on the journey. Most of life apparently consisted of being in a minority of one, a status worth going to some lengths to alleviate at events like your father's funeral. And old Emble had intrinsic merits too, seeming older than Robin, actually being richer and posher, also staid of demeanour, just the sort of fellow whom luck or good judgement could turn into a means of mitigating or even removing some minor disagreeableness like having to chat to an uncle or find an erstwhile business colleague a seat.

As things turned out the next morning, Embleton's relative richness came into play before the two reached their first destination. On understanding that he was expected to cross London by bus, sit in another train for a measurable time and then do some walking, he at once said that, instead of that, they would make the whole of the rest of their journey by taxi, and he would pay. To Robin, this was an unheard-of extravagance, but it seemed best to him to let matters take their course.

No doubt as some undiscussed part of his hostility to religious form, Mr Davies had clearly indicated a preference for the cremation of his remains over their burial. The crematorium was situated to the south-west of the suburb on the edge of what was still the countryside. Robin remembered going there before the war with a schoolmate whose mother had been killed in a street accident. He had disliked the place and found it frightening in some way not directly attached to its function. Faced with buff-coloured brick, it was a solid structure built on three sides of an asphalted square and adorned with details like spires and buttresses, which gave an ecclesiastical feeling not specific enough to offend anybody. Here and there were half-grown trees that, twenty years later, might with a bit of luck lend dignity and repose to the ambience.

On coming to the crematorium for the second time, Robin became aware that what he had found mysteriously unpleasant about the place before was its semblance to something he had at that stage never seen, and had still never seen except in news-reels and the like: an extermination centre on the east European model. At that moment, as he looked up, it seemed to him that the air above one the chimneys shook and rippled, perhaps at the upward passage of warm vapours. If he had been alone, instead of walking across the asphalt next to his mother with Embleton on her other side, he might have stopped in his tracks. But then suddenly his feeling of dread vanished and he was merely facing a small ordeal.

The three of them came up to the little knot of their fellow-mourners: George, Elizabeth, Margery, bearded Roger her husband, neighbours, cronies, relatives, a man or two from the dead man's office, another man or two of uncertain provenance, perhaps the local Ratepayers Association. Embleton came in very handy here, by prearrangement constantly introducing himself, stating his name in time to conceal Robin's total unawareness of other people's. Near the end of the round came someone he could not place at all, a woman in her early thirties with not much of a complexion but a good deal in the way of a figure, dressed for a funeral perhaps but only in the second place. She batted greenish eyes at him and sent him the kind of knowing smile he could have done with getting more often.

'Hallo Robin,' she said. 'Don't say you've forgotten me.'

The accent did it. 'Dilys!' he said, giving her a quick familial kiss on the cheek. Trying not to seem too ingenuous to be true, he said to Embleton, 'My cousin from Wales – my second cousin actually I suppose I should say.' He introduced Embleton, meanwhile keeping a weather eye open for Cousin Emrys, who he had heard was turning up but had instantly fallen out of his mind. There was the old fart, he soon saw, in three-quarter view, wearing his farmer's best suit, talking earnestly to a ratepayer or perhaps a chief clerk; long might he continue to do so. Robin went on agreeing with Dilys and Embleton that it was a sad day but there had been a good turn-out, until he saw an unidentifiable but unmistakable aunt-figure closing in from his other flank and went over to where his mother was standing with Margery and George. He laid his hand on her arm.

'How are you feeling, Mum?' he said without thought.

'I was just saying, dear, I wish your father had chosen to be buried after a proper church service instead of just having this done. I don't like this place.'

224

'He didn't believe in things like church services, Mum,' said George.

'No, he didn't, but he's not here, is he? I don't say I believe in it, but I'd like to have it done like that. So would a lot of other people, I shouldn't wonder.'

'You ought to have said before, Mum.'

'Oh no. No, I didn't mean I want it changed. We've all got to respect his wish. It wouldn't be right to go against his wish, he was very clear about it. It's up to us to do as he asked. It's our duty to do the last thing we can for him.'

Tears were running down Mrs Davies's face and the silence round her was spreading.

After a moment, Margery asked, 'Can I get you anything, Mum?'

'No thank you, dear. I would quite like to sit down.'

'Let's go inside.' George nodded to somebody out of Robin's view and the four of them began to move. George added, 'Have you got that piece of paper, Mum, you know, with the . . . That's it.' He took the typed half-sheet his mother passed him.

The temple or secular chapel or whatever it was that they entered would have held about two hundred persons if full. Those who came in now settled themselves on several rows of fixed benches with backs that would have reminded some people of pews, but of course were not pews. Down the middle of this auditorium there ran a sort of elevated wooden gangway that ended at a sort of stage with curtains of tussore or another shiny material drawn back. Near its top there rested on this gangway a closed coffin that looked to be of very recent manufacture. Not far from it in turn, and to one side, there stood a sort of unelevated pulpit sufficient to hold one occupant sitting or standing, and to this George made his way. Mrs Davies sat between her other two children. Bearded Roger, Elizabeth, Embleton were near. An indifferent recording of some archaic quasi-religious piece of music made itself heard for a minute or so, at the end of which time it was abruptly quenched. George got to his feet and silence fell.

'We are here to witness the cremation of Thomas Owen Davies,'

225

said George in a strong voice. 'That is as much as his expressed wish allows me to say. He strictly forbade any further pronouncement to be made on this occasion than the following lines of prose, the source of which he has not given.'

The principle defect of human life (George read) is not that it is short, nor even that when it ends, it ends for ever, but that from an early age we are aware of these unpleasant facts. Here is the final proof, if such a thing were needed, of the non-existence of God in any accepted sense. An impotent God or a wicked God remain available, though not to the present writer.

How should we behave, we who cannot believe in God? In prosperity, with kindness and self-restraint, in adversity, with patience and fortitude. We may notice that these good qualities are closely similar to what believers see as desirable, and we may admit that the one set may be historically derived from the other. We notice further that believers follow their precepts about as much or as little as we follow ours. But what of the most conclusive test of all?

Does apparent belief reduce the fear of death? No, no more than it reduces the grief of the bereaved. These things and many others being so, we may conclude that the difference between belief and unbelief is a mere matter of language. But perhaps that matter is not so mere. Is it seemly to articulate piffle?

'That's all,' said George from where he stood, and was seen to murmur a few inaudible words. He pressed some switch in front of him and the coffin, bumping slightly from time to time, made a slow progress down the gangway to the stage. When it had come to a stop the curtains closed and hid it from view.

'There were these two buttons set into the wood of that pulpit thing, not marked in any way but I was nearly sure the fellow had told me left for music, right for, well, the end of the proceedings. Thank God he and I between us got it right or the business would have been over even sooner than it was.'

'You did jolly well, George,' said Robin effusively. 'I'd have been absolutely petrified, standing up there in front of all those people.'

He spoke effusively for reasons that included his being well into his second gin and tonic in the private dining-room of a large pub that was evidently used to accommodating post-cremation lunch-parties. His mother, no longer weeping, no longer saying anything either, had been taken off by Margery and a local woman friend. In fact, of a company of fifteen or so only four were women, three assorted wives and Dilys. It was extraordinary, Robin considered, what a difference that girl had made to what would otherwise have been an occasion replete with melancholy and/or boredom. She had made it a better-than-bearable section of life simply by her presence, or if that was not quite true of the spirit in which he viewed her it was true to the letter of events so far. After recharging his glass he moved to her side, determining at the last minute to do so purposefully rather than by apparent chance.

'Nice of you to come all this way,' he said.

'Oh, I was in London in any case,' she said, and went on to speak of her husband's move to a job in marine insurance there without making it clear what part, if any, she played in his household.

'I expect you manage to get about quite a bit.'

'Not so much as you might think, perhaps. How about you?'

'Oh, so-so,' he said, wondering what on earth they were supposed to be talking about, as distinct from what they were talking about.

'I see that nice girl, is it Nancy, she's not with you today.'

'No,' he said heavily, sorrowfully, as if Nancy could hardly be expected to leave her iron lung or padded cell for such a frivolous outing.

'Do you still see her?'

'Well, yes, you could say that. But I manage to get to London quite a bit.'

'Do you like Indian cooking?'

When very hungry, he had quite enjoyed a couple of dishes

supposedly of that kind in Oxford. 'Oh, I'm mad about it,' he said.

'If you can let me have a bit of warning I'll do you a bhindi gosht you won't soon forget.'

'I'm looking forward to it already,' he said, and might perhaps have added something about stuffing her paratha for her had he thought of it in time. 'How do I get in touch with you?'

'I'll give you a number where you could leave a message. In a minute.'

They took their places at the table. To get himself next to Dilys there without resort to violence, Robin had to have Cousin Emrys on his other side. Well, at least it was somebody he knew. The old fellow was beginning to show his age, gone a little pouchy in the face, which was no less red than ever, and deaf in one ear, unfortunately the one further away from Robin. Very soon he was showing a half-grapefruit who was master. When he had nearly finished it he turned his head sharply and stared at Robin for a space. 'Don't you want your cherry?' he demanded.

'My what? I'm sorry, I don't think I—'

'Your cocktail cherry, *myn*. If you don't want it I'll give it a home. It is Cousin Robin, isn't it? Haven't seen you for years, boy.'

'It's very nice of you to have taken the trouble to come, as I was saying to—'

'I thought I should put in an appearance. Actually it's quite convenient for me, I had to come to London to see a bloke at the Ministry, but I'm afraid it means I'll have to rush off as soon as this is over.'

'Oh, well perhaps—'

'Hey, that was a funny old carry-on in that cremation place, wasn't it? What did you make of that extract or oration or whatever it was that your brother read out? Did . . . your poor father ever talk to you in that strain?'

'No. But it didn't surprise me that he'd chosen it for the occasion.'

'I wonder where he came across it. Of course, he used to read a lot, your father, didn't he? In a restless kind of way, as if he was looking for something he was afraid he'd never find. Pursued by shadows, he was. Not a happy man. Though I suppose this isn't quite the time to . . .'

'No, I suppose it isn't.'

Robin's attention was half distracted. Reviving old memories, a hand had brushed against his knee under the table. Confidently assuming it to be one of Dilys's, he had grasped it firmly, to hinder it from perhaps exploring further as much as to convey ardour. The infiltrating hand, having snatched itself irritably away, pushed into his own what felt very much like a small piece of paper. This he conveyed easily and unobtrusively to his jacket pocket. Good. He now had the number where he could leave a message for her. Splendid.

He looked up after this easy move to find Embleton's eye on him from the end of the table. Robin grinned ruefully and sketched a wave, and the other man's glance passed unhurriedly on, and short of telepathy there was no real possibility of his guessing what was afoot. Nevertheless in that passing moment Robin got from somewhere else an unwelcome reminder of who and what he had left behind in Oxford. It displeased him to have to suspect that, behind this chit-chat with Dilys just after his father's funeral, there had been a touch of the same theoretical amorousness as he had shown with Nancy after taking in Dr Wells's letter. For two pins, Robin told himself, he would pluck Dilys's note from his pocket and tear it to shreds. But he thought that would look peculiar, so he left it where it was.

They came out of the pub under a sky that had turned cloudy. It seemed a long time before everything had been said that should have been said and everybody bidden good-bye. Robin and Embleton gave George and Elizabeth a lift in their taxi, and that seemed to take a long time too, but most of the train journey back to Oxford passed in a flash. When Robin woke up in his corner he and Embleton were alone in the compartment and it was dark outside. They smiled at each other.

'Thank you for coming down,' said Robin. 'Before I fall asleep again.'

'Not at all. It was well worth it from my point of view. I hope I was some use.'

'You certainly were. What a day. What a do. You never met my father, did you? Since we were at school, I mean.'

'Then, yes, but a couple of times since. Not for very long.'

'I wonder what made him decide to have that stuff read out. Or rather I'm pretty sure I know. Oh, it must have tickled him to think of everybody having to listen to it in those circs. Especially Cousin Emrys. Dad would have been sure he'd be there. A way of telling him pretty straight he hadn't, that's Dad hadn't, come back to Mother Church in the end the way Cousin Emrys was always betting he would. Bloody Welshman.'

'I had a word or two with Cousin Emrys before lunch. He reminded me strongly of your father.'

'Dad would have hated to hear you say that.'

'I'm sure, not that I mean I think they're identical. Emrys is full of self-assurance, for one thing, which your dad certainly wasn't. But I was going to ask you about that stuff, you know, what he got your long-suffering brother to recite. Where did it come from, any ideas?'

'It sounded to me like a translation of some bit of nineteenth-century bullshit.'

'It didn't sound like a translation to me.' Embleton noisily rubbed his chin, dark with stubble at this hour. 'Bullshit, well yes, but quite vigorous on its level. And nineteenth century, don't forget your father was born in and must have done a lot of his growing-up in it, correct?'

'Emble, are you getting ready to tell me my dad wrote that stuff himself? Not a chance, he wasn't up to it.'

'Our elders, my boy, are up to more things than we might think. Anyway, of several points that struck me about the bullshit, one was the absence from it of a very important character in this connection, to wit, Christ, using the word for once to denote the founder of

230

the religion that bears his name. When people call themselves unbelievers, it's always God they don't believe in, Christ doesn't get a mention. I suppose for some he's included in God, but most of them just don't bother with him. A mistake, I'd say. Christ's much nicer than God, he hasn't got that capricious, arbitrary, prohibitive side, he's more human, what? You start feeling it's worth making an effort to do what he wants you to do, even in cases where . . . the size of the effort called for . . . may appear to be . . . excessive.' A great yawn rounded off the paragraph.

But for train noises there was silence till Robin said, 'Do you believe in, well, Christianity?'

'I can't say I do, but I have been into it a little. Worth going into, don't you think?'

'Maybe.'

First getting up and stretching elaborately, Embleton rubbed condensation off the window and peered out. 'Here we are. From what you've told me about him in the past, Robin, your father sounds to me like somebody who'd given up Christ, or thought he had, but couldn't quite bring himself to give up God, in spite of what we heard today. Or as seen there. Hence all the time he spent trying to stop you doing things.' Outside in the corridor, Embleton went on, 'It's tempting to see God's hand in that. He's a jealous God, you remember, and he'd certainly have wanted to punish your dad for such rebellious thoughts. And your dad's seed. In fact he, i.e. God, did his customary neat job of visiting the sins of the father upon the children.'

The train stopped and they got out of it into light and darkness. Robin said, 'Well, thanks a lot, Emble, for that exposition.'

'Don't mention it. Actually there's one other small bit. If you remember, God doesn't content himself with just visiting the sins of the fathers upon the children, he goes on visiting them even unto the third and fourth generation. So if you and Nancy or anyone else ever have children, watch out.'

Robin said nothing. He had put his hand into his pocket with the firm intention of closing it round the piece of paper there and dropping it underfoot. But then again he let it stay, this time on the principle that you never know.

Over the next couple of weeks, Robin and Nancy discussed several courses of action aimed at causing her to miscarry and tried one or two. They were handicapped by among other things lack of knowledge and also by lack of any obvious routes to it. At that time and place there was nothing in print, not even clandestine print. The only person in Oxford Robin felt he knew well enough to confide in was Embleton, but to judge by parts of their conversation after the funeral it seemed plain that Embleton would not do for this purpose. He lacked the required spark of irresponsibility. Robin's college mates were irresponsible to a fault, but he shied away from asking them his questions in any but a hypothetical spirit.

'When you put their ideas together they don't add up to much,' he told Nancy one evening. 'A fast ride on the back of a motor-bike along a bumpy road doesn't strike me as very promising. I suppose there are motor-bikes for hire. I know how to ride one.'

'I can't see it shifting him.' Nancy pointed to her middle. 'Are you sure it's not a joke?'

'Drinking a lot of gin and getting into a bath as hot as you can bear it and lying in it as long as you can bear it. Not any old time but on the day you'd be having your period if things were normal. I like that last point. Makes the whole thing sound quite practical.'

'I can't think where I'd do that. What other suggestions?'

'Well,' said Robin, consulting a notebook. 'Two chaps recommended falling down a flight of stairs. It's a man's world, isn't it? Pills from a chemist. Nobody seemed to have any idea what pills or which chemist. Having it – removed surgically. At least that's certain. But it's expensive. And also against the law. Which means it's hard to fix up.'

How hard it was Robin perhaps knew better than Nancy. Two days previously he had gone to see Dr Wells in his surgery.

'Thank you for trusting me, Mr Davies,' said the doctor when he had heard the story. 'But I fear I must tell you immediately that there's no way in which I can help you, either directly or indirectly. As you yourself acknowledge, any attempt I or anybody else might make to interfere with the course of nature in a case like this would be illegal. And even if I knew someone who might be prepared to put aside his scruples and his respect for the law in a good cause . . .' Here Dr Wells paused for so long and sat so still that Robin wondered if he would ever go on. But in the end he did. '. . . I should not be free to put you in touch with him. Until there's a change in the law, which won't happen in my lifetime, I have no alternative. Given my responsibilities.'

'Of course, doctor, I quite understand. I just thought I had to try you.'

'For my own satisfaction I wish I could convey to you and, to both of you how very much I wish I could do as you ask. But I can't. Forgive me.'

'Nonsense, you've been very kind.'

'Please, Mr Davies, let me ask you to drop any other plans you may have for terminating this pregnancy. If you know where to look, and I'm not going to give you a hand there either, you'll find a common back-street abortionist who will do the job for an exorbitant sum and at the substantial risk of infecting and quite possibly killing the girl in the case. How would you feel then? At the very least she runs a risk of being rendered barren for life, a prospect normal young women view with abhorrence. It's your duty to see to it that your girl understands all that if you decide to go ahead regardless. But I beg you not to, not to go ahead. It might be a better world if unmarried mothers suffered no stigma, I don't know, but I know it's better to suffer any likely amount of intolerance than to be sterilised or poisoned or murdered. Good day to you, Mr Davies. As I said, I'm sorry I can't help you.'

The evening after Nancy and Robin discussed ways of causing her to miscarry, she turned up looking mysterious and perhaps excited. She carried something in a paper bag which she put down on the bed.

'What's that?' he asked her. 'A goody for my supper?'

233

'Do you remember me telling you I've got a chum who's a nurse at the hospital?'

'Vaguely. What's she called?'

'There, you've forgotten her name. Good. You don't need to know it.'

'What? What's going on?' He picked up the paper bag.

'Careful, better let me do it. Now.'

And very carefully Nancy took from the bag a small hypodermic syringe in a transparent wrapping and some notably small bottles holding a clear liquid that Robin guessed were in all probability called ampoules. She faced him expectantly.

'What's this stuff?'

'It's got some Latin name. You inject a dose of it into a pregnant female and in half an hour to an hour she isn't pregnant any more. It's usually used on animals but it works all right on human beings too. I thought we might try it tonight.'

Robin was greatly disconcerted. 'But you can't just . . . Who's to inject it into you for a start? I tell you, I'm not going to.'

'Don't worry, chops, I wasn't going to ask you. I can do it myself, I know how to from doing the dogs at the kennels. Money for old rope.'

'But at least it would make sense of a sort to wait until your period's due.'

'It's due tomorrow, actually, and I can't see a few hours making any difference, can you?'

'But . . .'

Nancy had an answer to all his objections, which grew pro - gressively weaker both in themselves and in the intensity with which he urged them. It would undoubtedly be most satisfactory if matters could be resolved so easily, or rather simply. And cheaply. And surely no qualified nurse who was also a chum of Nancy's would put her, Nancy, at risk in a way that could be so directly traced back to her, nurse. And Nancy herself seemed to have quite made up her mind. And he was not going to have to do anything.

At nine o'clock that night, Nancy stuck the hypodermic needle into her arm, an event Robin minded more than he thought he was going to, though he managed to endure it by looking away at the last moment. Then she got into bed in her nightdress and started reading a book called *Harvest Heyday*. Robin sat down in the better chair of the two and read, or tried to read, the *Anabasis*, or, to give it his private alternative title, *How to Fuck up a Good Story*. It occurred to him in the process that the name Xenophon must mean speaker of a foreign language. Nothing else did. Round them a thermos-flask, a hot-water bottle full of hot water, a large packet of cotton-wool and a selection of towels stood ready.

At about nine-forty Nancy, who had fallen asleep, woke up and looked over at Robin.

'How are you feeling?' he asked, coming closer.

'Oh, just the same. I feel a bit sleepy, but then I've been asleep.'

'You've gone very white. Well, rather white. Here.' He passed her a hand-mirror.

'I say, I have, haven't I? That must mean something's happening.'

'Isn't anything happening inside you? Or can't you tell?'

'No, it all seems exactly as usual. I'd better give myself the second doo-dah.'

'What? What are you talking about?'

'She said, my friend said, the full dose is two of those little bottles. She also said twice or three times that much or more couldn't do me any actual harm.'

'I wish you'd told me that before.'

'Now I remember.'

He started to object even less heartily than at the outset and with the same lack of result, but he still felt no less inclination to look away when the needle entered Nancy's flesh. When that was done she lay down again, it seemed quite contentedly, though not to sleep, he thought. He tried the wireless, but it only made a noise like a giant's frying-pan and the task of finding a station was beyond him, so he turned the set off again. He looked at the *Oxford Mail*, and continued to do so even after he had noticed that he was forgetting as fast as he read. When he looked at Nancy, still lying with her eyes shut, his feelings moved as often before from admiration for her uncomplaining fortitude to irritation with her for dragging him – where? Somewhere he had no wish to go, anyway. Then, again as often before, he went back to admiring her. And felt negatively grateful to her.

After some incredible lapse of time like twenty-five minutes, she abruptly sat up in bed and looked at herself in the hand-mirror.

'Gosh, I'm whiter still, aren't I?'

'Not by much I'd have said, but I can't really tell because I've kept looking at you in the meantime. How do you feel?'

'You mean in any way at all? Anywhere at all?'

'Well yes, I suppose I do.'

'It'll take me a minute to make sure.'

'Take as long as you like.'

Nancy lay very straight in the bed breathing rather noisily through her nose, her eyes tightly and yet somehow unevenly shut. After a great swallow, she said, 'No, I'm sorry, I feel absolutely completely like I did before. I've sort of been everywhere in me.'

'Including, you know, down there?'

'Especially there.'

They went on as they were a few minutes longer, not moving much or saying anything, like a pair of conscientious sceptics giving some celebrated ghost a scrupulously fair chance to show itself. Nothing happened apart from a single one of Nancy's incredibly brisk and insignificant sneezes. Then she got up and had a quick bath and put on a woolly and skirt and they went along to the pub for a late drink. No more was said of the supposed miracle injection, except that a couple of days later Nancy told Robin that her chum said she had been misinformed, and that its effect would if anything have been to reinforce the status quo inside her.

'I think we'd better go and have a word with Mrs Pendry,' said Nancy.

The thought of their doing so, especially with reference to the topic under discussion, roused Robin from the lethargy into which he had briefly sunk. 'You can't be serious. She'd, she'd chuck us out of the house.'

'I am serious and she would not chuck us out of the house.'

'What makes you think she wouldn't?'

'She didn't when I, when she first realised.'

'You mean she knows!' said Robin, even less lethargically than a moment earlier. 'You mean you told her! What a stupid bloody—'

'She knows but I didn't tell her.'

'Telepathy then, was it?'

'Oh, don't be ridiculous, Robin. She said I was looking down in the mouth, and after a bit I said I was in trouble, and she said was it what that sounded like, and I said yes, and that was it. And she was very sympathetic'

'When did this little chat take place?'

'Two or three days ago. And yes, we've had quite a few chats since I came to live here, me and Mrs Pendry have. You're not here quite a lot of the time and I get lonely.'

'Of course. There's no need to be cross,' he said, but in no very conciliatory tone.

'I'm not cross.'

Perhaps not, but he thought she looked it, sounded it. There was a faint flush under her eyes he had not noticed before and thought might be a result of her condition. Now she lowered her gaze. When he put his arms round her she held away from him at first, but not for long.

'I'm sorry,' he said, 'I suddenly got a bit frightened.'

'So did I.'

'No need to, for either of us.'

'No,' she said. 'No, of course there isn't.'

Robin had naturally seen Mrs Pendry's sitting-room in the basement a number of times but never for long at a time, always in his supposed capacity as lodger's friend. On these earlier visits he had found the place amiably untidy, the large semi-circular table, a couple of chairs and the floor on either side of the fireplace covered with the debris of fingernail make-up and scratch meals. He had found this disorder amiable because it seemed to go with the image of a free-and-easy landlady, one who was not against a spot of misbehaviour, indeed in favour of it if anything, provided the parties kept themselves to themselves. But now, after a period of notice sufficient to prepare for a rigorous barrack-room inspection, he went down the stairs with Nancy to find everything almost starkly neat, no eggshells with runnels of yolk coagulated on the outside and very likely a cigarette-end dropped inside, no stained tufts of cottonwool, no topless bottle of hair-tint or nail-varnish, just the baronial frontage of the wireless, the tall pear-shaped birdcage containing no bird, and underfoot, only patchily to be seen before, the heavy rugs in rather stern good taste.

Mrs Pendry had a deep voice for a woman who was not also an American. She used it to say to Robin, 'So we've got ourselves into a little difficulty, have we?' in a way that incongruously suggested it was a bit daring and even posh of him to have rendered somebody pregnant. 'Well, perhaps there's something we can do.'

He was mildly surprised to hear himself saying, 'It's awfully decent of you to let us come and talk to you about it, Mrs Pendry.'

Mrs Pendry at any rate showed no surprise. She turned to Nancy and said, 'Just run over the dates and times and whatnot again, will you dear, just so I know where we are,' and Nancy obliged, and Robin started to feel more secure and less hopeful by the minute, and Mrs Pendry said several times in not so very different ways that she thought she had the picture and it was an old, old story.

'Do you think you can help us, Mrs P?' said Nancy, a little soon, Robin thought.

'Well now, that depends. Can I tempt either of you to a cup of tea? I don't have to go out of the room, I've got the electric kettle and the caddy and everything in here.'

Despite this inducement Nancy smiled and shook her head and Robin said he was fine, thanks, and really not to bother on his account.

'It's no trouble.' Mrs Pendry ogled him slightly and he noticed with some relief that she was too watery-eyed and generally shagged-looking to appeal to him, even, he estimated, when he was pissed. Nevertheless his interest quickened when she said, 'Oh, Mr Davies, or can I call you Robin, dear, can I offer you a glass of gin, Robin, I find a mouthful or two of it very comforting at this time of day. Oh good, you'll keep me company then. Nothing much to put in it, I'm afraid, I'm out of lime-juice but might I suggest a splash of soda. My husband, he was of a scientific turn of mind, he used to say the bubbles get the drink to you faster, hence the popularity of champagne at weddings and functions. He was a chemist, I think I told you, Nancy, he had this business in Pontypridd, a shop selling toiletries and so on and he made up prescriptions at the back. Of course, a man in his position, people were coming to him all the time with their troubles and upsets. I remember one young mother whose little baby just wouldn't be got off to sleep.'

Mrs Pendry remembered in some detail. At one point things sounded as if the little baby concerned was going to turn out to have been got off to sleep permanently, and Robin's interest quickened a second time, but no, and it subsided again. It declined another notch as a story about drains unfolded. On the other hand, he began to hope that if this type of stuff kept up much longer he might be able to get away without ever having to pursue the matter that had brought him here, a false hope in the long term, he was aware, but more and more attractive in the short. Quite soon after he had formed this thought Mrs Pendry said, 'He stood no nonsense from anyone, my husband. Particularly over the sort of spot of bother you two youngsters have got yourselves into. He used to say to, well, I'm talking about respectable people now, not riff-raff, oh yes, we had our share of them too, he used to say you've got a straight choice. *Either* you dose yourself with all manner of pills and powders and thoroughly upset your system, and it can be quite serious, and twenty to one it won't do what you were hoping it would do, *or* you decide on surgical termination by a qualified medical practitioner. Which is safe, painless, quick, and certain. But it has one drawback, one disadvantage. It costs money. There it is. I'm afraid there's no getting away from it.'

So saying, Mrs Pendry took a cork-tipped cigarette from a case made of some cloudy yellowish material. She neither used a holder nor had conspicuous rings on her fingers, but compensated for their absence with her long scarlet-painted fingernails. Robin wanted fervently to be told straight away how much money, but thought again.

'Thank you very much, Mrs Pendry, for being so patient with us and so sympathetic, because as you seem to have somehow guessed we, we're very much a' – short rueful laugh – 'a pair of babes in the wood in this, er, area, but I do appreciate how very practical and helpful you've been already . . .'

It was not quite spot-on, too humble or more likely not humble enough, but there was no question but that it was on the right lines. 'Because I know some people and you're friends, a hundred pounds,' said Mrs Pendry, with a sad smile that told him, if he had needed telling, that there were no reductions from that figure for anything whatsoever. 'Unreturnable. I dare say it sounds a lot of money,' she went on, 'but it is absolutely inclusive. No extras, no nothing, that's it. Prices are really shocking these days, aren't they?'

Robin nodded eagerly and said, 'As you'll understand, Mrs Pendry, Nancy and I'll need a few days to make up our minds and think how we can raise a sum of that size, if indeed we can,' which took only a short time in the saying but was quite long enough for him to reckon, firstly, that the old girl was whacking it on in fine style, since of the few bits of consensus among his college mates had been that the price for a grade-A London job was a hundred, secondly, that the amount in question would buy him about forty thousand of the full-sized kind of cigarette that Mrs Pendry was currently smoking and, thirdly, that he and Nancy might go further and not just fare worse but fail to fare at all.

Some of this, though perhaps not all, would have been in Mrs Pendry's mind already. At any rate, she answered his last remark by saying generously, 'As long as you like, dear, it's entirely up to you,' though when she added, 'but don't forget it'll take me a little while to get things set up,' it was in a sharper tone.

Afterwards, Robin told Nancy, 'Bit of luck, wasn't it, Mrs Pendry turning out to be able and willing to give us a hand like that?'

'Yes, wasn't it, but—'

'Something almost uncanny about it, as if we'd somehow seen it coming.'

'I think she was the one that saw it coming.'

'What?'

'Well, only the week before last she told me, terrifically casual, that if I ever found I needed any help over anything, she hoped I'd remember she was a good friend of mine, and then the other day it came back to me, she'd said her husband had been a chemist, and I thought, well, there we are, worth a try. A chemist in Pontypridd. I didn't mention it to you because I was afraid if I did you might give it away we'd been talking about her.'

'I see. I think.'

'But I was going to say, what about that hundred pounds? You haven't got it handy, have you, by any chance? Because I haven't.'

'No,' said Robin, 'but I know somebody I can ask to lend it. No, my turn not to mention something. Just to put your mind at rest, it isn't the vice-chancellor of the university or even the principal of my college. That was quite a strong gin she gave me, you know.'

The next afternoon Robin took the train to London. When he got out he had only a few minutes' walk to his destination, a house in a terrace built about the time of the first war. He went up a couple of steps and pressed the middle bell of three. After no great interval his brother George came to the door.

'Oh,' said George without delay. 'Well, you can take yourself off and lose no time about it, Robin, the answer's no.'

'What are you saying? You don't even know what I was going to—'

'Oh yes I do, and the answer's no, you can't bring Nancy here and I'm not going to lend you or give you or let you have any money, not a bean, so you can take yourself off.'

'Hey, George, half a minute, you haven't even given me time to tell you—'

'I knew what you were after the moment I saw you standing there. What other reason would you have for coming to see me all the way from Oxford without ringing me up first to make sure I'd be in? No, you reckoned if you pitched up on the doorstep I wouldn't have the heart to send you away. Well, you reckoned wrong.'

'Chap's got a mind like a razor,' said Robin.

His brother glared at him and showed more real anger than he had before when he said, 'Oh, I suppose I've got to ask you in now you're here, curse you, though I'm still not going to help you. *Fuck* you, Robin.'

So far, thought Robin, George had behaved predictably, even if he had got to the object of this visit rather fast and become as cross as he had rather fast too. Silence and pretended shame seemed called for. Robin followed down the gloomy hall, where there was an inferior-looking table scattered with inferior-looking items of mail and no other free objects at all, unless the dark-green lino on floor and stairs could have been counted as surplus to absolute necessity. These stairs were probably just broad enough to allow two unencumbered persons to pass on them, not that this contingency would often have arisen. On the first-floor landing a door with a lock in it and a numeral screwed to it led into a small space surrounded by doors or doorways. Although Robin had been here before he never remembered between times which led to which room. The one George led the way into, however designated, was a study with books, papers and, sticky-taped to the wall, a school-timetable and kindred matter from which Robin superstitiously averted his eyes. Also visible was a desk with a rotatable chair behind it where George sat himself down, pointing his brother to the only vacant seat, a stool that had a cork top and a general bathroom look.

'Is this an interview?' asked Robin. 'Because if it is—'

George cut him short with a sweep of his hand. His manner had mellowed to a fairly steady exasperation. He said, 'If you'd prefer a nice cosy chair with your little niece at play round you, you just say the word.'

'Where is she at the moment?' This question acknowledged the fact that the child referred to could not have been within hearing and still undetected.

'Out with her mother, as if you didn't know. Another bit of good timing on your part. Well, I suppose you'd better get on and tell me what you've come to tell me.'

Robin did so, giving an account of recent events that omitted among other things anything distinctive about Mrs Pendry, whom he reduced to some trusted chum or other of Nancy's. At the end he said, 'If I ask you something, will you promise not to get angry?'

'Certainly not, but I might consider trying. What do you want to know?'

'Is there anyone you've heard of in London who might be able to—'

'No there isn't, and if there were you'd never hear about them from me. I promise you faithfully. Why, is there something dodgy about this what, this chum of Nancy's? I mean something over and above the chance of her dying and you going to gaol.'

'I don't know, there's not much I do know about whatever it is and don't look like getting to know till I hand over the money. It's just, well, you can understand, George, I want to keep my options open as long as I—'

This attempt at self-justification was misguided. George said with renewed annoyance, 'Yeah, you've always been a great one for keeping those buggers open. I can remember you when you were about twelve, not saying whether you were coming to the pictures or not till the last moment in case you got a more attractive offer from somewhere. Good old O. O. Davies Dad used to call you, standing for Options Open. Have you talked to a doctor about this business, a real doctor?'

'Not just *a* doctor, none other than the estimable Dr Wells, who wouldn't touch it with a barge-pole or mention anyone else.'

'Of course he wouldn't. Did he tell you anything you didn't already know?'

'To be honest, he did. He said there was quite a risk of Nancy ending up sterile as well as dead, so to speak.'

'Don't be funny, Robin. Not to be able to have a child would ruin Nancy's life. Why don't you marry the girl while you've got the chance? Don't tell me, you want to keep your perishing options open. And no, I'm not being funny, I don't think those options of yours are funny in the bloody least.'

'All right. I quite agree this is a serious subject. It's my life and I intend to do what I want and not do what I don't want for a bit longer, with your permission. I don't think I've asked you this before, if I have I've forgotten what you said. How do you find marriage after how many years is it, five?'

George drew in breath to answer this question, but let it out again when a nearby door banged open and what sounded like a small crowd of people surged into the flat. After a thump as of a door-knob striking a piece of furniture, a series of heavy footfalls became audible, either of somebody with a peculiar gait or of a young child coming down as hard as possible at each step. A voice also sounded, elusive as regards its actual words, but identifiable as a child's less from its timbre than its tremendous volume. By this stage it seemed that no more than two persons had in fact arrived.

To Robin, one of his brother's great virtues was his inability to keep a straight face at such junctures, let alone put on a frown as their father might have done. 'Wouldn't you bloody well know,' said George, getting to his feet with caricatured haste. 'Right on cue. I'll have to go and do some welcoming home.'

'Must you?'

'Unless you want Marian to come bursting in to be welcomed in here.'

'Off you go then, George. I'll follow when things seem to have settled down a bit.'

Robin was given to telling himself, and others who would listen, that the advent of children was one of the things about getting married he expected not to enjoy much but was resigned to, unlike some other things. The weakness of that position was that the distinction embodied in it tended to become eroded at times like the present. Even as he got as far as this place in his thoughts a cry, or yell, of affected delight rang out from the next room and made him unable to remember how he had ever for a moment fancied he had resigned himself to having children. Well, to go on indefinitely lying doggo in here, however alluring, was not practicable. At a similar moment on his last visit here, George had sent little Marian to fetch out her kind but shy uncle, and the bugger was not above working the same kind of dodge again. Robin began to move. He was not much cast down by George's refusal of financial aid, which he took to be temporary only, nothing more than an attempt to make him sweat for a while.

He entered the sort of central section of the flat, part kitchen, part sitting-room, part just place to be. Marian, who looked and was dressed like a miniature girl rather than a mere undifferentiated lump of child, was getting on to a hard chair by the difficult route up and over its back. She seemed to be trying as hard as she could to use up energy but showed no sign at all of running short. Her head had no particular role in her climbing activities so she shook it randomly about on its neck. Any adult who went on like that, anyone over about ten, in fact, would be taken for a dangerous lunatic. George stood by, presumably to catch his daughter if she fell; Elizabeth was at the gas-stove, perhaps boiling an egg. Robin made no move to intervene.

'I understood Beatie was going to give you tea,' said George.

'So she did,' said his wife. 'Cake and all that.'

'But this one looks as if it's expecting to be given something like tea all over again.'

'Yes, that's right. Hallo, Robin dear, how lovely to see you.'

He went over to Elizabeth and they kissed affectionately. As usual at such times he appreciated her total femininity and wholesomeness and her almost total lack of looks. George seemed to know his feelings in the matter and not to care about them one way or the other, which once or twice in the past had nettled Robin slightly. Could it be that another man, admittedly one who knew her rather better than he did, saw in her something hidden from him, or what?

There was no time to speculate. Marian seemed to catch sight of him and flung up her arms in what he took to be greeting, but when he approached her chair screwed herself elaborately round, so that her legs and buttocks remained more or less in their former position while her face was turned away from him. When last seen, it had held an expression of horror or at least dismay. He was uncertain how to proceed.

'Say hallo nicely to Uncle Robin,' her mother told her.

Marian untwisted herself with great vigour and at once. 'Hallo Uncle Robin hallo Uncle Robin,' she began to bawl, repeating a designation that to Robin himself had connotations of baldness, pipe-smoking and golf. Then Elizabeth put some food in front of her and she shut up and attacked it in the spirit of someone registering appetite in a silent film.

'There's no doubt about it,' said her father, watching her, 'all kids are pissed all the time, or perhaps I'd better say drunk, I don't mean on alcohol, but drunk none the less. Then of course, with a few exceptions like the one in here, all women are pissed.'

'You mean drunk,' said Elizabeth, 'but thank you for the mention.'

'Queers are pissed, at least the ones who don't mind you knowing about them or are even quite keen for you to know about them.'

'What about the ones who do mind, or would mind?' asked Robin. 'Surely they're *drunk* too?'

'Sorry. All right – those ones sort of know how to hold their liquor. There are some straight men who are drunk all the time, mostly aristocrats and actors. Then other straight men are literally pissed, oh shit, *drunk* all the time, and lastly there are the ones who are sober in both senses except when they're pissed on alcohol. I mean drunk on alcohol. Christ.'

'You don't sound particularly sober yourself,' said Elizabeth. 'Have you been knocking it back on the sly?'

'Nothing since last night.'

'Well, congratulations on turning out in the end to belong to the righteous minority who see things steadily and see them whole.'

'Well, it's my ball,' said George. This post-childhood catch-phrase, meaning roughly that the originator of any kind of game could fairly expect to win it, was long familiar to Robin, but he was mildly miffed to find that Elizabeth knew it too.

After some experiment, Marian had evidently found that eating in the plain sense of putting food into the mouth, mashing it with the teeth and finally swallowing it, need not severely limit the noise made by the eater. You simply hummed as loudly as you could in the intervals when your mouth was shut and produced a wordless singsong the rest of the time. This lasted a minute or so until she incautiously laid down her spoon and was at once seized bodily and borne away by her mother. The access of indignant yelling this produced became more bearable at a distance, behind a closed door and finally when overlaid by the sound of running water.

'Just for the record, that was her being quite good,' said George.

'Christ, and I suppose you're going to tell me you get used to it in the end.'

'Am I fuck. Or rather it depends what you mean by *it*. Nobody could get used to a noise et cetera that's changing all the time except that it stays horrible. What you do sort of get used to is having a horrible noise going on for large parts of every day.'

'Can't you shut yourself away from most of it or go to the pub when you're not out working.'

'Surely you don't imagine a woman changes into something else just because she's become a wife and mother, do you? Locking myself in my study is skiving; going to the pub or anywhere else at all with the grudging exception of school is sneaking out or in severe cases buggering off. I'm not expected to do much except be there but be there I must or face the consequences. In a way you can see their point, I suppose. Well anyway.'

'Still, at the moment you've presumably done your bit for a bit.'

George shook his head to and fro. 'Oh dear. There's a chance I might be deemed to have done my bit if I stand there and watch Marian being tucked up in bed, a process known as putting her down, as if she were a dog.'

'Except that when you put a dog down, he stays down.'

'True, O king. After it's over we could go to the pub.'

'Sneak off, you mean?'

'Go more or less openly. It's always easier when you're around. Two or more men can seldom be considered to be sneaking off anywhere.'

Perhaps through difference in age, George liked pubs more than Robin, set more store by them. A day without a substantial visit to one was to him not much of a day. He had more than once feelingly described the rude awakening of a contemporary of his at finding, soon after marriage, that he was expected to spend most of his evenings with his new wife, not with his mates down the boozer as formerly. The contemporary had been a bloody fool, to be sure, but George saw his point. At other times he was given to gloomily forecasting the end of the pub as a male refuge: women had gained a foothold there during the war, and according to him they were not going to give it up in a hurry.

Tonight at least he seemed cheerful enough. With a contented sigh he put down a couple of pints of best bitter on the small round table where Robin sat, and with a large gesture clawed the transparent wrapping off a fresh packet of cigarettes.

'I like this place,' he said.

'Nice and quiet, anyway.'

'You know where you are in a place like this.'

Indeed you did, thought Robin, and taking in now the sombre tones of walls and floor, untouched for twenty years, the grey-clad customers sitting in ones rather than twos and the cheer-up pinks and light greens of the prefabricated lampshades, he could see a tenable case for being somewhere else, always provided it had drinks in it. He hoped that no woman worth the name would mind very much being driven out of here.

'You know, Robin, it's sort of funny in a way that you should be telling me you've got old Nancy into the pudding club at last.'

'Oh really?' Like many before him to have heard such an exordium, Robin judged it was about time somebody handed him a good laugh.

'Yes. You see, I've recently put Elizabeth into the very same club.'

'You mean on purpose, I take it.'

'Well, yes, I suppose so. Yes, we'd talked about it.'

'On purpose and for the second time of asking. I see.'

'Don't try and make it sound as though you're the sane one and I'm the raving lunatic,' said George, with a return to his exasperated manner. 'At least if I am barmy, so's everybody else. Or nearly everybody else. I'm not talking about bright sparks like you.'

'You'll be telling me marriage is nothing without children in a minute.'

'I'd be telling you that already if I thought it would do any good. Not nothing, by the way, just less, when you're young anyway. Now listen, do you imagine any husband says to himself, I feel like having my days and nights buggered up or at least continually disturbed by a small, noisy, often unclean, violent egomaniac with a five-second attention-span; I know what I'll do, I'll put the missis in pod. Perhaps unfortunately, it happens to be the only way of producing offspring, and not just any old offspring but yours and hers. There.'

'Where?' said Robin rather offensively. 'What a funny thing to want to produce.'

'I was a bloody fool to think you might get a glimmering of what I was driving at.'

'In the last hour I've had more than a glimmering of marriage from the inside.'

'You've got marriage on the winkle, Robin.'

'Thanks anyway for letting me know why you've gone in for it. I always rather wondered before.'

'Oh bugger off. I married Elizabeth in the first place because she was the only girl I'd ever met that I never wished wasn't there and she feels the same about me.'

'Has she told you she does?'

'Strictly no, but she'd have told me if she didn't.'

'You've drunk that rather fast, George.'

'We've been having such a fascinating conversation.'

'Have we time for another pint?'

'Why might we not?'

'Well, I don't know, do I, I thought we might be declared to be, what, hanging about in the pub.'

'Hanging *on* in the pub is more the phrase, but you've got the general idea. No, we're all right provided we're back indoors in say half an hour from now.'

Not long afterwards the pub began to fill up and become noisier, largely it seemed owing to the incursion of a couple of groups of stocky, dark-complexioned men who called out to each other in strange accents. They were poorly attired but apparently full of self-confidence and loquacity.

'Welshmen,' explained George. 'We're not far from the station here and somebody told me they're redecorating at the Load of Hay.'

'You don't know that, that they're Welshmen, I mean. The Geordie noise is quite similar at this sort of distance.'

'Nature's Welshmen. Imagine what Dad would have said about them.'

'While we've got a moment, George, I want to have my say. It's not supposed to be a very logical say or an at all admirable say and no doubt a right mess we'd be in if everybody thought like me, but it's what I think. I wish I could be like you, I wish I had the makings of a good father . . .'

'Whatever that is and whatever they are.'

'. . . but I can't see myself ever feeling about the whole business, well, anything very different from what I feel about it now, that's to say apathy relieved with horror. Whatever happens. I should have added a fair dose of incomprehension back there, but we mustn't get bogged down. As regards the main part, the sexual part, I simply want very strongly and seriously to stay free a few years longer, before I give in to all the pressures and settle down to bloody old monogamy. To *accept* monogamy – sorry, George.'

'Don't mind me, Robin, but you're mistaken if you think all married men accept monogamy.'

'You're not going to tell me you've . . .'

'No I'm not, because to start with I haven't. As yet. Thank God. But I've been tempted all right, especially when the old girl's been giving me a going-over for sneaking off somewhere. I've even been given a greenish light or so. But as I say, I haven't. Much to my relief. I don't think they go together very well, what you call monogamy and, well, non-monogamy.'

'What keeps you on the straight and narrow?'

'Reluctance to feel a shit. I realise some people don't mind feeling a shit and some may even like it. Also to some people it's just another name for a low sex-drive.'

'What do you say to that?'

'Look, I thought this was supposed to be your say. All right, what I say to that, after why don't you fuck off, is I think apart from a few sad cases everybody's got about the same amount of sex-drive as such and it's other things about them that make the difference to the way they behave. But get on with your say, if there's any more to it than a second look at keeping your options open.'

'Just, Nancy and I suit each other very well in a lot of ways but not in all. And imagine what sort of start the two of us would have if we'd had to get married. And you're the very picture of a man who'd never dream of looking at his watch.'

Back in the flat, Marian was singing quietly to herself, in other words yelling rhythmically at a volume short of fortissimo. At no particular point the sound cut off abruptly and was followed by the silence of sleep or death. No doubt preferring the first alternative, George and Elizabeth sat in the kitchen as if turned to stone, then after a minute or two ventured to cast their eyes to and fro. Nothing shifted its position for another minute or two, at the end of which cautious, limited movement evidently became possible to them, as to a couple gradually throwing off some disabling enchantment. Finally George spoke in a normal tone.

'She's off,' he said.

Even after this all-clear Robin formed his words with caution. 'It's . . . is it always like this?' he managed to ask.

'Better than average, if anything,' said Elizabeth. 'She's been quite good today. Well . . .'

'Yes, but that was this morning,' said George.

'How long is she likely to stay off?'

Elizabeth gave a short laugh. 'Oh . . . half-past ten, eleven. Midnight,' she said, letting her fancy wander. 'She's been known to sleep right through to the morning.'

'What sort of time in the morning?'

'Oh, six, six-thirty.'

Robin felt some curiosity about what usually happened after that, but not enough to make him ask Elizabeth another question. George said, 'When she does, that's my signal to get up, after she's done her bit of burbling.'

'What we call her dawn chorus,' said Elizabeth.

'It's my job to stop her doing whatever she's trying to do. Recently it's been trying to make Elizabeth a cup of tea and pouring it all over the floor.'

'She can't use the stove, but tea-leaves and cold water are not much more fun to clean up than real tea. And all the clobber as well.'

'But she's very grown up compared with some her age,' said George.

The two dropped the subject with some evident reluctance. Not for the first time, but rarely with such emphasis, Robin was brought up against the fact that he knew absolutely nothing about married life beyond what he would have gathered from a not very informative article in a magazine. He considered the experience should have reinforced his determination not to get married himself, but all it seemed to have done was cheese him off with a sample of what he was in for, whatever he did, not just accepting parenthood but entering into the spirit of the bugger.

This mood deepened when George, having got up spontaneously to announce he would walk him to the station, did so. It was raining, but not hard enough to wet them seriously in those few hundred yards. It was also dark. The streets were not crowded, but there were enough people in them, moving rapidly enough, for Robin to become aware of his small and shallow experience of the city he had been born in, not because he had been brought up near its distant edge but inevitably, not at all exceptionally. He would live and die without having found out anything much about it, anything personal to him, perhaps nothing worth remembering about anything.

At his side, George said, 'It's not that I doubt your ability to make the station unescorted, even though it is dark and wet.'

'I'm relieved to hear it.'

'I have a cheque here in my pocket for a hundred pounds which I'll hand over when we're in the dry somewhere.'

'Oh, that's marvellous. But I've been thinking about that, George,' said Robin, though he was unaware of having done so, 'won't you be needing all your spare cash for this extra nipper you say is coming?'

'Oh, he's not turning up until the spring. Plenty of time for you to pay me back, old man.'

'Yes. Still, make it eighty. I'll scrape the odd twenty together somehow.'

'That might hold things up. Quicker the better.'

'What made you change your mind?'

'Elizabeth has quite a lot of time for you, you know, remarkable as it might seem. She's also got a fair amount of time for Nancy, which makes life a bit tricky. So have I. Well, the thing is, Robin, to start with I was against the whole idea of Nancy having an abortion because of the risks involved, meaning the very real and concrete risks. . . .' George stopped speaking for a few minutes because two elderly and bizarrely accoutred but large persons were pushing a kind of lofty cart along the pavement towards and now between him and Robin. 'Risks of Nancy dying or being made infertile for the rest of her life,' he went on when the hindrance was past. Then you let me see something of your own position in the matter, nothing unexpected, just going a bit further than I'd heard you go before, and I made up my mind the worst thing that was likely to happen was you marrying Nancy because she was pregnant. Or, a good deal more likely, her having an abortion on the cheap. So if you'll just come under here a minute.'

George drew Robin into the shelter of a jeweller's shop-front and took from his wallet what was indubitably a cheque for a hundred pounds drawn by himself and made out to bearer.

'This is very good of you, George.'

'It is rather, yes,' said George, and added without affection or humour, 'Evidently you have a way with you. Perhaps the result of years of insisting on getting whatever you might happen to want. Let me know how things turn out, but for Christ's sake don't say anything to Elizabeth, unless the worst comes to the worst, you understand?'

'I won't breathe a word. But won't she have guessed we've been talking about something?'

'I've told her you felt like talking about Nancy, which is true in a sense.'

'Won't she press you for details?'

'Don't you worry your pretty little head about that, dear boy, I'll think of something harmless. Now, you know where you are, over the bridge and turn left. Give our love to Nancy.'

He was gone, walking briefly back the way they had come, in a hurry to get in out of the rain, of course, but also, Robin suspected, to get away from him. He had been conscious of George's disapproval in the past, but until today it had stayed unexpressed, or expressed only in the bantering fashion of their ordinary conversation, easily discounted or forgotten. This, especially its last couple of minutes, was going to take some shaking off, if indeed it ever could be. Robin saw now that the reason why he had been less than thoroughly dashed by having his request turned down to start with had been that all along he had believed George would come round in the end. But at the same time, that original refusal had excused him from contemplating what getting the money was going to make possible. The most solid, unarguable bar to Nancy's abortion had been removed, and here he was trying not to wish it were more firmly in place than ever. As he walked to the station entrance he had a kind of confused, semi-visual impression of something sharp cutting through Nancy's flesh, and he stopped on the wet pavement and put his hands over his mouth.

But only for a short time. After it had passed he took several slow deep breaths and groaned to himself. He had never thought, and nobody had ever said, that what was necessary was also easy to contemplate. Nothing on such a scale could be easy.

Robin's train was standing at its platform almost empty. He found a comfortable corner seat without any trouble.

By the time Robin got back to Mrs Pendry's lodging-house he had his feelings in order. He would face Nancy in the character of a man who had successfully but not surprisingly tackled a medium-sized obstacle in the way of a desirable objective, and he put on a calm, assured expression to match. He noticed on his way up that the light was on in her room; yes, she would be there, waiting for his news.

She was sitting in the chair with arm-rests, not the ideal perch for a standard-sized girl seriously reading a book, though she had one open on her lap. He saw her remembering not to put it aside and spring to her feet at the sight of him. Almost at once he saw something a little harder to see and much harder to seem not to have noticed: despite his efforts she read in him signs of satisfaction and her face fell, not so much fell as was struck by pain and fear.

After another moment that look was replaced by one of alert curiosity not much easier to ignore.

'How did it go?'

'He gave me the cash.'

'Oh, you must be pleased.'

'Well, it's what . . . I was hoping for,' said Robin, with some difficulty because what he would much rather have been saying to her was that he had been pulling her leg and that actually George had thrown out his appeal or that he himself had lost the money, dropped it, thrown it out of the train window in a fit of perversity, madness, anything that might explain why the two of them would not after all be travelling down wherever it was, he to make barely imaginable arrangements and generally be on hand, she to endure whatever was to be endured, in a couple of days' time.

All this had been waiting to be thought of and passed through his mind in a flash. After no more than an average conversational pause she was asking him with average concern if he was all right and he at once came back and said he was fine, thanks, but it had been rather a hard day, what with one thing and another. He had never felt so close to her nor had less idea of what to say to her. He knew, or thought he knew, that the right course of action now would have been a furious, mind-obliterating act of sex, but he would not have been able to remember a time when he had felt less inclined to any such thing. He asked her politely how she felt and how she had got through the day, and she politely told him. In the end he went along to the pub and drank one after the other a small neat whisky, a large glass of Empire port and a pint of draught cider. He had read somewhere that a London prostitute, who no doubt knew something, had recommended this triad of drinks as the cheapest way of ceasing to be sober, and taken in quick succession they certainly made him feel rather ill. At the same time he was in a better state to confront Mrs Pendry as arranged before he came out.

This time Nancy got to her feet when he came into the room. He thought she looked a bit pale, but she seemed normal when he kissed her, not tense or jittery. He put his hand on her breast and felt her calm heartbeat.

'Shall we go down straight away?' he asked.

'No point in hanging about.'

'Might as well get it over.'

Mrs Pendry's sitting-room was not quite as tidy as it had been on their previous visit. No actual detritus of food or make-up was to be seen but a painted tin tray and used tea-things stood and remained at one side of the semi-circular table and a china ashtray advertising a brand of cigarette overflowed with lip-sticky butts.

'Well,' said Mrs Pendry in her amiable voice, 'you've certainly raised the wind in double-quick time, Robin. Shall we get that side of it over now and out of the way?' When he had made a correct deduction and passed George's cheque across, she picked up what looked like a magnifying-glass in a heavy silver frame and peered through it. 'Now this Davies. . . George Davies, he'd be a relation of yours, would he, Robin?'

'He's my brother and I—'

'Of *course*,' said Mrs Pendry, mildly aghast before time at the thought of any doubt in the matter. 'Now I suggest I take charge of this as from this moment and undertake to see to it that everybody concerned receives their due rights on the understanding that you trust me to do so, okay?'

'Okay.' Robin nodded readily. It was true that he had and looked like going on having nothing in writing, but if they meant to skin him then skin him they would, which was a comforting thought. 'We're in your hands,' he added with conviction.

'Yes. Well, you two, we've had a stroke of good luck. I was on the phone just now to Molly Humphries, that's my friend in Cardiff, and it seems that the surgeon concerned, Dr Beck, has had a late cancellation for an appointment in two days' time. So what I suggest to you is this. You'll want to go down to Cardiff with Nancy, won't you Robin, so I think the two of you should get the train tomorrow afternoon and when you get there you take the bus to Molly's place and settle in there for the night. Then the next morning you go round to the clinic, it's only a couple of minutes' walk, and then you just have the little op, Nancy, which is about as serious as having a tooth out, and you stay in the clinic for the rest of that day and overnight, and then you're free as a bird. It's not really necessary to stay on all that time, but the clinic people recommend it and Dr Beck insists on it – oh, he's a great perfectionist, is Dr Beck.

'Now,' she continued brightly, 'here endeth all the official details and the rest of it, unless there's anything either of you would like to ask me.'

Nancy looked at Robin, who said, 'Oh, just, er, Mrs Humphries' address. I don't think you . . .'

'Of course, of course, yes, I thought I had one of her cards by me, but I can't seem to put my hand on it. It's – have you got a pen, Robin?' At Mrs Pendry's dictation he wrote down details that meant nothing in particular to him, after which she went on, 'Fancy me forgetting, I mean I know Cardiff isn't the size of London but it's not Nether Wallop either, imagine walking out of Cardiff station and going up to the first person you saw and asking them to direct you to where Molly Humphries lives. Anything else?'

'Not really, but you've been so good to us that I don't want you to be out of pocket,' lied Robin. 'You've had all these telephone calls to make and they must have run you into money. If I could make a contribution?'

An expression of genuine pleasure, along with serious respect for his conscientiousness, made Mrs Pendry's face less shagged-looking for a moment. 'Oh, my dear Robin, there's really no need in the world, but if we said two pounds that would be more than generous.'

He handed over the notes at once, thinking of their four erstwhile companions in his wallet and more dimly of the fund-raising he must do in the morning. He had thought well of his act of spontaneous generosity when he planned it on the train back from Oxford, but the degree of its success passed expectation. Mrs Pendry poured gin, offered cigarettes, beamed at them both, if such a thing could be said of a human countenance. After proclaiming closer friendship by being boring about the times she and Molly Humphries had had together, she went as far as telling them something of Dr Beck, that although admittedly of foreign descent he was thoroughly British in the ways that counted, speaking wonderful English, fully qualified at places like Warsaw and Latvia, a very warm-hearted man but a perfect gentleman, experienced to the nth degree in this particular little bit of minor surgery, which by the way was technically known as *curettage,* meaning just clearing things up, which was all it boiled down to really. Robin's opinion of Mrs Pendry rose throughout this exposition. In the circumstances it was unnecessarily nice of her to make soothing noises. And also in the circumstances there was no point in wondering what proportion of the fee she retained for herself, how much went to Molly Humphries, and more besides. In the last category there featured the question why Mrs Pendry, though careful not to write anything down, had told them so much more than a single name and address in Cardiff. Confidence, absent-mindedness, tipsy garrulity? Well, for the moment, and with luck for ever, that could be left unanswered.

The next morning, Robin found the figure of Dr Beck occupying his mind. It was presumably encouraging that the fellow could be described as thoroughly British in all the ways that counted, though what these might have been in Mrs Pendry's mind seemed debatable. Robin hoped that being at one's best when things were going badly was not among them, or would not be seen to be. But then that other thing, being – what was it – a very warm-hearted man but a perfect gentleman, surely anyone unique in this way could be expected to be distinguished in others. How wonderful was his English going to turn out to be?

By revolving such matters, Robin managed for a time to keep at some distance what was really interesting about Dr Beck: how much of a doctor he was. In search of further distraction as much as information he went to the big dictionary in his college library and looked up *curettage* – a lonely merit of the way Mrs Pendry had pronounced the word was its clear guide to the spelling. The word itself was reticently defined as use of the *curette*, but the entry under *curette* was as unreticent as he could have wished:

> A small surgical instrument like a scoop, used in removing a cataract from the eye, wax from the ear, granulations, dried mucus, etc., from the throat, uterine cavity, etc. . . .
>
> 1888 *Brit. Med. Jrnl.* 11 Feb 288 My present practice is to curette in every case of disease of the uterine mucous membrane.

Well, if they had been practising *curettage* at least since 1888 the chances were they were pretty good at it by now. The picture that formed briefly in Robin's mind was enough to send him into a dark corner of the library, there to gasp and swallow for a minute or so while moisture issued from his eyes. Recovering, he said to himself he must have a bit of a hangover.

He and Nancy went out to lunch at the cheap municipal restaurant they often used, but neither seemed to have any appetite.

'At least eat up your cheese,' she said.

'You take it, I couldn't eat a thing.'

'Don't be silly, there's no reason why you shouldn't eat, I'm the one that mustn't. I know because my sister Megan had to have something done once.'

'That's not till tomorrow, and anyway it's just I couldn't get anything down.'

It was a relief of a kind that quite soon they had to go off to the station and enter on the first stage of the progress that would in time bring them to Dr Beck. Robin took with him the leather music-case, once his father's, that in the past had held books or papers but this time pyjamas and shaving-tackle as well, Nancy a large string bag containing among other stuff two nightshirts and, after consultation with Mrs Pendry, two dark-blue packets of sanitary towels. Like some wretched club-organiser person, Robin had settled on a recounting of childhood experiences as a promising conversational opener for the journey, but found when it came to it that Nancy was either asleep or looking out of the window in apparent lassitude nearly all the time he was not himself asleep.

Arriving at Cardiff, they found themselves in the midst of hurrying or strolling people who had no attention to spare for them. Robin stopped in an unfrequented corner and faced Nancy.

He said in one breath, 'There's something I must tell you but it's not that I'm going away now or any other time because I'm going to be with you every moment I can I promise faithfully.' He smiled and added, 'Do you believe me?'

'Yes I do.' Nancy's face and whole bearing had shown some alarm from an early moment, but the signs of it had vanished before he was half-way through his short speech. 'So whatever it is it can't be absolutely terrible.' She put her string bag down right in the corner and turned back to him expectantly.

'Don't be too sure,' he hurried on. 'This is the last moment when we can turn back without any trouble. No, don't worry about the hundred pounds, that's not important. It's—'

'But it must be. What is important then?'

'Your health and your safety.'

'I thought we'd been into all that. I'm a big strong girl, you said so yourself. And it's only a sort of minor op.'

'They'll put you under so it's not minor by definition. You must realise.'

'Don't worry about me, I've thought about it and I can face it. We agreed it was best all round.'

Unseen by Nancy, Robin clenched his hand. 'There's a risk you may end up not being able to have another baby.'

'You mean ever? Oh. How big a risk?'

'I don't know. It can happen because of infection.'

'You don't know? You didn't say anything about this before.'

'All right, I'm saying it now. All I can tell you is there's a risk.'

She looked away in the direction of the street, where it was dark and looked rainy. 'Do you think I should take a chance? It can't happen often or people would know about it, wouldn't they?'

'I don't think I have a vote on that. You decide.'

Looking at him again, an uncomfortably penetrating look,

Nancy said in her unresonant voice, 'All right. All right, I'll chance it.' She picked up her string bag and made to move on.

'I agree with you it must be a small risk,' said Robin. 'But I can tell you, if there's anything in this set-up I don't like the look of, I'm whipping you out of it right away.'

There was no room on the bus for the two of them to sit together and from where he was, in the middle next to the aisle, nothing intelligibly connected could be glimpsed, only parts or outlines of buildings, innumerable lights, moving vehicles, unfamiliar names on posters and above shop windows, pedestrians intent on their business. When they left the bus it had most likely brought them less than a mile from the station, and yet the spot seemed deserted, the house in darkness. A light rain was falling. It was time for the sinister stranger to appear, and sure enough there came into sight and hearing somebody who fitted that description, a tall man in a long mackintosh limping and creaking towards them. Then, when he was still some yards off, Nancy called and pointed.

'Powys Crescent! There! Odd numbers on the other side. It must be just here. Yes!'

As if by the agency of a telepath, a light instantly sprang up in a downstairs room of the house she indicated. When Robin looked round for the limping man there was no sign of him. A few seconds later Molly Humphries had opened her front door and was introducing herself. Robin worked out later that she must be a controlling figure in the whole enterprise while Mrs Pendry operated an out-station, so to speak, and no doubt others functioned at Cambridge or Caterham. But just then he was so relieved and elated that for the moment it slipped his mind what Nancy and he were here for.

Molly Humphries was soon producing gin. To look at, she was enough like Mrs Pendry to have passed as her elder sister, with similar attention to the condition of hair and fingernails, but her voice was a good octave higher. Molly's quarters were a good deal more opulent, spread over a whole house as it seemed and including an extensive clock that had lots of its works on view and an oil painting of sociological-historical tendency. This showed a large country mansion with a lord and lady in its drawing-room, a couple of laundresses in its laundry, brewers in its brewery and so on. There were books, too, of recent publication by the look of them, but of authorship quite unfamiliar.

Sipping at his second Booth's and angostura, Robin wondered whether he might be destined for some heroic bender of unpredictable outcome. But before long Molly Humphries interrupted their careless chatter about rising prices and spreading shortages and where would it all end.

'If you don't mind, we should be on our way in a minute,' she pronounced gravely. That's to say round to the clinic to meet Dr Beck.'

Nancy said quickly, 'Does that mean he's going to do the operation straight away instead of in the morning?'

'Oh no, dear, no, nothing has changed, it's just that the doctor likes to meet a new patient well before it's actually necessary, *and* he likes to give a new patient a first look at the clinic and at him in advance, you see. He says it's beneficial to all concerned. Oh, he's very thoughtful, you know, the doctor.'

Dr Beck proved to be so thoughtful that he kept the three of them waiting no more than a couple of minutes when they arrived at the clinic referred to and were shown into its waiting-room. Like other parts of the establishment they had seen, this was hearteningly respectable and even humdrum in appearance, devoid of anything that dated after about 1930 or harked back to the last century. Into it there bustled a small round figure in a grey chalk-stripe suit that was a little tight round the middle. Its wearer was about fifty, with abundant grey hair and a chubby though pale face that revealed nothing certain about his origins except that they could not have been English. He was already laughing when he crossed the threshold, or rather chuckling in an easy, contented way. Treading lightly, he hurried up to Molly Humphries and in rather flamboyant style near-kissed her hand, then moved along to where Nancy and Robin sat.

'Beck,' he announced, stooped over Nancy's hand and vigorously shook Robin's, then did some more chuckling and went on with a good imitation of ferocity. 'So here we have the wicked young couple who have got up to their dangerous games and have found themselves in a small difficulty. We must see what we can do about it.'

The doctor spoke almost without accent but pronounced unstressed syllables more precisely than a native speaker would have done. A solitary flash of gold was to be seen among his teeth. He had drawn up a light chair and now leant forward on it facing his three visitors, hands on knees and elbows turned outwards. In what followed he still chortled now and then and kept a smile on his face throughout.

'Fortunately we're in a good position for this, thanks to the development of modern medical techniques. What has been until nearly the other day something quite difficult is now something that for the patient is easy, quick, painless, and holds no bad after-effects, eh? For the doctor, not so easy at first but has become easier with practice. And I've had very much practice.' The doctor gave a roguish wink, then made a show of comparative seriousness. 'Also necessary is a good modern clinic, which I assure you we have here, and well-trained staff and nurses who are also very nice to the patients. Now . . .'

Quite suddenly Dr Beck's expression and manner became stern, almost grim, 'I must ask . . . Nancy . . . some questions, nothing awful, but important. You won't see me taking a note of your replies, but nevertheless I'll be recording them . . . in here.' He tapped the side of his head slowly several times. 'Here is my notebook, where I shall record what's necessary, you understand?'

The questions that followed did now and then approach the awful, though without actually getting there, being mainly concerned with dates; Nancy showed no reluctance in answering them. Robin had cheered up inwardly at his first sight of Dr Beck, and still felt more comfortable than he had when the three entered the waiting-room. He might have felt better than that if the doctor's

264

present unsmiling behaviour had not been somehow too much like his earlier cheerful behaviour in seeming a bit on the whole-hearted side. He still sat forward on his chair, lips pushed out and eyes half shut as he listened and cogitated, all mobility and eyes wide open when he spoke. But this section lasted only a short time, and he was perfectly businesslike when he took the party on a selective tour of the clinic that excluded anything in the nature of an operating theatre but included the small private room Nancy would occupy the following day. Its bed had not yet been made up and no one would have called it over-furnished, but it was nice enough, Robin supposed. Two nurses dressed like nurses were introduced and were also nice enough. The place in general showed itself to be on a scale that made him wonder slightly whether it did all the abortions for the whole of South Wales and Monmouthshire, or the fact was that the inhabitants of Cardiff itself were exceptionally ignorant as well as immoral, or some amount of legal surgery went on here too. It, the place, certainly looked clean, totally hygienic, free of any and all infectious organisms, though it must have been true that there were few such places of which that could not be said.

The four of them had reached the hall again and Dr Beck was saying,

'If you ladies will excuse us for a few minutes I will snatch this young chap from you to say to him a few things that might offend your delicate ears,' and he politely opened the waiting-room door for them. Then, motioning to Robin to follow, he strode off back the way they had come. Round a corner he rapped at a smaller door and entered the room behind it so briskly that anybody inside would have had no time even to cry out, but there was nobody. It was like the room that was to be Nancy's except that there were no chairs in here.

'Sit down for a moment.' The doctor indicated the bed and Robin sat on it. 'Just a couple of small points, Robin. Now I haven't examined Nancy this evening, I didn't think it would be a good idea, but I will tomorrow, quick but enough, you know. I think I can see already she's very healthy and I'll find nothing. Yes. Now one important thing for you to do, or rather not to do, is not to play those naughty games with her that have brought you this difficulty, not for four weeks at least. You must understand something important about this system. You see, Nancy's system, all female system, goes like this. When the womb has stopped from being pregnant, it's *wanting to be made pregnant again*. Don't let this happen, Robin, or you'll be in serious trouble this time. You understand, eh? Four weeks. No games for four weeks.

'One last point. It must be too late to ask you to change your way of life, and we know that the human race is destined to continue, but I ask you seriously to consider whether you and Nancy and people like you are behaving in the wisest possible way. Surely it would be better otherwise.'

Robin was not sure he understood what Dr Beck was getting at, but he thought he recognised the tortured sincerity of a man who knows that whatever happens his money is safe. At the same time it had to be admitted that for a short time he had spoken as if he meant what he said. He muttered something about one's limited choice in such matters.

Not much surprised or disappointed, the doctor nodded his head. 'Very good,' he said, and went on without interval or change of tone, 'I see that you shaved very well this morning.'

'What? I always shave carefully. Every day.'

'Of course it's a pity I don't see you every day.'

Dr Beck, his mouth slightly open, was either staring at some object behind Robin and to his right or just happened to be looking fixedly in that direction. Robin was afraid to make any move and could think of nothing to say. He tried to assume a thoughtful expression, as if he were searching his mind for possible questions to ask. Five seconds or more went by. Then, with a visible jerk, the doctor resumed the breezy manner of his first appearance in the waiting-room.

'Well, that seems to be all, doesn't it? Remember what I said, old chap, about behaving yourself for the next month, eh? And now we mustn't keep the good ladies waiting.'

'Back already?' said Molly Humphries when the men returned.

'Yes, it turned out we had nothing much to discuss between ourselves. Everything absolutely straightforward. Now, before you go, is there any more information I can give you, on any point whatsoever? Please think carefully.' The doctor paused, not for long but long enough for him to have become all solicitude when he spoke again. 'Very good. I'll see you tomorrow morning at nine forty-five, please. Nancy, my dear, try not to worry because there's nothing to worry about, I promise you. You're healthy, you're young, you're not hysterical. I *know* . . . all will be okay.'

'What did you really think of that doctor?' Nancy asked Robin later that night.

'I thought he was fine. A bit of an actor, but all doctors are to some extent.'

'So you said before. Isn't there anything you didn't want Molly to hear?'

'I don't think so. I thought he was a bit of a joke, I suppose. Just in his manner. All that chuckling.'

'Did you trust him?'

'Yes, absolutely,' said Robin without hesitation.

'What did he really say to you when he had you on your own?'

'Just what I said. Oh, he did go on quite a bit about what he called no games for a month afterwards. That was when I finally decided I trusted him, actually.'

'Why then?'

'Well, I thought if he hadn't told me what he did tell me, he'd have another customer along in a few weeks, I mean the same customer. I mean another—'

'I see near enough what you mean. Anyway, you trust him.'

'Yeah. What did you think of him?'

'I thought he was sort of shy. He's got to keep up this front of being the great wise doctor who never has anything go wrong, it's no wonder he goes a bit far, not a care in the world one minute and tremendously serious and professional the next. After all, he's taking a risk too, isn't he?'

Later still that night the two of them got into the bed in what they were supposedly supposed to think of as their room, a rather small room situated above the hall of the house and heated only by a single-bar electric fire that made a lot of noise but at least came on when switched on, needing no coins to set it going. Supper, consisting of cheese omelettes, bread-and-butter and cups of warm tea, had been served in the uncomfortable and not over-clean kitchen by an overalled woman whose name and official designation Robin never learnt. After the meal there had been some hands of rummy with Molly Humphries, who had changed into a dress of some shiny green material with scalloped cuffs and said a hasty good night to him and Nancy when the doorbell rang. A man's voice was soon to be heard, a Welsh voice, then, after some time and from some distance, the sound of laughter and of music from gramophone or wireless. Finally an upstairs door shut. Robin and Nancy tried to make a joke and a story out of this, but not for long.

The bed they eventually got into was rather small, like the room, or more accurately was somewhere between a quite good-sized single bed and a pretty tight double bed. Neither of them took up a lot of room so they were not greatly constricted. However, they were pushed close enough together for some sort of embrace to be firmly indicated. The particular kind of embrace that should have come next seemed no less firmly indicated, but that was only to start with. After a minute or so he found he had nothing much to go on with, not enough, in fact. Such a thing had not happened to him since the time before he met Nancy and he was put out, though not as much as he might have been in the absence of anything else to claim his attention.

'Let's go to sleep,' said Nancy. 'We've got an early start in the morning.'

'So we have. D'you think you'll be able to get to sleep all right?'

'I should think so, I usually can. We've had a long day with the journey and everything. Anyhow I'm going to have a jolly good try.'

She turned on her side away from him and he fitted himself

against her. As usual she had pulled her hair in round her neck, so there was none of it about on the pillow to tickle his face. Sleep seemed to him far distant, but he set about switching himself off a bit at a time and tried to lose control of his thoughts, especially to get rid of the one that told him against his will that his incapacity just now was a good sign, showing as it did that his loathing of what was to be done to Nancy the next day ran deeper than he had supposed – correction: even deeper than he had felt. Christ, he wanted to yell into the darkness, that's exactly the kind of crappy stuff that landed you in the—

'Are you awake?' asked Nancy very quietly.

'M'm? Yes.'

'Do you think I'll be able to have a bath in the morning? Here, I mean?'

'I don't see why not. That's to say I'm sure there'll be no difficulty.'

'M'm. I'm not going to like asking. I don't want to put anybody out.'

'You wouldn't be, not in this sort of house. Would you like me to ask her for you?'

At this generous offer Nancy thrashed about a little in the bed. 'Ooh, would you?'

'Sure, no trouble at all.'

'Oh bless you,' she said, invisibly reaching behind her and patting him on the hip. 'I was really quite dreading that.'

'Would you like the light on?'

'You have it on if you want but not for me. I'm going to sleep.'

After that he lay and listened to the silence, which was actually not very far off real silence. Nancy could be quite a noisy sleeper, wailing or grunting, but only in the day, in the afternoon, completely soundless at all times like the present. The street, Powys Crescent he remembered, was quiet, with a murmur of distant traffic that fluctuated but never noticeably rose. In the house nothing moved, the gentleman friend of Molly Humphries having departed or fallen asleep long since. Robin rehearsed what he would say to her about Nancy's morning bath. It appeared to him to be about the right size of problem for him to cope with.

The part of Robin's mind that had congratulated him on his sexual inability overnight had also warned him to expect unpleasant dreams. In fact as he drifted off to sleep he tried to prepare himself for castration fantasies, nightmares in which his father, chuckling like Dr Beck, pursued him round a crematorium, science-fictions about being a foetus in search of a womb. As it turned out, all his unconscious could sink to was a tediously literal account of a lecture on late-Latin verse-forms. He could not even have pointed to anything that could be called wakefulness, sleeping most of the night through in one go that ended only when Nancy stirred and stretched.

For a moment he was bewildered, then remembered well enough what was to happen that day. He shut his eyes again and tried to reason with himself. First he considered the alternatives to what was to happen. Possibilities that were not really alternatives, like somehow finding a willing and impeccably qualified doctor who was more what, more suitable in some nebulous way than Dr Beck, could be discarded at once. The only true alternative was to allow the pregnancy to come to term, one which in the privacy of his own mind he felt he was in a position to call letting the baby be born. By the time that took place, the baby's mother might be in one of two possible stations in life, married or unmarried. For practical reasons, married meant married to him, Robin Davies, and unmarried meant abandoned by him. Of these two possibilities, the second was not unthinkable in the least, it was as thinkable as anything he had ever thought, but that was as far as it went. The only pair of alternatives he had was, as always, abortion and marriage.

Every time so far he had got to this stage there had been a conflict, sometimes prolonged, but in all cases ending in a clear win for abortion. This morning the issue seemed less straightforward. Resignedly he reached for his supporting arguments. It, abortion, was Nancy's choice of two as well as his, and, while making his own position clear at all times, he had never put the slightest pressure on her to choose as he had done. Footnote: if she had the right to choose as well as he, he had the right to choose as well as she, in that women owned only fifty per cent of any foetus they might carry. On the other hand, it was true that women ran one hundred per cent of the physical risk of any abortion, and while those who let others take such risks on their behalf were never going to look very good, in this case he had at least seen to it that the risk-taker understood all the risks before agreeing to take them. Next point: perhaps in one sense abortion was murder, but he would shoulder all that by himself, treat it as a matter between him and God, so to speak. Just then a query new to him presented itself: had Nancy considered the murder aspect, and anyhow how was a chap who let a girl take a large moral risk on his behalf going to look? He booted that one out of his mind as not having appeared before the closing date and quoted in his own support his favourite Shakespearean snub: ''Twere to consider too curiously to consider so.'

Finally, and briefly, and not even considering his own interests in the matter: as George and Elizabeth and everybody else would have fervently agreed, he was almost an ideal non-husband for Nancy, being selfish, self-indulgent, lazy, arrogant and above all inextinguishably promiscuous by nature. A picture or series of pictures of the pair of them married swam up: her crouched in a hovel with babies, him entertaining a tart in a flashy restaurant, or her passing round the cucumber sandwiches to other fecund young mums while he craned out of the boxroom window with a telescope pointed at the girls' school playground with a stand up to his neck. He could grin about it all from where he was but the reality would be no fun for anybody.

Robin had settled any doubts he might have had. Of the only two possible courses he had settled on A and quashed B. He had a moment of terrible compunction when he opened his eyes and saw the actual Nancy in her nearly outgrown oatmeal dressing-gown, dark hair in straggles, on the way out of the narrow bedroom clutching her sponge-bag, but promptly remembered his undertaking to negotiate a bath for her and set about approaching Molly Humphries on the subject. In the intervals of doing this he thought briefly of what was to come and said to himself that today's Robin, even the rest of this year's Robin and successors, all were bound to feel dreadful qualms now and then, but as today receded a feeling of thankfulness, of relief at having been spared worse, would supervene and eventually triumph.

For the next hour or so Robin succeeded quite well in keeping shut down any higher mental faculties he might have said he possessed. Having successfully taken a bath, Nancy appeared in the kitchen, where he was settling down to porridge, toast and tea. As instructed, she ate and drank nothing, at once bearing the *Western Mail* off to an easy chair in a corner away from the table. To his eye she looked reasonably comfortable, reasonably calm, though anyone might have noticed that every so often she pressed her lips tightly together, or have wondered how attentively she was reading. She sat in a posture familiar to Robin, with her legs tucked up on the seat not so much under her as beside her. Once or twice she looked up at him and gave a cheerful smile, like a good child on a journey signalling to his parents that all is well.

When the time came Robin abandoned rather than finished his breakfast, which although not unpalatable had not been easy to get down. Out of tact or indifference Molly Humphries had left them alone together, so he went in search of her and found her at a small bureau writing letters. He noticed that her fingernails were not very clean as well as being painted.

'We'll be off in a few minutes, Molly.'

'Would you like me to come with you?'

'Don't bother, we can manage.'

'Are you sure? Actually you'll be fine with Paul, he takes care of everything.'

'Paul?'

'Paul Beck. He used to be called Pavel or something but over here most people call him Paul. He told me once he was a count or something. Perhaps that's got something to do with his attitude to helping girls like Nancy out of their difficulties. Some of the fellows in that business are in it just for the money, let's face it, but Paul's different. I'm sure he'd work for nothing if he had to. You see, he's an idealist.' She spoke as of a Comanche or a vegetarian. 'Oh, I'm sorry I had to love you and leave you like that last night but an old buttie turned up out of the blue, in Cardiff for just a couple of days on business. I don't suppose you've got any firm plans for later as yet so I'll see you back here around six, say six-thirty, give you a key then if you want one, okay? I expect I'll be out this evening. On the town.'

Molly H looked sidelong at Robin in a conspiratorial sort of way, a way somehow incorporating the information that he would be wasting his time should he think of drawing her into any conspiracy of his own, a thought that had not actually occurred to him. A little earlier she had managed to pass him the message that her dealings with Pavel/Paul contained no personal element beyond respect. Oh really? In that case how and where had the two of them met?

He hoped he would never need to know the answer to this question, any more than others about the Pendry-Humphries-Beck-Uncle Tom Cobley et al. organization, if it deserved the term. He went up to the bedroom above the hall and found Nancy sitting on the bed with her loaded string bag beside her.

'Ready?'

'Yes.'

'We've got plenty of time but we might as well be off I suppose.'

It was a cloudy, damp day outside but no rain was falling. The streets were too noisy and crowded for them to have conversed on their way to the clinic. Seen in the light, the building proved to be two substantial terrace houses knocked into one and, not very recently, painted a dark grey. There was no external indication of what went on inside its walls, which by the look of them might just as likely have sheltered a small private school or largish firm of solicitors. Robin rang the only bell in sight and they waited on the step for perhaps half a minute. In that time Robin noticed that Nancy, who had turned away to face the street, suddenly turned back again. When he looked himself he saw a pair of middle-aged women halted side by side on the pavement and apparently watching him and Nancy as they stood at the door. Instinctively he made some sort of angry sweeping gesture at the two and they started to move on in some disarray.

'There are some people who'll stare at anything,' he remarked to Nancy, who gave no sign of having heard. Almost at once the door opened and a girl in a dark-grey overall let them in and took them as far as the entrance-hall. Just at that moment an old woman came into view. She wore a dressing-gown and was walking slowly and with difficulty on the arm of another girl in dark grey. The first sight of her was enough to put it beyond doubt that some of the doctoring at this place was all right, legal, above board. For some reason this revelation greatly heartened Robin. Before the old woman had moved out of sight, a tall bespectacled one of intermediate age appeared and gave a smile of professional greeting.

'Now, you're Mrs Shaw,' she told Nancy. 'Like Bernard Shaw the writer. You're a few minutes early, which is good. If you'll just come with me.'

They soon reached the small room Robin and Nancy had seen the previous evening. It was just the same as it had been then except that now the bed was made up. Nancy put her string bag down on it.

'Right,' the lady in the glasses said pleasantly. 'If you'll just get undressed now, Mrs Shaw, and slip your nightie on, and get into bed and try and relax. The bathroom's just across the way and a few yards to your right.' She turned to Robin. 'If you'd like to wait in the waiting-room you're very welcome. We must see if we can't find you a cup of tea. I'm afraid Mrs Shaw will have to wait a bit longer for hers. You did remember not to eat or drink anything this morning, I hope, dear?'

'Oh yes,' said Nancy, 'I mean I haven't eaten or drunk anything.'

'Good girl. Well, if there's nothing more I can do for you I'll be off. But before I go, now don't either of you let anybody know I said this, but we've done hundreds here and there's been no trouble with any of them. Dr Beck's one of the best in the world, and we think we're quite good ourselves.' She smiled. 'So – good luck, both.'

She was gone. Robin found that the cheering effect of the sight of the frail old woman had spent itself. For the moment he could find nothing to say, though he tried hard.

After a pause, Nancy said, 'You might as well go too, love.'

'I'll stay as long as you want me to.'

'No point, honestly. I'll be all right.'

'Really? Are you sure?'

For another moment it seemed to him not so much terrible as ridiculous that men and women had had and used the gift of speech for centuries and learnt to say the most complicated and important and special things to each other at all sorts of times, and now here were a couple of them with only stuff like this to utter. It was as if words had been the wrong idea from the start.

Did Nancy feel this or anything like this? She was saying, 'I'll do as she said and get undressed and lie down. She was nice, wasn't she? I took to her. Off you go, now. I've worked out what I feel about this. It's got to be done and I've come to one of the very best places to have it done and I might as well face it and after all a lot of women have it done these days and I bet a lot more wish they'd had it done when it's too late. Robin, please go and I'll see you in a little while.'

'You press that bell and tell them to fetch me and I'll come running.'

'Yes, now off you go.'

She turned her back and started taking things out of her string bag. He stood and wondered whether to embrace Nancy and give her a special kiss, but decided against it on the grounds that it would make their parting seem too important, not that it was not important but she had sounded as if she wanted it played down. So dithering

275

he called to her, 'See you very soon, then, love.' Receiving no reply, he went out.

Robin had reached the door of the waiting-room when he halted and again stood and considered. He could think of nothing more that he might have said or demonstrated to Nancy, usefully, relevantly said, etc, but perhaps he ought to have attached more weight to the idea that what you unusefully and irrelevantly said, etc, at such times had its own scale of importance. To put the matter more directly, he bloody well ought to have given Nancy a hug she would remember all her life and said all sorts of things to her neither of them would remember beyond the time it took to say and hear them. More directly still, he had been scared of a few tears. He swung round and, not without a certain moral glow for at once acting on the admission of error, went back the way he had come.

What happened next happened quickly. As he reached the shut door of the room where he had left Nancy, he heard a sound from inside he hardly had time to name before he was through the doorway and hurrying over to where she was lying face down on the bed. He noticed scattered on the floor near her were things she had brought in her string bag – hairbrush and comb, two oblong blue packets with rounded corners, a clean nightdress out of its folds, a sponge-bag with strings drawn, a tattered paperback book – together with the emptied string bag itself. There was an open packet of paper handkerchiefs within her reach by the pillow. He reached her side at the moment when without other movement she reached for the packet of handkerchiefs and pulled a fresh one out. She was crying hard, so hard that it was as if she was trying to get rid of all the tears she would ever shed, moaning between sobs on a hopeless, inconsolable note.

At once and acutely, Robin was aware of a jumble of feelings in himself, some he knew now he had been trying with fair success not to acknowledge, others of whose existence he had been altogether unaware. He dropped to his knees by the bed, spoke her name and called her darling, but had the sense not to ask her what was the matter.

Perhaps she had taken no notice of his arrival, perhaps she had not noticed it at all. Either way, she uttered now a strange and dreadful sound that was neither weeping nor speech and turned her face towards him, wet, flushed, rumpled, her eyes already inflamed and puffy. With difficulty and frequent sudden pauses, she said, 'I asked you, I told you to go, because I was afraid this would happen, I could feel it coming on, but then, before, I thought I could stop it from happening, only I knew it would if you stayed any longer, but it happened anyway.' Without warning she sat up, then swung herself round to sit on the edge of the bed. After a gulp or two she went on, 'But now you're here, I suppose I might as well tell you why. It's not so much not liking the idea of what he's going to do, the doctor, I'm sure I shan't feel a thing. It's more, well, it's more the idea of having it taken away, thinking of what it was going to be and won't be now.' Robin made to take her in his arms but she drew back. 'No, I want to tell you and you don't want your jacket mucked up. It's silly really, because I'm sure there'll be others, only they won't be this one. You see, I told you it was silly, didn't I? It's not as if, I mean I've known all the time it's got to be done.'

Fresh tears stood in her eyes and she tried to push them back with her fingers. Robin watched her for a few seconds before picking up the string bag and starting to refill it.

'What are you doing?'

'What does it look as though I'm doing? I'm getting us ready to leave.'

'What are you talking about. Dr Thing'll be here in a minute.'

'That's why we've got to get a move on. You'd better smarten yourself up.'

'What? But we can't just walk out now.'

'Oh, we can't, can't we? Just watch us.'

'But you've paid all that money.'

'So they'll have nothing to get at us for, once we're away from here. Come on.'

She had picked up her comb and started to wield it and was wiping her eyes with another paper handkerchief. 'Are you really and truly sure about this, Robin?' She blew her nose. 'Because unless you really are—'

'Shut up and get ready to move before I change my mind again.'

'You're not to do that.'

'I'll give you three minutes.'

Nobody even looked at them as they made their way out of the clinic, which was a great relief to them both and a mild vexation to Robin. He would have liked the chance of sending a message to Dr Beck or, better, confronting him in the flesh and saying something like, 'Thank you for your advice, which had something about wise behaviour in it, hadn't it? Well, here we go. And yes, I have shaved today and intend to do the same tomorrow regardless of your wishes. And ha ha ha ha ha and fuck off.' Or perhaps just the last two words, but them he quite deeply wanted to say to Molly Humphries' idealistic pal.

'Where are we off to now?' asked Nancy, whose eyes looked merely as if she had not been able to close them all night, much better than earlier.

'Pick up my stuff from Molly's, that's if I can get in.'

He managed with seconds to spare. Having dropped Nancy some way down the street for concealment, he was about to ring the bell when the door was thrown open by Molly herself, attired for the outdoors in a reddish tweed coat with a high neck and carrying a small umbrella.

'All going well, I trust?' she asked him.

'Oh yes, I just popped back for a couple of things.'

'You've cut it fine. I'm late already so you'll understand if I don't stay to see you out. Slam the door shut when you go.'

Without saying she would see him later, in fact without saying several things, Molly Humphries moved off. He hung about long enough to see her turn the opposite way to where Nancy had halted. That was a relief. He was afraid of Molly as he was not of Dr Beck and wondered what he had noticed about her that made him so, but he had forgotten that as soon as he had started to leave for the third and last time. What was in his mind, where it was not in the least welcome, was a short but vivid replay of Milnes licking at an ice-cream cornet in the school tuckshop and saying with all his old authority, 'Never promise anything or agree to anything while a woman's crying.' But when he caught sight of Nancy standing about in her belted overcoat in the chilly street, smiling and waving to him, he told himself that from that moment on he would never again think of Eric Milnes, whose very name he had forgotten for years till a few seconds before.

'Have you got everything?' asked Nancy. 'Good, well, can we go to the station now?'

'The next decent train isn't until—'

'We can wait for it there, can't we? There's bound to be somewhere to sit.'

'I think we'd do better in a—'

'I'd like to get as near as I can to not being in Cardiff any more.'

In the station refreshment-room, Robin got them both cups of Bovril. 'Do you feel safe yet?' he asked.

'Oh yes, I've felt safe in one way or another ever since I saw you starting to put my stuff into that bag. But I'll feel safer when we're actually on the train.'

'You mean you're afraid Dr Beck might come rushing in here and drag you back to that place by force?'

'I know it sounds silly.'

'I know what you mean, though. Will you still feel safe in only the one way or completely when you're on the train? Well, you said me packing up your stuff made you feel safe in one way. So what are the other ways of feeling safe, if any?'

'I shouldn't have brought it up,' she said, starting to blush, 'I was hoping you weren't going to notice. I honestly don't like saying this, and it's not my place, and of course the main thing is me not going to have the baby taken away, but I mean I don't see how I can just sort of go and have the baby like having something else like a holiday. I mean what about the baby?'

'Oh, the *baby*.' Robin tried to look as if he had indeed failed completely to reckon with the baby, but soon broke into smiles. 'I was hanging on for more suitable surroundings, but they may never turn up and anyway how can it possibly matter where one says it?'

She gazed at him with surly suspicion. 'Where one says what?'

'Will you marry me?'

Her expression did not change. 'You wouldn't say that unless you meant it,' she stated in as flat a tone as might have been thought possible for an urgent question.

'I was never more serious in my life,' he replied, lowering an internal safety-curtain to keep out of his thoughts anybody with a name beginning with M. 'Oh God, she's crying again.'

'Sorry, it won't last long this time. Different sort of crying, see. Anyway, er, is it possible for me to have a drink? I mean, you know, an intoxicating drink.'

'Here? I shouldn't think so for a moment. And anyway you ought to eat something, surely.'

'I'm not hungry.'

'You haven't had anything all day.'

'I'm still not hungry.'

'Do you really want a drink?'

'Never mind. I can't imagine what made me ask.'

'Oh yes you can, I can tell. Out with it. Now we're getting married we've got to tell each other everything.'

'All right, but it's terribly childish. The way I reckoned, I wanted to dance round the room, but I knew I couldn't, but I thought if I'd had a drink it wouldn't matter, because people would think I was dancing because I was drunk instead of barmy.'

'Jesus.'

'I said it was childish.'

'Different sort of Christ, see. There may be something I can do. Let me have a go now.'

Robin got up and went across to the counter, where an emaciated but colourfully made-up girl in her twenties presided over a large smart-looking tea-urn, some rows of bottles and a glass-sided receptacle that contained pork pies, sandwiches, some desiccated sprigs of parsley and a lonely tomato. When he came back he was carrying two glasses half full of a straw-coloured liquid in which strings of bubbles rose.

'This won't be very nice,' he explained, 'but it does seem to be a drink of a sort. British champagne-type wine is what it seems to boil down to. I thought at first I'd say you'd come over queer but then I remembered we were in Wales so I said it was your birthday. Hold your glass up to the young lady now and do a, you know, a cheerio.'

Nancy did as asked and then suddenly said, 'We are properly engaged, are we?'

'We are properly engaged. I'll get you a ring as soon as I can borrow some money. There, what more can I say?'

'Nothing I suppose.'

Returning from Cardiff something like twenty-four hours earlier than expected, Robin and Nancy had to find somewhere to spend the following night. Nancy said that now that they were properly engaged they should stay at a hotel of some sort and, within reason, never mind the expense, recouping themselves if necessary later with a loan from the Botley old girls. She also seemed to think that any decent hotel would recognise and welcome as virtually married any couple who seriously thought of themselves as properly engaged. He pointed out the flaws in these positions without feeling able to recommend an unheralded descent on Mrs Pendry, whose telephone number made a strange and ominous noise when the telephone operator tried it. More to defer a decision than anything else, he rang his brother George. After announcing his identity in the recommended style, Robin said he and Nancy were in London.

'Oh yes. And?'

'Well, and I don't suppose you could put us up for the night, could you?'

'Christ!' howled George into the telephone, and Robin just had time to think it an extreme response before the distant voice changed direction and merely bawled, 'Get her down off there! Who let her get up on there?' A confusion of voices followed, Marian's prominent among them, and Robin had plenty of time to reflect on an aspect of his own subsequent life. Returning, George said down the wire, 'As regards your staying the night, I'm afraid—'

'The reason we're a bit disorganised is we've changed our minds. Er, Nancy's not going to go and see that man after all.'

'What? What man? What?'

'You know, the man she was going to go and see. We're getting married instead.'

'Oh, bloody good! Well, pretty good. Well, anyway. This means I get my hundred quid back, I take it. Get that child out of here,' said George without bothering to shift his mouth from the mouthpiece.

'I'm afraid things aren't quite as straightforward as that.'

'Oh shit. They never are, are they, things? Anyway, or rather *anyway*, congratulations, especially to you, little brother, and come round as soon as you like. Though even if you hang about there'll still be bags of time for you to have a nice game with Marian before you give her her bath. It'll be good practice for you. I'll be sure to let her know you're on your way.'

Marian stopped yelling and running about for several minutes at the sight of her Auntie Nancy. The two had always got on well together. When they had settled down to some very elementary playing with toy building-blocks, Robin felt some satisfaction at what this boded, but also the faint disquiet of a man who sees his future existence being shaped for him without consultation. Later, Nancy and Elizabeth set about getting the small girl off to bath and bed with an urgency and attention to detail more in keeping, he felt, with preparations for getting somebody off to Antarctica. 'Pissed,' was George's mouthed comment. 'As farts,' went Robin's faithful reply.

In the pub, Robin did his best to explain about the non-availability of the hundred pounds. When he had finished, George said, 'I can't help feeling that someone along that line ought to be as pleased as Punch for having their cake and eating it, but I can't seem to decide who.'

'The woman in Cardiff is my educated guess. Hardest thing on two legs.'

'I thought to start with I'd give you the hundred as a wedding-present, but then I thought just the cancellation of a debt, that's a pretty lousy wedding-present.'

'Oh, I don't know.'

'Let's leave it for a bit, not that there seems much else to do. Elizabeth's got an uncle who had a nasty stroke the other day. He's known to have a soft spot for her and also not to be hard up for a few bob, so, well, who knows?'

'Jolly handy that would be.'

'I'm sorry if I got on my high horse slightly when I passed you the cheque the other day. I don't think I realised how painful it was going to be for me. There's nothing like lending somebody some money for waking you up to the bloke's moral shortcomings.'

'That's all right, George. Thanks again for the loan.'

'All the same, don't you go running away with the idea that after all this you've somehow lived to fight another day. It may not be exactly up to me to raise the matter, but when and I didn't say if like President Roosevelt you notice something moving and fuck it, for Christ's sake do it on the quiet, all right? And the fact that everybody's quite sure you'll go on pleasing yourself doesn't make you wonderful and free and like that turd Mellors in *Lady Chatterley's Lover* – yes I've got a copy at home, yes it is the unexpurgated edition and no you can't borrow it and no it's no good anyway—anyway, what I was going to say was, all it shows is you haven't bloody well grown up.'

'If everybody at my wedding party's going to be as nice to me as you've been I declare I shan't know where to look.'

'Drink that up and have another. Sorry, Robin, but you do rather ask for it, you know. When do you propose telling Mum about this? She went back home yesterday.'

'In that case I could ring her tonight, and then perhaps go down some time tomorrow.'

★

Robin and his mother, each holding a cup of tea, sat in their usual seats on either side of the drawing-room fireplace, where that afternoon a small coal fire burned. Outside it was so thickly overcast that in here the standard lamp was on. This piece was a comparative novelty, but piano, pelmet, occasional table and all were the same as ever.

'So I got out of there as soon as I decently could,' Mrs Davies was saying. 'It, it isn't Margery, though I do wish she'd try harder to control those children, but she's sweet to me. But between ourselves, Robin, it's that Roger with his rules and regulations. I mean what's the point of growing a beard if you're not going to be a little bit free and easy? Still, what do they say, you never really know a man till you've lived in his house. Those children are scared of him which shows you can go too far the other way.'

Here Mrs Davies gave a wince and a scowl, perhaps at the thought of bearded Roger and his régime. She began to rub her left shoulder and winced again.

'What's up, Mum?'

'Old age creeping on, dear. I've been getting these twinges of rheumatism in my shoulder and round there. It's this horrid damp weather.'

'But you are pretty fit generally, aren't you? George was saying how well you were looking when he saw you.'

'Oh yes, I mustn't complain. I've always been rather a one for little aches and pains. As you know.'

'I hope you'll tell me if you want anything done.'

'Now you didn't come all this way just to discuss my ailments.' Mrs Davies moved her left elbow to and fro. There, it's gone now. What were we talking about?'

'I was going to ask you what your plans were, Mum. Were you thinking of staying on here?'

'I don't want to do that any longer than I can help. It's not a very big house but it's really too big just for one person. Worth a bit, though, these days, and there's the furniture. I thought I'd sell up and then, you do remember Joy Carpenter, of course you do. She's on her own too, and we always said we'd throw in our lot together if we both found ourselves in that position, we've often discussed it. We've both got a bit put by and we thought we'd open a little teashop, you know, anchovy toast, strawberry jam and cream scones kind of thing, somewhere outside Henley or Woking. We're driving down to look at a couple of places on Thursday, Joy and I, we've made up our minds we're going to do something with what's left of our lives.'

Mrs Davies stirred her tea and sipped it carefully. She seemed to be wanting to say more but to be uncertain of how to set about it. Hesitantly, on the alert to change course at once if he turned out to be going wrong, he said, 'How's that son of hers, Jeremy isn't it, I remember I had lunch with him down the road during the war. Does he—'

He was on target. His mother sat up straight, then took her time settling her cup and saucer back on the tea-tray before saying in a lowered voice, 'He's got a place of his own now, somewhere near Sloane Square I believe. He comes and sees his mother every so often, she tells me. Doesn't encourage her to come and see him. Well . . .'

'And he's all right is he?' Robin considered this question a small masterpiece of vagueness.

'Huh!' Her short disrespectful laugh was not a noise he associated with his mother. 'Well, I suppose in one way he's very much all right,' she said, 'in a part of London where I gather you can more or less come and go as you please. If you want to hear what he does for a living, then I'm afraid I can't help you.'

'He'll have found something pretty unstrenuous if I know Jeremy.'

'You never knew him very well, did you? I remember you went to tea there a couple of times in their old house when the father was still alive. Mind you, dear, that Jeremy, now there was a funny sort of chap if you like. Do you remember him going to gaol rather than have anything to do with the war-effort? Well, that wasn't the only thing they threw him in gaol for. You know what I'm talking about, don't you?'

'Remind me,' said Robin, who needed no reminding.

'Jeremy was caught behaving indecently in a public lavatory. With a soldier, of course. His father knew a couple of the magistrates from the golf club and got part of the case left out. But there are no two ways about it, Robin, Jeremy Carpenter is a homosexual.'

Robin wanted to laugh and cheer when his mother brought out the word, pronouncing it in a way that suggested she had seldom done so before, though not lowering her voice. His reaction came partly from sudden embarrassment, partly from sheer surprise. He would have been as well prepared, rather better perhaps, for a mention from that source of the Tiger Mark VI with 88-mm guns. When he answered he tried not to overdo his appreciation of the justice of her diagnosis.

'M'm, I agree,' he said. 'I think I spotted it years back.' He shook his head dolefully.

'I suppose he hasn't ever . . .'

'No, never.'

'But you quite like him, don't you? Well, I don't *dislike* him myself, it's no business of mine but I can't seem to feel at ease with him. But evidently you don't mind.'

'No, I've no feelings against them, against homosexuals, though I'm bloody thankful I haven't a single drop of that in me,' he said, just to be on the safe side, 'but they can be most amusing to talk to, and Jeremy for one, Jeremy's very bright too. Though not quite as bright as he thinks he is,' he added, now speaking exactly as he felt.

'Well, obviously that's the voice of the modern generation, the ones who grew up in the war years. I expect somebody like me, I must seem quite early Victorian in comparison. All I say is, we're not all the same, some of us have tried to keep up with the times. I know Joy Carpenter thinks I tend to go too far sometimes these days. I saw you give me a look just now when I didn't mince my words.'

Robin could think of nothing whatsoever to say, so he contented himself with looking tolerant and with leaving undisturbed the present mood of confidence, of confidentiality between himself and his mother. The fire was burning low but he left it. After a moment she said, 'You don't mind if I talk for a bit, do you, dear?'

'Rather not, Mum, you go ahead.'

But again she paused. Robin made up the fire. Before he had quite finished, his mother spoke suddenly. 'I'd expected things to be different with your father gone, naturally I had, but I hadn't bargained for how different. He was a rather unusual man, your father, but we'd been married so long, thirty-five years, in that time I suppose I'd forgotten that or perhaps I just stopped noticing. He was very shy, you know, didn't like letting his feelings show in public. But at the same time he was very loving. He was very fond of you and Margery and George but he was afraid to, I think he probably didn't know how to show it. I always thought he was a little hard on you, Robin. He was disappointed in a way at how the other two had turned out, I couldn't see why. Margery's pretty silly but the odds are she gets that from my side, anyway not his fault, and surely there's nothing much wrong with George bar a bit of bad language, but no, your father was going to do his best to make sure of you. No one was going to be able to say he'd neglected you.'

She smiled. He had a spontaneous vision of an early life spent under conditions of parental neglect, a paradise of cigarette-smoking, tossing off, cutting games, cutting school, looking at feelthy pictures, using language fit to make George gasp, belching, farting and, in the background, vaguer images like large-scale chocolate thefts and afternoons with French maids. But for the moment he conscientiously put all these things out of his mind.

'He wasn't going to use religion on you the way his own father had on him. He hoped you'd ask him questions about religion and the rest of it, but you never did, not that I'm blaming you. Anyway, he was going to try to make you into something like himself regardless, I could see it and I could have told him it would never have worked. I loved your father, he was so much nicer to me when we were on our own than he ever let show to another living soul, and I tried to be a good wife to him and do and say what he wanted even when I didn't really hold with it deep down, what could I do but take his side, even over you, no, please don't say anything, Robin dear, and it's only now he's not here any more that I realise or can say to myself he tried to make me into somebody I wasn't, or only half was. He did it for the best, I'm sure he did everything for the best. Like most people.'

Robin waited for his mother's tears, but it was soon clear that none were coming, so he just took some time over lighting a cigarette.

'What made me feel as bad as anything was all the business about that nice girl Nancy. It was ridiculous and very wrong of him to order her out of the house like that, well you know I thought so at the time. What I want to say to you now, I did what I could for you and her but it wasn't enough, but I couldn't have gone against him, I wouldn't support him but I felt I couldn't defy him, what could I have done, I couldn't have anything to do with her behind his back. I think perhaps that was wrong of me but it's all over now. I hope you don't hold it against me, dear.'

'I understand completely, Mum.'

'You're a good boy, Robin, you've never been one to bear grudges. Well, now that's out of the way, I'd love to see her if you don't think she'd mind.'

'She'd love to see you but she's been afraid you'd think she was intruding. I'll tell her. Mum,' said Robin, going straight on, 'she and I are going to get married. Very soon.'

'Oh, I am delighted, dear,' said Mrs Davies, and mother and son warmly embraced. Then she said, 'I can't say I'm surprised, but I am so pleased and thrilled. But what's wrong? Going to have a baby, is she?'

'Yes. How did you guess?'

'What? Not much guesswork needed, dear. Well, again I'm not surprised, I suppose I am a bit that you didn't take care of things better. But anyway, I can't say I'm thrilled by that part. A wee bit disappointed in fact.'

'Sorry, Mum.'

'In my experience starting off like that is starting off on the wrong foot as you might say. But I expect that's only the old stick-in-the-mud in me talking. Anyhow, one thing I'm not is shocked. I've seen too much of life for that, even an old stick-in-the-mud living in south London. I promise not to make Nancy feel awkward about anything. Well, for what it's worth I give the two of you my blessing. The three of you. I can't help feeling pleased about that.'

That evening at Mrs Pendry's, Nancy said to Robin in a tone no doubt intended to sound light, 'I'm afraid my day wasn't as successful as yours seems to have been.'

'Oh dear. What went wrong? Do you want to tell me now or will it keep till we're sitting in the restaurant?'

'I'd sooner tell you now with nobody looking at us if you don't mind. You tell me again first, what day are we getting married?'

'Friday. It's the soonest they could do it.'

'Yes, you explained about that. Friday, so I was right. Not that it makes any difference. They say, that's my mum and dad, they won't come to the ceremony whenever it is.'

'Well, it's not as if they'd be missing much. A couple of minutes in the registry office. Some ceremony. A real corker, what?'

Nancy glared for a moment at that, but it was in a reasonable tone that she said, 'I can see why it doesn't matter much to you either way if they come or not, but it matters a lot to me. However short and sort of automatic the ceremony turns out to be, it's all the wedding I'm going to have and it may be silly of me but I want my mum and dad to be at it.'

'I'm sorry, love, I should have known better, I wasn't thinking. Of course it isn't silly of you to feel like that. Is there any more gin?'

'Only in Mrs Pendry's cupboard downstairs perhaps. You finished the bottle that was here yesterday. We could go along to supper if you like.'

'You never want a drink, do you, feel like one? Wait a minute, you did in that refreshment-room.'

289

'That was different, you see that. As regards in the ordinary way, I worked out wanting a drink must be like I feel when I feel I could really do with a cup of tea multiplied by about ten. Tea tastes nice, too.'

'What else did they say, your parents, apart from they wouldn't come?'

'Are you sure you wouldn't rather go to the restaurant? Well all right, my dad did most of the talking. He wasn't shouting or anything like that, but he kept saying I'd let them down, that's him and my mum. They'd trusted me, they'd put me on my honour, and I'd let them down. They thought they'd learned their lesson from how they'd carried on with my sister, like Victorian parents he said, and how that had turned out, and lo and behold . . .'

'You'd let them down. How did I come out of it?'

'Oh, very badly. Terribly badly. From what my mum said in particular. She'd thought you were a nice decent type of boy who respected your obligations to do this and not to do that and so on, and, well, lo and behold again, you've turned out to be nothing but a common seducer. I'm sorry, Robin, but that's what my dad said, those very words.'

'M'm. I can see how it must look to him.'

'I can't imagine how they managed to go on thinking we'd been content with just holding hands all these years. They were young themselves not so long ago.'

'Perhaps they're putting some of the blame on me for their own mistakes, you know, for taking the line of least resistance, just letting things slide.'

'Is that supposed to be funny?' asked Nancy.

'But perhaps not. Anyway, d'you think it would do any good if I went to see them?'

'I doubt it, not for the moment.'

'We've only got a moment, just till Friday.'

'Let's discuss it over supper. Then I can tell you more of what my dad said about you. I'll just nip along to the lav and then we'll be off.'

Left alone, Robin tried to sum up his position as he sat in the chair with arms. He had not often bothered to look round the bed-sitter while partly living in it and, now that he seemed about to move on, had little more reason to. But the row of Nancy's make-up stuff and bathroom stuff along the top of the squat greyish-brown chest of drawers, the snaps of parents, sister Megan with baby and various relatives on the mantelpiece above the diminutive electric fire, Nancy's shoes on floor, dressing-gown on hook, letter-case on bed, made him aware of the time that had passed since his first sight of them, gave him a feeling of having missed something indefinably important through lack of curiosity, lack of attention. This room was the first place in his life where he had even intermittently lived with somebody, somebody whose embraces were beyond compare the most wonderful in his life. At least he had not missed any of that.

Marrying that somebody was going to mean more than just more of the same. In fact it had on several recent occasions seemed to him that any resemblance between his present condition and the one busily coming his way was going to turn out to be not much better than purely coincidental. *Sure* Nancy was going to be there or just round the corner all the time instead of merely most of it, *of course* he was going to be able to make love to her whenever he felt like it, *natch* there would be severe, partly unforeseeable snags and checks in his way, unforeseeable in that the only means of finding out about them was to run into them personally. And that covered no more than life at home, which anyhow could not start until he had accomplished the gloom-enforcing task of finding somewhere to lead the said life in. Next came the life of a married undergraduate, which was dead certain to harbour all sorts of unforeseeable and specially nasty bits of nastiness all its own. After that, if not jostling it, came money. Oh . . .

Robin had worked his way through most of the maledictions known to him, passing over each in turn as far too puny for the occasion, when Nancy reappeared in the doorway and he cheered up at once. He thought he had never seen her looking so pretty or healthy or pleased about most things. He stood up.

'Ready?' she asked.

'Yes.'

As often, they dined, or had a sort of evening meal, at a place called the Refuge off the High Street, known to some as the Chinese, though it had never been known to serve any food even distantly associated with that land. Some of what they did serve was not closely associated with food from anywhere at all, but nearly every dish came to the table hot where appropriate and always in generous quantities. They were quite nice to you as well, though too inefficient to make it count for much.

Without having to be prompted, Nancy was as good as her word and told Robin more of what her dad had said about him. This ran, in part, 'According to him you're the kind of Welshman who gets Welsh people a bad name. Very charming on the surface and treacherous underneath. I'm only telling you what he said.'

'Which you don't agree with on the whole, at least not necessarily. That's a comfort. What did you tell him?'

'I said he didn't know you.'

'And he asked you whose fault that was.'

'Words to that effect, yes.'

'M'm. I'm only half as much as a Welshman as he is, less, having been born and brought up in England. I always think of myself as English. If it matters.'

'I said some of that too.'

'Yes, well, it doesn't sound as if it would do much good if I went to see them, does it?' Like Latin questions beginning with the particle *num*, this one expected the answer no. In fact it devoutly hoped for that answer, and would not have been asked at all had Robin not thought equity required that he should have asked it a second time.

She answered it by shaking her head and he silently blessed her.

'M'm. Is there any chance they'll change their minds at the last minute and turn up after all? Or are they perhaps acting up on purpose just to give us a bad time for a couple of days?'

Just then a waitress, a girl of eighteen of the type sometimes described as slatternly, though in reality good-natured enough, planked down a plateful of cheese omelette with chives in front of Nancy, who thus had a few seconds to consider her reply. This time it was fully verbal.

'No,' she said.

'Oh, I see.'

A few minutes later, Nancy said, 'I've remembered something else my dad said about you. No, it was my mum. No, it was my dad. I know it doesn't matter which really. Or at all. Anyway, he said you were the kind of man who thinks only of his own pleasure.'

This Robin heard with definite indignation. He said, 'I'd like to know how he makes that out, I must say. If that's all I was interested in, what the hell does he think I'm doing getting married to you? Jesus Christ.'

Nancy thought about that. 'You mean if you'd really been thinking of nothing but your own pleasure you'd never have got so that you were going to get married to me, is that right?'

'*No* of course I don't. No, I mean that the kind of man your father was thinking of, the kind that's interested only in his own pleasure, you know, a rake or a libertine like in Restoration comedy,' said Robin rather wildly, 'they're quite heartless and a different kind of person altogether.'

'Different from you, you mean?'

'Completely different.'

Robin was reconciled to the prospect of several discussions of this sort. What he would willingly have done without as accompaniment to this one was the presence at a nearby table of a couple of queers that might or might not have constituted a queer couple. Limited experience had taught him to be chary of applying that label to strangers, even mentally, but he had not much hesitation with these two. In the way they looked at Nancy and him, one of them turning his head quite a way round to do so, and then at each other, it was tempting to see amused superiority over a boringly conventional and also inept pair of straights. Robin resisted the temptation for a moment, glanced away, glanced back and saw more of the same. Right. Now he was visited by a less tempting temptation, namely to go over and punch the offending heads. This one he decisively rejected on several grounds, not excluding the fact that both members of the pair looked perfectly capable of some effective head-punching on their own accord. So what was he to do? Without thinking he reached across the table and found and grasped Nancy's hand. At once she gave him a brilliant smile and almost as quickly the smiles of the supposed queers seemed to him to turn forced and unnatural. Perhaps all of it – *all* of it? Well, what there had been of it – had taken place in his mind. Either way the neighbouring duo could go and fuck themselves.

'What are you grinning at?' asked Nancy, who had noticed nothing.

'That was no grin, that was an affectionate beam.'

In this case equity made no requirement.

The next morning Robin went round to college, his first visit there since the end of the previous week. Apart from picking up any mail, his purpose was to telephone his mother. He could have done so from Mrs Pendry's if necessary, but in the circumstances he felt like avoiding the likely presence of the lady. She might still have been having a difference with him over the aborted abortion. When that news was broken to her she had seemed partly delighted, as she might wholly have been at the thought of being co-recipient of a hundred unreturnable pounds, but at the same time suspicious that he had found Dr Beck, Molly Humphries and the rest of the set-up disreputable, beneath him in some way. He meant to keep as far as possible clear of her till the end of time, or at any rate till the end of Nancy's time under her roof.

Two communications awaited him in the porter's lodge, one a note in porter's handwriting time-dated earlier that morning and asking him to telephone a London number recognisable as George's, the other a serious affair on college stationery. When divested of its envelope this informed him that the Dean would like to see Mr

Robin Davies in what proved to be less than five minutes from that moment. He took a quick pee, grabbed a gown off a hook in the lodge, combed his hair, straightened the tie he was opportunely wearing and hurried into the back quad.

The Dean was perhaps fifty and so not much more than half the apparent average age of dons. He taught English language and so had had little to do with Robin in the matter of studies. He leaned considerably to one side when in a standing posture, had a habit of pushing his left cheek outwards with his tongue at intervals and usually wore a hairy brown suit with flaps on all visible pockets. His sitting-room was remarkable only for the number and variety of clocks in it. After some small-talk he said in his disconcertingly normal voice, 'As you're no doubt aware, Davies, full term in this university began on Monday and some of us have been hoping to see something of you. There was a College collection on Saturday, a formality in your case, but you failed to attend it or send an apology for your absence.'

'I'm sorry, sir, I forgot.' In some sense Robin had been aware of such matters, but until just now they had lain at the very back of his mind, among German aircraft silhouettes and Caesar's Gallic wars. He spoke with mild contrition.

The Dean was shaking his head. 'I haven't asked you here to reprehend you, merely to make an appeal. We know that these have been difficult times for you, we were sorry to hear of your father's death, and this together with your age and record of service under arms has inclined us to overlook any irregularities in your conduct so far. I hear too, unofficially, that you're about to get married. Is this the case?'

'Yes, sir. It'll be a quiet wedding.'

'Just so,' said the Dean. His left cheek bulged for a moment. 'May I offer you my congratulations? Also, I'm afraid, the suggestion that while you're in college this morning you call on the college secretary and notify her of your intention, orally will do very well. Now forgive me for seeming to pry, but what are your plans as regards a honeymoon?'

'Just the weekend,' said Robin, improvising at top speed. 'We're thinking of going away in the spring when the weather's better.'

'Very wise in my view. Also a relief to hear of, I confess. To be open with you, Davies, it's felt that you've gone far enough. We like you and are proud of you and expect great things of you, but if you continue to ignore, I might almost say to flout, the rules of the college and university we shall have to take action. Action in the form of a term's rustication at the very least. Don't make us do that.'

'I understand, sir. Can I have until next Monday?'

'On the understanding that you do a full day's work that day and thereafter.'

'I promise.'

'Good. Another thing I might advise you to do while you're in college is to look in on your tutor. Not a bad fellow, is he, old Hayes?'

'I've always got on well with him.'

'Once you're used to the way he blinks all the time when he's talking. Anyway, he's worried about you. I'm sure he'd be glad to see you even if only for a couple of minutes. If he's got a pupil, interrupt him. If he's not there leave him a note. Half a dozen words will do.'

'Right, sir.'

'Well, I feel in much better spirits now than I felt a few minutes ago. I dare say you do too, Davies.' The Dean pulled back a hairy brown cuff. 'I was about to suggest a glass of sherry, but you may agree that ten past ten does seem a little on the early side.'

The words were hardly out of his mouth when one of the nearer clocks, a small contrivance incorporated into the belly of an oriental despot in porcelain, made a hoarse whirring noise, chimed six times in rapid succession and as abruptly fell silent. The Dean, now canted over as far as Robin had ever seen him, burst into peals of unaffected laughter and waved him confusedly from the room.

Business with the college secretary and old Hayes was soon over. Then Robin installed himself in the pay-telephone booth in the lodge and called his brother's number. Almost at once it was repeated in female tones at the distant end.

'Elizabeth? It's Robin here. How are you? And how's the family? Good. Do you happen to know what George wants from me? Not there by any chance, is he?'

'No, I'm afraid not, and all I happen to know he wants from you is a hundred quid. Actually it was me who felt like a word with you.'

'Oh. Well, here I am. Fire away.'

'If what I'm going to say, if you think it's a funny sort of thing to discuss over the phone, well, I don't want to drag you up here for two minutes' chat . . .'

'Or feel like dragging yourself and Marian up here for the same. I'm dying to know what it is.'

'. . . and this way you can always ring off if you feel like it. Anyway, Robin, what it is, it's about Nancy. Now, that girl, oddly enough but if anybody was ever in love with anybody then she is with you. Did you know that?'

'I think so, and on my side I'm very fond of her.'

'Is that all? Aren't you in love with her? Or do you consider you've done all that could reasonably be required of you by agreeing to marry her? Come on, are you in love with her or not?'

'Well, I must be, mustn't I?'

'Oh you must, must you? What have you said to her about what you feel about her? That you reckon she's not a bad old stick when you get to know her?'

'To be quite honest I can't remember.'

'Have you ever told her you love her?'

'I thought actions were supposed to speak louder than words.'

'Not those words, not by much. And not to a girl like Nancy. She told me she was sure you did love her even though you hadn't said so. I know what sure means when people say it like that, they don't mean sure, they mean they hope, surely to God it must be like that, it must be if there's any justice in the world. It amazes me that a bright chap like you who can't plead total ignorance of women should contemplate even for a moment getting married to a girl like that in this day and age without having told her he loves her not once but a couple of thousand times. You stupid *bugger*.'

'I couldn't make it sound convincing at this stage,' protested Robin, if I suddenly started telling her I loved her now she'd see through it.'

'Another good thing from your point of view about having this conversation over the telephone rather than face to face is I can't give you the tremendous bash in the chops you deserve. Unconvincing? You could convince the public hangman out of stringing you up. You haven't said the necessary words because of some childish scruple or bit of integrity out of one of your favourite books. *Balls* to it.'

What was perhaps an incompetent imitation of an air-raid siren immediately followed these words, suggesting that Marian was at any rate not dead yet. Few words were added, except for a certain amount of repetition and arm-twisting on Elizabeth's side. It occurred to Robin as he rang off that all talk of a male militia, of men spontaneously uniting in defence of their interests against the encroaching female, misrepresented the situation. Men operated something like a confused, poorly armed guerilla-type rabble; women, in comparison, ran a highly trained, superbly equipped SS panzer corps complete with parachute brigade and grenadier back-up. So powerful was this impression that it was with some hesitation that he rang his mother, the least intractable female he had ever known.

The first part went entirely as expected. He ran over the arrangements for the forthcoming marriage and she presumably took note of them. Then she said something about looking forward to meeting Nancy's parents for what would be the first time.

Robin said, 'I'm afraid they won't be coming, Mum.'

'What? Are you sure?'

'Apparently they said Nancy had let them down terribly. They'd imagined they could trust her and then by the time they found out they couldn't, it was too late. That's it.'

'What did they say to you?'

'Oh, apparently they've put me down as somebody who just takes what he wants.'

'Well, that's not so . . . Robin, why do you keep saying apparently this and apparently that? What did they actually say to you?'

'We haven't, the three of us haven't in fact got together to discuss it.' In Robin's universe, direct lies were to be avoided whenever possible, but some selective heightening of the truth was sometimes acceptable. 'Nancy said it would be better all round if I kept out of their way.'

'I see. Now it can't do any harm if I just have a quick word with them and see if there's any way I can help. Have you got their telephone number by you?'

He had it and gave it. 'What will you say to them, Mum?'

'Just tell them to have some sense and pull themselves together and stop cutting off their nose to spite their face. Now before you ring off, dear, let's run over the registry details once more.'

That evening Robin telephoned his mother again.

'Yes. Twice. I spoke to them both. Robin, I'm afraid I didn't do any good, I didn't get anywhere with either of them. Not at all what I expected.'

'Listen, Mum, I'm sorry, but it rather looks as if you'd better go and ask them to their face. Faces. I don't mean now – in the morning. I'll come with you.'

'I'll ring them again. You stay there.'

'Good sport, Mum.'

When his mother called him back, she told him, 'I spoke to them again, but it was still no good, but they did say they'd see me, but they said there was no point.'

'But anyway, we're expected there in the morning.'

'I suppose so. What time is that train you were talking about?'

Robin spent that night in his room in college, by Nancy's choice rather than his own, following some pissy custom she knew of whereby bride and groom should meet for the first time the next morning immediately before the ceremony. Since the bride-to-be would be doing without wedding-dress, bouquet, bridesmaids, page, parson, church, bells, choir, organ, confetti, photographers and reception, to name a few, the groom-to-be felt he should accede to the proposition. He slept poorly, perhaps because he could not quite drive out the thought of his mother ringing up at two-thirty or five o'clock to make sure she knew the time her train left and he knew the time it arrived.

When Robin successfully met his mother at Oxford station, he noticed she was wearing a dark-blue costume suitable for a guest at a wedding, perhaps one in 1930 rather than nowadays, and about a size too large for her, but then he rather cleverly remembered that Joy Carpenter was probably about a size larger than she was. She looked quite serious so dressed but ill equipped to take on the Bennetts.

'We've got a good hour,' he said to her on the bus.

'That's more than enough for what I have to say.'

'Will you budge them, do you think?'

'I don't know, but you were quite right to get me to try. I've got to do everything I can for my sake as well as yours and of course poor little Nancy's.'

'Supposing they're out after all?' he asked her just before they got off the bus.

'You mark my words, they'll be in.'

And they were. Robin had supposed, or pretended to himself to suppose, that he was going to drop his mother at the Bennetts' and then bugger off out of it for a cup of coffee round the corner, but when they were approaching the front door and she told him to leave the talking to her, he saw he could never have let her face them undiluted. It struck him that when confronting Polyphemus or combating Scylla, notable adversaries as they might have been, Odysseus was at least free of the menace of boredom. He rang the doorbell.

The senior Bennetts, come to that, had never been much fun

even diluted. With fair success Robin had tried to come here as seldom as he could and, when he could not hold off any longer, stay as short a time as practicable. This minimising of exposure helped him to build up an image of himself as a scholarly recluse, shy of normal company, much more at home in an ancient library than he would have been in a young girl's bed, should he ever find his way to one of the latter. His spell as a prisoner of war had, needless to say, rendered him more reclusive than ever. So now, on only his second visit since returning to Oxford, he took in without much sense of over-familiarity such details as the wall-telephone that resembled the inside of a public box in itself and its attachments, this and the coat-cupboard where a small band of undersized terrorists could have hidden. But his sense of having strayed far from home ground was as strong as ever.

It was Mr Bennett who opened to them, no less tall than on Robin's first sight of him, but perceptibly thinner and lacking his previous look of being healthy against odds. He had a cigarette in his mouth, though for the moment not to his obvious detriment. He greeted them with something collusive in his manner, as if this encounter was indeed partly of his doing, and a look at his wife suggested whose idea it was not. Mrs Bennett's head seemed to have grown smaller over the years, most likely through a tighter arrangement of her hair rather than true cranial shrinkage. Her demeanour was not so much hostile as indifferent. Robin had never found it wholly natural to regard them as Nancy's parents and did not now. Neither of them looked at him.

Mrs Bennett seemed quite at ease, the only one there who did. She led the party into the room where the bar was, but no drinks were forthcoming that day. Indeed a pink and green cretonne curtain was drawn across the shelves where the bottles were or had been and the red-seated stools were standing on the counter. Robin would not have called himself a drinking man, and anyway the hour was not much less early than when he had visited the Dean, but he found the sight depressing. He thought he saw Mr Bennett send a brief wistful look in the direction of the curtained-off shelves.

Perhaps in compensation he took a hefty drag at his cigarette and shook slightly at some inner event.

When all four were seated at a low round table with a fluted glass vase of artificial flowers on it, rather in the manner of early customers at a teashop, it was Mr Bennett who unenthusiastically opened the proceedings.

'Well,' he said, 'the sooner we get on with this fandango the sooner we'll be finished, which I imagine can't be too soon for anybody's liking, so I'll just make two quick points. First, it'll be better all round if nobody says anything nasty or hurtful about anybody else, present or absent. Let's just get that established straight away, shall we? And secondly, it may help, er, our visitors to be assured that my wife and I have made up our minds that we won't be attending at the registry office today, and that decision will not be altered. Now is that clear to one and all?'

Robin thought so. He also thought that what he had heard was admirably brief from a Welshman with a captive audience. If the style was all that could reasonably have been asked for, the content was not. He, Robin, could on his own accord have wished for nothing better in its line than the absence of Mr and Mrs B from his wedding, except naturally for their absence from his life for a trial period of say fifty years. But then of course there were Nancy's feelings to be considered. Rather dully, but not unwillingly, he tried to imagine a future state of consciousness in which someone else's feelings, in this case his wife's, would seem to him as important and immediate as his own. Had George reached that state? Robin had no time to start wondering about that now.

'In that case,' Mrs Davies had been saying, 'what was the point of inviting Robin and me along here to put our point of view?'

With a patience that carried no hint of a display of that quality, Mr Bennett said, 'If you remember, Mrs Davies, neither Mrs Bennett nor myself invited anybody along anywhere to do anything. We, that's my wife and I, merely thought it would be, I don't quite know what to say, as it might be socially, personally unacceptable, to . . . to just not open the door to you or slam it in

302

your faces' (Saxon, thought Robin) 'and deny you the elementary facility of communicating your point of view' (Welsh).

'You're telling me it's going to make no difference what I say, whatever it is, you might as well be stone deaf and me reading out the daily paper.' Mrs Davies spoke steadily enough, though to Robin's eye she had turned a little pale. 'Well, now I'm here I suppose I can at least get you to tell me why you're going to let your daughter down on the most important day of her life and stay away when she gets married. I'd like to know what you've told her, that's if you're still on speaking terms with her, or perhaps you were just going to let her gradually realise you weren't coming.'

'That's none of your business, thank you,' said Mrs Bennett, glaring a certain amount.

There followed a sort of silent-film couple of moments in which Mr Bennett laid his hand on his wife's arm and she went through a hurried series of reactions, from a start or jump of sheer physical surprise through mild indignation to acceptance and gratitude. When this reached completion he said to Robin's mother, 'As Mrs Bennett has pointed out, what she and I may or may not have said to our own daughter is neither here nor there and certainly none of your concern, Mrs Davies. Still, I don't mind letting you know why we've made up our minds the way we have.'

'That's none of their business either, Frank.'

'Strictly speaking,' said Mr Bennett, speaking a little strictly, 'that's true, love, of course, but in practice we worked out what to say, didn't we, to the rest of the world and people like Rene and Bert, you remember, and I myself can't see any objection to telling, er, the Davieses something that won't be any kind of secret tomorrow morning. Or perhaps you have other ideas,' he finished with what Robin heard as a faint threat in his voice.

'Say what you've got to say, Frank.'

'All right, I will.' Mr Bennett addressed himself equally to both Davieses, 'It's strange you accused us just now of letting our daughter down, because that's exactly what we feel about her behaviour to us. We trusted her. We put her on her honour. And she's let us down. Simple as that. No need to prolong the agony. So, my wife and I decided to make known our displeasure as emphatically as possible. And more than our displeasure, I'd say our moral disapproval, if that didn't sound puritanical in a way none of us in this family have ever been inclined to. But yes, I'm afraid Nancy has revealed herself as in the deepest sense not fit to be trusted. It's a shame.' Mr Bennett's voice trembled with his last words.

Mrs Davies opened her handbag and brought out a small pink-bordered handkerchief and without disturbing its ironed folds dabbed at her nose. 'If I am to have a say – I'm sorry but I haven't got Mr, Mr Bennett's gift of the gab, so you'll probably catch me repeating myself and so on, I'll just have to do the best I can. Anyway, there's really only just one thing I want to say, and it's this. You can talk about your displeasure and Nancy not being fit to be trusted but, well, neither of you have said it but I'm not afraid to say it, the one who's caused all the displeasure and who's not fit to be trusted in a big way is this boy here. Look after number one, that's all you can trust him to do. If I know this son of mine he'll have been thanking his lucky stars his old father isn't here to tell him so. No, we all know there are women who lead young men astray, but Nancy, at her age, the very idea's ridiculous. Let's face it, it's still completely a man's world. If anybody led anybody astray, it was my son did it.

'So, I've nothing to be proud of him for, to say the least, but I'm going to his wedding. Oh yes. Not for his sake but for mine. I'm not one to take unnecessary risks, and that's what not going would be. I don't want to find myself some time in the future wishing I'd been there when it's too late. As they say, I put it to you, Mr Bennett, and Mrs Bennett, do you want that to happen in your family?'

To Robin, who had had the sense to stay quiet and not look at anyone during these speeches, it was already clear that the battle was won. More remarks were made on both sides, but it was not very long before Mrs Bennett broke into tears and left the room. Her husband followed her as far as the door, where he paused and looked back, seemed about to speak, then changed his mind slightly and hurried back to where Robin and his mother were sitting. From an inner pocket he took out a cigarette-case and opened it, but at once shut it again and put it back.

'Trying to cut down,' he said defensively.

'Go on, light up and be damned,' said Robin.

Within a few seconds each man had a lit cigarette in his mouth. Mr Bennett sent Robin a look in which a kind of envy could have been read. Then he switched that off and said in lowered tones, 'Well done. Mrs Davies, thank you for your cooperation.' He glanced at his watch. 'Just nice time. Now if you'll excuse me for a few minutes, when I'm with you again, I think we'll all have earnt a small bracer.' He looked at Robin a second time. 'You've got a lot to thank your mother for.'

As the sound of his cough, valiantly restrained until now, receded up the stairs, Mrs Davies said, 'Sorry I said all that about you, Robin. You can see I more or less had to.'

'That's all right, Mum, I could tell you didn't really mean it.'

'I didn't say I didn't mean it, dear, I said I was sorry I had to say it. You must know yourself it was true.'

'Oh.'

'All except the bit about me having nothing to be proud of you for. But I reckoned I could throw that in.'

'After all these years, parts of the marriage service, one or two of them sound rather strange now, it would be surprising if they didn't. Love, honour, obey, for instance – that word *obey* falls rather strangely on our modern ears, I think, and in say twenty years' time it might well not be there any more. But there aren't many like that. It's more a matter of, well, some parts of the service aren't easy to take in, to understand. One thing, though, hasn't changed and never will change and it's as easy to understand as it ever was. Marriage is a very special thing, it's for two people who love each other in a very special way. But I can see the two of you know all about that, and you're happy together, and you want to get on with your life together, so it only remains for me to wish you the very best of luck, and Robin, you may kiss the bride.'

The deputy registrar of births, marriages and deaths was a couple of decades young for this job, some might have considered, anyway measurably younger than the tremulous official in south London who had registered the death of Mr Davies. Before he could launch into one or other of the trite reflections that presented themselves, Robin took today's fellow at his word and kissed Nancy, who clung to him. It seemed as good a moment as any to follow Elizabeth's advice.

'You heard what the man said,' he whispered quickly, 'we're supposed to love each other in a very special way and that's the way I love you.'

Against his expectation he had been gripped by shyness after the first phrase, but he had got it all said well enough to make Nancy gasp and whisper back, 'Oh and I love you in an extra special way,' before clinging to him harder and starting to cry, which led to the arrival from the sidelines of her mother, also crying and starting to fold her daughter to her breast, and of his own mother, far from dry of eye as she was. Robin was aware that, however essential to the proceedings he might have been and indeed was, at this stage of them he was in some way superfluous. Mr Bennett, who arrived on the immediate scene a couple of moments later, evidently shared this view, recommended leaving the women to it and drew Robin aside.

'Well, that's done, then, much to my relief let it be said. If, er, if you and your new bride and your mother have nothing better to do, I suggest we might all partake of a wedding breakfast, an expression of uncertain meaning which it seems can include drinks and lunch. In fact to be quite open with you, Robin, I have a table booked for five at that hotel round the corner from here in a little over half an hour. If we go along there now we can set about filling in the time to some purpose. Well, boy, now you're one of the family I hope we'll be seeing more of you. Help to restore the balance of the sexes.'

They left the registrar's office, which despite a comparative sparsity of books and multiplicity of chairs managed to look more Oxonian than anywhere else in Oxford Robin had seen. Nevertheless he had indisputably got married, better say he and Nancy had got married, within its conspicuously panelled walls. He soon stopped focusing on the two of them and went back to the one of him.

Well, it was true, though totally unhelpful to consider, that he had done it now. It was also true, on the other hand, that quite large parts of what presumably lay ahead of him could be contemplated with equanimity at least. The prospect of having a small baby, then a larger baby, then a small child, then a being of the size and general condition of his niece, then a series of older versions spread over the following twenty years or so – of having such a creature in sight for long periods, in hearing for longer ones and seldom quite out of mind, well, again, it would happen whatever he did and there were palliatives like humour, George and the pub. And Nancy. She scored high in other ways too, of which probably the most durable was the fact that she never came near getting on his nerves, though he could think of plenty of more loving and no less true things to say about her. There was indeed every good reason for sticking to her and putting her first always. And what about the million or so bad reasons for not doing so all the time, reasons aged between sixteen and forty-five and distributed about evenly between Land's End and John o'Groats, to say nothing of their counterparts overseas? As to that, he had better take every chance he could of telling himself that after, in comparison with, the emotional effort of deciding to marry it would surely be a small thing, a succession of small things, to stay true to that marriage, to avoid not the temptation but the opportunity, the occasion, to identify the agents of harm and stay away, stay where it was safe. He remembered reading that saints were in the habit of strengthening their capacity to resist sin by exercising that capacity in imagination, as one might strengthen a muscle by exercise . . .

These thoughts chased themselves through his mind in the

half-minute or so it took him and the others to walk down the deserted stone stairway that led from the upper floor where the registry was to the level of the street. Mr Bennett pushed down the iron bar that opened the side door there and motioned Robin and Nancy past him. Immediately a girl going by looked at Robin or perhaps just in his direction and anyway for no more than an instant, but near enough and for long enough to arouse in him a fleeting sense of excitement and mischief. It was then too that Nancy took his arm and stepped out beside him, but there had been nothing for her to see.

'No doubt you've heard from Musgrave.'

'Yes,' said Robin. 'He wrote me a very nice letter.'

'I'm glad to hear it,' said Dr Wells. 'Musgrave is an outstanding diagnostician and a very able pharmacologist. Your mother couldn't have had a better doctor.'

'I didn't know she had a doctor at all, was under a doctor.'

'No. Well, Mr Davies, I'm sure Dr Musgrave will be in personal touch with you as soon as he returns, but in the meantime I thought I might ask you to call in here for a short chat. Forgive me for beginning with the obvious.' The doctor looked at Robin for a moment in silence. The loss of your mother so soon after that of your father must have come as a severe shock to you.'

'Yes, it was, it did.'

'My chief objective in asking you to come in is to save you any unnecessary feelings of discomfort and remorse and self-reproach such as I know from experience people in your sad position are all too liable to suffer from. Dr Musgrave and I are in the habit of comparing notes as in your mother's case and naturally I have my own experience to guide me. So I feel quite strongly inclined to inform you that the progress of her illness would not in my opinion have caused her any extremity of suffering, which is what you perhaps have hoped but not dared to believe. No doctor I know of ever tries to minimise what a patient undergoes, but I think it safe to say that your mother's physical pain was intermittent and . . .

most probably . . . never or not often extreme. I feel the same would have held true even of her final attack. One moment she was here, and the next she was not. In plain language, Mr Davies, she was dead before she hit the floor. If that's any consolation.'

'Yes it is, doctor. Is there anything to be said about my mother's mental suffering?'

'There I can't help you.'

'No, of course not.'

'But there was nothing that you or anybody else could have done to ease her pain or prolong her life. She had the best attention throughout.'

'I'm sure of it, Dr Wells,' said Robin, doing his best to make it sound as if he meant it, as he did just then, at least.

'Good. Now, is there anything you want to ask me? I can give you a couple of minutes to think, no longer I'm afraid because I have a rather full diary this morning.'

The doctor strode out of the room. There was nothing unexpected to be seen in it, except possibly for a dozen or so small cactuses in small pots arranged in a row along the window-sill. The rest was all cupboards, rows of books, file-containers, an old-fashioned set of scales with a weight-arm and a height-measuring attachment. Robin tried to think of questions to put to the doctor, but all he could do for the moment was visualise his mother as she had been in life, up to four days earlier. He had not seen her dead nor asked to do so. Her death had indeed come as a shock, more intense than his father's and not just because it had not been foreseen in the same way, or so Robin felt since first being told the news. No doubt Dr Wells had not meant to imply that the loss of his father had somehow merged with it. He had had moments of considering himself alone in the world, but merely as an abstract proposition; he for one would not have found it easy to take such a thing to heart while living in a North Oxford flat with a young wife in mid-pregnancy and a ginger kitten. So when the doctor came back he still had nothing to ask him and got to his feet in preparation for leaving.

Dr Wells held up his hand and said in his customary cheerful manner, 'I have just a couple of things to say to you before you go, Mr Davies. One of them is merely to emphasise something I've touched on already. It's very common, in fact I might say it's usual for a surviving child in your position to feel responsible, blameworthy in some way or to some degree for the death of a parent, quite needlessly so. Let me assure you most earnestly that to my knowledge you have nothing whatever to reproach yourself with.'

'Thank you for saying so, Dr Wells. Could I ask you, is it at all likely that my mother's death was hastened, brought on by nervous strain?'

'Some doctors would say yes. A majority of others, myself included, would say no, such a thing is possible of course but not in the least likely. Some deaths of your mother's kind occur, happen to occur, after some such strain. Others, many others, simply occur. You understand I can't lay down the law here.'

'Yes, I see. Well . . .'

'The other thing I wanted to say is that, yes, your mother died of a heart attack. That's a medical description. It might be more suitable and no less exact to say she died of a broken heart – I've some idea of how attached she was to your father.' Uncharacteristically, Dr Wells hesitated, and when he went on his mode of speech lost some of its habitual liveliness. 'Science doesn't recognise such an ailment.' He paused again. 'There has to be a physical disease for you to die of. I've seen . . . But I'm afraid my next patient is due at any moment. Good-bye, Mr Davies. Give my best regards to Nancy and, er, et cetera. I can't tell you how delighted I am that things there have turned out as they have.' For a few seconds the doctor's gloomy gaze became quite animated as he rose to his feet.

Robin emerged from the large converted house where the consulting-rooms were. His recently acquired car, an archaic but well preserved black-painted Morris saloon, stood near by at the kerb. It took him only a short time to reach it, get into it and drive off, but the interval was long enough for him to reflect on one thing in particular Dr Wells had said, that he, Robin, had no reason to feel remorseful over his mother's death or to suspect that he might have accelerated it. He would always be grateful to the doctor for saying so, but he himself would never be free of that shadow of guilt.

After no great interval he stopped the car outside the reddish cottagey building in remote Carshalton that housed Joy Carpenter. The lady herself opened the door to him just as he was about to knock on it and seized him in her arms. A glimpse of her face as she did so suggested that she was demonstrating a staunch resolve to prevent him, at least, from being snatched from her bosom. In the next couple of minutes he tried to put away this unkind thought, but was forced to notice how inappropriate any reference to literal bosoms would have been in her case. Indeed, poor Joy Carpenter might as well have been Jack Carpenter in drag for all the signs of femininity she carried, broad of shoulder, of generally cylindrical trunk and facially androgynous. Perhaps he had been wrong in guessing her to have been the owner of the navy costume his mother had worn to his wedding. She, his mother, had been only a year or two younger but would have been instantly recognisable as a woman if she had lived to be a hundred.

When Robin looked round the comfortable little sitting-room Mrs Carpenter followed his glance. There were fresh flowers on the mantelpiece and windowshelf.

'I'd just about got it nice for your mother and me. We were going to wait for the better weather before we thought seriously of moving. We had our eye on a nice place near Ashford where I used to know the people. We were going down to have another look in a couple of weeks' time. I suppose it's just as well we hadn't signed anything or made any definite arrangements. Yes, it is just as well.'

Robin followed this and more, giving an occasional serious nod, not letting it be seen that he had recently heard its substance at least once before. Mrs Carpenter talked on without much pause, but she was not easy in her manner, she was nervous of something or expecting something untoward. Then a person he failed to see properly approached and came into the house by the front door, and it was clear that this was what she had been looking out for. A voice Robin recognised called from the front passage.

'It's Jeremy,' said Mrs Carpenter unnecessarily, 'I mentioned you were coming down for lunch and he insisted on coming too. I hope that's all right.'

'What a marvellous idea, I'm so glad.'

'I thought you wouldn't mind.'

'Oh, terrific,' said Robin vaguely but forcefully, thinking for a moment of all the people who would have minded and no doubt had minded being on social terms with somebody of Jeremy's persuasion. He jumped to his feet as the door of the room opened, a warm handshake was exchanged and there was a certain amount of lively noise. Mrs Carpenter watched rather than listened, on the alert for any sudden outbreak of sexual behaviour or, contrariwise, belated explosion of disgust on Robin's part, as he might formerly have put it to himself. In a little while she said she had better start seeing about lunch, and went off. Jeremy turned to Robin and looked at him sadly and gave a nod that made unmistakable and sufficient reference to his mother's death.

'I hope you don't mind my turning up today,' said Jeremy, unconsciously echoing his own mother's words, 'I heard you were coming down and I asked if I could join the party. It seems simply ages since we met.'

Robin agreed it had been quite some time. Privately he thought the interval showed in Jeremy's face, at first glance unchanged in over ten years with skin as smooth, hair as glossy and abundant as ever, but at second or third glance lined round eyes and mouth and with a gap in the top teeth. Perhaps too the eyes themselves had become less clear.

He was going on. 'I reckoned if I arranged to just appear without letting you know in advance there'd be nothing you could do about it.'

'Why should I want to do anything about it?' asked Robin, who remembered using the same undercover approach himself not so long before.

'No idea. Look, do you fancy a short walk?'

'How short is short?'

'Two hundred yards, as far as the pub. I'm afraid it's not a very nice day but the pub isn't so bad as they go.'

No doubt it was not so bad as they went; it turned out to be physically habitable all right, but Robin thought it concentrated to an undue degree on subscription schemes, sweepstakes and the like, advertised on large cardboard notices in various unfamiliar inks. The landlord, a blank-faced fellow wearing a leather waistcoat of historical aspect, gave Jeremy a notably restrained welcome, indeed confined himself to a nod of small depth. Robin got another of the same when he ordered drinks.

'My word,' he said to Jeremy as they moved away, 'that chap fair knocks you over with the warmth of his welcome. Talk about old-fashioned ways.'

'Appearances can be deceptive, as you must have noticed. Actually Fred's a very decent good-natured sort of chap. Now. My mother tells me you're married, is that right?'

'Yes, as far as it goes. Did she say anything else, your mother?'

'Well yes, she did, if you must know. It was very sudden, she said, and she didn't half give me a look when she said it. Oh, I said, like that, was it? Just like that, she said, You're fond of her, though, aren't you? Your wife, I mean.'

Robin's response went into some detail, including the circum - stances of his and Nancy's trip to Cardiff and back, which nobody else had heard from him.

'You must like her a lot,' said Jeremy. 'You decide to marry her when it was all fixed up for you not to have to.'

'That wasn't how it seemed at the time. It's funny, sometimes I start thinking I might have liked her less, perhaps quite a bit less, and still not have been able to let her, you know, not have it. Oh, I wanted not to marry her all right, not her or anyone else. But then I also wanted a state of affairs that inescapably required us to be married. That's the trouble with these do-what-you-want merchants, it's always assumed you only want one thing at a time, like going for a swim. That's not very good, is it? Perhaps all I mean is not just wanting to have your cake and eat it, but absolutely having to have your bloody cake and eat it and either one on its own is no sodding good at all.'

'Well, that's a bit better, yes, but you surely don't imagine I've come all this way just to hear you nattering on about your domestic problems, do you?'

'I was beginning to wonder.'

'I wanted to see you in order to complain about my own difficulties. I don't expect you to suggest a remedy, partly because there isn't one, just to listen. For various reasons you're the only person I can tell and also want to tell, and I've got to start straight away or we'll have to go back before I'm finished, and there may not be a chance after that, in fact there may never be another chance, so would you like some gin? Decide quickly.'

'If listening is really all I'm expected to do, then yes. In fact yes anyway.'

Jeremy went and returned and said, 'So far so good. You lost your last chance not to have to listen to this when you mentioned wanting something that by definition it's impossible to have. What I want could likewise be described in that way, though there the resemblance ends, before it's properly started. My ideal world uses nothing but elements of the real world, your world, and yet it's much more different than anything uncovered by the remotest explorations of this planet.'

'If you're serious about wanting me to listen,' said Robin, sipping uniced gin and tonic without much enjoyment, 'I advise you to say things I might be able to take in.'

'I'm sorry, I let myself be carried away by the prospect of talking to somebody who can read and write. Did you know that queers are really very thick? Probably not, because of the undoubted fact that they're meant to be frightfully bright and ever so artistic. They seem to think that's just one obvious way they're of an altogether higher order of being than those ghastly women creatures. But they've got it all wrong, haven't they? I mean surely one of the great things about women is they're rather thick and *don't mind*. At least I've never come across a nice one or even an attractive one who seemed to mind. So a chap hasn't got to be on his best intellectual behaviour all the time. A woman tells her husband it's turned out nice again or it takes all sorts to make a world, and he says yes dear and starts filling his pipe and picks up the evening paper. Well, I realise I can't expect you to agree with that. It isn't supposed to be the whole story.'

'Let's just say I see what you mean. That, and that I expected this to be about queers, not women.'

'I know, it's this excitement of having someone to tell things to for once. Say anything that comes into my head, and plenty does.'

'What, you've got boy-friends, haven't you? To tell things to?'

'Keep your voice down. Wrong label for what I've got, if got is the word. A chap here and a bloke there, that's a bit more like it. No friends, no new ones anyway. Anyone I could call a friend I'd have to have got to know before he knew I was queer, and there's not much chance of that happening now.'

'Oh,' said Robin.

' Yeah. I only really like straight men, you see. They're the only sort I feel I could . . . Haven't I told you that before?'

'Very likely, I don't remember.'

'Never mind. Whereas the ones I lose my head over and chase after are pretty little things without much sex-drive either way who like being picked up and flattered and bought so-called presents and lent money, that's right, Robin, and in return permit certain familiarities to take place but only if they feel like it, which is of course less often and rather less whole-heartedly than you do.'

After a brief pause, Robin asked, 'And types like that, they're ever so artistic, are they?'

'Oh no. In a way they aren't really queer, a lot of them, according to me. I don't fancy interior decorators or antique dealers or even actors, it's more sailors and barrow boys and, well, I needn't go on, need I?'

'No. I mean please go on as long as you like.'

'Forgive me for asking, old boy, but have you ever had much to do with prostitutes? You know, whores?'

'Yes, I know. Yes, a bit, during the war. Abroad mostly.'

'Oh. Well, perhaps it's different there, I've no way of knowing. I tried them a couple of times, girls, years ago now, on a making-sure basis.'

'What did you think of it?'

'Well, I thought it was interesting, and good fun in the earlier stages. If I had to venture a criticism I'd have said it was a bit remote.'

'You could take them or leave them alone.'

'But both of them were perfectly decent girls, you know, they never even looked like trying to rob me or blackmail me or anything like that. They sort of put themselves out to see I had a good time. It wasn't their fault that I . . . I'm sorry about this pussyfooting round the subject, it's an easy habit to get into if you're like me. When you have one big thing that mustn't be given away you soon end up not giving all manner of little things away. So for instance queers are close about their movements even when all they've been doing is go down to the butcher for half a pound of neck of mutton. Where had I got to?'

'I'm not quite sure, you might have been somewhere near saying that whores had hearts of gold. I wouldn't blame you for not giving that away.'

'Female whores no doubt do a lot of bad things but I believe they'd draw the line at screaming at me to bugger off out of my own flat because they're in my bed with the window-cleaner. Yes. It's all different, utterly different, not a mere matter of, you know, for girl read boy throughout, it's . . . If I talked to you from now to midnight I still wouldn't have been able to explain it. Explain how it is, not why it is.'

There was a long silence. Robin said, 'Have another drink, Jeremy.'

'A quick one, then we must dash back or Mumsie will be afraid I've been getting into mischief and you've been covering for me. No she won't, or anyhow she won't say. She's really very good. Better than I deserve.'

'Be all right if we go for a spin in my motor after lunch?'

'Oh, super,' said Jeremy, staring into space.

'Haven't you got a steady bloke?'

'As I said, I only go for unsteady blokes. No, even that's only half true. What I really want is a promiscuous, thieving little tart who at the same time is the very soul of honour and fidelity. There. What was that about a drink?'

Serving Robin, the man behind the bar as before seemed afflicted by paralysis of the facial muscles and organs of speech. When the two left he beckoned Jeremy over and, out of Robin's hearing, offered a remark or two before nodding and turning away.

Outside, the sky had grown lighter. 'I think it's going to clear up,' said Jeremy vivaciously.

'What did that chap say?'

'Who, that landlord chap? Oh, he, er, he told me he thought it wouldn't be fair to refuse to serve me when I came in on my own because I never gave anybody any trouble. But then he explained that that didn't mean he was glad to see me in there and if I tried to bring in one of my mates another time he wouldn't serve us. That was what he said.'

'Christ. Anything you'd like me to do?'

'No. Well, you could stop scowling. Actually he was quite nice about it. As I said, he's a comparatively good-natured chap.'

'Don't apologise for him.'

'I'm not, I promise you. I'm just saying he could have con - veyed the same information in a much more offensive way. Believe me.'

'I do.'

'After all, he hadn't not let me into his pub in the first place. Hey, there was something I thought of back there, when you mentioned the fellows who keep on at you to do what you want, just before you started waffling about swimming and cakes and I don't know what all.'

They crossed the road and stepped over a pool of rainwater trapped by a blocked drain near the kerb. Apart from a wireless-repair van parked a few yards off and a vicar's-wife type, energetically push-biking past in bright yellow oilskins, the streets were deserted. Robin was quite glad to be out of the pub, where it had frankly not been much fun to be. For a short moment he reflected that it could not be much fun for Jeremy to be anywhere.

'What were you going to tell me you thought of?' he asked him.

'What? Oh yes. Two things, actually. One is, if what you want's something reasonable like buggering Boy Scouts, they'd tell you to go ahead and good luck to you and incidentally never mind whether the Boy Scouts want it or not. But if you happen to hanker after something that's frightfully bad form, like tarring and feathering beggars, then hold still while I fit this rope round your neck. The other thing I admit I'd thought of before a couple of times. The first completely free man will be the last one left on earth. He'll be able to do just whatever he likes, if he can think of anything.'

Not much more was said while they finished walking back to the cottage. The sun began to shine weakly just as they reached it. Mrs Carpenter had gin and tonic and a new box of fifty Player's waiting for them. A lavish meal followed, doubly lavish and also extraordinary at such a time: asparagus, roast lamb with mint sauce, spinach, carrots and roast potatoes washed down with bottled ale and augmented by apple pie and custard. Jeremy showed himself in good form as entertainer, as old friend, as affectionate and attentive son but not too much of either, and his mother was appreciative, relieved, cheered up, as near happy as she was ever likely to be now, Robin thought, without being easy in her mind for very long at a time. Her rather large face, small of eye and mouth but prominent of chin, seemed always about to lose its contentment in a puzzled frown, to betray uncertainty whether that last remark really meant what it said, some nervousness about the next but one. Then Jeremy, who had perhaps noticed nothing in particular, started an imitation of his coalman and Robin attended to that.

When the two of them went for the promised spin in his motor, the sun was still coming out at intervals but the lanes round about were damp and chilly, with fallen leaves showing here and there. Jeremy drowsed and perhaps dozed for a few minutes before grunting loudly, scratching himself and yawning.

'How did you think my mother was looking?' he asked.

'Oh, pretty well. She's very fond of you, isn't she?'

'Yes. Unfortunately I get on her nerves. She'd hate me not to come down but she doesn't really enjoy it when I do. Today was better than usual, thanks to you, dear boy.'

'Oh, I didn't do anything.'

'More than you know. It's a pity your mother died – I know it's more than a pity and so does my mother. She was really quite excited, toned up by the prospect of having something to do again, and now it isn't going to happen and there's nobody else and she's still here. To anticipate your question, she's got a sister, a cousin and an aunt in Canada, Rhodesia and an old folks' home respectively. Well, at least money's no problem, she's got a fair bit what she calls put by.'

'The very expression my mother used. I've got her bit now.'

'Hence this excellent motor, perhaps. Which reminds me, if you're going to take me to the station I suggest you turn its nose in that direction soon.'

The station was dirty and dispiriting, but a train almost immediately appeared and Jeremy and another man got into it.

'Have you brought anything to read?'

For answer, Jeremy brought out a book of poetry called *Another Time*.

'You still like him, then?'

'I had a devil of a job getting this into my mack pocket. I really only brought it to impress you.'

'You're just saying that,' said Robin.

'I was struck by a remark he made to someone, that his sexual proclivity was a symptom of arrested development. We're all about

319

eleven years old emotionally. No wonder he cottoned on to Homer Lane. Good advice for eleven-year-olds, do what you want, except most of them are doing it already.'

One of the troubles with that fellow, Robin said to himself as he went back to his car, was that you never knew whether to take him seriously or not take him seriously or take him seriously after all, which admittedly meant you had that much less reason to worry about him, which was perhaps what he intended. He took the road back to Mrs Carpenter's cottage to thank her for lunch, drink a cup of tea if offered one and tell her a few non-truths intended to be comforting.

4

Robin Davies parked his car, a product of the previous year, in the faculty area by the central block of the university and went over to the administrative offices. Here a porter uniformed in chocolate-brown explored a pigeon-hole and handed him a thin sheaf of letters and other communications. Robin nodded in acknowledgement and glanced at them without much curiosity as he mounted the main steps to the first floor and walked along to a door labelled DR ROBIN R. DAVIES READER CLASSICS DEPT. When the door was safely shut after him he went into a vigorous silent routine of obscene gestures involving most of the top half of his body and accompanied by the pulling of hideous faces. This sequence he performed every morning in term-time or nearly.

Having straightened his tie, he sat down on the hard chair behind the desk and started to deal with his mail. Most of it was official, or at any rate likely to be addressed to a reader in classics at a university college in the English midlands. One letter that was conspicuously neither of these things he opened ahead of its turn and skimmed through its contents, slowing down as he got near the end and smiling slightly in a way that had a touch or two of glee in it. When he had finished reading he put the sheets back in their envelope and locked the whole concern away in a lower drawer of his desk among others of the same general aspect. He laid aside the rest of his correspondence as not calling for his immediate attention and for the next few minutes checked through his notes for the lecture on Pindar's prosody he had shortly to deliver. When the time came he took his gown off its hook on the door and left the room.

It was a fine morning in early summer, a week or two before regular teaching was due to be suspended and students took to revision and last-minute work before the yearly examinations. Robin's way took him downstairs and across the open through part of the formal garden, or the remains of it, that had been laid out in the late nineteenth century when the college was built. As he moved among the laurel shrubs and stone figures he passed various pupils and colleagues and greeted them, not always as he thought they deserved. He gave out nods and smiles, showed respect where that might have seemed due, refrained from physical or perhaps just verbal assault where one or other really was due. The dance of rage of the sort he had performed in his room just now was partly a reassurance to himself that he was not yet sunk in complacency.

Such a sinking would have been at any rate understandable. The six years since he had come to teach here had brought Robin a modest prosperity. Although he considered he had still not got enough money, he was no longer grossly short of it. Hard work in research and teaching had brought him a readership and its increased salary earlier than even someone as well qualified as he was might have expected. A timely, carefully pitched book on the lesser-known Greek myths and a series of talks on the Third Programme, also published, had further strengthened his position. He had hopes of an Oxford fellowship in a year or two. The trouble, or one of the troubles, was that within that year or two he was going to have reached the age of thirty-five, an undismaying milestone to some who had left it behind, he had noticed, but none the less half-way to the old three score and ten.

He reached the literally redbrick building where he was to deliver his lecture and mounted stairs to the actual room. It had in it a wide blackboard on which, not for the first time that year, he turned an unfriendly glance. The thing was not there temporarily, on an easel, but incorporated into the front wall, and therefore, as he had remarked a couple of times, more suitable for some technical college than for a seat of learning. Today he gave that a miss. Before him sat or lolled fourteen youngsters, his first-year Honours class in full attendance. The hands of the lecture-room clock pointed to ten minutes past the hour, the statutory time for proceedings to open. Robin opened them.

A girl called Pauline Stokes was in her usual place at the end of the front row next to the window. Whatever Robin proceeded to say about Pindaric prosody, however deeply boring he sank or close to the tolerable he ascended, she kept her eyes on him. What this meant in practice was that she kept her tits pointed towards him. There was no question but that they were very good tits, and not a lot more but that she thought that, properly wielded, they would swing her a passage to some sort of Honours degree, even if only to one of the third class. He thought he must have managed to conceal from her, so far, two settled beliefs of his, first that those in his position were above things like tits, moved on some more elevated moral plane, and second that her face was no better than all right, certainly not up to her tits. When it came to the little blonde creature next but one to Pauline he might have had more trouble resisting temptation, had it not been for the useful tips offered him by a Latinist colleague, a veteran Ulsterman with teaching experiences in India. There were likewise two of these: one, nobody signing on who cannot distinguish between *in medias res* and *in mediis rebus* is to be taken seriously, and two, never lay a finger on them till they graduate. Both maxims had served Robin well.

He completed his lecture on time, answered a couple of questions, took a couple of books back to the library and came away with a couple of others, visited the common-room and drank most of a cup of its coffee, gave a tutorial, went and got into his car and drove out of the college towards where he lived. Soon he had moved out of the old part of the town and left behind the clothing and footwear factories on which its prosperity had largely been founded. Soon after that, green spaces began to appear ahead of him, beside him, a park with memorial gates, playing-fields surrounding school buildings, a golf-course where players moved. On the far side of a strip of common a line of houses came into view, built before the first war and forming part of a residential suburb, one no longer at its peak of affluence but still high-priced enough for Robin to have needed a large part of a handy legacy to buy a place in it.

The house he stopped in front of had a small garage built on to one side of it, but he left his car parked in the street, or crescent as it was imaginatively called. He righted a child's red-painted tricycle that lay overturned by the front door and entered the house. Everything he touched and saw there was in good order.

He walked through until he reached a sort of glassed-in sun-room off the kitchen that had actual sunshine falling within it. There seemed to be nobody about, and Robin lit a cigarette, sat down and picked up a newspaper, but it was a bare two minutes before there was a great commotion of juvenile arrival and a moment later two children came bursting into the room, making no great noise or disturbance in doing so but undeniably coming bursting rather than merely coming. Both were girls, the elder, called Margaret after her paternal grandmother, being a healthy half-grown development of the embryo her parents had been to so much trouble not to get rid of in Cardiff nine years previously. Margaret and her far smaller sister launched themselves on their father as he sat helpless in his basket chair. He took a commendably dry kiss on the cheek from Margaret and a moment later gave an unaffected scream of pain at the pinch inflicted on his leg not far from the ankle by four-year-old Tilly. Christened Matilda after a maternal aunt, she already had enough power in her fingers to mark her out for a successful career in physiotherapy or massage. So at least her father now remembered saying. Tilly's mother had taken some exception to this remark, which puzzled him until she confessed she had no certain idea of what physiotherapy might be and had thought by massage he must have meant rude massage. At that point she herself, Nancy, came in and quickly drove her offspring from the room. Rather as in the mode of their arrival there, little was used in the way of violence or threats and yet any witness would have agreed at once that she did more than simply shove and scold.

'Phew,' said Nancy, enunciating it as a proper word. She was wearing a denim jacket and skirt and a white top. She and her husband kissed in no mechanical style but putting as much or as little into it as most married couples who saw each other for a fair amount of most days. 'Lunch in ten minutes?'

'Fine.' It was the day in the week when Robin had to get back smartly, in time for a two o'clock lecture. Picking up his newspaper again but not yet going back to reading it, he asked without any great show of interest, 'Anything to report?'

'No, they've been pretty good really, on the whole,' said Nancy. She made it sound as if the girls were handicapped in some way.

'I've only just realised, what are they doing in the house at this time? I know they live here.'

'Half-term. Oh yes, I remember now, somebody rang up.'

'Really?' Now he did turn his eyes to the newspaper.

'A woman.'

'Oh yes? What did she want?'

'I don't know, she was rather peculiar. Asked where you were, and I said you weren't here, you were at work, and she wouldn't go away.'

'In my experience people like that either ring again or they don't.'

Nancy hesitated before saying, 'She had a cockney accent.'

'Fascinating.'

'It didn't stop her trying to be very haughty and toffee-nosed.'

'No, I don't suppose it would,' said Robin, having decided against saying that the expression toffee-nosed was one of disparagement and nobody *tried* to sound it.

'Anyway, she sort of, I don't know, she annoyed me.'

Unseen by her he grimaced, but mildly, without special effort, nowhere near the scale of his performance in his college room. He was back to normal by the time he lowered his newspaper and said gently, 'Upset you, hasn't it?'

'O Lord no, not *upset*. Just felt a bit puzzled, that's all.'

'Well, I'm afraid there doesn't seem much I can do about it from here.'

Such fuss, such prolonged fuss, was uncharacteristic of her, he considered. She had visibly dropped the subject when the telephone rang in the next room and he got up with alacrity. 'That's her again,' she said, 'I'd know that ring anywhere,' and a moment later he was making an unattractive noise into the receiver.

'Oh, may I speak to Dr Davies, please, Dr Robin Davies?' asked a woman's voice with something of a cockney accent and a perhaps toffee-nosed manner.

'Hallo,' said Robin, pitching his own voice up an octave or thereabouts above normal.

'That's you, Robin, isn't it, you can't fool—'

'Halloooooo.'

'Just let me tell you—'

'Hallo hallo hallo,' piped Robin, and disconnected. Having done so he exhaled deeply a couple of times, took a bottle of gin out of a cupboard and poured himself a stiffish drink. Normally such an action was banned during the day but a telephoning madwoman was not normal. Nancy found him sitting with his glass of pink gin in his place at the laid lunch-table when she came into the kitchen with Margaret and Tilly.

'Was it her?'

'I think it must have been, yes.'

'You got rid of her all right, then.'

'I just kept saying hallo, didn't you hear?'

'I was dying to listen but then one of these two started yelling. Anyway, she went off all right. Any idea who she was or what she wanted?'

He shook his head decisively. 'Not the faintest. Some poor deranged creature. A student's mum who thinks she or he has got a grievance. Anyway, if she rings again which I don't think she will and I'm not here, just put the phone down.'

'Cold soup to start,' said Nancy. 'Tilly! Matilda, would you kindly *sit* on the chair.'

Margaret, helping to dish up the meal, gave her sister a superior glance.

For the next forty minutes or so, Robin was very interested in whether the presumptively unknown woman would telephone again and what in that event he would say to her. As it was, the instrument remained silent throughout, but he was in his car and driving away from the house before he became capable of much in the way of connected thought. Even so, there was nothing constructive he could have done, or did do, until he reached his room in the main administration building and picked up one of the telephones there. It was on an outside line, a facility enjoyed by few of the teaching staff below professorial rank and only obtained in this case after a couple of years of hard trying.

Naturally Robin knew who it was that had tried to telephone him earlier, had in fact no difficulty in making an identification from Nancy's account. His call now was soon answered. By the time he went off to his lecture he had adjusted matters with Toffee-Nose to his satisfaction, preparatory to cutting her off altogether as an unacceptable security risk. Over the years he had got quite good at applying the closure.

Back again after his lecture, he spent a good deal longer composing a reply to his important letter of that morning. The task involved some consultation of diaries, railway timetables and other aids. But finally the job was done, the envelope stamped, the whole thing ready to be posted via not the box in the porter's lodge but, in best take no-avoidable-chances style, one handily situated on his way home.

Fine. Nevertheless the matter of Nancy remained very far from fine, to wit her awareness that there had been something not all right about that unfamiliar voice on the telephone, that particular one. There was no ordinary, material way in which she could have known anything whatever about Toffee-Nose, he was a hundred per cent sure he had given nothing away at any stage, nothing in Nancy's words or voice or demeanour hinted that she had any awareness of the truth. But something in her had known. It was frighteningly as if the truth had some way of communicating itself that took no account of ordinary possibilities or likelihoods or chains of logic. And she had gone on about it for an enormously long time, much longer than was reasonable.

Well, it was a warning.

The following week was the first week of students' revision and hence an opportunity for their teachers to go off on short trips elsewhere if so inclined. Robin was very much inclined. His short trip would include one night or possibly two in London and an assortment of meals, drinks, recordings with publishers, agents, BBC men, not forgetting friends. It sounded good, or assuredly would have done if he had had to recite it. But Nancy's invariable practice was to show no curiosity about where he said he would be at such times, nor even to listen when in the past he had started to tell her. All he had to do was say emphatically that he would leave in some childproof cache a telephone number where he could be reached in an emergency, and then not leave such a thing anywhere. There never was an emergency, not at the home end anyway.

Robin, carrying a remarkably sedate briefcase, caught a train that landed him at Euston station shortly after five o'clock. By six he was well settled in at a small and little-known but, outwardly at least, respectable hotel near the Fulham Road. These days he was not much given to introspection, but the lady known for the time being as Mrs Davies was going to be a little later than usual, and there was not much else to do except get drunk or start to, not a mind-filling activity as well as undesirable at the moment. So, away from the public eye, in fact in the inconsiderable bedroom, he lit a cigarette and started introspecting at a familiar point.

Why was he still pursuing his former naughty life? He could not have said he was unhappily married, indeed he could and would have said he found all three of them, wife and children, altogether lovable, even Tilly, not least when she was not to be seen or heard. It was hard to be at all sure about such a thing, but he thought Nancy herself was even better, more attractive than when he had first met her. Others might have said that he lived a dull life up there, but that life seemed to him to be fun enough to live as it was from day to day, in no actual need of bits of excitement thrown in. And if there had been anything high-flown or low-flown at work about imagined or psychological or displaced troilism, three-in-a-bed fancyings, he had always been and was now aware of nothing of the kind.

Then his tendency had been in position since the beginning, before so to speak there had been such a thing as marriage, before at any rate he had taken the least account of it as something possible in his life. With this established he presumably had to change his question and start asking himself why he was the sort of man he was, screwing around whenever an opportunity came along provided it had good tits, goodish anyway, and a face to match. Meaning no known case of anything that could have been called self-restraint on his part. Not quite true: what about the little blonde creature who usually sat next but one to Pauline Stokes in his first-year Honours class, and others of that general kind? Well, the reason for non-pursuance in such cases was nothing but fear of the sack and its effects, and even that might wilt one day before a well organised enticement or a sudden sense of having some spare time that pressingly needed to be filled. So the only curb on his sexual egotism was another and more cowardly form of egotism. Thanks a lot.

That seemed about as far as his introspecting was going to reach. There was something in his nature that said that was just as well, if all it was going to produce was a solemn outburst agonising over what was no more than a few harmless bits of fun. But there was something equally there that said no, the thing demanded to be taken seriously. No sooner had he said that to himself than his thoughts seemed to move apart like a pair of curtains to reveal the idea that his first question to himself had been the right one, and the answer to it was a grim determination not to let a bagatelle like a hurried marriage interfere with what he had always done or at least wanted to do.

This latest idea made Robin look forward about as eagerly to a nice spot of adultery as to a midwinter swim across the Thames in full evening dress, but by good luck only a short period of contemplation came his way. Almost at once there was a soft knock on the bedroom door, and when he called to the knocker to come in, it was his second cousin, Dilys by name, who entered. He had first got in touch with her for immoral purposes a rather discreditably short time after she had dropped her London telephone number on him at his father's funeral, but he took none of that into account as he shut the door after her and at once grabbed her in his arms. He always did something like that when they got together. Once, when the engagement had been taking place on her rather than his ground, he had unavailingly suggested that she should be naked on her first appearance. Now, if it occurred to him that she might have preferred to hold off until she had had a chance to sit down and pass the time of day, he gave no sign. Not that she seemed in the least reluctant to take part. A corner of his mind was room enough for the wish that some of his colleagues could see him now, especially old Brontosaurus-Brain who was supposed to run his department. Make the old fart twitch his tail.

Within a couple of minutes he was hard at it. The room, the air generally, was warm enough for them not to need any bed-covering on them. They still wore or had not finally tugged off an undergarment or two of their own, thereby lending their embraces a valuable effect of urgency. Dilys was a great shouter at these do's, but they had never had any trouble because of it and today he let her have her head, reasoning that here too was a handy mark of abandon. Such a thing was doubly welcome just now, with precautions having had to be taken against repetition of what had happened that fatal time with Nancy. Anyway, on the whole the thing was a great success.

'Thanks for not eating me,' said Dilys eventually.

'I remembered not to at the last minute.'

'You've come a long way since that fumble down on the farm.'

'I should have done, I'm more than twice as old.'

330

'I suppose you must be. But it's funny, in some ways you don't seem to have changed at all.'

'You have,' said Robin. 'You've got better.'

'Oh, there's gallant we're being, I declare.'

'I think perhaps you were a bit shy in the old days, you know, way back.'

'Really? Anyway, you couldn't say I was shy now, could you?'

'No, I couldn't say that.'

Dilys pushed her legs down the bed. 'No trouble getting away, then?'

'There never is. I think old Nancy thinks I do what I say I'm doing. Or else she knows she'll never run me down. Either way she can't have any idea where I am.'

'Lucky girl to have such a careful husband.'

Robin forbore to ask after Dilys's husband, out of tact and lack of interest, also because he had forgotten the fellow's name. Dilys herself gave no sign of wanting to discuss any such matter. At that moment, or else the next, she was asleep. He too slept for a short while. A short while after that the two got up, went out for drinks and an early dinner, went to a film, got back to the hotel in good time for an early night. They had hardly arrived in their room when the telephone in it rang. Without particular thought Robin answered it, and was very much surprised by what he heard from the other end.

'Hallo, Robin, it's Nancy speaking. Oh, I'm probably nearer than you expected, in the hall whatsit one floor down from where you are. I've been here nearly an hour, waiting for you and your girl-friend to get back from wherever you've been. Who is she, by the way, anybody I know? Who? Oh yes, I remember, all sort of hot eyes and tits. Are you fit to be seen at the moment? In that case I suggest you come down here and have a chat, unless you want me to come up and the three of us have a chat there. What? Look, mate, as far as I'm concerned you can tell her whatever you bloody well like.'

It was never clear to Robin, even at the time, what he told Dilys.

After a minute or two he went downstairs and found his wife in a small sitting-room affair he had not known existed. With its green-seated chairs and green-panelled central table it looked as if a limited number of dentists could rewardingly have conferred in it. Nancy was wearing a dress he had not seen before, with red and blue sea-creatures pictured on a white ground. She looked as healthy as ever, with clear eyes and pink cheeks. At her elbow there stood a nearly empty glass of what looked like ginger beer.

'I hope you don't mind,' she said, 'I had it put down on your bill.'

He shook his head, then nodded it.

'You must be wondering how I found you here,' said Nancy in an expressive, almost-lively tone, as if she had been starting to tell him a story about other people that was well worth listening to. 'That was the easiest part of the lot. I just went to an agency place that does that kind of work and they got one of their chaps to follow you. It does happen, you know, really as well as in films and things. The man at the agency said they'd never been so busy. About snowed under they were, he said. Something to do with the war. It was quite hard work, you know, lots of time on the telephone and sending photographs and so on, but as you see I caught you in the end. Pretty soon, actually.'

'How did you find the agency?' It was not what Robin most wanted to know, but for the moment he could not work out what that might be.

'Your brother George, he told me on the quiet to come to him if I wanted any help. He made the appointment for me and didn't ask any questions. Well, I felt I had to tell him a bit, like what it was all in aid of, but he just said he'd like to hear the full story any time I was ready. He's really a very nice fellow, your brother. No, I can see this isn't the time for me to be singing his praises. Not to you, anyway.'

'He hasn't been in touch with me at all about this.'

'No, I got him to promise to keep his mouth shut before I told him anything, and he's the sort of chap who – no, never mind.'

'I mean, honestly . . .'

'Honestly what, Robin?'

'Nothing. Carry on.'

'Oh. George is very fond of you, he just doesn't think much of you. Rather like me in a way. Well now, the next chapter's about what put me on to you.'

'I say, can we go out somewhere?'

'How do you mean?'

'I don't think I could face sitting here hour after hour listening to you telling me whatever you, whatever you feel like telling me. We could get a taxi-driver to take us to a quiet bar somewhere. I'm thirsty and I want a drink. I know that must sound a bit . . .'

'Never mind how it sounds.' For the first time some impatience entered Nancy's manner. Her eyes widened slightly. 'This isn't going to go on hour after hour. I have to leave in less than one hour to catch my train and there's no point in going anywhere else. I'm sure you can get whatever you want here, and if you're worried about Dilys Thing coming in and cutting up rough she'll have been out of this place like a cat in hell if I know anything about her sort. And a snip of you having to do what you don't fancy doing is just what the doctor ordered for you, Robin Davies. See that bell there? Well, I'd try pressing it if I were you.'

He meekly did as he was told. He did it meekly because there seemed to be no other way of doing it. He had tried bewilderment shading into muddled protest just now and had cut no ice at all. While he sat avoiding Nancy's eye and waiting for his ring to be answered, he kept on telling himself that what he was engaged in was not an argument, something you might win or lose or draw, it was more serious than that. And yet in a sense it was less serious because there was no point in trying to build a case. Trying as such hardly came into it.

The door opened so abruptly that Robin jumped and for an unpleasant instant he thought it must have been Dilys who was arriving. But no, it was a middle-aged man with grey hair cut very short and wearing a high-necked navy-blue tunic and trousers too much unlike ordinary clothes not to be a kind of uniform, but one that suggested some exotic provenance like the headquarters mess of a disbanded Polish or Austrian regiment of light horse. Unfortunately no clue was forthcoming in the fellow's manner of speech, since he said nothing, though he did suddenly lift his head in an enquiring way. Robin asked for two large whiskies-and-soda and a glass of ginger beer to be brought and identified himself. Still in silence and with no change of expression, the man withdrew, brought the drinks with unusual speed and again withdrew, leaving a great silence behind.

As he distributed the drinks – both of the whiskies for him, the ginger beer for Nancy – Robin was touched by the memory of impressing on her long ago the duty of acquiescence when he seemed to be, but was not really, ordering an alcoholic drink for her as well as himself. Yes, she had never needed telling again. Now she took a sip of ginger beer, put her glass down firmly and went on with what she had to say, and any improvement in the atmosphere was soon dissipated.

'Right. And by the way, if you suspect I'm enjoying this, well I am quite. It's taken a long time for my turn to come round. But it's here now, isn't it? For years and years I went on trying not to wonder what you got up to on your own, when I wasn't about, making myself not ask, and that was more or less all right until someone thoughtfully told me they'd seen you in London when you were supposed to be in Cambridge or somewhere, you and some lady were having a lovely time in a drinking club I think it was called. I still don't know why she told me, probably to do with you or me, I don't know.'

Nancy stopped speaking for over a minute and stared into or towards her glass. He became aware that he had a very poor idea of what she was thinking, no better than whatever he might have been able to imagine any woman of her general sort thinking at such a time as this, and when he tried to remember her as she had been in her life with him or at any earlier time nothing came into his mind. A great fear of being altogether alone swept over him, as if she might take from him not only herself and their life together but everything familiar to him, all his reference points, whatever made it possible to steer through the hours between waking up and falling asleep. But he could not put any of this into words, only wait for her to go on.

'Anyway,' she said, 'after that I couldn't keep it up any longer, pretending not to believe it and trying not to believe it and believing it at the same time. It was a struggle but then I happened to catch you just looking at I've forgotten who it was at one of our parties, and after that I was sure the other was true, and then . . . I had to try and drop all the nice things I remembered about you being so kind and sweet to me and how lovely it was.'

Nancy stopped speaking abruptly and held her hand out and up towards him, then said in a different tone and hurriedly, 'Don't come near me, don't come near me, please don't.' A second later she was weeping hard with her hands over her face and in between was trying to apologise for it and say she had not meant to. Robin did not have to think he ought to shed tears, but he hid them in case she should think he was putting it on or just letting the tears come. 'I'm sorry,' he said, furtively wiping his eyes with his fingers, 'no excuses, just me being a shit.'

She blew her nose into what he was nearly sure was one of his handkerchiefs and soon started to liven up again. 'What did you say about not having any excuses? Yes, quite right, you haven't, none that'll hold water anyway, and not only for this either. I expect you tried, though. I know I did. My dad used to say there was no excuse so lame I wouldn't make it for you. Honestly, when I think of it. You wouldn't come and see him and my mum because you'd got enough parents of your own, hadn't you, and that was why you never asked after them either, my mum and dad, and never even stopped to think how handy it was that they never came near you. And you never told me you loved me because it wasn't your way, was it, it wasn't a word you liked, was it, because even you had a funny feeling it laid sort of obligations on you. And you never called me darling, same sort of thing, just what your father used to call your mother. But I let you get away with it all, because I loved you.' There was no mistaking the dislike and contempt in her tone. 'I think I'd even have let you get them to take my child away and I don't know why you changed your mind and I don't want you to start trying to tell me, I couldn't stand going over it again.'

She picked up her glass but put it down again without drinking. 'I suppose even now I'm only doing this, telling you, because I'm fed up with you going on like you do without knowing about yourself. You said no excuses just now. But that's just another thing you say. Even now you still think you're not *really* to blame for yourself and what you do and don't do. If you do a bad thing or don't do a good thing it's because of the way you were brought up, what they taught you or fell down on the job by not teaching you, and the books you read because they were all the rage before the war, and anyway we're all, what is it, products of the age we live in. But when you, wait a minute, when you do a good thing or don't do a bad thing, like not starting to try and screw some female, then that's all *you*, full marks to Robin Davies Esquire and his marvellous natural sense of right and wrong, and if you think that's rather a posh way for me to put it, well I got it off you one time when you were going on about that American psychologist man and that queer poet with the funny name and D. H. Lawrence. That was years ago, you haven't said much about them recently, but I know what that is, that's you showing how we all stay the same after whatever age it is because we've all been *conditioned* by then. But I remember you said, when Tilly was just a baby, you said Lawrence's motto was just It's all right when I do it, without realising, I mean you didn't realise it was your motto too. That stuff you read didn't *condition* you, you chose it because it was what you wanted to hear. And that's really all I've got to say. Except nowadays I don't think you even get much fun out of what you do. You're just piling up a score, like a small boy with his airgun out after rats or rabbits or sparrows, it doesn't matter which. And that is all.'

'There's not much I can say, is there?'

'Not much, no. Don't bother. I was the one with things to say.'

'When did you stop loving me?'

She turned on him furiously. 'You want to hear the words, don't you, even though you haven't really much of an idea what they mean. Believe me, chum, there's nothing I'd like better than to be able to tell you I don't love you, and mean it. Do you think if I hadn't been I'd have come any of the way with you at all ? You don't stop loving someone just because you find out they're not worth it.'

'So you still do?'

'Oh shut up, Robin, will you please shut up.'

'All right. All right. But we're splitting up. I don't blame you, how can I?'

'Not unless you want to.'

Having said that very quickly, Nancy looked desperately about and upwards in a way he interpreted as referring to Dilys, to some other, to any other he might know of or hope for. Without thought or purpose, Robin said, 'I want to die. Hearing you say that, you being afraid I might go off with somebody else, that makes me want to die. I can't bear you being afraid of me going off after all the terrible things I've done. I just want to not be here to be able to think of a thing like that. I'd rather never be able to think of anything again than have to think of that.' He lowered his head until all he could see was the table with the green panels in it. For a moment he was afraid that he really would die, and then he wondered whether that might not be best after all.

Out of his view, Nancy swallowed and sighed and was quiet and motionless. He heard her get up from where she sat. Her voice said, 'I'm going now. Come home tomorrow if you're coming, but ring me first. We'll try again, but under different rules from now on. I haven't managed to get any further than the first so far, but that says you only get one second chance and if I ever, this'll have to do for now, if I ever stop being sure you're not trying to get away with something then I'm off for good with Margaret and Tilly, all right? You can have the three of us, or you can have everyone else. Not both.'

Nancy came round the table and stood close to him. 'Come on, look up, you idiot,' she said. When he did, he found she looked immensely tall from where he sat. There's just one more thing,' she said. 'Stand up.'

He wondered whether she meant to kiss him or spit in his face. In the event she did neither but half turned away from him and moved her right hand to somewhere near her left shoulder. He was doing as he had been told though was still not fully settled on his feet when she swung round and caught him a tremendous backhanded buffet on the right cheekbone. The force of the blow sent him staggering and he tripped over himself and would have fallen all the way to the floor if he had not half upset one of the green-seated chairs.

Before he could gather his wits she was starting to help him up. 'I'm sorry. I didn't mean to knock you over,' she said, sounding concerned. 'I haven't hurt you, have I, love? Are you all right?'

In a standing posture again, cautiously touching his cheek, he said, 'My Christ, you don't know your own strength.'

At once any tenderness left her manner. 'That was just to be going on with,' she said, gave him a single admonitory nod and went out.

Left alone, Robin found time to remember that classes were over at the college for the time being, and so he would not have to face them with a probable black eye. Then he said aloud, 'Of course I could end up with neither lot,' drained his second whisky-and-soda and pressed the bell again. The Herzogovinian hussar came a short way into the room and Robin ordered another whisky-and-soda and a ham sandwich. The waiter, or whatever he really was, held his head at an angle such as made it hard to be sure where he was looking. Any uncertainty on the point was removed when, in halting but obviously home-grown accents, he said, 'Your face . . . you've hurt your face.'

'I slipped.' Robin left it at that – why not? He repeated his demand for refreshment, spacing the words out.

Meanwhile the waiter seemed to become agitated. 'The lady

upstairs . . . she's gone,' he said after a great gulp, 'Left the hotel
. . . sir.'

'Oh, good,' said Robin comfortably. He produced a pound note
and handed it over. 'I'll just pop up there myself for a minute, then
I'll be leaving too.'

'Not . . . staying the night?'

'No, my plans have changed. Would you have my bill made out?
Oh, and bring me the whisky and the sandwich in my room.'

Upstairs, Robin examined his face in the mirror. He could think
of nothing to do about the red mark on his cheek, so he left it. Then
he rang George.

THE HISTORY OF VINTAGE

The famous American publisher Alfred A. Knopf (1892–1984) founded Vintage Books in the United States in 1954 as a paperback home for the authors published by his company. Vintage was launched in the United Kingdom in 1990 and works independently from the American imprint although both are part of the international publishing group, Random House.

Vintage in the United Kingdom was initially created to publish paperback editions of books acquired by the prestigious hardback imprints in the Random House Group such as Jonathan Cape, Chatto & Windus, Hutchinson and later William Heinemann, Secker & Warburg and The Harvill Press. There are many Booker and Nobel Prize-winning authors on the Vintage list and the imprint publishes a huge variety of fiction and non-fiction. Over the years Vintage has expanded and the list now includes great authors of the past – who are published under the Vintage Classics imprint – as well as many of the most influential authors of the present.

For a full list of the books Vintage publishes, please visit our website
www.vintage-books.co.uk

For book details and other information about the classic authors we publish, please visit the Vintage Classics website
www.vintage-classics.info

www.vintage-classics.info